The Gerasimov Doctrine

Michael Crawshaw

First published in 2023
This edition published 2023

ISBN: 9781739572501

1

'God, I am good.' Karl Kristensen affirmed this declaration with a gentle rocking of his head. 'I'm up there with J.F.K., Martin Luther King and Churchill.'

'You don't want to be up there with them.' His secretary pointed to the sky.

Karl grunted, sipped water from his bamboo bottle then settled back in the leather seat to read a report.

The Gerasimov Doctrine calls for a 4:1 ratio of non-military to military actions. Controlling the information space, political assassination, targeting critical civilian infrastructure …

Same old.

He set it back on his lap and turned instead to look out the window at the rocky greens erupting from a blue Baltic. It had been another good day in a year that kept getting better. He'd become President of Finland before his thirty-fifth birthday. Next on the agenda, installing the missile system that will keep his people safe. And like Churchill, he would not be deterred by the enemy's sabre-rattling. He would never surrender.

The car swerved suddenly.

'Careful,' he said, mopping water from his lap.

'That wasn't me,' the driver replied implausibly. 'It must have been the automatic lane-keep.'

Karl said nothing, but he was confident who was at fault. Computers don't make mistakes.

'Mister Kristensen.'

Was the driver about to protest his innocence again?

'I think we're being followed.'

Moon eyes reflected in the rear-view mirror.

Karl's bodyguard turned to look out the back window. 'The Audi?'

'The Mercedes behind.'

Karl looked over his shoulder. 'Press?'

'Not driving an S-class,' replied the bodyguard, unclipping the cover on his shoulder holster. 'Speed up and see if they follow.'

Needing no second invitation the driver slammed the accelerator and the car lurched forward.

Ignoring flashing lights from an oncoming bus they overtook a fast-moving BMW then took a bend at a speed Karl would not have hit on the straight.

'They're not following,' said the driver. 'False alarm.'

You were the one who was alarmed, thought Karl. But he said nothing. Just made a mental note to get a new driver. A metallic clunk brought his focus back to the present. 'Why did you lock the doors?'

'I didn't,' said the driver.

'The computer again?' asked Karl sarcastically. 'I don't like to be locked in. Unlock the door.'

'I told you. I didn't lock them!'

'And you can slow down now.'

'I can't. The brakes aren't working.'

'Slow down!' screamed the guard as they drifted into the outer lane on a bend. 'Kill the engine.'

'I can't.'

'Crash the gears.'

'It's stuck in automatic.'

The guard punched a fast dial. 'This is the security detail for Karl Kristensen. We are travelling west on the 189 outside Porhonkallio. Driver has lost control of vehicle. Urgent assistance needed.'

A bend skidded by. A salivating sea called from the bottom of the cliffs.

'Whoa!' shouted the driver, straining to turn the steering as the car swung out round the next bend onto the other side of the road. 'Now the power steering has gone.'

The driver edged into the nearside rock face to drag the car slower. It bounced back into the road. Into and over the crash barrier. Falling weightless, Karl desperately wanted to tell his people that even without him they must not flag nor fail, they must go on to the end, defend our country whatever the cost may be. Never surrender …

2

'Where's my money?' Mickey Summer was calm. As calm as possible for someone who had just mislaid his life savings.

'I don't know,' replied the solicitor. 'But it hasn't arrived in our account.'

'I sent it yesterday.' Deep breaths. One, two, three, four. Mickey pulled his wallet from his pocket, fished out the transaction slip. 'I've got it written down here. Priority Payment Customer Authority. Account to be debited Michael J Summer- that's me. Beneficiary name, Hartley Solicitors – that's you. Payment amount two million pounds. That's real money. A lot of it.'

'I've seen the picture of the slip, Mr Summer. You sent it earlier. But I'm afraid the money has not arrived.'

'Well, it's no longer in my bank account.' Should have walked round with it in a suitcase. Never trust a computer. 'We just press on and it will turn up. Right?'

'Until the money arrives, I am unable to forward it to the Marshall's solicitor and complete the purchase.'

'We are going ahead with this, mate.'

'Hopefully so.'

Definitely so. Mickey turned. Helen was struggling out the front door of the flat with the dog in a cage. It was her idea to get a dog, she chose one that weighed twenty kilos and yet her eyes were glaring at Mickey. She could be a travel agent for guilt trips.

He signalled that he would come and take it off her then went back to the call. Helen's ears were blocked from swimming, but he lowered his voice just in case. 'Mate. The van is packed. And I am driving it to our new house. Right now. So, you just get your end sorted.'

'Might I suggest you go round to the bank instead and chase up the money? I have tried ringing, but I can't get through.'

'Try again.'

Mickey cut the call.

'Problem?' Helen's right eyebrow arched. Seemed her ears were not so blocked.

'Just the solicitor,' said Mickey, going over to take the dog.

'The solicitor?'

'A boring technicality.' Like two million quid gone missing.

'But you're worried.'

She always could read him. 'Come on. Let's go to our new home.'

Mickey squeezed the dog and cage into the last available space in the back of the Luton. He shut the doors and slapped the side of the van as if it had just won the Champion Hurdle. 'Would you believe it? Everything we own, and some we don't, fits in the back of one van.'

'Are you worried?' Helen asked again.

'About how little we own?'

'About this technicality.'

'Just the money transfer from our bank to the solicitors. It's stuck in traffic.'

Helen pursed her lips but said nothing as she walked to her car.

'The address is in the sat nav,' said Mickey. 'See you there.'

He waved her off then climbed up into the van, familiarised himself with the controls and pulled away into the narrow streets of Hoxton. His phone vibrated in his pocket. Tempting to answer it but not while controlling a seven-meter monster.

When he reached the suburbs, he switched on the radio. Some racket on Radio 1 and a DJ that loved the sound of his own voice. He turned it off. His phone vibrated again. More comfortable behind the wheel now, he pulled it out. Four missed calls. One from Helen, two from the solicitor and one from Slick Jimmy. The last one could be important. He pulled into a bus stop and called back.

'Mickey! Just in time, mate.'

'For what?'

'Flying Magpie's withdrawn from the three o'clock at Haydock. Pulled up lame in the paddock. Desert Cloud is a brilliant front-runner, so it's all hers. She's come into tens but that's still a steal. Wanted to give my old mate a chance of easy winnings.'

'And use the weight of money to shorten the odds so you can cash out.'

'There's gratitude.'

It was still a good tip. 'Problem is, I'm moving house and I've got short term cash flow issues. Can you do me a favour?'

Silence except for the engine.

'How much do you want to put on?' said Jimmy finally.

'Five bags.'

'Five thousand pounds? To be clear.'

'That's it.'

'Done. Catch you later.'

Mickey killed the call and resumed driving. It got trickier again in the narrow, leafy lanes of Hertfordshire. Just short of his destination he pulled over to let a car pass and scraped the side of the van on the hedgerow. Should be damage he could clean up. But turning into his new driveway he clipped the brick gate post. That would cost. Never mind. New house ahead.

Helen stood in the drive; arms folded. Mickey waved enthusiastically. She didn't wave back. Beside her Mr Marshall, his face red and pocked like a long-fallen apple, raised a hand half-heartedly.

'Wotcha!' Mickey said, lowering himself from the cabin.

'I've been ringing you,' said Helen.

'Can't use the phone while driving. The Old Bill don't like it. Everything all right?'

'No, it is not,' said Marshall.

'What's up?'

'There appears to be a problem with your financing.'

'I don't have any financing,' explained Mickey. 'I'm a cash buyer.'

'You don't have the cash to complete the purchase.'

'What is going on, Mickey?' asked Helen.

'I told you. Just some technicality. The solicitor is chasing it up. One tick.'

He hit dial back. The solicitor picked up before the second ring. 'Mickey. I've been trying to get hold of you.'

'You've got the money?'

'No. But I know what the problem is.'

'Go on.'

'There's something wrong at Royal Shire Bank. All accounts

have been frozen.'

'A computer glitch?'

'I don't know, but that explains why your money hasn't come through.'

'But my money is still safe in Royal Shire?'

No answer.

'My money is still safe in Royal Shire?' Mickey repeated.

'There are rumours Royal Shire is going under.'

'Don't be daft. Royal Shire can't go bust. It's majority owned by State Financial. Too big to fail and all that.'

'That's what they said about Lehman Brothers.'

And Bear Stearns. But State Financial was much bigger. It couldn't go bust. It really couldn't.

'What is it?' Helen asked.

He raised a hand to appeal for time. 'What do we do?'

'There's nothing we can do at this point. You can't complete the move.'

'Can't we sign something to make it clear the money belongs to the Marshalls when the accounts get unfrozen?'

'That wouldn't work.'

'Have you got any better ideas?'

'I'm afraid not. I did think it was risky putting all your money in one bank.'

'Did you now. I don't recollect any such conversation. We call that jobbing backwards in my old line of work.'

Mrs Marshall came out of the house and joined the gawkers. 'Is there a problem?'

'Not really,' said Mickey, convincing no one, least of all himself.

'What's this about Royal Shire going bust?' asked Helen.

'Just rumours,' insisted Mickey. 'It's owned by State Financial. Biggest bank in the world. They won't let it fail. But just as a precaution, they've frozen all transactions. Just a temporary thing.'

'So, you can't actually buy our house,' announced Marshall with a tone of recrimination that really deserved a punch in the face.

Hang on. If Desert Cloud had come in, he would have fifty thousand pounds to put forward. Maybe the Marshalls would take that as a non-refundable deposit. If they move today and he finds the money, happy days all round. If he doesn't Mickey forfeits the deposit, and the Marshalls get their house back. 'Give me a minute. I've got an idea.'

Away from wi-fi the phone was slow. Eventually the results for Haydock Park came up. First place... Darling. Who the bleeding 'ell was Darling? He scrolled down the runners and riders. Desert Cloud came in fifth.

'What's your idea?' asked Mister Marshall.

'Never mind.' Mickey put away his phone. 'Everything will be all right. We just can't give you the money today. But when they unfreeze the account, everything will be sorted.'

'Really?' asked Helen, her hands clasping her head.

'Really. Everything will be fine. Trust me.'

'We need to get this house.'

'I know.'

'The flat isn't big enough for us. At least it won't be soon.'

What?

Helen pulled him to one side. 'I'm pregnant. I've just found out. I was going to tell you once we'd moved in.'

A baby? What else? He grabbed Helen and lifted her off her feet. 'That's amazing.' A shock but still amazing. No wonder she didn't want to carry the dog.

'So, you see, we really do need a new home,' she said.

'Everything will be fine. I'll sort it.'

Had to.

3

TruNews breaking news: Karl Kristensen killed in motor crash. The Finnish President died this morning along with his driver, secretary, and bodyguard when their Mercedes limousine careered down a cliff into the Baltic Sea near Porhonkallio in the Turku Archipelago. There have been allegations made that he was killed by the CIA because he refused to evict Russian people living in Finland.

Declan Lehane shook his head. 'You have to admire these Russian spin merchants. They make a ludicrous claim that the CIA killed Kristensen. Yet it'll sound entirely plausible to Russian listeners.'

'And to the conspiracy theorists and counterfactuals in the west who follow TruNews,' the monitoring agent added. 'It was just a car crash, wasn't it? No foul play.'

Declan shrugged. 'The driver was speeding round hair pin bends.'

'Suicide?'

'Unlikely. Clearances to drive a President are stringent. But it's suspiciously convenient given that Kristensen wants to allow NATO missiles to be based in Finland. We should look at it.'

'That's Langley's bailiwick.'

'If it's political murder it's hybrid war. And that's ours. Touch base with the Finnish police and see what they're thinking.'

The agent made a note in a pad. 'Meanwhile Russian troll farms are getting more prolific by the day. Look at this one. Seriously impressive A.I.'

Declan rolled over on his chair.

The agent angled his screen towards him. 'It posts about three times a minute, usually on the same themes of NATO aggression and American imperialism. Feeds off any comments and pings back instantly. Now it's onto the theme that the CIA killed Kristensen.'

Declan studied the screen. 'Reasonable quality but no nuance.'

'It's not nuanced but it's entirely coherent.'

'GPT-4?' asked Declan.

'Might even be fifth gen.'

'But it's still not sentient, right?'

'Not so far as I can make out. It's not trying to communicate anything. It doesn't really think up what it writes. It's still given prompts by its handler and then it spouts off. But it's very convincing.'

Declan made a note to tell Jennifer Seymour when they next met. The Director of the NSA had a bee in her bonnet about the Russians getting any edge on artificial intelligence. He dealt with some emails then grabbed his bag.

'Later. I'm off to State Financial.'

'Still don't see why you're getting involved in a cyber theft. That's financial crime.'

'That could also be hybrid war. It's a Latvian bank subsidiary that was targeted. Could be Kremlin fingerprints on the keyboard.'

* * *

Once check-in and transfers to airports were factored in, it was as quick to travel by Amtrak as fly from the District to New York. Besides, the rolling of the train sent Declan to sleep, a blessed relief that he rarely found in bed nowadays.

He woke to the peanut smell of brake dust and was on his feet beside the carriage doors before they opened. He skipped through Moynihan Hall and down to the subway. It was Saturday morning so there was plenty of available seating amongst a typically cosmopolitan crowd, eyes closed for snoozing or down into screens. Only one old man, probably about the age pops would have been, hands crossed on his walking stick, had his head up. Declan nodded. The old man took a second to register the unfamiliar, then smiled and nodded back.

'This the right line for Wall Street?' asked Declan, making conversation.

'Sure is,' said the old man, rocking forward.

They chatted until Declan's stop. Back in the sunlight the sidewalks of Manhattan's financial district were peppered with selfie-taking tourists and dressed-down office workers.

At the headquarters of State Financial a huge Stars and Stripes snapped in the downdraft. Declan jogged up the steps, sashayed through the revolving doors, and tapped over the marble floor to reception. The FBI Financial Crime team had set up an incident room away from the Security Operations Centre to keep those in the know as few as possible. This was on the fiftieth floor. Manhattan shrank into patchwork as Declan rode an empty elevator.

Apropos of nothing the cyber breach had been given a code name of Whiteberry and the word was written on the outside of the door. He opened it without knocking.

An old colleague from financial crime rose slowly from his chair, smiling, but only from one side of his face. 'Surprised to see you. Thought you were busy with the Russians. And chasing shadows in your spare time.'

Chuck and Declan had once got along well. But the relationship had soured. It had something to do with the Black Chamber enquiry. They'd started the investigation into this deep state group together. But given the high profile of those they'd arrested the Attorney General had handed the case over to a special prosecutor who had been getting nowhere fast. Declan was not at all happy about that and was holding the prosecutor's feet to the fire. But Chuck had gone cold. He seemed to have lost faith in the prosecution. He wasn't the only one. Most people had lost faith in it. It had started to feel like Declan was the only person who still believed the Black Chamber existed.

'I'm here,' said Declan, 'because Directors Seymour and Connelly figured the NSA and the Bureau should both look at this. And in around an hour we've got to brief the State Financial board. So, let's crack on.'

Chuck introduced Declan to the other agents from Financial Crime and the in-house IT guys from the bank. Declan helped himself to coffee from a flask on the side and eyed up a donut beside it. Remembering his cholesterol count, he cut it in two. 'Let's have a sit rep.'

'Situation is we're looking at the biggest cyber theft ever,' said Chuck. 'Seven billion dollars.'

'That's a damned big number,' said Declan. 'How?'

'Targeted spear phishing attacks that used artificial intelligence to create very believable bespoke messages for hundreds of staff at the Latvian subsidiary of the State Financial European subsidiary, Royal Shire Bank. All unique to each recipient. Written in perfect Latvian. One of them fell for it and gave the hackers chance to install a keystroke logger and away they went through their back door into the whole system.'

'The attackers also used malware to remove the statements and confirmations that would normally act as secondary controls.

The losses only came to light when the bank defaulted on margin calls on its own loans. That was Friday.'

'Any indications where the money went?'

'Cayman Islands, Granada, Jersey, Bermuda, Singapore ... you name it.'

The money would be impossible to trace without a huge task force. 'Attribution?'

'Nothing yet. But given it was a Latvian bank we're assuming Russians.'

'State or independents?'

'Is there a difference? President Pintov has given free rein to Russian cyber criminals to attack the west.'

'But you're just guessing,' said Declan.

'At this stage.'

'What do we know about the code?'

'It's a derivative of GameOverRed.'

Declan skipped a beat. The malware he had developed to attack the Great Firewall of China. His baby. Gone AWOL again. 'We issued a patch for that months ago. Why wasn't State Financial using it?'

'They were. But the Latvian subsidiary wasn't.'

'How come?'

'Human error.'

'Do we believe that? Could be an inside job?'

'That's also a possibility.'

Declan spent the best part of an hour getting up to speed and then his alarm sounded. Five minutes to the board meeting. 'We'd better get upstairs.'

4

With no athletes and few visitors left, the Olympic Park was as peaceful and green as you can get in inner London. It even had a beach. Mickey tried to pretend they were on a city break. Rather than homeless. But Helen was having none of it. They checked into a mid-range hotel and he suggested a stroll to the river. But she didn't want to walk on pavement. She wanted her easel and paints. Her subject was to be the red twisting Orbit Tower. He'd packed her painting stuff into the van first and it took twenty minutes to fish it out. In the process, most of the contents of the van had been revealed to any watching thief. By the time he'd retrieved it, Helen had decided she didn't want to paint a metal sculpture after all. She set off with the dog on an evening walk round the concrete jungle she'd first rejected. Mickey was not invited.

He sat in the hotel cafe and scrolled the news. Calls for a general election, a ministerial sacking, Russian military manoeuvres. Then the rumours of a black hole in Royal Shire's balance sheet. Worryingly there were no denials from senior management. Just some public relations plonker giving assurances that the bank would not collapse. Mate, you would be the last to know.

Mickey rang around his old City contacts. One told Mickey of a six-point-one billion loss. A disconcertingly precise number. But still peanuts to State Financial. Relax. The money would come back eventually.

When Helen returned, she'd already eaten. Mickey settled for the complimentary biscuits and an early night. He checked for news on his phone. Nothing new. Nothing to be done except get some sleep. But loose pipework in the ceiling rattled every time he drifted off. It was going to be a long, nervous night.

5

Dominic Steele, CEO and President of State Financial, sat impatiently at the head of the boardroom table, sunken eyes staring out any that caught his own. He cleared his throat as the wall clock flipped to the hour.

'Let me first introduce our guests. Special Agent Chuck Baldwin here is from the FBI's financial crime team. Declan Lehane is from the National Security Agency and formerly FBI.'

Smiles and nodded acknowledgements around the room.

'If you didn't already know,' continued Steele, 'we've suffered a cyber theft of seven billion dollars.'

No surprised expressions. Everyone did know.

'Time is of the essence if we are going to save this bank.'

That piece of news, however, was as much of a shock to most in the room as it was to Declan. They all knew Royal Shire was in trouble, but they didn't know it was a problem for the parent.

Steele turned and nodded to a thin man with a tie pulled up so tight Declan worried for his breathing.

'Royal Shire Bank has been the victim of a cyber theft,' explained tight tie. 'This has resulted in a loss of six point one billion pounds sterling, seven in dollars. Capital requirements were raised last month in Europe but …'

'How do you lose seven billion dollars?' asked a man with skin like mouldy jam. 'I mean how is that possible?'

'Perhaps we should explain that first,' said Steele. He turned to the head of IT. 'Please.'

The IT man picked up the hot potato and quickly put some distance between it and him. 'Our Royal Shire subsidiary has let us down very badly. Or more specifically the IT people at their Latvian subsidiary, Baltika Bank have. They were attacked by sophisticated AI spear phishing, but they were also not taking the proper defences against hackers. Someone made a hacking tool available as open source Metasploit modules …'

'Keep it simple,' snapped Steele.

'It's like a blueprint,' Declan interjected. He gave a look of reassurance to the IT head. 'It was the Chinese who made the exploit available.'

'What's the exploit called?' asked Steele.

Declan hesitated. Why was he interested? 'GameOverRed.'

Steele made a note in his pad then turned back to the IT man. 'Carry on.'

'The hackers adapted GameOverRed to hide the fact they were already behind the Latvian bank's firewall and withdrawing money. But it's been known about for months and Baltika's systems should have been able to defend against it.'

'I still don't see how hackers can walk off with seven billion dollars,' said jam face again. 'Just because the IT guys screwed up.'

'The hackers got a back door into the bank's financial systems and managed to cover their tracks so the bank couldn't tell it was bleeding assets.'

'They only discovered that on Friday,' explained tight tie. 'Royal Shire didn't have enough cash to pay margin calls on its own loans.'

'Unbelievable,' said jam face, shaking his head.

'We have plugged the cyber hole to prevent any further losses,' the IT head offered hopefully.

'How do we get our money back?' asked Steele. He turned to Chuck. 'If you guys catch the criminals, we recover our losses, right?'

Chuck puffed out his cheeks. 'I think that's unlikely.'

Declan jumped in. 'It will be very difficult to discover who did this. Harder still to trace the lost money. And impossible to get it back.'

'Are we insured against this?' Steele asked tight tie.

'Possibly. If we could demonstrate that the Latvian bank had taken all reasonable steps to prevent cybercrime.'

'But you don't believe they did,' Steele said to Declan.

'The Pentagon and FBI released a fix for the exploit. The Latvian bank could and should have stopped this attack.'

'So you blame Baltika's IT guys.' Steele cradled his fingers and stared at Declan. Did he know what Declan knew? How could he?

'I blame the criminals,' said Declan.

They spent another twenty minutes going over the same ground in more detail and then Steele asked all non-members of the board to leave. Declan was happy to oblige.

* * *

Alone with the board again, Steele cleared his throat. 'Who knows we're in trouble?'

'It's getting out in the press and social media,' said jam face. 'Royal Shire had to close accounts. It's rumoured to be going under.'

'The whole world knows that Royal Shire is in trouble. But who knows that we are too?'

'The people in this room and the guys who just left,' said tight tie. 'And we have of course notified the SEC.'

'It's only seven billion dollars,' said someone. 'We just transfer the capital over to RSB. Problem solved.'

'Except we don't have seven billion dollars of capital,' said tight tie. 'Our tier one capital ratio is already below three percent.'

'What about the Latvian government? It's the Latvians that screwed up.'

'Baltika is a fully owned subsidiary of RSB. It's a British problem as far as they are concerned. A collapse would not be systemic.'

'How about the British government then? They still have a stake in RSB. They can inject capital.'

'I tried,' said Steele. 'There is no appetite in Downing Street for another bank rescue. Especially not a bank that is essentially now American.'

'How about our government then?'

Steele shook his head. 'POTUS says: not my circus, not my monkeys.'

'What does that even mean?'

'It means no.'

'The Fed?'

'They've made it clear they won't be helping out.' Steele shook his head. 'Not a second time round. They know we have a way out of this.'

'Which is?'

Steele pursed his lips and looked around the table. 'We transfer back to us whatever reserves are left at Royal Shire and let it go under.'

A heavy silence settled. When it lifted, they moved to the practicalities.

'One final question,' said Steele. 'Why did the National Security Agency send their wonderkid, Declan Lehane, to investigate a bank robbery?'

'He's a wonderkid?'

'Remember the cyberattacks on the railways and energy infrastructure? Declan Lehane was riding shotgun on all that when he was at the FBI. He worked out it was Islamists. And that China was behind them. Got transferred to Cyber command and led the charge against China. He's a living legend in the Bureau and the Pentagon. President Topps has a soft spot for him.'

'We should be honoured.'

'We should be suspicious.'

'Why?'

'It was Declan Lehane that developed the GameOverRed malware used to attack China. The same malware these cyber criminals used to steal from us.'

'So, maybe he is here because of that special expertise?'

'Or maybe Declan Lehane is covering his backside,' suggested Steele. People exchanged glances. Steele turned to the Head of Legal. 'Is it possible to sue the FBI?'

'You'd be suing the government. The bureau will have indemnity.'

'Look into it.'

6

The Sunday papers devoted many pages to the emergency at Royal Shire Bank. They were long on speculation and short on facts. On social media the speculation was presented as fact. Mickey knew that they wouldn't really know what was happening until the stock market opened on Monday morning. Then RSB management and the Bank of England would have to clarify the situation. Until then they would just have to kill time.

They walked the dog on Hackney marshes, or what was left of them. Mickey remembered them stretching for miles when he was a boy. They had a pub lunch then another walk round the Olympic Park. Night fell early and he accompanied Helen to church. It was a welcome distraction before an Italian dinner with his phone turned off to stop him looking for news. Just before bedtime he turned it back on again to check. Still nothing, but share prices in Japanese banks had opened down on fears of exposure to Royal Shire. The pipes rattled again. He barely slept.

Dawn crept in through a tear in the curtain. Finally, he could stop trying to sleep. He sat up, stuffed two pillows behind his back and turned on the television, muted, with subtitles. There it was. A blood-red headline running along the bottom of the screen. Fact. No longer a rumour. Royal Shire Bank was bust. Needing a financial rescue.

The big question was whether it would be State Financial or the British Treasury. Whichever. One of them would do it. Time for work.

He dressed quietly then brushed his teeth with finger and soap. He left a note for Helen to take it easy then slipped out the door.

He was one of the first to arrive at the market and set out his stall methodically, stopping occasionally to check the news.

And the news was very bad. The worst possible. There would be no rescue of Royal Shire. State Financial and the British government had both ruled it out.

The bank was Hovis. Brown bread. Dead.

That cannot be. Someone else would step in.

He kicked a barrel of apples. Hurt his toe. Kicked it again.

Their life savings were tied up in that bank. If he couldn't get it back Helen would go nuts. He'd promised her everything would turn out fine.

An old woman came over and ordered some carrots. Get back to work. Focus on the present. 'That's three pounds eleven, love,' he said as he passed over the bag. 'Make it a nice round three.'

'You sure?' asked the woman with a smile. Everyone loves a bargain.

Now he was down two million pounds and eleven pence. 'Sure, I'm sure. You have a nice day.'

She moved on. He checked the news. Nothing more. Scrolled through some financial message boards. The word in the City was that Royal Shire might have struggled on, wounded for sure, but still alive. But what little money it had left was transferred back across the Atlantic late on Sunday night to protect State Financial's capital ratios. They pulled the plug.

He picked up an unsightly parsnip, snapped it in two and threw it as hard as he could into the green waste bin. Somehow, he was going to get his money back. Even if he had no idea how.

A familiar smile appeared.

'Morning, Jocelyn.'

'Morning, Mickey. Three kilos of Russet.'

Jocelyn always cheered him up. But even she couldn't manage that right now. He dropped a half dozen into a bag and placed it on the scales.

'Just shy of three kilos.' Mickey tapped on his calculator. Seventy-five pence times three came to … two million quid. 'That's two pounds twenty-five, love.'

She handed over a fiver, took her change and moved off with a breezy wave.

Well, she hadn't just lost two million quid. Back on his phone he came across a list of financial institutions that had dropped a big one investing in RSB. He wasn't the only mug in town.

Crosshairs Investments was one name that jumped out. His old pal Uli worked there now. He might have an inside track. He hit dial.

'Uli Slorer.'

'All right me old Viking. It's Mickey. How's tricks?'

'Hey, Mickey. How are you?'

'Got some issues to be honest, mate. Like to run them by you. Fancy a beer?'

'Is the Pope a Catholic?'

'See you in thirty minutes?' Mondays were always quiet on the market, and he could get Johnny on the next stall to mind the shop.

'They don't allow lunchtime drinking at Crosshairs.'

'Who's to know?'

'They do random breathalysers and blood tests. Not worth the risk.'

What had the world come to when you couldn't have a beer at lunchtime? 'What time do you clock off?'

'Six.'

'Six in the Lamb.'

7

Olga Federova smiled appreciatively at the freezing fog that had settled over St Petersburg. She liked the change of seasons. Moreover, she felt justified in buying the expensive quilted jacket and snow boots to wear on the walk to work. Outside a baker's, a queue shivered ferociously, and it made her think of the soldiers fighting bravely in Ukraine for the Motherland. When would this special military operation end? She could never talk openly about her reservations, but she was beginning to wonder how it could possibly be worth such loss of life.

The slow traffic on Linya Vo granted her safe passage to the foot of the glass headquarters of TruNews, where she paused at the revolving doors to greet her friend Ekaterina Albats.

'Brains before beauty,' said Olga, though if truth be told, Ekaterina had both.

They had been friends since they were teenagers in the Nashi anti-orange force promoted by President Pintov to defend Russia from dangerous pro-democracy activists. But whereas Olga had gone on to work in anonymity, underground in the cyber division of TruNews, Ekaterina had become the influential face of the news channel. Too influential in the view of some in the Kremlin. While still vehemently pro-Russian and supportive of the military, Ekaterina had cooled in support for Pintov and the Special Military Operation. She wasn't the only one. But she was the voice people listened to on national television. And a change in tone had been detected.

Consequently, Olga's department had been instructed to compile a dossier on Ekaterina's private life.

'We must have dinner,' said Ekaterina. 'Soon,' she called over her shoulder as she hurried away.

Olga would send her a reminder, though she doubted Ekaterina would fit a dinner into her hectic social scene.

After security Olga bought a coffee from the in-house vendor that had taken over after Starbucks withdrew from Russia. The coffee beans and water were just the same. If anything, it tasted better knowing it had nothing to do with imperialist America.

She took an elevator to level minus two. Here security was more serious and included the newly introduced iris scanner. Passage approved, Olga walked onto the cyber floor where over one hundred staff leant over monitors, heads bobbing like woodpeckers, claws picking at keyboards.

Once in the sanctuary of her office, she threw her coat on the stand and changed into slippers. She poured her coffee into a bone china cup that she'd bought in Odessa. She used to go there every summer and had no doubt she would do so again once the Special Military Operation was successful. She settled into an antique leather chair bought at an auction clear-out of St Petersburg Military Engineering University. It was sold as having belonged to Mendeleev, the father of the Periodic Table.

She sipped the coffee and tapped a ditty on the polished teak desktop as her computer warmed up. She checked her diary. It was clear as she'd instructed. It was going to be a busy enough day. Skimming down her email inbox a message from Bogdan glared out from the screen.

URGENT – need updates from Dmitri and Dragan.

One of her golden rules was to do the most important task first and then the most difficult. An update from Dmitri was the most important. Interaction with Dragan was always difficult. She savoured the last of the coffee then hit the intercom.

'Can you step into my office, please?'

Through the glass wall she saw Dmitri rise from his chair and amble over. He was short but muscular, even though he'd never seen the inside of a gym.

'Shut the door behind you, please.'

He pulled it to but didn't fully close it.

'How are you today?'

'I have a bit of a sore head. We celebrated hard all weekend.'

'Was that wise?' asked Olga. 'Drawing attention to yourself like that.'

He shrugged. 'Who's to know why we were celebrating?'

'Are we in danger of being exposed?'

'I've been careful as always.'

'The British bank RSB has collapsed.'

Dmitri smiled. 'Not bad?'

'Yes bad. You've been greedy. Now the British police and intelligence services will be looking for you.'

'Good luck to them,' Dmitri laughed. 'We withdrew and covered our tracks. Nothing can lead them to us.'

'Let us hope not. Keep me informed if anything changes.'

Dmitri took a few seconds to realise he had been dismissed, then pushed the door and returned to his desk. She messaged Bogdan with a summary of the conversation.

Now for the most difficult. Olga hit the intercom again.

'He's not in,' replied Dragan's secretary before she could ask.

'Please ask him to call me when he does come in.'

Olga stood up from the desk. Time to tour the floor. She paused at the door and looked about her. All across the room cyber teams with headphones were working in silence, except for the omnipresent cicada of keyboards.

The first person she met was the head of the troll farm. His red eyes betrayed the effects of the weed he'd smoked for breakfast.

'How's it going?' she asked.

'Good. There's a lot of heart-bleed on western social media for Kristensen. We're reminding everyone he was a fascist who was provoking war with Russia by installing missiles in Finland.'

'And that the CIA killed him?'

'Yes, that too.'

She walked along the group, smiling encouragingly whenever anyone caught her eye. She came to the end of the row where a young woman was monitoring the output from the adapted AI software.

'How's it going?' Olga asked again.

'Amazing,' replied the woman. 'The content is excellent.'

Olga stooped to read a post by some American redneck calling for NATO to intervene on the ground in Ukraine. The AI used its own 'intelligence' to reply that NATO had been interfering in Ukraine for years which is why Russia needed its special military operation. 'Very clever.'

'It's like it is human.'

Better than a human. Soon the AI tools would make the

woman and most of the trolling team redundant.

She moved on to the ransomware desk that targeted rich multinationals, locking up their files then charging for a digital key to release them. The levy was a paltry thousand dollars, which the companies almost always paid, and the team would throw in a complimentary PowerPoint presentation on how to prevent future hackers exploiting the same vulnerabilities. The team provided a genuine value-added service.

In fact, apart from Dragan, who really belonged to the dark side of Bogdan's business that she wanted no part of, all her cyber employees were good honest workers. Some were employed in legitimate activities such as research into security risks, like Ekaterina, and in helping the police monitor protest groups and rallies. None were the cyber punks of cliché. They were not rebels or anarchists. She did not employ those unreliable types. Her recruits were mostly well-adjusted university graduates. In another world they might be employed in constructive endeavour at a Russian Microsoft or Google. But even before sanctions the Americans had such a monopoly on the IT industry that the only jobs available to the bright young sparks in Russia were either with the FSB, on a regular income and a pension, or in cyber services, which paid better but was less secure.

Her phone rang. Dragan.

'Why aren't you in the office?'

'I work when I want to work.'

That was true of course and she wished she'd phrased it differently. 'Bogdan wants to know how things went.'

'I only talk to Bogdan.'

She sighed. Because of the nature of Dragan's work, he had his own office and reported directly to Bogdan with only a dotted line to Olga. She was fine with this arrangement as she wanted as little as possible to do with Dragan. But occasionally his refusal to communicate was frustrating. 'He simply wants to know if you had any problems on your trip?'

'No problems.'

'No encounters with the Finnish police or border control?'

'I said, no problems.'

She cut the call. In fact, she was relieved that Dragan did not want to talk. His car hacking had been murder. And he hadn't only killed Karl Kristensen, the American stooge, for whom Olga had little sympathy, but the other occupants of the car.

Olga might not approve of Dragan's work but Bogdan was the boss. He claimed they needed to do such 'political work' to keep onside with the siloviki. Like everyone in Russia, Bogdan was positioning for life after Pintov.

8

The high iron-and-glass structure of Leadenhall market left it airy and light, if a little cold in winter, and it had always been popular with smokers who could chuff away outside without fear of rain.

Outside the Lamb Tavern, Mickey found a tall table standing precariously on the cobbles. He ordered two pints of lager from a 'thirst-aider'. A couple on their phones at the next table were behaving like strangers. One bloke was reading a book. Used to be you went down the boozer for a pint and a chat.

'You all right there?' enquired a barmaid, setting down the drinks. 'Want me to turn on the patio heater?'

He pictured a polar bear on a shrinking ice flow and buttoned up his coat instead. 'I'm fine, love.'

'No worries.'

When had everyone become Australian?

Uli appeared without the longboat. He was sporting a new moustache that made him look like someone who could help police with their enquiries.

Mickey offered his hand. 'Do you know you've got something crawling over your top lip?'

Uli shrugged. 'My girlfriend likes it.'

'Cos it makes you look like her?'

They exchanged typical traders' banter as they recapped on who had done what since they had left the Quadra fund.

'What are these *issues* you wanted to discuss?' Uli asked eventually.

Mickey explained how he'd had all his savings in RSB ready to buy a house when the bank went bust.

'No way!'

'Way.'

'You know you'll get compensated eighty-five thousand pounds by the Financial Services Compensation Scheme,' said Uli.

'As everyone keeps telling me.'

'One hundred and seventy if it was a joint account.'

'It wasn't.' Helen had insisted on separate accounts but that was another story. 'Fact is, I've slid down the big snake and I'm back at square one.'

Uli took a sip of beer and wiped the froth from his moustache. 'Bit risky having all your money in one bank.'

'Usually, I have my nuts squirrelled away in various tree holes. But I had to bring it all together so I could complete on the house.'

'Bad luck.'

'I know. Somehow, I've got to make good again.'

'Like how?'

'I'm open to ideas,' said Mickey. 'RSB shares are still trading. I'm wondering if there is any chance of recovery?'

'It's just option money, Mickey. Don't go there.'

'Well, you guys at Crosshairs lost a packet as well. What are you planning to do?'

'We already cut our losses,' said Uli. He looked over both shoulders then lit a cigarette. 'It wiped out ten percent of the Special Situation fund. That's five hundred million pounds.'

'Did you see anything coming?'

'We heard rumours from a broker that the Latvian subsidiary was losing cash. Spoke to the RSB Finance Director. He told us not to worry. Next thing we know the bank is bust.'

'What are you going to do?'

Uli shrugged. 'Nothing we can do. Accidents happen.'

'Except this weren't an accident.'

'Agreed.'

'Who do you think it was?'

'It's the Russians, stupid.'

'You heard that from the police?'

Uli shook his head. 'Our head of cyber security heard from inside RSB. Plus, it was a Latvian bank. It's obvious.'

'The Kremlin sending a message?'

'Word is the St Petersburg mafia. But they would have needed the blessing of the Kremlin to do something as high profile as taking down a bank.'

'Why Latvia?'

'Do you read the papers?'

Not really. Too depressing. 'I know Russia is hassling the Baltic States now, but it's just sabre-rattling ain't it?'

'That's what we all thought before they invaded Ukraine. And it's the same thing now in Latvia. The Kremlin is miffed that Latvia is going to allow NATO missiles and heavy tanks on its territory. There was an understanding between NATO and Russia that a former Soviet bloc neighbour like Latvia wouldn't have weapons on its soil. It's like NATO can defend Latvia but it can't attack from there.'

'But that was all before Ukraine, right?'

'Correct.'

'Seems strange to bring down a bank instead of bomb the missile bases.'

'It fits with the Gerasimov Doctrine,' said Uli. He must have seen the blank expression on Mickey's face. 'Russian General. Came up with the concept of hybrid warfare, combining hard and soft power to achieve strategic aims. Proxy armies, disinformation, assassinations, cyberattacks, blocking grain shipments, stopping gas supplies etcetera. Bringing down a bank in Latvia disrupts the economy and sends a message that the neighbour next door is not to be messed with. Same thing with Karl Kristenson.'

'Karl Kristenson?' repeated Mickey.

'The Finnish President who was just killed in a car crash.'

'Missed that,' said Mickey.

'Well some don't think it was an accident. Nikolai Mishkin is certain it wasn't.'

'Who's Nikolai Mishkin when he's at home?'

'Russian dissident. Nose close to the ground in Russia.'

Mickey shrugged. He'd never heard of this Mishkin geezer.

And he hadn't heard about the car crash. 'Whatevs. But going back to the Latvian bank, that is interesting. I've been wondering whether we might get compensation.'

'You can get eighty-five …'

'Thousand from the FSCS. I know. You said. I'm talking about the whole lot. Sue for damages.'

'Sue who?' asked Uli, setting his drink down and looking interested.

'Pintov,' Mickey was just thinking aloud now. 'If we win, we get compensated from his frozen assets. That boat they've seized in Italy and whatever else they find.'

'I doubt you can take the President of Russia to court.'

'Well, here's another idea,' said Mickey. 'If RSB management were negligent because they didn't have their cyber defences up we could sue them.'

'Who said they didn't have their cyber defences up?'

'Stands to reason.'

'But the bank is bust, so you're not going to get any money back.'

'State Financial isn't,' Mickey pointed out. 'We could take out a class action. The Americans do it at the drop of a hat.'

Uli shrugged. 'You'd have to ask a lawyer.'

'I'm about to do just that.'

* * *

As Mickey approached Mitre chambers, he recalled the goose bumps he felt on his first meeting with Veronica to discuss his contract at RSB. That seemed a long time ago now. It might as well be as long ago as the construction of the white pillars and courtyards that belonged to the medieval world of the Knights Templar. It seemed odd to come here for advice on twenty first century cyber theft.

Veronica suddenly appeared from under an archway sporting a silk gown, white wig, and the same beguiling smile.

Mickey curtsied. 'No need to get all dressed up on my account.'

She shook his hand. 'One of the archaic conventions of working as a barrister I'm afraid. How are you?'

'Not good to be honest,' said Mickey. 'But I'll come to that. Are you well?'

She didn't reply. Her eyes moved up and to the left as if accessing a memory of something that had nearly been. 'Let's take a walk.'

They made small talk as they walked through the black gates into the wintry lawns of Temple Gardens and then Mickey explained how he had lost all his money in the collapse of RSB.

'I'm sorry to hear that.'

'That makes two of us.'

'You know about the Financial Services Compensation scheme.'

'It has been mentioned, but I'm down a bit more than that. Two million quid.'

'Two million? That's awful.'

'I'm fuming. Don't know who to be angry with but when I work it out, I'll clobber someone.'

'Don't do anything that will get you in trouble.'

Mickey smiled. It was nice that she cared. He watched her bend down to snap a head of seeds off a dead stem. She wrapped them in an empty crisp bag and put them in her briefcase.

'What are you thieving?'

'Fennel seeds,' she explained. 'They'll go to waste here. Are you a gardener?'

'I tried,' said Mickey. 'But I killed so many plants the garden centre has my face up on a wanted poster.'

She laughed quietly then asked. 'What did you want to see me about?'

'I'm wondering if there might be a way of getting my money back. Some legal action to take.'

'It's difficult to see an obvious route.'

'I've been reading around,' said Mickey. 'Wondering about criminal injuries.'

'But you haven't been injured.'

'Well it feels like I've been hit with a pickaxe. But I guess I'm thinking of emotional distress more than physical injury.'

Veronica took a seat on a bench by the fountain. 'That comes into play in cases of discrimination. But you weren't discriminated against.'

'How about fraud?' he asked, sitting on the bench, not too close. 'Fraud victims get compensation.'

'But you weren't the direct victim of fraud. The bank was. Really the government should step in and rescue the bank.'

'Can you have a word, because they're not playing ball.'

'And I see State Financial has turned its back as well,' said Veronica.

'That's another thought. How about suing the parent company for negligence?'

'That's a more likely route,' agreed Veronica.

Mickey's spirits lifted. The first sign of a breakthrough.

'But it won't be easy,' Veronica continued. 'You'd have to prove that State Financial management was criminally negligent in its cyber security. And it can take time for a class action case.'

'Like how long?'

'Many years.'

He didn't have that time. Needed to get Helen and baby settled in a new home soon.

'And you'd probably only receive a small portion of what you lost.'

Mickey puffed out his cheeks and for once was lost for words.

'Sorry I can't be more encouraging.' Veronica checked her watch. 'I'm due in court in ten minutes.'

They stood up and walked back through the gardens.

'Another idea I had was to sue Pintov.'

She stymied a smile. 'Was Pintov involved?'

'He'd have given it his blessing. I'm thinking I might get paid compensation from his seized assets?'

'I'm not aware that we have managed to identify any of his assets.' Veronica shook her head. 'Even if we have, those assets would be frozen. To be seized the government would need to pursue an Unexplained Wealth Order. And they have been notoriously unsuccessful at that in the past.'

They walked on through the courtyards and then over the Strand stopping outside the ecclesiastically feigned Royal Courts of Justice.

'I'm sorry I can't think of a way forward.'

'No problem. I'll find a way.'

'I don't doubt that.' She offered a hand. 'Nice to see you again, Mickey.'

'And you. See you round.'

Round. Like the big fat zero solutions he'd come up with so far. What was he going to tell Helen?

9

Director Connelly's silence unsettled Declan. There was none of the usual forensic questioning as he debriefed on his visit to State Financial. He seemed more interested in the view out the window of the Hoover building's brutalist lower trapezium.

Eventually, Connelly cut in. 'Has the GameOverRed malware come up?'

'Of course. The in-house IT guys knew about it.'

'Did Steele mention it?'

'He asked what the malware was called. I told him and he made a note on his pad.'

'Damnation.' Connelly turned to a different window and gazed out over the pleasing diagonal of Pennsylvania avenue. 'Does he know you wrote it?'

'The malware the hackers used is a derivative,' said Declan, avoiding the question.

'But you created the original.'

'What are you worried about?'

'That Steele will sue the Bureau.'

'We issued Microsoft a patch for GameOverRed more than a year ago. The Bureau is not to blame if people don't use it. Plus, the Stuxnet source code can be downloaded online and is adapted by hackers all the time. Nobody has thought to sue the CIA or Homeland.'

'Dominic Steele isn't nobody.'

'If we are going to lay blame anywhere other than with the cyber criminals then I'd blame Dominic Steele.'

Connelly turned back to face Declan. 'Go on.'

'The IT department at the Latvian bank didn't use the Microsoft patch. They were at fault. Management is at fault. Ultimately Steele is to blame.'

'That is very good to know, Declan. I'll keep that in my back pocket.' Suddenly Connelly switched back to his investigative self. 'Sounds like it might be an inside job.'

'We're exploring that possibility. Running background checks on everyone connected, especially compliance officers.'

'I'm not really interested in solving the crime here,' said Connelly. 'We're never going to bring anyone to court, are we? So don't waste resources. The priority is to keep GameOverRed out of the picture.'

'I still don't see how he can sue,' said Declan.

'It's not just a legal challenge. I don't want headlines saying the FBI nearly collapsed State Financial. You don't need the bad PR.'

It was only later, as Declan fought through traffic on Pennsylvania Avenue, that he replayed Connelly's remark. He hadn't used 'we'. Neither had the Bureau been the subject. Connelly clearly thought it was Declan who didn't need the bad PR. And there was only one explanation for that.

10

'You said everything would be all right!'

'It will be,' said Mickey. 'Don't worry.'

'Why shouldn't I worry?' asked Helen. 'You've lost all our money and we've got nowhere to live.'

'I'll get the money back.'

'From Royal Shire?'

'That's not going to work.'

She gripped her shoulder and began to sob. 'The solicitor said you should never have put all our money in one bank.'

'That's easy to say now.' Mickey put his arms around her. 'Don't worry. I will fix this.'

'How?'

'I don't know yet. But I will. I'm going to see DI Brighouse. Remember him?'

She wiped her eyes and looked up into Mickey's face. 'Can he help?'

'If he can't, he'll know someone who can. Meantime you should take it easy. Don't go into work today.'

'We're short-staffed.'

Because you can't recruit teaching assistants on nine grand a year, he thought. But he couldn't say that. 'You've got enough stress already without toddlers screaming at you.'

'Actually, I think I *will* take the day off.'

'Do that. Take it easy. And don't worry about the money. I'll get it all back.'

He smiled reassuringly. Though he hadn't the foggiest idea how he was going to manage that.

* * *

Stress leads to poor decisions and probably explained why Mickey had chosen a poncy wine bar charging twenty-five quid for a bottle of plonk when he was down to his last few pennies. Hopefully it would be worth it when Frank came up with some ideas on how to get his money back.

Frank appeared in the doorway. He shook the rain off his brolly, clocked Mickey, then raised one finger in the air as if dismissing him from the wicket.

'Good to see you,' said Mickey.

He shook Frank's hand firmly, then poured him a glass.

'I'm not really a wine drinker,' said Frank. 'Yorkshire bitter. Guinness at a push. But I'll give it a go.'

'How's tricks?'

'I'm in good health. So is the family. You?'

'We'll come on to that. You still with the Fraud Squad?'

'Economic crime,' Frank corrected.

'You still working there?'

'Why are you interested?'

'I'm looking into the collapse of RSB. I want to know who's responsible.'

Frank took a sip from his glass, winced then set it back down on the table and pushed it a few inches into the middle. 'Why is that?'

'I got badly burnt.'

'Thought you'd left finance,' said Frank. 'You decided to go back to the rat race after all.'

'Trouble with the rat race is that even if you win it, you're still a rat.' Mickey looked away. He had done the right thing leaving. 'I did quit to go work back on the market, like you say. But I had all my savings in RSB, ready to buy a house. When it went bust, I lost the lot.'

'You know you can get back eighty-five thousand pounds …'

'From the Financial Services Compensation scheme,' Mickey finished. 'It has been mentioned. But it's not going to do a lot of good. I had two million quid there.'

'Ouch.'

'And I want to get it back.'

Frank picked up his glass and tried another cautious sip. This time he seemed to find it more agreeable.

'So, come on then,' said Mickey. 'What do you know about it?'

Frank shook his head. 'It's not my investigation.'

'Don't give me that. You must know what's going on.'

'It's not my patch.'

Mickey frowned. 'Thought you was a mate.'

'On a personal basis I am.'

'Well then, on a personal basis, what's your hunch? Russians?'

'Probably.'

'Rumour is it's the Russian mafia. Reckon you'll catch them?'

Frank didn't take the bait. Took a good gulp of wine instead. 'It's actually not bad this stuff.'

'I hope so at twenty-five quid a bottle,' said Mickey. 'Do you reckon they'll get caught? Because then there might be a way for me to get my money back.'

'I don't think the Russian mafia do refunds,' said Frank.

'Some sort of criminal compensation,' said Mickey. 'I asked a lawyer who thinks there might be a way. Veronica. You remember?'

'I remember,' said Frank with a raised eyebrow. 'Look Mickey, if it is Russians, it would be impossible to prosecute given current relations.'

'But the money must have gone somewhere. If you can prove it was a crime you could confiscate it?'

'It'll be spread over digital currencies, gold, offshore accounts. Impossible to find.' Frank refilled his glass.

'Well, what are you going to do about this?'

'Nothing much, I suspect.'

Mickey shook his head. 'I know you boys don't bother with shoplifting anymore, but this is a bit more serious.'

Frank shrugged apologetically. 'I'm just telling you how it is.'

'I'll do it myself. Point me in the right direction. Where do I start?'

'Are you mad? You can't take on the Russian mafia.'

'I am mad. That's the point. Furious that someone has nicked my life savings. I don't care if it's the Russian mafia or Pintov himself. I'm after them. So where do I look?'

Frank sat back in his chair and studied Mickey. Checked the room and then said quietly, 'It does look to have been the Russian mafia.'

'I already know that.'

'St Petersburg mob. But how does that help you? You can't just fly over and ask them for your money back.'

'I don't know yet. You got anything more specific?'

'Yes. These people are specifically very dangerous. I strongly recommend you don't get involved.'

'Well, I am involved. And I reckon you still owe me for what I did in China.'

'You did quite nicely out of that, if I remember correctly. That's how you came to have two million quid to lose.'

'Don't give me that. I deserved a reward. Anyhow, what I made has all gone down with the good ship RSB.'

After a long pause, Frank said, 'Let me make some enquiries. I still can't imagine a way that you can get your money back, but if we're not going to investigate and you're mad enough to do it, I'll see what I can tell you. No promises. But I'll try.'

* * *

When Frank had left the bar Mickey scurried up the winding stairs. He stopped when his head was at street level and saw Frank pull up his coat collar against the wind and set off along the embankment.

Mickey climbed the last few steps. Out in the street Frank weaved in and out of the other pedestrians. Mickey nearly lost him passing the Houses of Parliament when a coach tipped out a ton of Chinese tourists.

He pushed through and carried on along the north bank of the Thames until he came to Lambeth bridge. He stopped behind a lamppost and pulled out his phone. He took a picture as Frank walked into Thames House.

Frank had also done well out of his involvement in China. Got a move into MI5. He'd said he was still in Economic Crime.

He was putting his phone back in his pocket when it rang.

Helen.

'All right love.'

'Mickey, I'm bleeding.'

11

Olga checked the latest profile reports prepared for the FSB. She took a personal interest in the file on her friend Ekaterina and was pleased to note there was no mention of their relationship. Ekaterina's girlfriend was mentioned, at length, and a relationship with a married man. Neither of which was illegal but would still provide Moscow with leverage.

She then checked a report on the anti-war protesters undermining the morale of the brave soldiers on the front. Of course, everyone wants an end to the war but protesting would not help. As she skimmed through the photographs one jumped off the page. It was the architecture student who lived in the apartment above her in Petrogradsky. No surprise there. A boy who wore white poppies and had yet to enter employment thought he understood the world better than President Pintov.

Her secure desk phone rang. Only one person ever rang it.

'How are you?' asked Bogdan in his distinctive Gulag slang. 'And how is your father?'

Bogdan was entitled to ask as he was paying for the proton radiation therapy. 'He is still very weak, but the doctors are satisfied with the treatment.'

'That is the important thing,' said Bogdan.

She started to talk through her daily report, but Bogdan cut in.

'Update me on Dragan. Still no problems?'

'He says not. But I don't understand why we need to be involved in that type of business. If the SVR want to assassinate a politician, they should do it themselves.'

'You know how it works, Olga. If something goes wrong, they can blame it on a rogue, over-enthusiastic patriot like Dragan. It's the same situation with Dmitri. Is he still in the clear?'

'He has fully laundered the money. He says it is untraceable.'

'I am not so confident. I think the Americans and the British will be looking for us. He went too far collapsing the bank.'

'Do we care? We're at war with them.'

'I don't care. And Mr Pintov is delighted. But it has angered my partner.'

Olga had never met this silent partner that Bogdan often referenced when he wanted to pass things off as beyond his control. 'Well, as I say, Dmitri says everything is safe.'

'I hope he is right. It is a very sensitive moment for my partner. If the British or Americans find Dmitri, they will find me. I do not care. But if it leads to him, things will go very badly for us.'

12

Whipps Cross Hospital's one-way system and signage must have been designed by a prankster, but Mickey eventually found the Emergency Department entrance. It was guarded by an 'Ambulances Only' sign that he was tempted to ignore, but he raced on to the car park and took the first space available. Blue badge. Tough.

They walked slowly. He didn't want Helen to panic. He was

doing enough for both. Helen told a male triage nurse about the bleeding. Her voice was higher than normal, and she spoke a little quicker.

A twenty-minute wait was nineteen too long but eventually another nurse took them behind a curtain. Date of last period? Six weeks apparently, so that's the age of the little one. Pulse, blood pressure, temperature, oxygen saturation all taken. Mickey stepped out when she wanted a urine sample.

The nurse left them in a waiting area. Helen was silent. Mickey had a hundred questions, but knew better than to ask.

When the nurse eventually returned her face gave nothing away.

'Everything appears to be fine,' she said, as if commuting a death sentence.

'Thank you,' said Helen.

'Shouldn't we get a scan?' asked Mickey.

'Not at this stage,' said the nurse, eyes on Helen. 'I'm going to refer you to the Early Pregnancy Unit. They'll call you tomorrow to discuss your symptoms and they'll give you advice or make an appointment to come in for assessment. That might include an ultrasound, but not every pregnant person needs one.'

Pregnant person? Pregnant woman, surely? He looked at Helen, but she apparently hadn't noticed.

'Thank you,' she repeated.

'But your high blood pressure is concerning,' said the nurse.

'Did that cause the bleeding?'

'That would appear to be a normal implantation bleed. But high blood pressure during pregnancy can increase the chances of having a baby who is preterm or low birthweight. You should discuss this at the EPU. Are you especially stressed at present?'

Helen looked at Mickey and then back to the nurse. 'I am.'

'I know it can be really hard, but you should try to avoid stress if you possibly can.'

Mickey made a pledge. Whatever it took he was going to get his money back and buy a home for Helen and the baby. End of.

* * *

The Parcel Yard pub was as busy as in its old days as the postal sorting office at Kings Cross station. Mickey was contemplating getting his second pint when Frank finally showed up at the top of the stairs. He came down them two at a time and glided over the floor on the balls of his feet. Something to do with strengthening his running gait he'd once explained.

Frank checked his watch. 'Sorry I'm late.'

'What can I get you?'

'Nothing.'

'I can't drink on my own.'

Frank looked at the nearly empty glass. 'Looks like you're managing fine. I can only spare ten minutes, Mickey.'

'Got to get back to the Economic Crime division.' Mickey winked then pulled up the picture of Frank walking into Thames House. 'You've been telling porkies.'

'We are supposed to be discrete.'

'Bit daft walking in the front entrance of MI5 then.'

Frank nodded to concede the point. 'It's not the end of the world if someone knows. We just don't offer it up unnecessarily.'

'Right, well now we've cleared that up maybe you can come again with what you know about the collapse of Royal Shire Bank.'

'It does look to have been the St Petersburg mafia.' Frank folded his arms and sat back in his chair. 'But I still don't understand what you think you can do about it, Mickey.'

'Let me worry about that. Come on. Got a name you can stick with a warrant?'

'Who would serve it?' asked Frank.

'I'll do it.'

Frank laughed. 'You probably would 'n' all. It's hypothetical in any case. There won't be any warrants issued.'

'So, you're still not going to do anything?'

Frank looked away for a moment then came back to Mickey. Motioned him closer with his finger and lowered his voice. 'Given your extraordinary losses and considering all you've done for us in the past, I've been able to arrange for a colleague to talk to you. She'll be better placed to explain the sensitivities and why we're not doing anything. And why you should also keep your big nose out of it.'

'Thanks.'

'I'll be in touch with arrangements.' Frank rose effortlessly to his feet.

Core strength from all that running.

'One question,' said Mickey. 'Before you go.'

'Go on.'

'Just something you said. A serious matter. More important than the collapse of a bank.'

Frank checked his watch again. 'Be quick.'

'No more porkies. Tell the truth.'

'I will if you ever get to the point.'

Mickey turned side on and touched his nose. 'Is it really a big one?'

* * *

Crossing Lambeth bridge Mickey paused briefly to take in the elegant main entrance of Thames House brooding ahead of him. The black bollards, doors and lampposts contrasted with the white Portland stone walls and high archway. He walked to a side entrance that Frank had told him to use. Collected his thoughts. Objective: get the inside track on the bank hacking and make money front running that information.

Through a bomb-proof door into a security room made of thick glass. Behind it armed guards stood serenely in dark blue uniform and Kevlar vests.

'Mickey Summer,' he announced on the intercom and read out the reference number Frank had given.

He was directed to place his jacket on the conveyer for the X-ray and put some ID in a small hatch. A moment later a door opened, and a guard appeared waving an electronic wand.

'Shoes off please, sir.'

'Hold your nose,' said Mickey as he removed them.

'Do you have any metal objects in your body; studs or surgical pins or anything like that?'

'Not that I know of,' replied Mickey, faint at the thought.

After passing the scan and a body search Mickey put his shoes back on. The guard tapped on the glass and the door opened again. On the other side he was met by a receptionist who led him down corridors bustling with smartly dressed, bright-looking people. Just like Threadneedle Street of old. The receptionist opened a door and ushered him into a meeting room.

Frank was already waiting with a colleague.

'Morning all,' said Mickey.

'Good morning,' replied the woman, raising a hand.

'I'm Mickey. But I guess you know that. And you are?'

'Let's use Jennie.'

Mickey took a seat.

'Jennie has been looking into the RSB collapse,' explained Frank. 'Certain matters are confidential but there are some things we are happy to disclose. Although of course this is strictly off the record. Do you understand?'

'I might have a big gob,' said Mickey, 'but I know when to keep it shut. Did I ever mention anything about our China adventure to anyone?'

'You didn't,' said Frank. 'Which is why you are here now.'

'Great. So, what can you tell me?'

Jennie cast a sideways glance at Frank. 'Attribution in cyberattacks is very difficult. It is almost impossible to determine by connectivity. The Russians no longer launch attacks from within Russia. They set up servers around the world under remote command and control centres.'

'But you do think it is Russia,' said Mickey.

Jennie nodded. 'It's probable, but not certain, that the FSB's 18th Centre developed the targeted spear phishing attacks and the malware, and they augmented the operation using cyber criminals to move the money into bank accounts.'

'Any clues on the cyber criminals then?'

'Nothing concrete.'

'I've heard it was the St Petersburg mafia.'

'Where did you hear that?'

Mickey hesitated. He didn't want to get Uli in trouble. The Russian dissident who Uli had heard it from had already agreed to meet Mickey and so it wasn't much of a porkie to give his name.

'Nikolai Mishkin.'

Jennie glanced at Frank again then turned back to Mickey. 'I'd take what Mishkin says with a large dose of salt.'

'But is he right?'

She hesitated. 'Again, nothing is certain. But digital fingerprints do point to a hacker known as Dmitri, other times Geneve, Hawaiian Fury or Torchlight. He's independent but he has been known to work with the St Petersburg mafia.'

'He has previous then.'

'Filleting accounts.'

'Is that what's happened with RSB?'

'Yes and no. Filleting with botnets is usually simply gathering codes and passwords and then siphoning off relatively small sums of money from thousands of accounts. That usually doesn't cause much damage because the daily limit notifications flag up the transfers and the theft is spotted and stopped. And as it is fraud the bank pays the customer back. And as they're small sums the bank doesn't really have a problem with it. A cost of doing business online you might say.'

'How was this so damaging?' asked Mickey.

'This used AI generated targeted spear phishing emails that were so much more convincing than the normal crude phishing emails people receive all the time and spot as fake. Eventually someone clicked and let the hackers into the whole system. They could then submit fraudulent and irrevocable funds transfers. Then they hid evidence by removing the statements and confirmations that would normally act as secondary controls. Nobody spotted they were siphoning off billions of pounds.'

'It sounds like you're well on top of this,' said Mickey, more hopeful than he had been for days. 'Are you going after Dmitri?'

She shook her head. 'He's already under sanctions and subject to travel bans and asset freezes.'

'Can't you get him for this crime as well?'

'The truth is ...' She hesitated, looked at Frank, then down at her hands.

What was the truth, and when might she get round to it?

'The truth is there's just no point. All we can do is learn what we can to prevent similar cyberattacks in future. There isn't any appetite for pursuing a prosecution.'

'Who's got no appetite?'

'Management,' she said vaguely.

'Our friends down river,' explained Frank, jerking a thumb in a southerly direction.

'MI6?'

'They're called SIS now.'

'Same difference. Why have they got no appetite?'

'Zero chance of prosecution. Plus, national security.'

'I don't understand.' Mickey turned back to Jennie. 'Russia invades Ukraine, it threatens Finland and Latvia. It collapses a British bank. Why are they being so wet?'

Jennie's face froze like a gargoyle while she considered her reply. 'If we can't prove it was Russians then it's just mudslinging and it weakens our position when we do have something concrete. We need to spare our punches.'

'Do you agree with this approach?'

'It's not for me to agree or otherwise.'

Mickey smiled. 'You think we should be going after them. And you, Frank?'

'It doesn't matter what I think,' he replied, just as unconvincingly. 'I brought you here to do you a favour. To show you that everyone thinks this is a lost cause. Give up on it.'

'But for me it's personal,' said Mickey. 'Like I told you, Frank, I've got to get my money back.'

'There's nothing to be done.'

'I'll see if Nikolai Mishkin has any ideas,' said Mickey mischievously.

Frank and Jennie exchanged looks.

'I'd really advise you not to get involved with Mishkin,' said Frank.

'Well let me talk to someone at MI6.'

'SIS,' Frank corrected. 'You're not going to change anybody's mind.'

He didn't want to change anyone's mind. He wanted to know what they were thinking. He'd already got one useful tidbit. 'Let me talk to them anyway.'

Frank sighed heavily. 'You are very demanding, Mickey.'

'Last request.'

'I'll see if I can find someone prepared to talk to you.'

They closed the meeting with small talk and then Frank chaperoned Mickey back to reception. Walking through the corridors of Thames House, Mickey got the feeling that a little bit of thread had come loose. It went by the name of Dmitri, and he was going to pull it and see how far the ball would unravel.

13

It was a ninety-minute drive across London and out into deepest Surrey, where most of Mickey's old City friends lived. However, none of them lived in a magnificent castle like Nikolai Mishkin, even if first impressions were spoilt by the vicious razor wire halfway up the walls. It seemed unnecessary, as the moat was twenty metres wide and Spiderman would struggle to climb the smooth ten metres to the battlements. People who fell out with Pintov clearly needed to take extra precautions.

Mickey edged the front wheels of the car onto the drawbridge then hesitated. Don't look down. Wet stuff a long way below. Focus on the towers above. He drove over, a little fast. Had to brake hard at the security detail. They checked his driving licence against a visitor list then punched a code into a panel on the castle wall. The portcullis rose, protesting its age with squeals and rattles.

Inside the walls a small, landscaped garden offered the only relief from a gravel courtyard. A guard escorted him through huge oak doors into a marble lobby, where a receptionist in an uncomfortably tight dress greeted Mickey and showed him into a drawing room that exuded wealth with heavy curtains, crystal, Renaissance paintings, and antique furnishings. Mickey parked himself on a chaise longue.

He didn't have long to wait before Mishkin arrived. He had a face like an unmade bed, but the one redeeming feature was wide, deep blue eyes.

Mickey stuck out a hand. 'Mickey Summer.'

'Welcome,' Mishkin replied without accepting the handshake.

'Nice pad you've got.'

'Indeed.' Mishkin took a seat on a Louis XVI armchair. Might have been original. 'Would you like a drink?'

'I'm all right, mate.'

Mishkin pulled a plastic water bottle from inside his jacket, took a sip, replaced the cap, tightened it securely then put it back in the pocket. 'Tell me a little about yourself, Mister Summer. You're a Cockney.'

'I am. And it's Mickey.'

Mishkin nodded. 'Nikolai.'

Mickey rattled through a potted history of his time in the City and his more recent past making a living on the market stall in Spitalfields and then losing everything in the collapse of RSB bank.

Mishkin crossed his hands under his chin and rested his elbows on the arms of the chair. 'How can I help?'

'You're on record saying you reckon the collapse was the work of the St Petersburg mafia with help from the state. I'm looking for any leads you might have.'

'And what would you do with them?'

'Not sure yet.'

'Take them to the police?'

'They don't seem interested.'

'They never are.'

'Might have to investigate myself.'

Mishkin produced a thin elongated smile. 'That's fighting talk.'

'I said investigate. Not fight.'

Mishkin nodded to concede the point. 'Even investigation can be very dangerous. This goes all the way to Pintov. If you got close, he would have you killed.'

'I'll keep socially distanced then,' said Mickey.

'He kills with impunity.' Mishkin sat back in his chair with his hands folded on the table. 'Over a dozen murders in Britain.'

'I've read about some. That guy who was poisoned with uranium …'

'Polonium,' Mishkin corrected. 'Alexander Litvinenko. A good friend.'

'Then there was that couple who got done by a nerve agent in Canterbury.'

'Salisbury.' Mishkin took another sip of water.

The door opened and a young lady popped her head in. 'Sorry to interrupt darling but you do remember we are having dinner at the Waldorf?'

'Yes. Yes.' He turned in his chair. 'This is my wife, Julia. This is Mickey Summer. He's thinking of taking on the Russian mafia and Pintov. What do you think about that?'

'Very courageous, Mister Summer.'

And then she was gone.

'Have you heard the name Nikolai Glushkov?' asked Mishkin.

Mickey shook his head.

'He was strangled with his own dog's leash. Nobody was prosecuted. Boris Berezovsky?'

Mickey had only just come across the name in his research into Russia. 'Another dissident.'

'Correct. There were multiple well-documented assassination attempts on his life and when they did finally get him it was made to look like suicide. But a German asphyxiation expert said that his injuries were not consistent with hanging. The marks on his neck were circular and not V-shaped. His face was discoloured instead of pale. There was also a fresh wound on the back of his head, and he had a fractured rib. The coroner recorded an open verdict. But he was murdered.'

'I'm sure you're right, but why are you telling me all this?'

Mishkin ignored the question. 'Mikhail Lesin. He died from multiple blunt-force injuries to his head, neck, torso, arms, and legs. He had "apparently",' Mishkin signed the inverted commas, 'bludgeoned himself to death by repeatedly falling in his room while drunk. Verdict: suicide.'

Mishkin retrieved his water bottle and took another sip, replaced the lid tight and put the bottle back inside his jacket. 'Doctor Matthew Puncher. Stabbed repeatedly with two knives and sustained wounds on his hands consistent with defending himself from a third-party assault. Police verdict: suicide. Scot Young. Plunged to his death on wrought-iron spikes. Police verdict: suicide.'

Another pause. 'Alexander Perepilichny. Despite having no history of heart problems, he died of a heart attack while out jogging in St George's Hill. Aged forty-two.'

'It happens,' said Mickey.

'It happens,' agreed Mishkin. 'But two autopsies proved inconclusive. Eventually his life insurance company ordered tests on his stomach contents and discovered traces of a deadly natural poison called Gelsemium, nicknamed 'heart break grass' because it triggers cardiac arrest if ingested.'

Mishkin edged forward on his seat and rattled off a list of other names without going into detail.

'Why are you telling me all this?' Mickey asked again.

'Two reasons,' replied Mishkin. 'First is that you will get no help from the British police. They turned a blind eye to all those murders, and they also don't want to know about Russian criminal activities. Even now after Ukraine. Too many politicians and others in authority who have been bought off by Russia.'

'And the second reason?' asked Mickey, not even believing the first.

'I want you to understand how a totalitarian state works. The siloviki in charge are unaccountable and can do anything. They can collapse a bank, assassinate a politician. Anything is possible. The thousands of deaths from Chernobyl are the best example.'

Mickey was reluctant to encourage Mishkin, but he had to point out that Chernobyl happened in the Soviet era.

'It's the same siloviki in charge. Same philosophy. The state had to maintain the position of invincibility. It denied there was any problem. Its own citizens could not leave the city, phone lines were cut. They continued with the May Day parades in Ukraine even though the air was radioactive.'

'Mate, I gave up history in year nine. Why is this relevant to me?'

'The people you are considering investigating are very dangerous.'

'Thanks. I've got that. But where should I start looking?'

Mishkin sat in silence a while and studied Mickey. 'Your friends in the intelligence community would be a good place to start.'

'Who says I've got any?'

'Frank Brighouse in MI5 for example.' Mishkin smiled and then went on to explain, 'I have thorough background checks performed on everyone who visits.'

'MI5 don't seem interested. No chance of a prosecution.'

'As I explained, they don't want a prosecution. But Frank might be able to give you information.'

He thought of the conversation they'd had. 'That's as maybe.'

'But what do you think you can do on your own?' asked Mishkin.

'I don't know yet. I haven't got a plan.'

'Are you prepared to travel to St Petersburg?'

'If I need to.'

'What would be your cover story?'

'Tourist?'

Mishkin shook his head. 'The Foreign Office advice is essential travel only. Important business requiring your physical presence. You could use your background in finance.'

Mickey tossed it over for a while. 'I could be an investor thinking of buying Russian equities. Meeting Russian corporates.'

'That could work,' agreed Mishkin.

'Any other ideas?'

'Your friend Ivan Kazbegi would also be a good person to talk to.'

'How come?' asked Mickey.

'He grew up in St Petersburg and had mafia links before he "ostensibly" cleaned up his act.'

Mickey was not exactly mates with the Russian owner of West Ham Football Club, but had done some advisory work for Kazbegi when he'd bought the club. 'I'll give him a call.'

'Keep me in touch,' said Mishkin. 'I'd like to help. Any leads you get, check them out with me first.'

With that Mishkin left the room. A guard escorted Mickey back to the courtyard where his car was waiting with the door open and engine running.

He survived the drawbridge and on the drive back to London an idea began to form. Not in a flash. More like candlelight flickering through fog. A cover story for poking around in Russia. And a corner to poke around in.

14

Halfway across Vauxhall Bridge Mickey's tracker alarm sounded. He glanced at the display. Five thousand paces before he'd had a sniff of breakfast. Legend.

In the distance the honey concrete and green glass headquarters of SIS looked like an escaped river monster that refused to be put back in the Thames. Mission today: find out whether MI6 were looking into the hacking. And get names to chase up.

He continued his slalom through commuters and tourists, arriving at the entrance just as it started to rain. The security check was thorough and included a full body scan.

'Do I go to my GP for the results?' Mickey asked.

'I've heard them all before,' the scanner replied, before passing Mickey on to a guard, who led him down labyrinthine corridors to a windowless meeting room that pressed upon his claustrophobia. He took a seat and dipped into his pocket for his phone before remembering it had been left at security. Nothing to look at. Nothing to do.

Mercifully, the door opened. In walked a short man with the fulsome smile of a restaurant owner undone by dandruff on his jacket collar. 'Peter Jones.'

'Mickey Summer,' he said, accepting the handshake. 'I really appreciate you seeing me. I know you don't usually talk to civvies.'

'Not at all, Mickey. After all you did for us in China, we owe you the courtesy of a friendly chat.' Jones cleared his throat. 'Frank tells me you are interested in the collapse of Royal Shire Bank.'

'Just wondering why we're not doing anything about it.'

'The Economic Crime Squad are investigating,' Jones pointed out.

'But they're only looking at what lessons can be learnt to

prevent future cyber thefts.'

'Important, don't you think?'

'What about catching the thieving geezers that done it? They nicked two million quid off me.'

'I'm sorry to hear that.' Jones affected a look of grave concern. 'In an ideal world the police would prosecute the perpetrators. But there is no realistic chance of any prosecution.'

'I've heard it's you guys that have kiboshed any investigation.'

'I'd be as interested as you to know who did this,' said Jones. 'But it has not been prioritised here for much the same reasons as it has not been with the police. Even if we found who did it there is nothing to be gained.'

That seemed implausible to Mickey. 'I've already worked out it was a cyber gang that operates out of St Petersburg,' said Mickey. 'And that's just little old me after a few days.'

Jones scratched an eyebrow.

'I was told that by Nikolai Mishkin,' said Mickey quickly, eager to protect Frank.

'Mishkin.' Jones repeated, brushing the dandruff off his collar. 'Yes, he's been offering his opinion to anyone who will listen to him. But even if we could prove it was a specific cyber gang in St Petersburg, we would never get them to court. The Russians wouldn't extradite.'

'Mishkin also thinks the collapse of the Latvian bank wasn't just criminal, it was political.'

'I wouldn't believe everything you hear from Nikolai Mishkin. However, undoubtedly this will have had Pintov's blessing.'

'So that's another reason to go after them.'

Jones leant back in his chair far enough for Mickey to worry he might fall over. 'We are not going to find Pintov's fingerprints on the keyboard and if we accuse him it will only strengthen his support.'

'How come?'

'Whenever the West accuses Pintov, he simply dismisses the accusation as lies to undermine him. The Russian people believe him, become fervently patriotic, and rally round him. Win, win for Pintov.'

'You're saying he's untouchable?'

Jones shrugged. 'Arguably.'

'You know that some of the big institutions who lost money are thinking of taking out a private prosecution against Pintov. Get compensation from his frozen assets.'

'Good luck with that one.' Jones laughed, but made a note in a pad on his leather desktop.

'It seems like we don't care about Russian aggression in Eastern Europe.'

'Believe me we do.'

'But you're not doing anything. Everyone is just standing by while Pintov thrashes around like a wild animal.'

'Good analogy,' said Jones. 'He is wild and angry. Under such circumstances the best course of action is to contain the animal and let it work off its anger.'

'You say that as if you think his anger is justified.'

Jones raised his palms upward. 'That's a conversation to be had at length with a good bottle of scotch.'

'So, you do think he *is* justified,' Mickey pressed.

Jones smiled. 'There is a view in some quarters this side of the pond, that NATO has been guilty of mindless corporatism. Growing for the sake of it. Croatia, Albania, Montenegro as examples. Losing sight of its original purpose. As for eastern Europe and the Baltic States and especially Ukraine, some might say that was just provocative.'

'So that's the plan,' said Mickey. 'Contain the angry bear. Don't provoke further.'

Jones just smiled again but said nothing.

'I'm not going to poke any bears but I am going to St Petersburg to have a sniff around.'

'I'd strongly recommend you let this one slide, Mickey. I'd be amazed if you found the culprits. I'm almost certain you won't get your money back. And I am crystal clear it would be very dangerous.'

'So is smoking.'

'I'd advise against that as well,' said Jones, pushing his glasses up over the bridge of his nose with a nicotine-stained finger.

'But you do it anyway.'

'Can't stop myself, unfortunately.'

'Me neither,' said Mickey. He got to his feet. 'Thanks for your time.'

All he'd learned was that SIS thought Pintov had some reason to be angry. It was disappointing but not entirely unexpected. He needed to shake things up a bit. Starting with Ivan Kazbegi.

* * *

Jones pulled up the file on Michael John Summer. It was impressive. There was a brief background history on his troubled childhood in London's east end, expulsion from school without qualifications. Minor criminal activities. Then a section on the bonus pool murders at Royal Shire Bank where he went from prime suspect to full exoneration from DI Frank Brighouse who was now at MI5. Then there was Summer's extraordinary help liaising between American and British intelligence during an insider-trading enquiry, which escalated into full cyber war with China and the uncovering of a suspected deep-state body in America called the Black Chamber. Mickey Summer was clearly very resourceful.

Jones called Frank Brighouse.

'Mickey Summer,' he said.

'Yes,' Brighouse replied cautiously.

'As requested, I explained the futility in pursuing these Russian hackers. Why we're not and he shouldn't.'

'What was his reaction?'

'He seems determined to go ahead on his own. He's even got an idea to sue Pintov.'

'Good luck with that.'

'That's what I said. But the thing is he could get himself into serious trouble, and after all he did for us in China, I sort of feel like we need to protect him a bit.'

'I agree.'

'Plus, it might blow up in our faces. We should look after him as best we can while keeping at arm's length.'

'So just keep him and us safe then?'

'Well. Of course I'd need to see anything he does discover however unlikely that is.'

'So why don't you investigate?'

Jones sighed. 'Unfortunately, I don't set intelligence priorities. Requirements do that. Even if they agreed we'd then have to wait for assessment from case risk. If they agreed to send in an officer, we'd first need background work from the data scientists and covert communications. You get the picture. Never going to happen. Instead, I have someone we know who has shown some capability and is prepared to walk right in.'

'Walk into danger,' said Frank. 'We should be talking him out of it.'

'We've both tried. But if we can't do that then we'd best keep an eye on him.'

'We?' asked Frank.

'You,' said Jones. 'Though keep socially distanced. If it blows up in Mickey's face and our masters in Whitehall ask us why we were poking around in this, we can say he acted alone.'

15

It was time for Olga's morning tour. Sprinkle a little love and affection on those who wanted it and keep a watchful eye on those who didn't.

She approached the first bank of desks and hovered over Dmitri's shoulder. His screen was filled with debit-card details harvested from spear-phishing, soon to be sold on the dark web for a few dollars a time. It was a far cry from the recent monumental bank theft.

'How's it going?' asked Olga.

With reflex reaction Dmitri blacked his screen and, without answering her question, asked, 'Where is Bogdan?'

Despite the early hour she guessed Bogdan was in his favourite drinking den, one hand on a bottle of spirits and the other on one of his girlfriend's laps. 'He's not in.'

'We need to talk about my bonus for the bank work.' Someone

on the team coughed ostentatiously and Dmitri corrected himself. 'Our bonuses.'

'You'll have to talk to Bogdan about that.'

'That's why I asked where he was.'

Olga had no idea what bonus arrangement Dmitri had struck with Bogdan. A lot of people had their hands in the air for a share of those billions, not least Pintov. But even if Dmitri had only negotiated a small percentage, as was typically the case, he stood to make a lot of money. Enough to walk away from all this. Except, he never would, because he was a cyber addict, and he would need his next fix.

She moved to the team targeting Finnish utilities and businesses. For months they had been progressing methodically through the intrusive stages to be ready ahead of the Finnish elections.

'All well?'

'We are just waiting for a green light from Yasenevo,' the girl said, referring to the district in Moscow housing the Foreign Intelligence Service.

Olga moved over to the desk targeting Finnish social media.

She looked down at a message on a screen.

Tom Gun: KARL KRISTENSEN was a victim of the war between America and Russia. Let us Finns stay out of it. #VoteFinnishFreedomParty

When she looked up again, she noticed Lieutenant Colonel Beratov marching across the floor as if it were a parade ground. Beratov was a typical jackboot FSB, with a background in the army. She presumed he had come, as he did every week, to collect the profile reports and ex-filtrated emails and data that might prove useful to the Kremlin. And to collect his brown envelope; the protection money for the 'roof' he provided Bogdan. No doubt he'd expect it to be fatter than normal because of the bank theft.

Beratov was especially red-faced and stiff as he strode into Olga's office. He looked at her with narrowed eyes as if looking into the sun and motioned his head sharply as a signal for her to join him.

She walked over, closed the door behind her and smiled. 'I have your usual.' She opened her safe, took out a brown packet and handed it over.

'Where is Bogdan?' he asked, without acknowledging the packet.

'He's not here.'

'I can see he is not here. I asked you *where* he is?'

'There's no need to shout. Is there a problem?'

'Yes.' Beratov glanced around the room. 'You need to make certain you have covered your tracks. Wiped your computers clean or whatever it is you do to make sure the bank attack cannot be traced back here.'

'We use remote servers for all our work,' she explained, not for the first time. 'It's all invisible.'

'The British have traced it to St Petersburg.'

'They're just guessing.'

'It would be very awkward if they traced it to us.'

'We are at war with the West. Moscow has given us free rein to cause trouble.'

'I'm not bothered about Moscow.' He stopped, looked over his shoulder then lowered his voice. 'As you say, Mr Pintov is supportive and looking forward to his share.'

'Why would it be awkward then?'

'If the trail leads here then it might lead to Bogdan's partner. And if that happens, we will all be in a lot of trouble.'

16

Second Lieutenant Timo Martinnen gunned his snowmobile into a clearing in the boreal forest. He halted, put the vehicle in neutral and walked up a sharp granite extrusion. Now he had a clear view of the source of the metallic thunder on the other side of the border.

He waved forward the cameraman and asked, 'Is this a good view for you?'

Surveying the Russian tanks manoeuvring below the cameraman replied, 'It's dangerous here. They can see us.'

'Don't worry,' said Timo. 'They want you to film them. This whole exercise is for show.'

Timo didn't know that for sure. And even if the intelligence assessment was correct there was always the possibility that some trigger-happy Russian might fire by mistake, or for fun. But from such a distance they'd be unlikely to be hit.

'Don't worry,' Timo said again.

Looking not in the least reassured, the cameraman swung the camera up from his hip and filmed.

Timo pulled up his binoculars and focused in on the new-spec turret of an upgraded T-90M tank. There was some debate about whether the explosive reactive armour could be circumvented by double hits from RPGs, but it was nevertheless a good tank. In any case its defensive capabilities were at the present time academic. Timo had no intention of pointing anything more aggressive than a camera.

He turned to his communications officer. 'Private. Have you managed to get through to base?'

The officer shook his head. 'The Russians are still jamming our communications.'

Timo pulled out his satellite phone. 'Patrol fifteen to base. Over.'

'Patrol fifteen go ahead.'

'We tried raising you on the radio but could not get through. Suspect the Russians are jamming our communications.'

'Patrol fifteen we can confirm that. Please give a sit rep.'

In under one minute Timo gave a summary of the facts without conjecture or speculation.

'Acknowledged patrol fifteen. When cameraman is finished send him back to base accompanied. You are instructed to keep as many men with you as possible and continue to enforce the border zone.'

'Enforce the border zone?'

'Those are your orders, Patrol fifteen. Next sit rep expected in thirty minutes or before if significant change. Over.'

'Over and out.'

Timo couldn't hide a smile as he slid the phone back into its case. Enforce the border! With ten men on snowmobiles against hundreds of Russian tanks. If the Russians did invade, he would defend his country as valiantly as the men and women in Ukraine.

Just as his own great uncle and fellow countrymen had fought off the Bear in the Winter War. Then the Russians had surged across the Karelian Isthmus in similarly superior numbers but were held back heroically at the Mannerheim defensive line.

He didn't know where the defensive line would be this time. But it wouldn't be here on the border. Timo would not be shooting tanks from behind a spruce tree. Because although the new T-90M was the fastest tank the Russians had in operation, it wasn't as fast as a snowmobile.

* * *

Turning up the TV volume, Edvard watched the tank manoeuvres with growing alarm. 'There must be hundreds of them. Maybe even thousands …'

He realised Katrina was neither watching the news nor listening to him. She was laughing at something on her phone.

'We are about to be invaded by the Russians,' barked Edvard. 'Doesn't that concern you?'

Katrina turned over her phone and looked at the television. 'We mustn't worry.'

'Why not!?'

'Because that is what Pintov wants us to do. The tanks are just for show. And they are in Russia not in Finland.'

'That's what everyone said before they invaded Ukraine.'

'Finland was never part of Russia like Ukraine.'

'It absolutely was. The city centre was built under Russian rule. We have thousands of Russian speakers. It's just the same.'

'They are just trying to influence the polls.'

'And if the National Coalition party get in with their policy of housing NATO missiles, those tanks could be rolling down the Aleksanterinkatu.'

'The National Coalition won't allow NATO missiles. That was Kristensen's mad idea. Everyone agrees it is too provocative. Besides, the polls show the Finns party leading.'

'That's worse. They are Russophiles.'

'Hardly. They just don't want to provoke Russia. That's sensible.'

Edvard shook his head. 'By being aggressive like this, Russia is playing into the hands of those who think Finland does need NATO missiles. It doesn't make sense.'

Katrina smiled. 'Pintov doesn't think like a normal person. But his generals know we would fight. And they have already suffered enough in Ukraine.'

'I hope you are right.'

17

Olga woke to the squeal of brakes and screech of tyres. A crash at the apartment block's front door was followed by feet drumming up the stairwell.

She sat up in bed. Were they coming for her? It had to be because of her association with Bogdan. Even though she was not involved in his mafia activities and frequently pleaded with him to stop them and focus solely on TruNews, the police would still have her down as a colleague. And now they were coming for her. She grabbed her mother's crucifix as the drumming grew louder. She looked at the door, expecting it to burst open like a paper bag.

But it stood firm. The footsteps passed by and on up the next flight of stairs. She breathed again.

Another smash and crash as a door fell upstairs. Boots on her ceiling. They'd come for the architecture student. Now that made sense. Screams and shouts from his girlfriend. She'd be in trouble too. Olga had seen the photo of her in an anti-Pintov T-shirt. She probably felt brave in the crowd. She'd simply been naïve.

The screaming stopped abruptly, suggesting they'd been knocked out or drugged. The feet shuffled past her door and down the stairs.

Olga crept to the window and teased the wooden slats on her shutters open just enough to see four men hog-carry the boy into the back of the police van. The girlfriend was transported in a similar fashion and dumped in a second. As the vans drove off slowly, Olga wondered what would become of her neighbours. If they readily submitted to re-education, they should be fine. If they resisted, they would be broken.

She sat back in bed with the duvet pulled up to her neck. It was too cold to get up before the heating came on. If it came on. Increasingly there were unexplained 'maintenance' issues that meant it never did.

Squeals from the first commuter train leaving Gorskaya turned her thoughts to the busy day ahead. She stretched to the bedside table and switched on the coffee machine. As it wheezed and spluttered, she checked her diary.

She added sweetener to the coffee and a smattering of full fat milk. The first sip of the day was the best.

She went to her in-tray. Most urgent today was an editorial that she needed to approve before release.

> *TruNews. Finland's long-established position of neutrality between East and West has been crucial to peace in the region for many decades. Membership of NATO has threatened that. But if it went further and Finland housed missiles on its soil this would be an act of war. Those Finns planning to vote for the National Coalition party must understand that Russia cannot tolerate NATO missiles so close to St Petersburg. Think very carefully before casting a vote tomorrow. Stay neutral. Stay friends with your neighbour.*

Simple. To the point. She ticked her approval.

Next, she checked the plans for cyberattacks in Helsinki and other areas that were strongly supportive of the National Coalition Party. The disruption would cause so much mayhem that it would lead to lower turnout. In rural areas where the Finns party was popular there would be no disruption and a higher turnout. Much work still to be done. But plans were ahead of schedule.

18

Like emperor penguins to the sea, the crowd shuffled off the cold terraces at the London Stadium. Mickey followed Martin to the Director's box where well-heeled fans were attacking the buffet and flutes of champagne with rather more enterprise than the Hammers had attacked their opposition.

'That new kid from the academy plays Cinderella football,' said Mickey picking up a cheese sandwich from a silver platter. 'Keeps leaving the ball behind him.'

'Give him a chance,' replied Martin. 'He has commitment. He lives, dreams and eats football.'

'If only he could play it as well,' said Mickey. He wandered to the glass partition between their room and the Chairman's lounge. On the other side were various Hammers legends, WAGS, assorted hangers-on, and the only person Mickey was interested in, club owner and chairman Ivan Kazbegi. He was shorter and with less hair than Mickey remembered. On either side of him, balanced precariously on stilettoes were young women that weren't his daughters.

Mickey had read that Kazbegi's political ambitions in Russia had been frustrated by Pintov's refusal to retire. Consequently, he had turned his attention to Britain, where he could mingle with politicians and celebrities in fine restaurants, on his yacht, at his glamorous annual charity fundraiser or here at the London Stadium. His schmoozing appeared to be working, for unlike other Russian oligarchs, Kazbegi had somehow escaped sanctions. There were calls from some quarters, the loudest being Nikolai Mishkin, for him to be treated like the others. Mickey hoped not, because the Hammers could do without the disruption of a change in ownership.

With an uncanny awareness, Kazbegi caught Mickey's eye.

Mickey winked and raised his glass. Kazbegi at first looked quizzical then held up a hand, seemingly in recognition.

Mickey wandered back to Martin. 'You said you were going to fix for me to meet Kazbegi.'

Martin, who was probably taller than anyone in the stadium except for the two goalkeepers, looked over the heads into the next room. 'We'll go see him at full time.'

'Sounds good to me.'

'You're not going to embarrass me, Mickey?'

'When 'ave I ever embarrassed you?'

'I haven't got time to go through all the occasions. Just remember, I'm doing you a big favour here. Kazbegi is my biggest client.'

'You're telling me your other clients are shorter!'

'Don't make jokes about his size. He doesn't find it funny. In fact, Mickey, don't make any jokes at all.'

They finished another flute of champagne and made their way back to the VIP seats on the halfway line.

The home team eventually took an undeserved lead courtesy of an own goal and somehow clung on for the full ninety minutes and an anxious extra six.

On the referee's whistle Mickey jumped to his feet and joined fifty thousand fans singing, 'Stand up if you love West Ham!' Then everyone sat back down as the singing morphed seamlessly into, 'Sit down if you hate Tottenham.'

The singing faded as people headed for the exits. Martin led the way to the Chairman's lounge. At the door, wired-up, beefy security guards patted them down and checked ID and names against some database.

In the centre of the room a crowd had gathered around Kazbegi and his entourage. Some guy was waffling on about Belarus. Kazbegi looked bored so Mickey cut in. 'Another three points, Ivan. Congratulations.'

Kazbegi raised his full glass of champagne. 'Another three points!'

The crowd joined the toast.

Kazbegi didn't take a sip.

'This is Mickey Summer,' Martin said to Kazbegi. 'He's a lifelong Hammers fan and one of the small shareholders you bought out when you took over.'

'I remember,' said Kazbegi. 'You did some helpful work for us on the valuation of the club. Thank you.'

'It's me who should thank *you*,' said Mickey. 'The club is in a much better shape since you took over from the clowns who were running it before.'

'I agree. But now there are some who want your government to take over from me!'

He laughed. People shuffled awkwardly but said nothing.

'That's a joke,' said Mickey. 'You put a billion plus into the club and just because Pintov goes on the warpath people think the government can nick it off you.'

'I appreciate your sympathy,' he replied. 'As I've said many times before, I am not close to Pintov, and I have absolutely zero influence over his policies.'

'The stock market doesn't believe that though, does it?'

'That's your area of expertise.'

'Kazbegi Holdings is growing exponentially because you are buying Russian companies on the cheap. And yet you are trading at a massive discount because the market expects you to get hit by sanctions.'

'Maybe it's a good time to buy,' said Kazbegi.

'I'm thinking about it,' replied Mickey. 'Sniffing around. Checking you've got no skeletons in the cupboard.'

'How is your anti-corruption campaign going?' Martin interjected, giving Mickey a gentle sideways nudge.

'Very well thank you, Martin. Though for the time being it's overshadowed by the war and sanctions.' Kazbegi gave some spiel about how he was fighting corruption in Russia, as he believed this was at the heart of all that was wrong in the country. The politics, the mafia, the war in Ukraine, the threats to the Baltic states. Apparently, they all stemmed from systemic corruption. He held court for ten minutes, still without touching his champagne.

When Kazbegi finally arrived at a natural end Mickey jumped back in. 'Do you think there's any corruption in Kazbegi Holdings?'

Kazbegi frowned and squinted at Mickey. 'I'm certain there is not.'

'Can you prove that?'

'I don't need to.'

'The stock market wants you to. That's another reason your share price is at a massive discount. Partly the threat of sanctions but also because the market assumes some of the hundreds of businesses in the holding company are bleeding cash through corruption. If you can prove otherwise and prove you're not linked to the mafia or to Pintov, then the share price will go through the roof when sanctions are lifted. Happy days again.'

'Well thanks for your time,' said Martin, trying to pull Mickey away.

Mickey snapped his arm free. 'Don't shoot the messenger, Ivan. Bankers like Martin won't ever tell you the truth for fear of making you angry. But I always tell it straight.'

'And why exactly are you telling me this?' asked Kazbegi, stroking his chin.

'Because I can fix it for you.'

'How?'

'Not here.' Mickey handed Kazbegi a card. 'Let's have a chat.'

Mickey felt the tug on his arm again. He winked at Kazbegi then turned and followed Martin out of the room.

'What are you playing at, Mickey? You just upset my best client.'

'Nah,' said Mickey. 'I got his attention. Probably the only conversation he'll remember today.'

19

Katrina pulled the bed covers up and curled her toes. 'It's so cold tonight. Are you sure the heating is on?'

'Yes, it is on,' replied Edvard. 'It's just that it's minus fifteen outside.'

'Can you check?'

Reluctantly he slid out of bed and pulled a jumper over his thermals. Leading with his bad leg he limped downstairs to the thermostat in the hallway. It was set to thirty degrees. He shuffled to the control panel in the kitchen. It was on constant.

And yet …

He checked the radiator. Stone cold. He moved to the boiler and pulled down the flap expecting to see an error message. None. The flame was lit. He turned on the hot water tap. It ran warm then too hot. The boiler was working, just not the heating system.

Nothing could be done about it in the middle of the night, so he went to the hall cupboard and fished out two sets of hats and gloves. Suddenly the lights came on, momentarily blinding his unadjusted eyes.

'Turn off the light,' Katrina called out from upstairs.

'It wasn't me. It came on by mistake.'

Keeping eyes closed he fumbled along the wall to the switch. Flicked it. The light stayed on. Flicked it the other way. It still stayed on. He opened his eyes fully and realised that every light in the house was on.

'What are you doing?'

'Nothing. All the lights are on. I can't turn them off.'

Suddenly Tchaikovsky's violin concerto sprang to life.

Katrina's head appeared over the railings. 'Have you gone mad!?'

'It's not me,' he screamed above the music. 'There must be a fault with this new internet of things you made us get.'

'Well turn it off!'

Edvard did not know how. But he did have a good old-fashioned answer to the music. He marched into the dining room and unplugged the music system. Still there was music. This time from the television that was on full volume in the lounge. He went through and unplugged that. Now his brain was starting to function. He went to the electrical panel in the hall cupboard and flicked down the lever for the light circuits. Shazam! The house was plunged back into darkness.

'Everything is fine now.'

In the morning he'd sort everything out. He headed back to bed, pleased at his old-style victory over modern madness. But then a shrill, persistent caterwaul forced him to jam his hands over his ears.

Katrina appeared at the top of the stairs. 'Is there a fire?'

'No,' he screamed. 'It's this stupid system. It doesn't work. I told you it was too clever.' He hurried back to the electrical panel and flicked the lever. But the alarm still sounded. He flicked it up and back down again. Still the deafening clatter. Why would it not go off? Think. Batteries! The alarm had a battery back-up in case a burglar cut the electricity supply. But where was the back up? Perhaps in the alarm cover.

He opened the front door and looked up at the alarm, flashing blue, unreachable five metres up the front wall of the house. He realised that alarms up and down the road were hooting and flashing in similar fashion. Not all. Presumably just those with the smart system.

Or maybe not so smart.

20

Declan stopped ten metres short of the car and made sure there were no passing pedestrians before he pressed the remote. The car unlocked without exploding. As it always did and probably always would. He was perhaps overly cautious, but it was a routine he'd begun when investigating a white supremacist gang who had a penchant for car bombs.

In similar fashion he left the door open when he started the engine. Any explosion would then have a route to escape and blow him out instead of trapping him in a metal compression chamber. In fact it was a different chamber that was causing his insecurity. The members of the Black Chamber were more than capable of blowing away an irritation like Declan.

Accompanied by Washington FM he drove nose to tail through the capital. The majestic Needle, the calm Potomac, Lincoln's back, and a side of the Pentagon that he passed almost within touching distance before hitting Interstate 66 which, despite bearing no connection to the famous route 66, always raised his spirits as he headed west.

They sank again as he arrived at Three Patriots Park, a drab seven-storey outpost of National Intelligence. The only thing it had going for it was its location. Tucked up against the crossroads of the Dulles Access and Fairfax County Parkway it made for easy access to Washington and, being only a dozen jumbo lengths from Dulles airport, it was handy for out-of-town visitors.

He parked up, took a black coffee and half a donut from the trailer café, and made his way to the office. Other members of the Hybrid Threat Group were already gathered round an oval table covered in papers, pens, laptops, and drinks.

Declan drew the blinds against the low November sun, waited

a minute for the clock to strike nine and opened the meeting with a roll call. This was primarily for the benefit of Chuck, for whom this was the first visit. Declan introduced the NSA staff and representatives from Homeland and Cyber Command and the Deputy Director of CIA Analysis, Steven Stotton.

He then kicked off with the first agenda item concerning the Russian GRU military cyber offensive unit. 'We're seeing a significant increase in brute force access attempts on dot.gov entities, energy, higher education, law firms, media. It's across the piece.'

'That's why we have the Shields Up initiative,' said the rep from Homeland. 'And CISA re-issued the advisory on multi-factor authentication. It's the most effective mitigation.'

'What I still don't understand,' said Declan, 'is why they are only probing and installing malware but not executing. Any ideas?'

'The same reason they're only talking about using tactical nuclear weapons. They're scared of how we would retaliate,' said the liaison from Cyber Command.

'How would we retaliate in the case of a major cyberattack?' asked Declan. 'Say they took down the Eastern Seaboard power grid.'

'We could do the same to the Russian grid and keep it down. But we might not do like for like. We might just shut down the Russian internet. That would be seriously embarrassing for Pintov.'

'Can we do that?' asked Declan. In the China crisis Cyber Command had struggled to get past the Great Firewall of China until he'd written the GameOverRed malware.

'Probably,' he said unconvincingly. 'Even if we can't, the Russians are worried that we can. That's why they're holding back. At least that's my theory.'

'Well, they didn't hold back on the cyber theft that almost led to the collapse of State Financial. Chuck, can you give us an overview?'

Chuck summarised what was known. 'Everything points to Russian actors.'

'Tell us something we don't know,' said Stotton. 'Like, who

specifically?'

'Elements of the St Petersburg mafia,' said Chuck.

'Which gang?'

'Probably a hacker who goes by the name of Dmitri or Geneve. But we can't be sure.'

'And they used your GameOverRed malware.' Stotton grinned at Declan. 'Is that right?'

'A derivative of GameOverRed, correct.' Why had he brought that up? It wasn't relevant.

'Do we think this is simple criminality, or hybrid warfare?' asked Cyber Command.

'It was a Latvian bank,' Declan pointed out. 'Moscow is mad about Latvia's planned NATO missile sites. They have motive. We're also not convinced a criminal gang could devise this exploit on their own.'

'For sure it wasn't simply criminal,' said Stotton. 'HUMINT from CIA station in St Petersburg says the plan originated in Moscow. Question is: what are we going to do about it?'

'Financial Crime is investigating,' Declan pointed out. 'It's not going to be throwing resources at it though. State Financial is safe. We can leave any heavy lifting to the Latvians and the British.'

'Do nothing, then.'

Declan ignored Stotton and turned the meeting to the next agenda item. He asked his man from Current Intelligence to take up the running.

'The Russians are manipulating the Finnish elections. There's a strong possibility that they assassinated the President, Karl Kristensen, who as you know wanted NATO missiles in Finland.'

'Can you run us through the analysis?' asked Declan.

'The Finnish police got a call from Kristensen's security detail twenty seconds before the crash to say the driver had lost control of the vehicle. We wondered why he didn't just pull over. We think his car could have been hacked. We searched open-source media and came up with pictures of a blacked-out Mercedes S class driving on the same road. Metadata shows the timing is perfect for it to be following Kristensen's car by around a hundred metres. No registration plate but we did a reverse image search and found what we think is the same vehicle in St Petersburg two days later.'

'Thanks,' said Declan. 'As well as probably assassinating Kristensen the Russians have had a tank battalion on the border for the last fortnight and there has been extensive propaganda on social media. Also sophisticated cyberattacks on pro-European households.'

'What are we doing about it?' asked Stotton.

'This hybrid threat group is tasked with assessment,' said Declan. 'That's what we're doing about it.'

'My understanding is that the purpose of this group is not simply to monitor hybrid warfare.' Stotton looked around the table. 'We should also take recommendations for action to Jennifer.'

'We do where we have any,' said Declan, trying not to be annoyed. 'Of course, everyone is also free to take proposals back up through their own departments. Frankly I can't think of any course of action to recommend.'

'You never can.'

Declan ignored the dig. 'Any other business?'

'Yes,' said Stotton. 'How about Pintov threatening the use of chemical and biological weapons and dirty nuclear bombs. That kind of hybrid war is a little more worrying than troll farms and political assassinations.'

'We discussed that months ago, and I gave Jennifer an extensive briefing on the threat.'

'And the action recommendation on that was also to do nothing.'

'Don't panic would be a more accurate summary,' Declan corrected.

'Easy for you not to panic sitting in Washington,' said Stotton. 'It's not your family facing the threat of attack.'

'We agreed as a group, including you, that the threat has been exaggerated. Chemical weapons accounted for around one in ten thousand deaths in World War 1. A similar ratio in Syria. And with a dirty nuclear bomb the detonation would cause more deaths than the nuclear fallout.'

'Not if the Russians blow up the Zaporizhzhia nuclear station.'

'That would be a major incident,' agreed Declan. 'But not one we can do anything about.'

The meeting closed without further incident, but Declan asked Stotton to stay behind.

When the room was clear he jumped straight in. 'You don't seem to believe in what we're doing.'

'I speak my mind,' said Stotton. 'You've already got enough Yes men. You should be grateful for my challenges.'

That was a fair point. It was healthy to have a sceptic on the team. That wasn't what was bugging Declan. And they both knew it.

'You are also often openly hostile to me. It makes things difficult for me.'

Stotton shrugged. 'You've made life difficult for a lot of people with your Black Chamber conspiracy theory. I guess I'm returning the compliment.'

'Have you had the call from Spitz?'

'I wouldn't be able to tell you if I had. But the answer is no.'

It was odd that Spitz had not yet investigated Stotton. 'Really?'

'Sorry to disappoint.'

Declan raised his hands in the air. 'Look it's no longer my enquiry. I'm totally out of the loop. But when you do get called, you'll have to stand down from your role here.'

'We'll cross that bridge if we come to it.'

'We will.'

Stotton walked to the door and turned round as he opened it. 'You know, you'd like the new Titanic movie.'

'Why is that?'

'It suggests there was a second iceberg.' Stotton grinned. 'Read my lips. There is no Black Chamber.'

Declan stared at the back of the closed door. He knew they thought he was a conspiracy theorist who had fallen down the rabbit hole. He was making a lot of enemies. The stress was giving him sleepless nights and headaches. But it would all be worth it when Spitz published his findings. Then he'd be vindicated. The members of the Black Chamber would be arrested. And Stotton could make all the wise cracks he wanted behind bars.

21

The presence of the Defence Secretary, Bob Bryson, signalled the gravity of the situation, and a frisson of suspense ran through those gathered in the Joint Chiefs of Staff conference room in the Pentagon E-Ring. The seats round the long table were mostly occupied with gold braid. Advisors such as Declan stood around the walls, elbows in.

General Horn, Chairman of the JCS, sat playing with a curl on his beard. He waited until precisely two o'clock then signalled the Joint Staff Special Assistant to close the door.

'Let's make a start,' he said in a voice scratched from years of barking orders and sucking on Marlboro lights. 'The business of the day is the situation in Finland and the Baltics.'

He motioned for the Joint Staff Officer who was sponsoring the topic to take the floor. The JSO hesitated, glanced at the empty chair beside him where General Dare should have been, looked at the door and then finally at Horn who again motioned for him to get on with proceedings.

'Apologies that time did not allow for pre-distribution of slides.' The JSO took to his feet and put a map of the Baltic States up on the screen. 'Now, there has been a lot of misinformation on the news channels so let me give you the facts. At zero-eight-hundred Eastern European Standard time which is zero-one-hundred Eastern Standard time, six Russian Flankers left Lida air base in Belarus and flew into Lithuanian air space on a route shown by the green line. They retreated before Lithuanian Air Defence could intercept.'

'My understanding is it was before they could even mobilise,' interjected Horn. Declan had heard the same. 'Is that right?'

'That's unclear,' replied the JSO. He was about to resume when the conference door burst open and in came General Dare, Head of European Command and NATO. He held up an apologetic hand as he marched to the empty chair.

Horn cleared his throat. 'I must remind you, General Dare, that procedures for the meetings of the JCS clearly state that late arrivals will not be allowed to enter the conference room after the door has been closed.'

'Apologies,' grunted Dare. 'I had to sit in on a call from NATO HQ, concerning matters arising.'

'Conflicting appointments are not considered an adequate rationale for late arrival. Exceptions to this policy must be coordinated with the Special Assistant before the meeting.'

'I'll make sure I do that next time,' said Dare unconvincingly.

Declan caught Jennifer's eyes. Her eyebrow rose. He wasn't the only one in the room uncomfortable at a four-star General being berated like a schoolboy.

Horn motioned the JSO to continue his briefing.

'At zero-ten-hundred hours a battalion from the Russian 1st Guards Tank Army arrived west of Grodno, on the border with Poland,' he pointed to a red block on the map. 'At the same time airborne units from the 76th Air Assault Division landed to the north. Meanwhile six Backfire bombers flew just inside Belarus's border with Poland. Most alarming of all,' he paused for effect, 'we believe two Satan missiles have been primed for deployment. One in Krasnoyarsk and the other in Orenburg. Each missile has a range of six thousand miles and can carry sixteen warheads. It could destroy an area the size of Ukraine,' he paused for effect again, 'or Texas.'

While the JSO went on to outline various issues and concerns that had been identified by the Service and Combatant Commanders and Joint Staff in the preceding Operations Deputies meeting, Declan's mind drifted to the candy bowls scattered around the room. He managed to resist, though surveying the girth around the room others would do well to do the same. He'd heard that a previous Special Assistant, presumably having come to the same conclusion, had replaced the candy with fruit. Rather than earning him a commendation for prolonging the lives of the country's senior military command he was transferred to another post. The bowls had been filled with candy ever since.

The briefing was coming to the sharp end of proceedings and Declan refocused.

'What do the Russians claim they are up to?' asked Horn.

'Demonstrating that they are capable of defending Belarus

from Western aggression,' replied the JSO.

'Is it a prelude to invasion?' Horn pressed.

'Not in our view.'

'Okay. But if it is, what do we do about it?'

The JSO pulled up a fresh chart. 'We sharpen our defence of the Suwalki Gap.' He circled a stretch of land on the border of Poland and Lithuania. 'If the Russians were to take control of the gap, they would control territory all the way from the Russian enclave of Kaliningrad on the Baltic Sea right through the Russian ally of Belarus back to Russia proper. The Baltic states would be catastrophically cut off from NATO allies.'

'Precisely how do we sharpen our defence?' asked Horn.

'We match them up on the ground by moving tanks and men into the gap.'

'Which tanks and men exactly?' asked Horn.

The JSO nodded appreciatively at Horn's teeing up of his next slide. With a laser pen he drew a circle round a tank in south Lithuania. 'We have Lithuania's Iron Wolf mechanized infantry brigade, which is reinforced by a German battalion with Marder and Leopard tanks and self-propelled howitzers. This unit is additionally reinforced by Czech, Dutch, and Norwegian mechanized infantry companies. We move them all down to the gap.

'Plus at Orszyz,' his laser pen circled another tank in northeast Poland, 'we have our own squadron equipped with Abrams tanks and Bradley scout vehicles. They are partnered with Poland's 15th Mechanized Brigade as well as a British light reconnaissance company and a battery of Croatian Vulkan self-propelled rocket artillery and Romanian air-defence missiles.'

This wasn't Declan's bailiwick, but it sounded like a hodgepodge. Furrowed brows around the table suggested others were thinking the same.

'You think you can co-ordinate that?' asked Horn.

'That's what we've done in training,' said the JSO, averting his gaze.

Horn pursed his lips and took a deep breath. 'Let's discuss the tank manoeuvres on the border with Finland. Might that be a prelude to invasion?'

'That's possible,' said the JSO.

'I am very worried about Finland,' said Bryson. Declan didn't think the Secretary of Defence looked particularly worried, but he never gave away any signs of emotion. 'It's a soft target. There are nationalists around Pintov who are furious at the humiliation in Ukraine and are looking for an easy victory somewhere to restore pride.'

Horn looked down the table at Jennifer. 'What do you think the Russians are up to, Jennifer? Are we facing a new war in the Baltics or Finland?'

'The hybrid war has already begun,' Jennifer replied, with the calm authority that Declan admired. 'They are manipulating the Finnish elections, not least by assassinating President Karl Kristensen. They've collapsed a bank in Latvia. There's been a constant stream of propaganda for internal and external consumption that could pave the way for military intervention. This is precisely the softening up we saw before they invaded Ukraine. Hybrid war right out of General Gerasimov's playbook.'

'I'd like to hear more about the propaganda,' said Horn.

'Let me pass on to Declan Lehane, who many of you know. Declan chairs the cross-discipline Hybrid Threat Group.' She offered an upturned palm.

Declan stepped forward from the wall. This was his chance to reassert some of the authority he'd lost with his Black Chamber prosecution. Almost everyone he'd arrested in the Washington Country Club that day was sitting in the room. And thanks to Spitz's unwillingness to push forward the prosecution they were confident they were not going to be found out. They were all angry. Some deliberately averted their gaze. Others were staring at him. Hoping for him to mess up.

He cleared his throat. 'For those who do not know, the Gerasimov Doctrine is hybrid warfare as proposed by Russian General Valery Gerasimov. It proposes the use of non-military operations such as assassinations, propaganda, disinformation, hiring thugs for political rallies, blackmail, kompromat, maskirovka, nuclear threat, energy supply squeezes, sabotage of industrial infrastructure, etcetera. All of it. He proposed that unconventional warfare such as this was more effective and had less collateral damage than conventional war. Use both and you have hybrid warfare.

'For years Russian cyber propaganda and disinformation campaigns have been running the message that the Baltic States should be part of the Eurasian Union not the European. They were once part of Russia, and they should never forget the treatment under the Nazis. At the same time, they are propagating the idea that the ethnic Russians in Finland and the Baltic States suffer discrimination and are generally among the poorer paid. So, if Russia went in it would be to defend them, just as it defended the Russians in the Donbas. It would claim its occupation was humanitarian intervention. That's the narrative that is already running.'

'Thank you,' said Horn, turning to General Dare. 'If Russia does invade Finland or the Baltics, can we stop them?'

'The battalions we have in the field function as tripwires,' explained Dare. 'They put NATO skin in the game. If Russia wants to invade the Baltics, it will have to fight and kill NATO soldiers deployed there, not merely overrun small Baltic militaries. That would invoke Article 5 and make a vigorous NATO counterattack more likely.'

'What if they avoid the NATO troops?' asked Horn.

Declan knew that to be a real risk. Dare nodded and bridged his hands. 'Given the small number of troops NATO has deployed, Russian forces could bypass our tripwires and focus on securing the surrounding towns and countryside. They could then claim to have occupied the Baltic States to safeguard Russians and preserve the peace in the way Declan described. We would then be in a position of having to mobilise public opinion in favour of us going in and liberating them. That's a different matter altogether.'

'What do we do to mitigate that risk?' asked Horn.

'We put NATO troops in the towns and capitals. As a deterrent.'

'Any other views?' Horn looked around the table. None were forthcoming.

'Very well,' said Horn. 'Our primary objective is to protect the Suwalki Gap, to maintain a land route into the Baltic States if we need to go in. The secondary objective is to put troops and equipment in the Baltic state capitals to lengthen the NATO tripwire. Are we all agreed on this response as the recommendation from the Joint Chiefs?'

'Agreed,' they answered, a few heads nodding for good measure.

'Then I will take this to the President.'

22

From the top floor of the Gherkin, in the offices of Crosshairs Investments, Mickey looked down at a grey Thames snaking under a Millennium Bridge that never could manage the impossible task of linking the brutal Tate Modern with the classical beauty of St Paul's. Similarly, HMS Belfast tried unsuccessfully to bridge the ages between the jagged Shard and the imperial Tower. Now Mickey would have to bridge the gap between the market stall trader he was today and the financial trader he used to be. He had to persuade Uli that he could get back to where he was. First, he needed to convince himself.

'Great place to work,' he said, turning back into the room.

'The worst,' said Uli. 'It takes me ten minutes to get down to the street for a smoke. Ten to get back up. I've been forced to take up vaping.'

'Better for you.'

Uli pulled a vape pipe from his pocket, inhaled, then blew out a plume of vapour. 'I preferred the Quadra Fund offices in Mayfair. I could walk outside in the garden square and enjoy a smoke in the fresh air.'

Leaving that contradiction aside, Mickey summarised what he had discovered since they last met. That all the indications were that the collapse of RSB was the work of the St Petersburg mafia aided by Russian military cyber intelligence. But the legal avenues to get compensation looked closed.

'We'll have to do it ourselves,' said Mickey.

'It's the Russian mafia.' Uli frowned and tilted his head to one side. 'What can we do?'

'I haven't worked out the details yet,' said Mickey.

'Details!' Uli laughed. 'Do you even have a vague plan of action?'

A kernel of an idea had been forming, but he didn't want to reveal it just yet. 'How much does Crosshairs Investments spend on cyber security defence?'

Uli shrugged. 'No idea.'

'You spent thirty-two million last year. UK banks in total spend about seven hundred million. Each year. All on cyber defence. How about spending a tiny sum on investigation?'

'Even if we could prove it was the St Petersburg mafia, then what? There'd be nothing to gain.'

'Let's find out who precisely did it first. Then we can think about how to get compensation.'

'Our expertise is investing money,' said Uli.

'And that's just where I'd start.'

Uli immediately looked more interested. He took another tug on his vape and blew out the side of his mouth. 'Tell me.'

Mickey smiled. First line of defence broken. 'I need a cover story to be sniffing around in Russia. I'll run an investment portfolio. That way I can talk to Russian brokers, visit companies, look for good companies to invest in, bad ones to avoid.'

'We can't trade Russian equities. They're sanctioned.'

'You can't, but I can. Legally. If I set the fund up in Switzerland or Turkey for example.'

'But you were a trader in developed markets,' said Uli. 'Not Russia.'

'Same difference. Buy good companies. Avoid bad. It's not rocket science.'

Another tug and Uli seemed to concede the point but then he tensed up again. 'There is one major flaw in your plan.'

'Go on,' said Mickey, knowing what Uli was going to say.

'You don't have any money to build a portfolio of Russian equities.'

'Thanks for offering,' said Mickey. 'That's exactly where Crosshairs fits in.'

'Last time I checked our outreach programme didn't stretch that far.'

'I don't want charity,' snapped Mickey. 'Russia is a classic risk-reward investment. You give me as much money as you're comfortable with. Give me a hurdle rate. I take twenty percent over that. You keep the rest.'

Uli puffed out his cheeks. 'You're asking a lot, Mickey.'

'I'll also need a fighting fund.'

'For what?'

'Expenses. Travel to Russia. Hiring private investigators. Might need to stuff a few brown envelopes.'

'You can't do anything illegal, Mickey.'

'Only joking.' Though he wasn't. It was the wild east. Who knew what went on out there. 'Just give me an expense account to start with. You can pull the plug anytime if you don't like the way it's going.'

Uli said nothing, but Mickey could tell his interest was piqued.

He pressed on. 'Russian stocks are trading at a massive discount right now. It's indiscriminate. Even Kazbegi Holdings, which is as blue-chip as they come, is trading at a thirty percent discount to fair value. And you can buy that without any compliance problems because Kazbegi has not been sanctioned. If I can prove Kazbegi has no links to the mafia or Pintov, then when the Russian market bounces back the shares will go through the roof.'

'If the Russian market bounces back.'

'If,' agreed Mickey.

'How will you go about proving that Kazbegi is clean?'

'With Kazbegi's help. I've already run the idea past him.'

'You talked to him?'

'Yesterday. After the Hammers game.'

Uli took another drag as he re-evaluated. Smoke fell from his nostrils. Smaug eyeing a mountain of gold. 'You are finally starting to make some sense. You're essentially talking about a Russian recovery fund.'

'You've got it.'

'Which has a lot more chance of success than taking a baseball bat to the Russian mafia and asking for your money back.'

'I'll still explore that,' said Mickey. 'Best way to avoid mafia links in the investments is to uncover them.'

'I guess so.' Another tug on the pipe. 'Maybe it's more like a special situation fund.'

'Call it what you want. And I'll need analysts to do the research. I could hire them but that would take time. Best if you give me a couple of yours that you've already vetted.'

'Possible.'

'At least one of them needs to speak Russian,' said Mickey. 'And we'll need secure premises. Again, I can rent that, but you can vouch for the security at Crosshairs.'

'Anything else, your highness?'

'Fresh flowers and chocolates in my dressing room.'

Uli stood up and walked to the window. The low sun had worked through an opening in the clouds. A last hurrah before winter set in. 'I'll put the idea to Crispin.'

'What's not to like? There's almost no downside for you. I take all the risk.'

23

The cyberattack on the Latvian electricity grid had been conceived in Yasenevo, the vulnerabilities identified by GRU military intelligence, and the malware devised by the cyber brigade in Tambov. But there would be no state fingerprints because it would be executed by Igor's team using remote servers in Iran and North Korea.

Olga, Bogdan and Beratov had gathered around Igor's desk, and he was enjoying the attention. She had never seen him so animated.

'Nothing that we are going to do is especially complicated in itself,' Igor admitted. 'The skill is in the co-ordination of the strikes.'

'Josef here,' he gave a signal, 'is launching a DNS attack on the Latvian utility call centres.'

Olga noticed a frown appear on Bogdan's forehead. Already the old Vor was struggling to understand the language. 'Perhaps you could explain, Igor.'

It was Igor's turn to frown. She motioned her head sideways at Bogdan, and Igor's face cleared. 'A denial-of-service attack floods the switchboard with fake phone calls. Then genuine electricity customers will not be able to ring in to report the power outages we are about to cause.'

Igor turned to another of his team. 'Now we gain access to the control centre at the electricity company.' Igor pointed at a huge free-standing monitor. 'This is a display at the AST control centre showing the substations across the network. They are currently all blue, which means they are allowing electricity through. Now we have control of the operating systems we can open the circuit breakers.'

One by one the lights turned red.

'What's to stop the real operators taking back control and closing the circuit breakers?' asked Beratov.

'Good question.' He turned to another desk. 'Ready with the KillDisk?'

'We're ready.'

'Go ahead.' Igor turned back to Beratov. 'We are now sabotaging PCs and servers across the electricity company. They will still be able to send people to substations to manually close the breakers. But that will take many hours.'

One section of the large screen was now fully covered in red lights.

'We have cut the electricity supply to three hundred thousand Latvians,' Igor declared proudly.

Olga gave Igor a smile of encouragement.

'Very good,' said Beratov.

'What is good about it?' snarled Bogdan. 'We make no money. We risk being identified by the Americans or British, but we don't get any reward from this work.'

'You get the blessing of President Pintov,' corrected Beratov.

'I don't need Pintov's blessings anymore.'

The air sucked from the room.

Beratov spoke first. 'He is still the President.'

'He has that title,' Bogdan conceded. 'But the siloviki are now running the country. Pintov is still one of them. But no longer the most important.'

The silence was finally broken by the tapping of keyboards as people went back to work.

Olga returned to her office, still in shock that Bogdan had been so openly dismissive of Pintov. That was dangerous talk. For all of them.

24

Finsbury Circus Garden was empty except for Mickey and a grey squirrel that scrambled up a London plane tree as he approached.

Uli arrived shortly after, tugging on his vape.

'Wotcha,' said Mickey. 'How's the pillaging going today?'

'Pretty good.' Uli nodded. 'I've been doing well out of pairs trading government bonds.'

'Glad to hear it. Even more glad to hear you've got news for me.'

Uli nodded and took a pull on his vape. 'Do you want the good news or the bad news first?'

'I always take good news first. Might not have to worry about the bad news if I get hit by a meteorite.'

'The good news is Crispin thinks it's a very good idea to exploit dislocations in the Russian market. That's how Crispin puts it. Plus, he knows you. He thinks you'll do a good job. He's not bothered about your lack of experience in Russia. Thinks it might even be an advantage so long as you have a good analyst on the team and get your feet on the ground in Russia.'

'Now the bad news.'

'Compliance won't let us. It's a big red flag with a hammer and sickle on it. While sanctions are in place we can't invest in Russian stocks, even offshore.'

Mickey's heart sank. He'd got himself fizzed up on this idea and had assumed Uli would get the go-ahead from Crispin.

'Do you want the other good news?' asked Uli.

'There's two parts?'

'Crispin is happy to invest from his personal account. So long as he's not the only investor. He thinks you need to raise thirty million.'

'How much is he prepared to put in?'

'Fifteen.'

'It's a start.'

'Do you think you can raise the rest?'

'We,' Mickey corrected. 'Do we think we can raise the rest?'

'What do I get out of it?' asked Uli.

'A three percent arrangement fee for whatever you bring in.'

'Make it five.'

'Deal.'

Finally, a breakthrough. Mickey cupped Uli's head in his hands and kissed his forehead. 'Beauty.'

25

Following a weekend of violent anti-Pintov demonstrations, a tentative calm had settled over Moscow. Police were everywhere and two of them watched Olga closely as she exited the subway. She smiled to assure them that this citizen was on their side. One returned the gesture. The other, expressionless, looked up and down the length of her body.

Halfway along the underpass a rakishly thin, duvet-draped, drug user held out a hand and muttered, 'Help a hungry soldier.'

He was missing a leg, God help him. Ordinarily Olga did not give to beggars, but she made exceptions for soldiers and this man also had the native Siberian accent, round face, and eyes of her father. She dropped some change in the paper cup and walked on, smiling at two more baby-faced policemen as she exited in front of the Olympic Plaza shopping centre. An unwittingly camouflaged police transporter was parked near the entrance to the blue and white building. Passing another van outside the Olympic Sports complex, she arrived at the European Medical Centre, declaring its name proudly from the rooftop in giant letters. Olga could not be the only Russian to think it was overdue a name change.

Inside, she negotiated the corridors on autopilot then paused outside the oncology department to vigorously clean her hands with the alcohol rub whose smell she had come to hate. She took a deep breath and pushed through the swing double doors.

Her father was flat on his back, mouth open, saliva slithering out of one corner, staring at the ceiling.

She wiped his mouth with a tissue. 'Papa.'

He blinked, but otherwise no movement. His mouth remained open.

'It's me, Olga.'

He tried to speak but only the faintest whisper escaped.

Using the control panel, she manoeuvred the bed until he was sitting upright. His eyes opened.

'Water?' Without waiting for a reply, she held the plastic beaker to his lips just as she hoped he had once done for her. He took a few sips. 'Better?'

He nodded.

'How are you?'

'I want to go home.'

'I know,' she said.

They both knew that even if the new radiotherapy gave him another couple of years, the encroaching fog of dementia and Parkinson's meant he would live out the remainder of his life in hospital.

If she were a more dutiful daughter, she would look after him. Sacrifice her job and bring him into her home. Just as Papa had made sacrifices to look after her when Mama died. Giving up his salaried job-for-life in the FSB and taking odd jobs that could be fitted around Olga.

She assuaged her guilt by remembering that her position allowed him to receive treatment in this private hospital. The nature of her employment meant she was not officially employed and not registered for Obligatory Medical Insurance or for Voluntary Additional Insurance. But she had Bogdan. As soon as he heard about her father's illness, he promised to personally take care of all medical expenses. And the word of a Vor was better than any insurance policy.

They caught up on his latest treatment and other events in the hospital since her last visit. Then Papa wanted to talk about the world outside. He listened intently to developments in Finland and the Baltics and took a keen interest in Pintov's falling popularity and the siloviki who were manoeuvring to replace him. His medium and long-term recall of people and events always amazed Olga given he would never remember what he'd eaten for breakfast.

A dementia nurse had described the memory bank as like a bookcase. The disease slowly, randomly removes one book at a time, primarily the books close to hand that have been read most recently. But the classics and the heavyweight encyclopaedias and atlases on the bottom shelf remained in place. Papa could talk about the history of Russia all day long. They had to be careful when talking about Pintov because Papa was fiercely against him. It frustrated her that he never could explain why he hated a man who had done so much good for the country.

Eventually the dinner trolley rattled around the floor and Olga took that as the cue to leave.

'Are you not staying for lunch?'

'They don't serve visitors,' she reminded him.

'Share mine. I can't eat it all.'

It was borscht, which she liked. And she was hungry. She savoured the smell of the red beetroot soup, filled with meat and vegetables. But he was so thin she couldn't possibly take any.

A nurse arrived and sat on the edge of the bed to feed him.

'I must go, Papa. I'm sorry.'

'That is all right. I have work to do.'

'Work?' Olga struggled to keep a straight face.

'My writing.' He opened a bedside cabinet and withdrew a notebook and pen.

'What are you writing?'

'A letter,' he replied.

'Who to?'

'To you.'

'Can I read it?' she asked offering her hand to take the book.

'When it is finished,' he replied, closing the notebook.

'I look forward to reading it.' She kissed his forehead. 'I'll see you soon.'

26

Mickey met his new colleagues in a room filled with phones, printers, and plasma screens. A painfully thin Russian in his mid-twenties called Vlad, and Carmella, a severe young American from Newark, not to be confused with New York, she insisted.

He poked around in their backgrounds and discovered that Vlad's father had been imprisoned then exiled for campaigning against Pintov and still had connections to opposition politicians that might prove useful.

Carmella had gone to Harvard, which was impressive. Less so her unhappiness at being shunted onto Mickey's desk from her trainee role on the Socially Responsible Investment team. Mickey consoled her with the thought that in the murky waters of Russian business she'd probably gain useful insights.

'Thanks for coming on board anyway,' he said. 'I'll be honest. We're sailing into the unknown. But the downside protection for you guys is that you have a lifeboat back into Crosshairs. If it all goes wrong, you go right back to what you were doing yesterday.' Their shoulders slackened a little. 'If it goes well, you'll have gained invaluable experience. In the meantime. We'll have a lot of fun. Sound alright?'

Vlad exchanged glances with Carmella but said nothing.

'Spit it out,' said Mickey. 'Full disclosure.'

'Something has been worrying us,' said Vlad. 'Do you think this work might be dangerous?'

'Fair question.' To which he didn't really have an answer. He wandered to a window and looked down on the Lloyd's building. Why had they let a plumber design it?

'I mean we are basically at war with Russia,' Vlad pressed.

'I'll be the only one going to Russia,' Mickey pointed out. 'You'll be working in London,'

'If we upset Pintov that won't matter.'

'There's no reason for Pintov to get upset with us buying Russian equities.'

'But we are also investigating the Russian mafia.'

Fair point. 'Let's make sure we keep your names out of everything.'

They exchanged looks again and nodded, somewhat reassured.

'While we're doing full disclosure,' said Mickey. 'I have been worrying that this work might be too difficult for you. Not the financial analysis but the investigative work.'

'Why did you hire us?' asked Vlad, folding his arms. 'If you don't think we can do it?'

'Because I've been told you're smart and techy and the best I can get. But I still want to ask the question. You've got no training in intelligence gathering. Maybe I'm asking too much.'

'We are trained in information gathering and analysis,' said Carmella. 'That's what we do. It's the same methodology. Sift the available information and analyse.'

'I guess so,' said Mickey. 'But you're not on the ground in Russia. You don't have agents like the CIA does.'

'We don't need them,' replied Carmella. 'There is plenty of open-source intelligence that we have access to. As for human intelligence ...' she smiled. 'That's you.'

'Agent double O Summer!' said Mickey. 'Brilliant. Let's get to work.'

He showed them an advert he had mocked up based on similar from CRIMESTOPPERS for a reward for information on the hacking of Baltika bank. It specified that the information had to lead to an arrest or be of significant use to law enforcement agencies.

'Which law enforcement agencies?' asked Carmella. 'Russian or British?'

'Either. Or American, Latvian, whatever.'

'A reward of ten million rubles is too much,' said Vlad.

'It's only about one hundred thousand pounds,' Mickey pointed out.

'Too much,' he repeated.

'How can you have too big a reward?'

'It raises the bar,' said Vlad. 'Someone who has maybe only heard a rumour will not think passing that on will earn them so much money. Others might be frightened that such a big reward will make them visible to the authorities.'

'I would also make it less official,' said Carmella. 'Don't mention arrests and law enforcement agencies.'

Mickey thought about it for a moment. 'How about a reward of one million rubles for information deemed to be of significant use to our enquiries?'

Vlad and Carmella both agreed and Mickey high-fived them. 'The dream team has made its first decision.'

They tweaked the advert a little further, Vlad translated it into Russian and then, using fake ID, he posted it on Russian social media. Carmella fired off the advert to thousands of Russian email addresses she had bought on the dark web, and to everyone on LinkedIn based in Moscow and St Petersburg.

Mickey preferred his usual modus operandi. He picked up the blower and rang through a list of Russian journalists. Most didn't want to help. Some gave hints that he should be looking towards St Petersburg, but they didn't want to say more than that. However, a woman called Dina said she would talk but only in person in St Petersburg, and he would need to prove he was not working for the FSB.

'How do I do that?' he asked.

'Nikolai Mishkin,' she said, before cutting the call.

His new best mate.

Later that afternoon Vlad and Carmella briefed everyone on what they'd been up to. Vlad had filtered out a lot of conspiracy theories about the Baltic bank being brought down by the CIA and found a bona-fide human rights campaigner who had heard it was the St Petersburg mafia.

Carmella had dismissed numerous invitations from dubious sounding men to rendezvous in Moscow or St Petersburg but had found plenty of chat on dissident groups suggesting the bank collapse was done with the blessing of Pintov in response to Western sanctions.

Over a matter of days, they garnered more leads and information. One name kept popping up. Semyon Bogdan, a St Petersburg mobster.

Mickey called Mishkin. 'Mate, you said to come back if I got a lead and run it by you. How about Semyon Bogdan?'

'St Petersburg mafia,' replied Mishkin. 'Wouldn't be at all surprised if he had something to do with it. Not personally. He can't work a mobile phone. But someone in his outfit. He owns the media company TruNews and it has a cyber arm.'

'Thanks. Also, Dina Kuznetsov?'

'Dina is an investigative journalist,' replied Mishkin.

'She'll talk to me if I can prove I'm not FSB. Gave me your name as if you'd be a reference.'

'Consider it done.'

'Cheers.'

Mickey cut the call and turned back to the team. 'We need to get all the information we can on Semyon Bogdan and his businesses.'

'We'll run his name by Sherlock,' said Vlad.

'Who is Sherlock?'

'It's a service run by the Kremlin. Gives you the address, telephone number, date of birth, tax number, companies or domain names registered in that person's name, IP address, user ID, vehicle identification number, passport number, mobile ...'

'I get the idea,' interrupted Mickey. 'How come you have access?'

'Crosshairs bought a small Moscow insurance company. They have access so they can see if clients are likely to sting them.'

'Awesome. We also need to work on Kazbegi Holdings. Kazbegi may have a dodgy past but for a long time now he's been playing a straight bat. He's got nothing to do with Pintov and the government acknowledges that. He hasn't faced sanctions, but the shares are still trading at a massive discount. It's probably going to be our top pick for the recovery fund.'

'I agree,' said Vlad. 'It's a screaming buy.'

'Can you knock together a presentation on Kazbegi Holdings. Short on text, big on charts and diagrams. Breakdown of the businesses by assets and earnings and by geography, everything in Russia in red. Just something to show him that we've already made a start.'

'Show who?'

'Kazbegi. I'm fixed up to see him tomorrow.'

They looked suitably impressed. Things were starting to fall into place. There was just one major hurdle to clear. How to tell Helen of his plan to travel to Russia without sending her blood pressure through the roof.

* * *

Helen tucked a curl into her swim cap as she waded out into the water. She normally swam in just a costume, but she'd put on a wet suit in case the cold-water shock was bad for the little one. Even then it was cold getting into the water. She took a deep breath and launched. Rapid, random reflex strokes then the arms stretched out further and more slowly into something resembling a swimming motion.

As she moved away from shore a loon without a wet suit came out of the water. The blood had drained from his prickled skin.

'Giving up already?' asked Mickey mischievously.

'Why don't you come in yourself?'

'Not today, mate. I left my dry suit at home.'

'It's good for you,' the man persisted.

'So is spinach. I don't do that either.'

The man shivered away to the changing rooms. Mickey turned back to check Helen was still above water. She had some bottle. As she drew near, he picked up her towel tent and held it ready for her to dive into.

'Thanks,' she said.

'How was it?'

'Amazing! Just what I needed to clear my head.'

'That's great.' Mickey would rather a lobotomy, but he knew a swim always picked her up.

'The estate agent called,' she said. 'I wasn't sure whether to tell you.'

'Tell me what?'

'The Marshalls still have the house on the market. They've moved to their new house and it's standing empty.' She shrugged.

'I know we can't buy it, that's why I wasn't sure whether to tell you. But I thought you should know.'

Brilliant. She's teed him up nicely. 'Well, I do now have a plan to get our money back.'

'Really,' she mumbled from under the towelling.

'But it will involve me travelling to Russia.'

'What!?' Wide eyes popped out from under the towelling. 'Are you insane? We're at war with Russia!'

'We're not at war,' said Mickey.

'As good as.'

'I know it's a little risky,' said Mickey. 'But I've been given the opportunity to run a Russian recovery fund. Just as a one-off. It's a chance to get the money back to buy the Marshall's house.'

'Mickey, I understand your frustration at losing the money, but going to Russia and putting yourself in danger won't achieve anything.'

He said nothing. She was processing. That was a good start.

'At least think about it very carefully,' she continued. 'Don't make any rash decision.'

Mickey zipped his mouth. Cashed in his chips. A successful first round had shifted Helen's position from questioning his sanity to cautioning against making any rash decision. What's more, she seemed genuinely concerned for his welfare. No longer mad at him for losing all the house money.

* * *

Mickey sheltered from the light drizzle under the central bay of Marble Arch and thought about the appointment with Kazbegi. Objective: get him to invest in the recovery fund or give a mandate to review Kazbegi Holdings. Ideally both. Bang on eleven o'clock a limousine pulled into the closed nearside lane and flashed its lights. The window slid down and the driver asked, 'Mickey Summer?'

'The one and only, mate.'

A door opened and Mickey jumped in. As the car slid silently down Park Lane a man fiddled with the controls of the electronic device on his knees. On the screen red and green columns rose and fell playfully.

'Are we making an album?' asked Mickey. 'Because I forgot to bring my spoons.'

'Turn off your phone please.'

Mickey complied. 'Where are we going?' he asked, as they passed Hyde Park corner.

'To your meeting.' The man switched off his gadget and placed Mickey's phone in a heavy black case.

Mickey gave up on the conversation and watched South Kensington pass by. The art-deco façade of Harrods, the red-brick terraced houses and mews. They circled a block a couple of times and then the driver headed west with renewed purpose.

They arrived at a new office block in Ealing and entered a meeting room with soft furnishings and floor-to-ceiling windows offering a nondescript view that could be found anywhere in west London. The gadget man closed all the blinds and set up his counter-surveillance equipment. The coloured columns danced again. Mickey waited patiently.

Kazbegi arrived and Mickey handed everyone a copy of his presentation on how to increase the value of Kazbegi Holdings by selling unethical activities and making the financials more transparent.

'The real black hole is the equity accounted subsidiaries in Russia. We need transparency on what these businesses do. Identify which you want to keep and increase your holdings so you can fully consolidate. Sell the others. As for TruNews. It's a Pintov mouthpiece. You should sell.'

'That is the reality of running a media business in Russia. If you are not for the state, you are soon closed.'

'You should sell,' Mickey repeated. 'And you should sell the stake in Arktikugol in Svalbard. It's loss-making and it's old-economy coal mining. I don't really understand why you bought a stake in the first place. You just seem to have propped up a loss-making state business.'

'I like the old economy,' said Kazbegi. 'I have a lot of new-economy exposure with my Lithium and Nickel mines. What if the Green Economy doesn't take off? We'll still need coal.'

Mickey could tell he'd not convinced Kazbegi, so he moved on. 'I also think you should sell the legacy businesses you got in the early privatisations.'

'Why is that?'

'Because you got them on the cheap. Some might even say you stole them. Whereas the ones you've built up there's no question about their legitimacy.'

'All of my businesses are legitimate,' insisted Kazbegi. 'I was born into a poor family. I made my early money selling vodka in the Soviet days.'

'Selling on the black market,' Mickey pointed out.

'In communist times everything was sold on the black market. After vodka I moved into buying and selling cars. And then I bought and sold oil and other commodity businesses. I was a trader like you.'

'Just a good trader?' asked Mickey. 'Or did you have help from Mr Pintov?'

'I had no help from anyone. People like me were the mid-wives of capitalism in Russia. And it was a difficult birth. Gorbachev's Law of Co-operatives allowed entrepreneurs like me to set up businesses in Russia for the first time since the days of the Tsar. I was twenty years old when I started importing German cars. I used my vodka money. I could have lost everything. It was a gamble.'

'But you also bought state industries in the privatisations for almost nothing.'

'I didn't set the rules,' snapped Kazbegi. 'It was that crazy drunk Yeltsin, advised by western bankers like you who set them. They liberalised the prices of bread and rent, which squeezed the poor. Then they held down the internal prices of natural resources like oil and gas and minerals but opened their sale up to the world markets. Why?' Kazbegi shrugged. 'Nobody has ever been able to explain why. It was madness. I could buy oil for a dollar a barrel in Siberia and sell it for forty times that in the City of London. And it was all perfectly legitimate. The British government knew this, otherwise they would not have let me buy West Ham.'

Kazbegi paused as he sat back in his chair.

'The mafia used their new wealth to expand into prostitution, drugs, weapons, human trafficking, cybercrime and other illegal activities. Businessmen like me used our new wealth to expand the economy by developing legitimate businesses in media, energy and manufacturing. However, sometimes bad businesses would evolve inside the legitimate businesses. Like weeds, as you describe in your presentation. I don't want them, but they grow anyway. And you are correct that I must constantly pull them up and throw them away.'

'So why haven't you thrown away Bogdan?' asked Mickey.

'As I told you, I barely have any contact with him anymore.'

'Why did you ever?'

'The mafia realised the new businessmen like me were making a lot of money, legally. More than they were making illegally. They moved in. To survive against them I needed protection. That's how I became involved with Bogdan. He was my krysha.'

'Krysha?' asked Mickey.

'It means roof. Providing protection. But that was a long time ago. I severed all connections with him years ago.'

'Except your shareholding in TruNews, which he runs.'

'It's purely a financial relationship.'

'As I said, you should sell it.'

Kazbegi studied Mickey in silence a while, then said, 'There may be something in your proposal, but this isn't the time to be selling Russian businesses. With sanctions in place, I won't get a fair value for my holding.'

'Can I make a suggestion?'

'Please.'

'I'm going out to Moscow and St Petersburg to visit companies. I'm building up a special situation recovery fund for when sanctions are lifted.'

'That may be a long time.'

'Perhaps, but this is the time to do the research. Might you be interested in investing in the fund?'

Kazbegi shook his head. 'As you've just outlined, I already have a lot of investments in Russia.'

Fair point. 'While I'm out there, I could also take a closer look at your businesses, including TruNews. I can do a valuation for you, like I did for West Ham. I'll also look at your equity accounted businesses and then I can make a more concrete proposal about what to buy and sell.'

Kazbegi sat in silence for a while as he flicked through the presentation. Finally, he looked back up at Mickey. 'What do I have to lose? As you are out there in any case you won't need paying.'

'I ain't running a charity.'

'I'm a reasonable man. If you bring back anything useful, I'll reward you fairly.'

Perfect. Now he had two money-making ventures on the go.

27

Olga jumped in a Yandex taxi outside the hospital entrance. 'Passazhirskaya station, please.'

'Passa …?' the driver said in a Central Asian accent, she guessed Kazakhstan.

'Leningradsky,' she offered the more familiar name and was rewarded with a toothy smile.

They had only moved a few hundred meters when the traffic slowed and then came to an abrupt halt. Anti-war protestors were out again, and this time had blocked the road at the entrance to the Olympic Plaza. The placards and banners made demands for peace. Peace. Yes. Olga wanted peace. Everyone wanted peace. That is what the boys were fighting for.

The protestors were naïve, but they weren't stupid. They wore hard hats, goggles, and capes to protect against water cannon. Many wore masks. And it wasn't to stop the spread of any virus. They deployed hand signals rather than using mobile phones that could be traced, and they moved around rapidly, like tadpoles in a pond, to make identification more difficult.

'Why do they support the Nazis in Ukraine?' asked the driver. 'They should be supporting the glorious Motherland.'

'They don't want more young men to die,' replied Olga, oddly irritated by the immigrant's fervent nationalism.

The driver caught her eye in the mirror. 'You agree with these people?'

'Can you let me out please?' she replied without answering his question. 'I'll be quicker walking.' She settled the fare, stepped out and dialled the office. 'Are you monitoring the demonstration at the Olympic Plaza in Moscow?'

'Of course. We've harvested and passed on personal details as usual. Why?'

'I happened to walk right into it. Just checking.'

'It's about to be broken up. Don't get caught up with them.'

'I won't.' Olga cut the call and secured her phone in a zipped pocket. Despite her assertion, she found herself inexplicably drawn towards the crowd. She stopped just five metres short of the police barriers. Although the demonstrators were loud and energetic, they didn't seem angry. Many were smiling. Why were they so happy? The country was under attack from the west.

She turned at the sound of commotion behind. A mob approached wielding batons and metal bars. They marched ten across and fifty deep in ubiquitous black jeans and, despite the near freezing temperatures, torsos bare except for extravagant tattoos. They ran with fists held up on the end of gym-manufactured arms.

Olga recognised some as St Petersburg muscle that Bogdan sometimes hired. Riot police stood aside as the mob kicked over barriers and moved in, swinging fists and weapons indiscriminately. Some demonstrators threw defensive punches and fired pepper spray. Most just screamed and backed away, falling over, curling up on the floor, taking the blows. A young man lay motionless, blood pouring over his white office shirt. A nurse crawled out from the scrum; her eye swollen like a purple tulip.

This wasn't the way to deal with the protestors. They needed to be arrested and re-educated. But she was powerless to stop it. And the police were enjoying the sport.

After several minutes OMON riot police finally arrived. Like well-trained dogs, they stood to attention on the whistle, impressive in their pressed blue and grey camouflage and the shining round black helmets from which they drew their cosmonauts nickname. At a signal the OMON dispersed into the demonstrators and dragged away the wounded to grey vans.

With the protest broken, the barricades were removed. The police waved cars and pedestrians forward. A sort of normality returned, although Olga's legs were still shaking. The demonstration for peace had achieved nothing but violence. As if the world didn't have enough of that already.

28

It was just like the good old days. Mickey on a foreign jaunt flying business class at someone else's expense. Which was just as well. The ticket cost three thousand pounds because of stratospheric jet fuel prices and sanctions that made it a nine-hour flight via Turkey instead of five direct to St Petersburg.

On the approach to Pulkovo a steward woke him to request he buckle up. They bounced down the runway and taxied to the terminal. He received a cool reception from border police who took his fingerprints and a DNA swab. While these were checked they scrolled through his phone and quizzed him on the reason for his visit. They weren't impressed with the recovery fund story, but snapped to attention when he mentioned that he was also doing work for Ivan Kazbegi and was able to prove it by showing an email from Kazbegi's secretary fixing up their appointment. That was like waving a magic wand.

And so it was that an hour later than expected he emerged into the arrivals hall to see a chauffeur bearing his name on a whiteboard. With light, late-morning traffic they sailed breezily into St Petersburg.

Marble lions guarded the entrance to the restored nineteenth century Royal Palace. The commissionaire doffed his gold cap.

'My name's Mickey. I'll be staying a few days.'

'You are welcome, Mickey.'

Two bellboys fought for the bags. He gave them one each.

Muzak seeped around the hotel foyer like poison gas.

He offered up his passport to a severe receptionist who could have come from border control. She copied his driving license and credit card and asked him to show his travel insurance, sign a health declaration, confirm his address and date of birth, and sign a few more pieces of paper in Russian that he didn't understand. Finally, she gave the room key to the older of the two bellboys who led Mickey to the lifts. Up to the third floor and into an oak-panelled room. He squished the lavender pillow, acknowledged the tinkle of the fountain in the courtyard, and slipped each of the boys a one hundred ruble note. They took it like winnings on the Grand National and backed out of the room.

Mickey freshened up in the bathroom and then, with time to kill before his meeting, he left the hotel and strolled the pavements of Nevsky Prospekt. The warm yeasty aroma from a patisserie sucked him in. He bought a chocolate salami and ate it as he window-shopped. St Petersburg fashion appeared to be sober colours for men and violet, pink, and olive for women. A maternity dress stood out. But that would be tempting fate.

He thought of ringing to check all was well but when he checked the time, he realised she'd be at the open swim session. Keeping her fitness up for her and the baby. Meanwhile Mickey needed to make sure they had a house to live in.

* * *

Mickey's first meeting was with Pawel, an old colleague who now worked for the St Petersburg office of the largest private client broker in Russia. Meeting objective: introductions to promising listed Russian companies. Simple. Even for Pawel, who had always been a bit of a slacker. Liked to do nothing and then rest afterwards. But even he could manage this.

Pawel came down to the foyer, waved at Mickey and approached with a smile and a slight limp. Rumour had it that he'd got on the wrong side of the mafia in the early days of the Russian stock market, and someone had shot his knee cap.

'Good to see you, Mickey,' said Pawel as they shook hands. 'You haven't changed a bit.'

'Good to see you too,' said Mickey. He couldn't return the compliment on looks. Pawel had not aged well. The hair was thin and lank. Eyes red.

They played catch-up on former colleagues as they made their way to a meeting room. Waiting for them there was a young woman with black hair plastered tight.

'Pleased to meet you,' she said in perfect English, with an American accent. 'I'm Tatiana.'

'Mickey Summer.'

'Tatiana runs our ethical investments team,' explained Pawel.

Tatiana had a presentation pack titled, 'Socially Responsible Investing in Russia'. She took Mickey through it. At the end there was a complicated but useful table with a hundred companies showing exposure to dozens of different categories. Alcohol, arms, energy, tobacco, gambling ... Almost every company had question marks against them.

Mickey looked down at the list. 'I'm surprised you don't have corruption and mafia connections as categories.'

Tatiana nodded. 'For sure they are areas of concern. But we don't have the tools to search for that.'

'Do you imagine Kazbegi Holdings would get a clean bill of health if you did?'

'For sure.'

'Is it the most blue-chip company in Russia?'

'We say red chip, but yes, it is.'

'But looking at your list it could clean up a little more.'

'It could.'

'How about TruNews?'

Tatiana frowned. 'It's a private company. It's not listed on the market.'

'I know, but Kazbegi Holdings has a stake in it, so I'd like to know what you think.'

Tatiana looked at Pawel then back to Mickey. 'We haven't researched it. But the man who runs it is probably mafia.'

'Semyon Bogdan?' asked Mickey.

'Correct.'

'Can you fix me up with a meeting?'

'Why would he agree to meet you?' asked Pawel. 'He doesn't have outside investors in TruNews.'

'Tell him I'm a banker with ideas on how to make him rich.'

Pawel shrugged. 'I'll try.'

They spent the rest of the meeting talking through other possible investments and Pawel made a note of the companies that most interested Mickey. He promised to send him accounts and fix meetings with management. It had been a useful meeting and Mickey returned to the streets of St Peterburg uplifted and ready for his next encounter.

* * *

Mickey sat at a pavement table at an empty tavern and waited for the journalist Dina. His phone rang. But just as he was about to answer it rang off.

A short, pencil-thin woman in a leather coat approached. Holding up her phone she said, 'That was me.'

He opened his mouth to introduce himself, but she raised a hand to stop him.

'Turn off your phone please.'

Mickey did, then passed it into her open hand.

'I'll give it back to you after our meeting.' She placed it inside a heavy case.

'It's soundproofed,' she explained. 'Even though you turned it off the microphone could still be working.'

'You think my phone is bugged?'

'You're not a celebrity or a political activist, but you are British. It's just a precaution. I check my phone every day to see whether Pegasus is on it.'

'Doesn't your horse have his own phone?'

'The Israeli spyware,' she explained.

He stuck out his hand. 'Mickey Summer. Pleased to meet you.'

'Dina.' She avoided the handshake, but her eyes smiled behind the heavy spectacles.

A waiter arrived with pen and pad ready.

Dina ordered sparkling water. Mickey followed suit. They made small talk about the weather and the sights of St Petersburg that she recommended Mickey visit. After the waiter arrived with the drinks Dina switched into serious mode.

'Why have you come to Russia?'

'I'm investing in Russian equities,' said Mickey.

'But you also want to find out who hacked Baltika bank.'

'That's right.'

'What did you tell the border police?'

'I'm doing some business advisory work for Ivan Kazbegi.'

Dina looked as impressed as the border police. 'And why are you interested in the hacking of Baltika? Are you a policeman?'

'I'm just a guy that lost a lot of money when the bank collapsed.'

'And you think you might be able to get it back? Is that it?'

'Maybe.'

She stymied a laugh. 'How?'

'I don't know. Maybe I can't.' Mickey shrugged. 'But I think the criminals shouldn't get away without being identified at the least.'

She studied him as she sipped her water. 'You want revenge?'

It did sound stupid. 'I'm not sure what I want. But the prime suspect is a hacker known as Dmitri or Geneve. He's working under Semyon Bogdan. But I need more than rumours. I need evidence.'

'You've heard of TruNews?'

'Of course. It's a TV station. Pintov's mouthpiece.'

'It also has a cyber-security business. But that is cover for illegal cyber activities. Your hacker probably operated from there.'

'Thanks. I'll investigate that.'

'What would you do with any evidence you find?' asked Dina. 'Take it to the British police?'

'Or the Russian.'

This time she produced a warm, toothy smile. 'If it is Bogdan's people behind the hacking you have no chance of a prosecution in Russia. He is very popular in the community because although he is a lifelong mafia man and everyone knows it, he does charitable things. He is like your Robin Hood. A thief of the people. He's so popular he's going to run for Mayor. People talk about him possibly replacing Pintov.'

'If he's committed a crime then don't the Russian police have to charge him? They can't all be corrupt.'

'Stealing from a Latvian or British bank isn't a Russian crime.'

Fair point. 'If I got evidence, maybe you could expose it in your paper?'

'My readership wouldn't be very interested. It's not really a Russian story.'

'But if everyone thinks Bogdan is a good guy this would be another angle.'

'Bogdan has zashchita.'

'Sorry to hear that. Is there a cure?'

'Zashchita means a team of lawyers, PR specialists and media influencers that protect their client's image. Even if you had evidence that Bogdan was behind the collapse of RSB his zashchita would spin it as another Robin Hood story. Stealing from the British to compensate for sanctions.'

Without any prompting from Mickey, she then moved onto the general injustices in modern Russia. The surveillance, hounding, suppression of opposition. Mickey listened. She seemed to need to unload.

'Sounds like a mess,' he said eventually. 'Are you not tempted to just leave the country?'

'I have thought about it. Especially since Ukraine. But it's my homeland. There are plenty of decent people living here. Why must all the good Russians go and leave everything to the mafia and the stupid serfs who are just as culpable for believing the propaganda.' She removed her glasses revealing indentations on her snub nose, cleaned them on a napkin and popped them back on her head.

'Going back to Bogdan. How do I go about investigating him? Where do I start?'

She bit her bottom lip. 'You are correct that not everyone is corrupt. Try official channels first. The Ministry of Justice, the Prosecutor General....'

Mickey scribbled the names and other suggestions on a piece of paper. 'Can I trust these people?'

'You can't trust anyone. Some are honest and trying to fight corruption. Some are not. It's difficult to tell who the good guys are. But you might come across someone who wants to be brave. They won't personally take on Bogdan, but they might help you do that.'

'Thanks.'

'If you do come up with any leads then let me know. I may be able to help.'

A heavy-set man in a brown suit suddenly appeared beside the table.

'I believe this is yours,' he said in perfect English, offering Mickey a leather satchel.

Mickey reached out but Dina slapped his hand. She grabbed Mickey by the arm and pulled him to his feet. 'Let's take a walk.'

She led him down the street and flagged a taxi.

'Where are we going?'

'Away,' she said as they climbed in. She pointed to a man with a camera on the other side of the street. 'You were being filmed. If you'd opened the bag, it would have been caught on camera.'

'What was in the bag?'

'Drugs? Stolen goods? Maps of Russian troop deployments? You take the bag and seconds later that man's colleagues come in to arrest you.'

'He was a policeman?'

'Or FSB. I recognised the face from somewhere.'

It was a close escape.

'I also have a camera,' she said taking off her spectacles and showing him the lens. 'These are to protect me from false arrest. What the camera sees is played in real time on a friend's computer. Even if they take my camera, I will have evidence.'

Her phone rang. She turned to one side and spoke at length in Russian as she made notes on her pad. After killing the call, she turned back to Mickey. 'That was my friend who has used facial recognition software to identify the man. Eduard Beratov. He is a Lieutenant Colonel in the FSB.'

'Why is he after me?'

'Probably because you met me. That's not what a normal businessman would do. I suspect they wanted to take you in and find out what you are up to. I'd advise you to go back to England.'

'A few minutes ago, you were all for me investigating Bogdan,'

Mickey pointed out.

'That was before I knew that the FSB are watching you. Go home.'

'I'm enjoying myself and it's nowhere near bedtime.'

They drove in silence for a while and then the car pulled up beside a metro stop. 'This is where I get out.'

'Thanks for your help.'

She sighed. 'I still recommend you go home to the UK, but if you are going to stay then get a bodyguard.'

'They can be expensive.' Mickey had considered it but had baulked at the cost.

'I don't know the rates, but this isn't an area to save expenses on. Get a cheap hotel. Eat cheap food. Don't use cheap security.'

'That sounds like good advice.'

'This is the best you can get,' she said writing a phone number down on a slip of paper. She then took his phone out of the hardcase and handed it back. 'Don't use this phone to ring the number. Buy a new pre-paid and a packet of SIM cards. Change the card after each call and drop the old one down into the sewers.'

It had started so well with Pawel, but it suddenly all seemed a lot more serious. Maybe Helen had been right. This was madness. He didn't want Dina to leave him alone, but she opened the door and stepped out onto the pavement.

'Stay safe,' she said.

'Where to?' asked the driver in English.

Mickey hesitated. The airport seemed sensible. However, even if he did go home, he needed to check out of the hotel first. 'The Royal Palace, please.'

29

The President's bomb-proof limousine had been left behind in Moscow. It was too large to fit on the speedboat and impractical on the cobbled streets of the medieval port of Daphne, and the dirt mountain roads winding along the foothills of the snow-flanked Mount Athos. Moreover, the security threat from the local population of monks and mystics had been assessed at level one, almost as safe as the President's dacha on the shore of the Black Sea.

Abbot Tryphon made all the small talk as the Toyota pick-up climbed away from the turquoise bay. Dust infused with forest chestnuts blew in through the open window and for a moment all the President's troubles were forgotten. But a pothole sparked a spasm in his spine and snapped him back into the present.

'Who is with us? Who against?'

'This is very difficult to know,' said the abbot. 'Only Pantokrator is openly against and recognising the Ukrainian Orthodoxy. As for the others, I am not sure where they stand.'

'You should know. I know. Philotheou and Karakal are with us.'

'They closed the doors of their monastery to the Bishop of Odessa, but that does not necessarily mean they will break with Constantinople. They do not want a schism in the church.'

'Too late for that. Constantinople created the schism when it made the Ukrainian church autocephalous. Everyone must decide which side they are on. Helandariou is also with us.'

'You are so sure about the Serbians?'

'I am sure. And the Bulgarians in Zografou. Who are the waverers that I must bring on board?'

'All of the others,' said the abbot. 'It is not so easy for them. Even for me. I am Russian, but like all twenty monasteries on Athos I am under the authority of Constantinople.'

The President's eyes narrowed. 'Istanbul is a Muslim city. How can it be the centre of our Christian Church? Moscow should be the first among equals.'

The President was about to develop the point when he was thrown forward in his seat as the truck braked. A party of tangle-bearded monks floated across the road. They resumed the journey in silence and arrived finally at the cupolas and medieval architecture of the Russian monastery of Panteleimon.

The abbot took the President on a tour. First to the monastery bell, the largest in the world and audible across the entire peninsular. Then to the library filled with shelves of leather-bound tomes, parchments, and jewel-encrusted icons. Then to the relics, including a stone from the tomb, a bone of Joseph and finally the pride of the monastery, the venerable head of the Great Martyr Panteleimon.

The President then requested time to relax before the meeting. He was shown to a simple cell with a single bed, a wooden table and chair, and a cross on the wall.

'Would you like to be informed on developments in the outside world?' asked his secretary, standing uncertainly in the doorway.

'Let the outside world look after itself. I am about to reclaim Russian leadership of the Orthodox Church.'

'I'll leave you in peace,' said the secretary, shutting the door.

The President lay down on the hard bed, closed his eyes. And prayed.

* * *

'The crab wants beef stroganoff tomorrow.'

The COMINT on the Joint Service Signal Unit in Cyprus recorded the phone call and relayed a copy to Fort Meade. There it aroused the interest of a signals analyst. She escalated it to the SIGINT Directorate head, who quickly discovered that the boat from where the call was made was Turkish registered and owned by an Indian billionaire. She agreed that it was a million to one chance but to be safe she escalated it to the Operation Group Director, who decided to run it by Declan.

'The crab wants beef stroganoff tomorrow,' the Director read aloud. 'This was a conversation in Russian and crab is a common nickname for Pintov and stroganoff is a dish Pintov likes.'

'Is that all?' asked Declan.

The Director shifted his weight. 'Mount Athos is an orthodox Christian enclave that Pintov has visited previously. I've requested more intel, but because of the time sensitivity I thought I'd show you what we have now. It's just possible.'

'You can't really think Pintov is on that Greek island? What would he be doing there at a time like this?'

'I don't know.'

'Where's his guard? The nearest Russian ship is in the Black Sea.'

'Maybe he's gone in under the radar.'

Declan shook his head. 'It's a Turkish registered boat visiting Mount Athos. Two Russian crew members who call the owner a crab, probably as an in joke because he behaves like Pintov.'

'But what if it is him and we miss the opportunity?'

Declan liked to go with gut instinct. His said it was nothing. But the gut instinct of several people along the reporting line had been to pursue it further. He decided to do the same. 'Call Hurlburt and get some eyes over that island. Let's see what's going on.'

'I'll do that.'

'Make it a Reaper.'

'You want the drone armed?'

'Hell yes. If it *is* Pintov. We'll give POTUS an option.'

30

The gathering in the refectory at Panteleimon looked lost in the Julian Calendar. Abbots, elders, and assorted hangers-on from all twenty monasteries, plus the sketes, cells and hermitages, sat on wooden benches eating a simple meal of fried sea bream served with fresh brown bread on a pewter plate, accompanied by a glass of home-made wine. The conversations meandered through everyday secular life on the isolated island, some ecclesiastical discussion, and occasional speculation as to the identity of the surprise guest who had yet to appear.

After the meal, staff cleared and wiped the tables. Wood scraped on stone as the monks turned chairs to face the front. When the room was settled, Abbot Tryphon said a prayer asking for the Lord's intervention on proceedings. Then he turned and nodded at the monk waiting by the door. He opened it, and the room gasped as President Pintov walked in.

'Our most honoured guest today needs no introduction, so I will simply invite him to speak.'

The President was pleased that they were in shock. It showed the security arrangements had worked. 'Thank you, Abbot Tryphon. Thank you, all. Thank you for coming to talk with me today.'

He removed his tie, undid the buttons on his shirt collar and pulled out his cross. 'This is my baptismal cross. Thirty years ago, I went to Israel to get it blessed at the Lord's Tomb. I did as Mama instructed and then put the cross around my neck. I have never taken it off since. I keep it under my shirt. I do not think a man should show off his belief. It is inside his heart. So why do I show you? To prove that I am a Christian? I do not need to tell you wise and holy men that this symbol proves nothing. Only God will decide if I am a true follower of Christ. I show you simply to demonstrate that I always keep Christianity at the heart of what I do.'

The President talked at length, with impeccable humility, about his Christian faith, the conflicts between his atheist father and orthodox mother, the difficulties in expressing any faith during the communist era and his own personal battles between right and wrong.

'So why am I here today? You men are wise,' he said again. 'You know already. When the Patriarch of Constantinople made the Ukrainian church autocephalous, in direct opposition to Patriarch Krill of the Russian Orthodox church, he created a schism.' He paused and looked around the room. 'Constantinople took this action. Constantinople caused this schism. Not Russia. Constantinople has lost all credibility and it should also lose its position as first among equals. Patriarch Krill has decreed that the Russian church will have no communion with Constantinople. I ask each of you here to consider your own communion. You have Christ as your leader in spirit. You have the Superior of the Holy Supervision as your leader on Mount Athos. You do not need Constantinople.' He looked around the room. 'Or should we call it by its real name of Istanbul. The largest city in the Muslim country of Turkey. Constantinople is no more.'

'I object!'

Wide eyes turned toward the flowing white beard of the Abbot of Pantokrator. 'Ecumenical Patriarch of Constantinople is not history. And he remains *primus inter pares* among the churches. You are a politician. You cannot teach us about canon law. Politics and religion should be kept separate.'

'Thank you, Abbot Visarion, for opening the debate,' said

the President. After a moment for translations at various speeds, relieved laughter rippled around the room.

'Religion and politics are intertwined. But we should be governed by common sense. And common sense should be based on moral principles first. And it is not possible today to have morality separated from religious values.'

'Was it moral for you to invade Crimea? That is why the Patriarch was forced to make the Ukrainian church autocephalous.'

'Thank you for that question,' said the President. 'It was in Crimea that Grand Prince Vladimir was baptised before bringing Christianity to the rest of Russia. In addition to ethnic similarity and a common language, Christianity was the most powerful unifying force amongst the various tribes in the Eastern Slavic world and key to the creation of a Russian state. Crimea is of sacred importance to Russia, like the Temple Mount in Jerusalem for the followers of Islam and Judaism. That is why we needed to regain control.'

'And why did you invade the rest of Ukraine?'

'We did not invade. Ukraine is part of Russia. It has been for over a thousand years since the days of Kievan Rus. We gave it some limited freedoms as a republic and then as an aligned country. But Nazi influences have spread there, and we had to remove them with our special military operation.'

'And here on Mount Athos? What does Russia want?'

'We want to help you be independent.'

'You want a mini-Gibraltar. A toehold in the Mediterranean. Look out the window. Look what they are already building.'

The monks turned to the window, some having to stand up to get a view. Down in the harbour an extensive breakwater had been extended far out into the turquoise bay.

'We are building a larger harbour where we will be able to dock small ships. Nothing too large. We wish to preserve the tranquillity of the peninsula.'

'Militarising the harbour! How will that preserve the tranquillity?'

'Because we will stop the Turks from coming here.'

'The Greek government will do that.'

'Greece is a weak outpost of Europe.'

'We have the protection of many countries, not just Greece. Our monasteries have Patriarchs in Serbia, Bulgaria, Romania, and we have monks here from America, Australia, Canada, and all around the world. We have many friends.'

The President smiled. 'We have a saying in Russia. Many friends, means no friends. These countries will not protect you. I am approaching the end of my days. I will go to meet the creator. Maybe this year, maybe next. Soon. I am not acting in my personal interests. I am acting only in the best interest of Orthodox Christianity. I want this to be my legacy,'

'We are part of Europe. We do not need Russian protection.'

Now the President laughed. 'Europe is France and Germany, and they are growing de-Christianised, with immigration policies turning them into a dangerous mix of Islam and atheism. And their Christianity is corrupted. They allow same sex marriage. They now have a gender-neutral God. You must not be corrupted by the Europeans. Russia is the only Christian country that is strong enough to protect you. And if you pray for spiritual guidance, you will know that this is true.'

31

In the space of one hour NSA's assessment of the probability of Pintov being on Mount Athos had jumped from one percentage point to eighty. On his way to the Security Council meeting, Declan passed through the watch floor to check the very latest intelligence. It, and the surge room beyond, were running at full revs, fusing the latest information for the decision-makers who were already gathered in the JFK Conference room. Declan took his place standing against the wall behind Jennifer's seat.

President Topps called the meeting to order and then asked the Director of National Intelligence to set the scene. Asimov pulled up live footage of a luxurious powerboat getting ready for departure and a man being shepherded under a blanket along the quay. Asimov started to outline the mosaic of evidence that suggested it was Pintov, but the President cut in.

'The briefing notes say eighty percent probability. Is that still your assessment?'

'It is.'

'Then I'll take that. I don't need to know how you calculate it. We're running out of time. Can the Greeks arrest him?'

'We don't believe they have the capability at such short notice,' said Bryson. Declan wasn't sure how the Secretary of Defence came to that conclusion, but he looked confident.

'Do we?'

General Horn cleared his throat. 'The closest SEAL team is on the Theodore Roosevelt in Souda Bay, Crete. They couldn't get there in time. We have the Arleigh Burke in Alexandroupoli port. We have already scrambled a marine unit on to it and the ship is moving to intercept. However, that speed boat can travel at over one hundred miles an hour. If she leaves at top speed she's not going to be contained.'

'Give me some options,' the President demanded.

'We could try to destroy the boat while avoiding fatalities and give time for the Arleigh Burke to get there.'

'Is it possible to hit the boat without killing anyone?'

'The Reaper is pretty accurate. So long as the boat isn't moving. Once it's at speed a Tomahawk from the Arleigh Burke would be a safer option. But still a risk of fatalities.'

The President turned to the Secretary of State. 'Bex?'

'I'm not comfortable with any of this. If it goes wrong and it isn't Pintov, we've murdered an Indian businessman. If it is Pintov, we've assassinated a Head of State of a country we're not even officially at war with.'

'I agree with Rebecca,' said Bryson. 'We can't kill him.'

'How about the Ukrainians. Have we told them yet?'

'No,' Horn shook his head.

'If we give them the information and they go kill Pintov,' the President shrugged, 'well then that's their business, isn't it?'

'We'd still be complicit,' said Bex.

'But less so.'

'I don't think the Ukrainians have the capability,' interrupted

Horn. 'Their ATACMS only have an accuracy range of two hundred miles. It is five hundred from Ukraine to Mount Athos.'

'What about the fighter jets?'

'Theirs only have a range of four hundred miles. They'd need refuelling and they'd have to fly over Romania, Bulgaria, and Greece. All of that involves NATO.'

'How about the F-16s?'

Horn nodded. 'They have a range of five hundred, but they've been lent on the condition they don't leave Ukrainian airspace.'

The President went back to Bex and the Attorney General to rehearse the legalities of a drone strike. It seemed to Declan that if the President knew for sure it was Pintov, he would order it and hang the collateral. But because it was only an eighty percent chance they were holding back. But Declan knew how that eighty percent assessment was made. It was almost impossible to get higher than that because of in-built caution. It was obviously Pintov, but they wouldn't trust their instinct. He couldn't stop himself. He jumped in.

'If I may Mister President, could I just draw your attention to something happening in real time.' He motioned to the screen where the suspect, still under a blanket, was boarding the boat. 'The blanket is being used because they know we have a drone above them. That means the boat has military grade high resolution radar. And an Indian businessman wouldn't care if he was being watched, wouldn't have gone to a Russian monastery and probably wouldn't have Russian speaking crew. It's Pintov.'

The boat pulled away from the quay, turned a tight circle then raced out of the harbour. 'And he's getting away.'

General Horn suggested the President, Asimov and Bex follow him into the breakout room. All eyes in the conference room turned to the boat on the screen. It was soon in open water and flying towards the Turkish coast. A map displayed the positions of the speedboat and the Arleigh Burke. Watching the movement of both for just a minute it became clear that the destroyer was not fast enough to intercept the speedboat. A caption appeared at the bottom of the screen showing the distance to Turkish waters in miles. Twenty-five.

Still the President remained in the breakout room in earnest discussion.

Twenty miles. How long does it take to deploy a Tomahawk? A matter of seconds. They still had time.

While they continued talking in the breakout session a heavy silence settled over the conference room.

Fifteen. Did the President realise Pintov was getting away? Did he have a monitor in the breakout room showing what they could all see. Should he go into the breakout room and tell them?

Declan glanced at Jennifer. She shook her head.

Finally, the gang of four emerged. They took their seats slowly.

'I'm not going to order a strike and risk an assassination,' said the President. 'I'm not prepared to set that precedent.'

And with that the President closed the meeting and left the room. Most of the cabinet followed. Declan, Jennifer, General Horn, and a handful of others stayed and watched the boat cross into Turkish waters.

What an opportunity missed. What had been said in the breakout session? In fact, why had they gone into breakout? What did Asimov, Bex and Horn have to say that couldn't be discussed openly?

Perhaps they thought it was in American interests to let Pintov go. Perhaps they were all members of the Black Chamber with a warped view of the world that they had sucked the President into.

32

Safe in his hotel room, Mickey locked the door and stood with his back against it. Housekeeping had made the bed, folded his shorts and sweater on a chair and cleared away his empties.

He still hadn't made up his mind whether to go or stay, so he checked flight times to Istanbul. From his wallet he pulled out the card for the bodyguard. May as well be guarded on the trip to the airport even if he was going home. He dialled the number. A woman's voice answered.

'Hi, my name is Mickey Summer. I need to hire a bodyguard.'

'Who gave you this number, Mister Summer?'

'Dina.' Mickey managed to pull the journalist's card from his wallet using only one hand and read her surname. 'Kuznetsov.'

'What is your business in St Petersburg?'

Mickey gave a summary account and explained that he had been approached by the FSB and that was why he wanted a bodyguard.

'I recommend you go back to London,' said the receptionist. 'We could safely escort you to the airport.'

Someone else who thought he should go. They were getting his back up. He'd decide if he stayed or not. He might cut his trip short, but he wasn't running away just yet. 'I need protection, not travel advice.'

'That would be the best way to protect you.'

'Look, can I speak to whoever is in charge?'

'I am in charge.'

Fairy snuff. Called that one wrong. 'Well, I ain't going back to London just yet. I've got business meetings set up. Are you able to help me or shall I look somewhere else?'

'I can help. I can provide twenty-four-hour personal protection at a charge of two thousand dollars per day plus add-ons.'

'Add-ons?'

'Depending on where you go and how dangerous the situation might become, I might have to hire additional personnel.'

'That's fine. When can you start?'

'Lock your door. Pack your bags. I'll be with you in one hour.'

'Wait! You don't know where I am.'

'I do.'

The line went dead. Mickey stepped over to the door and locked it.

He dialled the office on his new pre-paid. He figured the call still could be monitored so he was careful not to give much away. He gave Vlad the names of the companies the Russian broker had recommended and asked him to dig into them.

'I've also got a name for you to check out. Eduard Beratov. Run him through all the databases and social media checks and see what comes up.'

He then pulled out the piece of paper on which he'd written the names Dina had given. He started at the top and dialled the office of the Russian Prosecutor General.

A lady answered in cheerful Russian.

'I'm very sorry,' said Mickey. 'I speak very little Russian.' If she'd tested him the full list was da, nyet and Spartak Moscow.

'That is all right. How may I direct you?'

'I am Detective Inspector Moran of the City of London police. Could you put me through to the Prosecutor General?'

'What is your enquiry relating to, Detective Moran?'

'I'm working on the collapse of Baltika bank.'

'Just a moment please.'

She left him listening to classical music. He guessed it was Russian. Tchaikovsky was the only composer he knew to be Russian. And he wasn't sure of that.

After ten minutes she put him through to a man who asked abruptly, 'What do you want?'

'I'm working on the collapse of Baltika bank, and I was wondering if we could compare notes. Who am I speaking to?'

'I work in the Deputy Prosecutor's office. We are not working on that case.'

'Maybe you should be,' said Mickey. 'We think the theft was carried out by a cyber gang linked to the St Petersburg mafia.'

'Where did you get this information?'

'Intercepted communications,' Mickey bluffed.

'And this is with the City of London police with whom you work, yes?'

'That's right. I was …'

'There is no Detective Inspector Moran working for the City of London police. Whoever you are please go away.'

Click.

Silence.

Mickey replaced the receiver. Using the same ruse, he rang several other offices. The Russian Criminal Investigations Division, Internal Affairs, Interpol, the mayors of Moscow and St Petersburg and the City police departments. Most calls were dead ends. But occasionally a name was suggested of someone who might know more. Then knowing one name he could ask for and being able to reference the name of the person who had passed him on, he found people became more helpful. Slowly through the course of his enquiries he began to build a picture of names and places to investigate further.

The name Semyon Bogdan was top of the list.

* * *

Mickey jumped at a knock on the door. Was it the bodyguard? Or someone that the bodyguard needed to save him from? He slipped into his shoes and tied his laces. Might need to kick someone. Might need to run. He tip-toed over to the door and peered through the keyhole. A tall woman and a male the shape of a paving slab.

'Who is it?' he called out.

'The security detail you asked for,' came the reply from the woman.

Mickey breathed out, unlocked the door, and opened it.

The woman walked into the room, leaving the Slab in the corridor. She was six feet tall, slim and with straight black hair curled down to high cheek bones. Under the sharp suit was a muscular and athletic body. Could look after herself in a fight for sure.

'Don't do that again,' she said with a glare that could bevel granite.

'Do what?'

'Open the door to a stranger.'

'Right.' Though how would she have got in otherwise?

'Turn off your phone please.'

Mickey did as he was told.

She offered a hand. 'I'm Angelina.'

'Mickey. Pleased to meet you.'

'I suggest again that we escort you to the airport.'

'I understand. But I'm going to hang around a couple of days.'

'We have a saying in Russia. God keeps those safe who keep themselves safe.'

'I'm hoping my Guardian Angelina will keep me safe.'

'As you wish.' She smiled. 'Give me your phone.'

He explained that the one in his hand was a pre-paid on the advice of Dina. His original was in a cupboard wrapped up in clothes.

'Can I have them both please. I'll check for spyware and give them back to you later.'

He handed them over and she placed them in a metal box.

'Here is a new credit card.' She looked down at his bag. 'Is that all your luggage?'

He nodded. She picked up the bag with two fingers then stepped out into the corridor. Mickey followed her. The slab turned out to have the name of Leonid. He led them to the fire exit and down a staircase wrapped around the elevator shaft.

They emerged in the dim light of an underground car park and walked quietly to a black car that the man opened with a key rather than the fob. Mickey guessed so as not to attract attention. He drove away without turning on the headlamps.

'I forgot to check out,' said Mickey.

'I took care of it,' said Angelina.

'I get a credit card and you pay my hotel bills. I like the way this relationship is starting out.'

'I'll add the bill on to expenses,' said Angelina. 'And by the way, this isn't a relationship, and you should cut down on the drinking.'

33

Arriving at the giant black box of Fort Meade, Declan turned off the radio and found a parking space. He jogged to the entrance, holding off the light drizzle with a copy of the Washington Post, swiped through security, grabbed a latte, then worked his way through the maze of corridors to the Cyber Security Directorate's operation room.

It was buzzing with hundreds of staff at neatly spaced work-stations. He made his way directly to the team working on the Latvian bank attack.

'Any developments, Charlie?'

Charlie rubbed his hands enthusiastically. His job was entirely desk bound and he took no exercise. But he was a bundle of nervous energy that left him rail thin. 'The TruNews troll farm has been using a command-and-control centre in Islamabad to get round the censors. The Latvian bank hackers used the same centre.'

'Co-incidence?'

'I don't think so. And neither do the British. They have identified the hacker as Dmitri, other times known as Geneve, Hawaiian Fury or Torchlight.'

'Good work.'

'There's something else.'

Charlie pulled up an advert for a financial reward for information on the hackers behind the Latvian Bank robbery. 'It's anonymous but we traced it to a UK hedge fund called Crosshairs Investments.'

Declan wondered if he'd heard correctly. 'Why is a hedge fund investigating a crime?'

'To somehow make money,' said Charlie. 'Why does a hedge fund do anything? For that matter, why do any of us work?

'I'm not motivated by money,' Declan countered.

'Would you do the job if it didn't pay?'

Let's think about that a moment. 'Probably not.'

'There's something else. Guess who runs the money?'

Declan shrugged. 'No idea.'

'Your old pal Mickey Summer.'

'Mickey? I thought he'd given that up?'

'Seems not. And guess where he is right now.'

'St Petersburg?'

'Got it in one.'

'Let's keep an eye on him.'

'Why don't you give him a call?'

'This investigation is under the radar. Mickey doesn't do under the radar. He's the white flashing blob front and centre.'

34

Mickey let out a whoop as he shut the limo door. 'Lock up your skeletons! Mickey Summer, financial sleuth, and scourge of bad management is back.' He settled down in the limousine's soft leather and closed his eyes.

'Tired?' asked Angelina.

'No. I'm buzzing. All this rushing around. Need to calm down.'

'We have a saying in Russia,' said Angelina. 'Ride slower, get further.'

Pawel turned round from the front passenger seat. 'You've had a busy day. We visited eight companies. And you got to see senior management each time. Finance Directors and Chief Executives. Before sanctions you would probably have only got to see investor relations.'

'You certainly fixed up a first-class tour, Pawel.'

'And you'll remember to show your appreciation.'

'Don't worry. When we invest, I'll make sure the trades go through your bank, so you get the commission.'

Pawel glanced at Angelina then back to Mickey. 'I prefer cash. Shall we say five thousand dollars? Cut the inside out of a hardback book and put it in the hole. Then hand it to me when we next meet.'

Mickey shrugged. When in Russia do as the Russians.

'Which companies impressed you the most?' asked Pawel.

'I liked the engineering company. It's a pity it supplies a Russian weapons manufacturer though. I can't invest in that. The med tech business was interesting. High risk of course. I liked what I saw of Kazbegi Holdings. But I already did. Seems like a slam dunk safe bet.'

'It seems like it, yes. But before you invest in Kazbegi Holdings you need to visit TruNews.'

'Tomorrow, right?'

'Yes. He's agreed. But he said you'd better not be wasting his time.'

He dropped them at the hotel in darkness. Angelina and Leonid retired to adjoining rooms. Mickey would have gladly gone to bed, but he'd arranged a zoom and soon his screen was filled with the smiling faces of Vlad and Carmella.

'What have you got for me?'

'Eduard Beratov is a Lieutenant Colonel in the FSB.'

'Good. That means I can trust the journalist who told me that. What else?'

'He earns eighty thousand rubles per month,' said Vlad. 'That is at the high end of the range for FSB officers. However, he earns nowhere near enough to afford his lifestyle.'

'Tell me more.'

'Nothing came up when I ran his name through the databases. But when I ran his mother's and sister's I got a different picture. The mother has a two thousand square foot apartment in the Kutuzovsky Prospekt. You've heard of that, right?'

Nope. 'Nice?'

'It's like Park Lane in London. The apartment is probably worth two million pounds. She also owns seven plots of land in the Noginski district, a development area just outside Moscow.'

'Is she a property developer?'

'She's seventy-eight and in a care home. There's more. We checked the records at St Petersburg Traffic Police. Beratov's sister owns a Mercedes-Benz S-class, a Jaguar XJ, and a top of the range Range-Rover.'

'Maybe the sister likes nice cars,' suggested Mickey, continuing to play Devil's advocate.

'She lives in Volgograd.'

'Go on.'

'We checked the Russian Border Control database. Travel records show that before sanctions Beratov flew to around twenty foreign destinations including the Caribbean, United States, Maldives. Some of those trips were by private jet.'

'He's not shy about flashing the cash,' said Mickey.

'He's not hiding anything,' agreed Vlad. 'His social media pages are full of pictures of him on holidays with beautiful girls. And there are posts from nights out at the most expensive night clubs in St Petersburg and Moscow. He has clearly got another source of income.'

'And I guess it's not a milk round,' said Mickey.

'He works for Bogdan.'

'How do you know?'

'A lot of the social media pictures show him with Bogdan. He's Bogdan's krysha.'

'A roof,' said Mickey, remembering what Dina had said.

'Exactly. He makes sure the police don't poke their noses into Bogdan's affairs.'

Mickey still wasn't sure why he'd tried to frighten him away, and he wondered again whether it was such a good idea to see Bogdan. But why would Bogdan agree to see him just to do harm? Easier just to not meet. 'Great work.'

'We've not told you the best yet,' said Carmella. 'The Friday night just before Baltika collapsed he was out at Blank nightclub in St Petersburg, doing cocaine and making spritzers from champagne.'

'So what? You said he likes to splash the cash.'

'He wasn't picking up the tab. That was a hacker named Dmitri who goes by various other names such as Geneve …'

'And Hawaiian fury,' interrupted Mickey. 'MI5 told me about him.'

'That's right. Anyway, he's the one throwing the party and posting on social media. Celebrating his winnings from the cyber-theft of Baltika.'

'Can you prove that?'

'No, but it's probable.'

'Can you pull together a video of all that evidence, with dates and pictures of Beratov and Dmitri and Bogdan and the cars and the property?'

'I can. But what are you going to do with it?'

'Not sure yet. How did you get on with Bogdan's business interests?'

'I've sent you a report.'

'What's the summary?'

'On the surface everything appears legitimate. The jewel in the crown is his fifty-percent stake in TruNews.'

'Who owns the other fifty percent?'

'Kazbegi Holdings has twenty percent. Then there are various other investment vehicles. Impossible to trace.'

'Why did you say on the surface everything appears legitimate?'

'Because that's as far as we can see. But he wouldn't need a krysha if he wasn't also doing illegal activities. He also has an interesting wife.'

'How come?'

'She spent eight hundred thousand pounds at Harrods in the two years before sanctions, using fifteen different credit cards all billed to a credit card company that is a subsidiary of Kazbegi Holdings. She bought ...'

'Kazbegi Holdings? Are you sure?'

'TruNews also has a small stake in the credit card company.'

'I suppose that's not altogether unusual. All these tangled webs of investments must overlap sometime.'

'Bogdan's wife also bought a house on Bishop's Avenue for nine million pounds and a golf club in Surrey for six. Both were bought through a special purpose vehicle registered in the British Virgin Islands and, so far as we can tell, she doesn't know one end of a golf club from the other and she's never set foot in the house. She stayed at the Ritz when she travelled to London.'

'Very interesting,' said Mickey. 'I never did like the idea that Kazbegi holdings has a stake in TruNews. I told Kazbegi that from the get-go. Now I'm totally certain he needs to sell his stake.'

'Are you still planning to see Bogdan?'

'Tomorrow.'

'Is that a good idea?'

'I'll be fine. I've got bodyguards remember.'

35

Declan took a seat on a bench in an otherwise empty circle in Stanton Park and admired the equestrian statue of General Nathanael Greene, the fighting Quaker. From the children's play area came squeals and laughter, and then a little more distant, Tod Spitz appeared from under a late cherry blossom overhanging the path.

The Special Counsel had left the Bureau a year before Declan joined. But the shared heritage meant that Declan had access to Spitz that he would not have otherwise.

Spitz took a seat and checked his watch. 'Apologies,' he said, slipping the metal strap off his wrist. He pulled out the crown and turned it a notch. 'Watch running slow. What did you want to see me about, as if I can't guess?'

'Yes, the Black Chamber enquiry,' said Declan. 'Wondering where it's at.'

'Almost complete. Ready to send to the Attorney General.'

'Stotton told me you hadn't contacted him yet and I wondered if that was true.'

'You shouldn't be talking to Stotton about the enquiry.'

'You know how it is.'

Spitz produced a head-masterly frown. 'Well, he's correct that I personally haven't been in touch. But he has been interviewed by one of my staff.'

'He's still in the frame?'

'I wouldn't say that.'

Declan frowned. 'Who is, then?'

'We made good progress on Lawson Ladyman,' Spitz replied. 'Though I really shouldn't be telling you this.'

'Thanks. Who else?'

Spitz straightened his back and rubbed his hands together. 'Our enquiries haven't found evidence that Ladyman colluded with anyone else.'

'Nobody else?' Had he heard correctly? 'Are you out of your mind?'

'Let's keep this civil, Declan. We're on the same team.'

'We were. I'm not so sure now. I handed you a room full of suspects and all you can nail down is Ladyman.'

'We've done a thorough investigation. That's where it's at.'

'How many people have you got on your team?'

Spitz took a deep breath. 'Seven attorneys. Twenty support staff.'

'Only seven attorneys?'

'They interviewed over one hundred witnesses and reviewed ten thousand documents. We also had the assistance of Langley's Internal Counterintelligence Investigation unit.'

'Muller had fifteen on the investigation into Russian meddling in 2017. And this is way bigger.'

'If you recall, Muller ruffled an awful lot of feathers without making anything stick. The Attorney General isn't keen on me making the same mistake.'

'Ladyman can't be the only one you can bring in.'

'We might have a misdemeanour charge for Biggerstaff as well.'

Unbelievable. Spitz couldn't have come up with so little. 'What about Stotton? When the cyberattacks on our country were happening, Stotton was liaising with the cyber jihadists behind it.'

'He says he didn't make the connection.'

'What about the SEAL team raid on the Syrian cyber team? Langley ordered that to cover the tracks of the cyber jihadists.'

'The Pentagon ordered the attack.'

'QED. Collusion with General Horn.'

Spitz frowned and shook his head. 'They thought alike. They agreed on strategy. But there's nothing to suggest they were part of any deep state group ...'

Declan held up a hand to stop him. 'The Chinese.'

'What about them?'

'Hue Wing would give evidence. He told CIA Beijing about the cyberattacks months in advance and they just ignored him. How can Stotton explain away that?'

'They couldn't trust the source. Hue Wing was the son of the number two in the Politburo and worked for State Security.'

Declan was practically hyperventilating. He tried to slow his breathing. 'Have you got nothing on Senator Martin?'

'No.'

'Asimov?'

'No.'

'General Horn?'

'No.'

'Surely Biggerstaff must get more than a misdemeanour charge?' Like Ladyman, he also had previous for sexing up the evidence for weapons of mass destruction in Iraq. This time round he had been the handler for the ISIS double agent coordinating the cyberattacks on America. He was a slam dunk.

'Biggerstaff's defence is that he was just following Ladyman's orders.'

Declan shook his head, discovered a crick that had only just come on and massaged it aggressively. 'Have you offered Ladyman a plea bargain?'

'He isn't interested.'

'But you are going to prosecute him?'

Spitz said nothing and checked his watch again.

'What are you considering?' Declan pressed.

Spitz sighed. 'Mishandling classified information. In trying to protect his asset, Azizi, he did suppress classified information and he misused his authority in ordering Financial Crime to stand down their own investigation into Azizi.'

'That's all?'

'That's all I will be recommending in my report to the Attorney General. He'll decide whether to prosecute.'

'Don't file the report yet,' Declan pleaded. 'Go bold. Empower a Grand Jury. Issue subpoenas to anyone at those drinks in the Washington Golf and Country Club. Ask them why they were there. Get them to testify under oath.'

Spitz sighed. 'We both know they won't agree to that.'

He was right. They would never volunteer to go on trial. 'Can I ask you another question?'

'Quickly.'

'Why do you think the Bureau was told not to investigate Russian involvement in the near collapse of State Financial?'

'I have no idea. You'd be better off asking Director Connelly that question.'

'He just said it's orders from above. And you may not be aware of this, but yesterday POTUS had a chance of taking out Pintov.'

'Really?'

'But he got talked out of it by Asimov, Bex and General Horn.'

'I have no insight into that, but I would imagine POTUS made his own decision after listening to their input.'

'Or it could be the Black Chamber pulling the strings again?'

'My enquiries have not uncovered any Black Chamber.' Spitz stood up slowly, clearly a pain in his right knee. They shook hands again and he wandered off.

Declan waited until Spitz had left the central area and dug a cell phone out of his pocket. He dialled Connelly's office.

'It's Declan. I really need to speak to Director Connelly.'

'I'm sorry,' replied his secretary. 'He's left for the day.'

'It's urgent.'

'Everything is always urgent with you, Declan.'

'When can I see him?'

Tapping on a keyboard. 'As it so happens Director Connelly wants to see you in any case. Friday at two?'

'I need to see him before Friday.'

'I'll ask him if he won't mind you talking to him during his warm down after his morning workout. I'll message you if he's OK with that.'

* * *

The echo of footsteps in the empty entrance lobby of the Hoover building reminded Declan of his occasional visits during the lockdown madness.

He made his way to a fitness room full of weights and pulleys and running machines. Declan had never got on with gyms. Partly he didn't like the foul air and having to wipe other people's sweat off the equipment. Mostly it just left him tired and aching without the uplift he got from running outdoors. Though he hadn't done much of that lately.

Connelly had finished his workout and was laid on his back on the floor, arms out like a fallen signpost.

When he saw Declan, he hauled himself to his feet and touched his toes. 'Still running to keep in shape, Declan?'

'I've been struggling to make time.'

'I miss running,' said Connelly, stretching his quads. 'But the knees won't allow.'

He seemed to be looking for sympathy, but Declan wanted to get down to business. 'Apparently you wanted to see me, sir.'

'Where have you got to with the RSB collapse?'

'You asked me to drop it. Told me to leave it to the British.'

'I told you not to waste too much time on it,' Connelly corrected him. 'But I'm more interested now than I was.'

'Why is that?'

'Steele. As I feared, he's considering suing the Bureau for developing GameOverRed. That's where he'll go unless we can give him someone else to blame.'

'We're fairly confident it's the St Petersburg mafia.'

'Can you put together a robust case?'

'We hadn't been thinking along those lines,' said Declan. 'But we could. We've identified the principal hacker. We think he was working from the cyber arm of Russian media outlet TruNews.'

'That would be good, to be able to throw a corporate at Steele,' said Connelly. 'Why do you want to see me?'

'The Black Chamber enquiry.'

'I might have guessed.'

'Spitz has got jack shit, other than a charge against Ladyman for mishandling classified information whilst trying to protect his asset.'

Connelly stretched out a hamstring. 'I heard.'

So why hadn't Connelly called Declan to express his own disappointment? 'That's just nowhere near good enough.'

Connelly shrugged. 'It is what it is.'

'Let me take over. It's my enquiry after all.'

'Not anymore. The attorney general gave it to Spitz. I can't do a thing about it.'

'But Spitz is running scared of these guys. He practically admitted that to me.'

'He is right to tread carefully after the flak we got with the Mueller and Coney investigations. We can't be accused of political bias again.'

'But this *is* political,' interrupted Declan. 'That's precisely what is going on here. The Black Chamber is a deep state body that has been illegally influencing US foreign policy. And for many years.'

'Except that you found no proof that such a body exists. And it looks like Spitz is coming up blank as well.'

Declan shook his head. 'Ladyman will get a few years in an open prison and then collect his reward from an unnamed account in the Bahamas. Biggerstaff is probably getting away scot-free, even though he was the asset handler that Ladyman was protecting. And remember this is the same guy who got away with sexing up the report on WMD in Iraq.'

Connelly didn't answer. He picked up his sweat towel and water bottle and headed towards the changing room.

Declan followed.

'Anything else?' asked Connelly.

'I guess not.'

Connelly turned at the changing room door. 'You know your Black Chamber enquiry made a lot of waves in Langley, the Pentagon and on the Hill. Now that Spitz looks to be pulling up short you and I both will have to eat some humble pie.'

'Just because Spitz doesn't have the balls to go after the Black Chamber, that doesn't mean I have to eat any pie. They all know they're guilty. I'll get them somehow.'

'When did you last take a holiday, Declan?'

'I'm too busy for holidays.' Though he knew he could do with one. If only to get some sleep.

'Once you've got us clear of Steele then I want you to take one.'

'Is that an order?' asked Declan.

'I'm talking to you as a concerned colleague, not your boss.'

Declan looked into Connelly's eyes. He looked sincere.

'I appreciate that.'

* * *

Declan had handed over the Black Chamber members gift-wrapped, but Spitz had screwed up. They had got away with manipulating government policy to pursue regime change in China. They'd done the same in Iraq. Now they were dragging their feet over Russia because they didn't want regime change. Innocents would die. His brother already had.

He felt too angry and confused to show up at work, so he headed to Greenbelt Park and wandered out on the perimeter trail. The Virginia pine and oaks had lost most of their leaves, but the understory of holly and scrub was a calming green. He didn't know his birds, but there were white throats, golden crowns, breasts of every colour. A small deer picked its way across the forest floor before it noticed Declan and spirited away.

He checked the time on his phone. Mom would be up, and he hadn't called her in days. He sat down on a fallen tree trunk and dialled.

'Hi mom, it's Declan.'

'Is everything all right?'

'Sure. How are you?'

'You don't normally ring so early.'

'I'm just taking an early morning walk in the park. It's a fine day down here. What's it like in Baltimore?'

There was a pause. He guessed while she went to look out the window. 'A little overcast, but I'm not complaining.'

'You should get out.'

'I'm going for a walk with Alice later.'

The conversation meandered round Alice's replacement hip, the camper van blocking the street, the biker gang that drove by late on Saturday night and the missed garbage collection.

Declan would have happily traded concerns.

'You still working on your Black Chamber investigation?' she asked as if reading his mind.

'Remember I told you that a special prosecutor has taken over the enquiry. I'm back working in Fort Meade.'

'How is the prosecutor getting on? How many of them has he got?'

Declan sighed. 'He thinks he's got enough evidence to send the main man to jail.'

'That's a start.'

'It might be that's all he can get.'

'But if he finds one person guilty it can't take much to find the others.'

'We'll see, Mom.'

He finished the call and headed back along the trail. Ladyman going to jail would at least be something. Not sufficient punishment for causing a war that had taken his brother's life. But something. He paused in a clearing and looked up at the mackerel sky. 'I'm still trying, Josh.'

36

The agreed rendezvous was a disabled-parking place overlooking the Neva. It flowed below. They waited above. Flowed and waited.

Angelina grew increasingly anxious, looking out the windows. Front, left, right, back. Repeat.

'Normally I keep my clients as far away as possible from people like Bogdan. It's your business, I know, but I still don't understand why you need to see him.'

'I've got a business plan to show him.'

'We have a saying in Russia …'

'Another one?' asked Mickey. 'You like your sayings, don't you?'

'Live with the wolves, howl like a wolf.'

'Why would Bogdan want to harm Mickey?' asked Pawel, from the driver's seat. 'Mickey is bringing him a business proposal. If he doesn't like it, he just says no thanks.'

Mickey wanted to change the subject. He pointed to an impressive bronze statue of a horseman. 'I'd put money on that horse if I knew the jockey.'

'That is Peter the Great,' said Angelina frostily. 'Some would argue the greatest ever Russian.'

'How about Catherine the Great?' Mickey didn't really know anything about her.

'She was born a Prussian,' replied Pawel. He pointed through the window. 'As you are taking an interest in Russian culture, behind the horseman you can see the golden dome of St Isaac's cathedral. The long yellow building to the left is the Admiralty. Behind it you can just see the top of Alexander Column in Palace Square. This celebrates Russia's victory over Napoleon.'

It reminded Mickey of the Monument tower in London, but instead of a golden orb on top it had an angel with a cross. He wondered why Alexander didn't feature but he didn't want to encourage Pawel. He wasn't in the mood for a history lesson. Thankfully a police car pulled up alongside a beast of an armoured limo behind it and a second police car behind that. A uniformed policeman and a man in a brown suit exited the first car.

'That's the FSB guy who approached me when I met Dina,' said Mickey. 'Lieutenant Colonel Beratov.'

'We should leave now,' said Angelina, tapping Pawel on his shoulder.

'It's fine,' said Mickey. 'I found out he works for Bogdan. He has every reason to be here. Besides, he's with a policeman.'

Angelina shook her head. 'That's no comfort.'

Beratov approached the driver's window and barked something in Russian.

Pawel called over his shoulder, 'He wants to see your ID.'

Mickey fished out his passport from his inside jacket pocket. Beratov studied the ID then passed it back through the window.

'Poydem so mnoy.'

'He wants us to go with him,' Angelina translated.

Mickey, Angelina, and Leonid got out onto the pavement, but Beratov said something to Pawel and signalled for him to stay in the car.

'Explain that he's a financial advisor,' Mickey said to Angelina. 'He's not just a driver.'

'He knows who Pawel is and he has some previous business with him. I don't know what, but he can't come.'

Mickey didn't need Pawel, other than the introduction which he'd already arranged. He let it drop, though he did wonder whether the 'previous business' might account for Pawel's limp.

They transferred into the limousine, the police cars turned on their lights and sirens and the cavalcade moved off.

Beratov leant back with an outstretched hand. 'Phones.'

'Am I due an upgrade?' Mickey asked as he handed it over.

'Passcode?'

'One, four, four, two.'

Beratov looked through the phone as they continued the journey. Palaces and fine buildings passed by before giving way to a leafy residential area. At the end of a cul-de-sac behind tall security fencing lay a dappled-red dacha with corner turrets.

In the driveway German shepherds snarled and strained at their leads. Armed guards at the front door checked ID again and relieved Angelina and Leonid of their guns. They were then escorted through wood-panelled rooms furnished with sculptures and brightly coloured paintings of Jesus, Mary, and unknown saints. On to a windowless inner room with a huge mirror.

They waited in silence.

Mickey drummed his fingers on the table. 'Bogdan's probably putting on his makeup.'

'He's watching us,' explained Angelina. She nodded to the mirror.

Mickey smiled and blew a kiss.

As if on cue a panel opened in the wall and a guard waved them through. In the next room, a sofa-sized man lounged in tracksuit and slippers. He had knife tattoos on both arms, a big black moustache and a huge crucifix hanging from a thick gold chain round his neck.

Mickey stuck out a hand. 'I'm Mickey Summer.'

Bogdan eyeballed Mickey for a few seconds then almost crushed his hand.

He said something in Russian.

Angelina translated. 'He wants to hear your business proposal.'

'Great,' said Mickey. 'I have a presentation to show him.'

Bogdan growled something.

'Just talk,' Angelina explained. 'You have two minutes.'

Mickey switched into elevator pitch mode. 'You need to prepare now for life after Pintov. You need to position all your businesses, so they do not need the patronage of Pintov. So that they can stand on their own. Focus on TruNews as the centre of a media empire. Turn the cyber division into a cyber defence consultancy and cut out illegal activities, such as cyber hacking. Sell businesses that make a low return on capital. Buy out the minorities in your good businesses. Produce clear, consolidated accounts. Then list this new cleaned-up business in Moscow and be ready to list it in the UK, when that becomes possible again.'

When Angelina had finished translating, Bogdan stood up,

turned, and walked out through another door hidden behind a panel.

Mickey sighed. He'd come all this way. Managed to get in to see Bogdan. But then failed to have a conversation. He hadn't even got to show the presentation. It wasn't mission critical, but it would have been useful to have a proper meeting with Bogdan that he could tell Kazbegi about.

Beratov motioned towards the door. In silence they retraced their steps to the front entrance. Angelina and Leonid retrieved their weapons. They walked back to the limousine. The police escort had left. The limo driver opened the passenger doors and Beratov got in the front.

'We can find our own way home,' said Mickey. It had been an annoying waste of time and he didn't want any companions on the way home. He certainly wasn't going to make small talk.

Beratov turned in his seat and looked over his shoulder. 'We're going to the offices of TruNews. Bogdan will talk to you there.'

* * *

Beratov led up the entrance steps, through the revolving glass doors and into the atrium. Angelina signed in their weapons. A red-haired female security guard patted her down, while a man with a scar from ear to chin did the same to Leonid and Mickey.

'Naughty!' said Mickey, as Scarface undid his belt and ran his fingers round the inside of his trousers. He took a knee and padded down Mickey's trouser legs. Then said something in Russian.

'Take off your shoes,' Angelina translated.

'Hold your noses,' said Mickey.

Scarface examined the shoes, felt inside then handed them back. Mickey put them on, tucked in his shirt, did up the belt, then joined the departing posse. On the top floor of TruNews Beratov showed them into a room, told them to help themselves to water, then left.

Mickey walked over to the window. A kaleidoscope of construction over centuries. Baroque stone, Soviet-era concrete, and modern glass, all dissected by a grey Neva peppered with boats and barges.

They waited almost half an hour before the door finally opened. Two guards took up positions either side of the opening. Then in came Bogdan, now dressed in a suit, accompanied by a young man and a steely-eyed lady.

They sat around an oval table and motioned for Mickey to join them. Angelina sat beside him. Leonid remained standing.

The lady spoke in a calm voice. 'I assume you don't speak Russian.'

'I'm learning English first,' said Mickey.

'Then I will interpret when necessary. My name is Olga.'

'Great. I have a short presentation to show Bogdan.'

Mickey handed out packs and this time Bogdan accepted his. Mickey turned to the summary page, which was pretty much the elevator pitch he had given back at Bogdan's house.

Olga translated. Bogdan motioned Mickey to continue.

He walked them through the presentation. Stop-start for the translation. The suited man was an accountant of some sort and asked a lot of questions. It turned out that Olga wasn't just a translator. She ran the cyber division. She and the accountant and Bogdan talked among themselves for a time.

'What are they discussing?' Mickey asked.

Angelina shrugged. 'I don't understand.'

'They're speaking Russian, right?'

'Yes and no. It is a dialect that evolved in the Gulag and among the Vory. They throw 'fe' and 'nya' in the middle of normal words. I can't really understand but my sense is that the lady agrees with your plans and the man doesn't. Bogdan is open-minded.'

Eventually they stopped and Bogdan spoke to Mickey.

Olga translated. 'The reason we make these provisions and other charges every year is to lower the amount of tax we pay. If we do what you suggest then yes, we will show higher profits, but we will also pay more taxes.'

'But you will raise the market value of the company,' explained Mickey.

'Bogdan doesn't care about the market value of the company,' the accountant jumped in, speaking good English. 'Because he is not selling it. The only way for him to take money out of the company is in cash.'

'But if the company was listed on the stock market, he could pay himself share options each year and sell them and that will make him more money than the cash he is taking out of the business now.'

Olga translated for Bogdan.

'Explain what you mean about cleaning up the business,' said Bogdan, who had discovered he could speak good English too.

'Accounting transparency is the first thing. Investors need to trust the figures. That's easily done. The second thing is to dispose of any activities that are illegal.'

'We don't have illegal activities,' he said.

Nobody in the room believed that. Olga even raised her eyes to the ceiling.

'I mean activities that might look illegal,' said Mickey. 'Like the cyber work you do for Pintov at TruNews. Like hacking into Baltika bank for example.'

Bogdan said nothing. Didn't acknowledge it. But didn't deny it.

'And you need to distance yourself from Pintov.'

'Pintov was great for Russia for many years,' said Bogdan. 'But now this war with Ukraine and NATO. It is a disaster. For everyone.'

'You should say this in public.'

'I will be silenced.'

'People say that Pintov can't touch you. You have a good name because of your charitable work. You control TruNews and public opinion. Some say you might even take over from Pintov.'

Bogdan growled something that didn't get translated. He flicked through the presentation again. This time asking Olga the occasional question in Russian. It started to get heated between Olga and the accountant.

Suddenly Bogdan snatched the presentation packs from the other two and tore them up in his massive hands. Mickey would have needed a saw. Bogdan dropped the two halves in a waste basket. His own pack he placed in a locked drawer. 'Do you like Pelmeni?'

'Pelmeni?' repeated Mickey.

'Dumplings of meat and fish,' said Bogdan. 'It's Siberian cuisine. You'll love them.'

* * *

The restaurateur greeted Bogdan with a deep bow, then hurried over to help the Maître d' escort a party of four from the outside table, where they were midway through their main course.

They made no complaint, avoiding eye contact with those who had displaced them as a posse of waiters transferred their plates and drinks inside. Even if they didn't know precisely who Bogdan was, it was clear from his appcarance and that of his entourage that he was not a man to argue with over seating arrangements.

More waiters reset the table and turned the patio heater on full. Bogdan sat facing the street. His men had blocked off both ends to stop passing traffic. Presumably to protect Bogdan from lead. And not the type that came in petrol.

The owner returned and after another exchange in Russian, and without consulting Mickey, a waiter served everyone mulled wine.

'*Na Zdorovie!*' Bogdan toasted with a raised glass.

'*Nostrovia!*' returned Mickey.

'Very good. You can speak Russian.'

'Just the important words.'

Bogdan laughed. 'Are you a family man?'

'I'm married.'

'Children?'

It didn't seem right to mention the baby. 'Not yet.'

Bogdan frowned. 'You must have children. Without children it is only half a life. Your passions? What do you like most about life?'

'West Ham United.'

'Ah! That is Kazbegi's club.'

They discussed the strengths of the English and Russian football teams, then meandered through Andrey Arshavin, Olga Korbut, Elvis Presley, King Charles. Bogdan was warm and humorous. It was difficult to conceive of him as a gang-master with blood on his hands.

Inevitably the conversation turned to the war in Ukraine and the confrontation with NATO. Bogdan was keen to ensure Mickey understood the Russian perspective, that the West has always been opposed to Russia and now it was helping Ukraine's west-leaning, puppet government.

'You see it isn't as simple as the media in the west say. You think it is just the war of a madman.'

'Before you sounded against the war?' Mickey pressed. 'Do you approve or not?'

'I approve officially.' Bogdan looked around the room. He was even afraid to speak openly. 'But you ask me in private and no, of course I don't approve. Thousands of young boys killed. The economy collapsed. Pintov didn't ask permission. He just started the war. Him and his stupid siloviki.'

'Who should he ask for permission?'

'The *avtoritety*. People like Kazbegi and me and all the other business leaders. We run the country.'

'How will it end for Pintov?'

'Everything ends in death.' Bogdan looked around again. A man from another table looked to be eavesdropping. 'Let's speak no more about this.'

The Pelmini was served swimming in broth and black pepper. It was tasty and warm, especially good as the outside patio heaters weren't quite doing their job. Through lunch they talked more about politics and war.

When a natural break arrived Mickey again broached the subject of cleaning up the businesses.

'Why do you need to be involved in illegal activities?' asked Mickey. 'Drugs and prostitution, for example.'

Bogdan said nothing.

'I agree with you,' said Olga. She reddened slightly. 'That is, I agree that it would be a bad idea to be involved in criminal activities. There is no need. TruNews is a successful media company, and we should focus on these activities.'

'And what about your cyber division?' asked Mickey. 'Is that involved in criminal activity?'

'Not according to Russian law,' she said.

'How about collapsing the Latvian bank?'

'Is that criminal?' asked Bogdan, again not denying his involvement. 'Sanctions have hurt our economy. People steal a little back. We have a saying in Russia, even a bishop will steal if he's hungry.'

Well, this bishop has stolen my life savings. But he kept that to himself. 'It is criminal in the eyes of the west.'

'We are not in the west,' said Bogdan.

Mickey let it drop. He'd pushed things as far as he dared, and he was now as certain as he ever could be that Dmitri the hacker had been working for Bogdan. The conversation drifted back to everyday life. Eventually Olga said she had to leave, and the accountant left with her. Mickey and Bogdan finished off another bottle of wine and then Mickey also made his excuses. He offered to pay the bill, but Bogdan explained that there wouldn't be one.

As they drove away from the restaurant Angelina asked, 'Did you enjoy that?'

'I've had worse lunches.'

'You certainly enjoyed the drink.'

'Leave it out, will you. I was just being sociable, so I got Bogdan to lower his guard. And it worked. He basically admitted that they did the cyber-theft of Baltika bank.'

'It was you that lowered your guard. Laughing and joking with Bogdan as if he is an ordinary human being.'

'I didn't notice any green skin or antennae. I know he's got some dodgy dealings but that's just leftovers from his criminal past.'

'It's the present,' snapped Angelina. 'I don't know what exactly, but he's certainly involved in criminal activities. And not just cybercrime. Olga didn't seem to view that as criminal, but she agreed he should cut other criminal activities out of the business. Whatever they are.'

They travelled the rest of the journey in silence.

Mickey resolved to take a short nap and sober up before doing more work, but when he arrived back at the hotel the receptionist said he had a visitor waiting in the bar.

Sitting on a leather settee was Olga.

37

Declan entered the situation room in the White House West Wing just a few seconds before President Topps, which didn't leave time to dip into the selection of sandwiches laid out on a trolley on the far side of the room.

'Okay,' said Topps as he took his seat. 'The big item is new Russian military manoeuvring in Europe. But before we get to that I am becoming increasingly concerned that we are losing the PR war with the Russians.' He turned to the Director of the NSA. 'I want to understand what we're doing to counter Russian propaganda, Jennifer?'

Jennifer sat upright and bright-eyed like a startled meerkat. Declan knew this had come from left field, otherwise she would have given him a heads-up. 'Which propaganda in particular?'

'All of it,' snapped Topps. 'Like the preposterous claim that the CIA killed Karl Kristensen, that Latvia is persecuting Russian speakers, Ukraine is full of Nazis, Russia is defending itself from NATO aggression. This baloney is all over our own social media.'

'We're doing our best,' said Jennifer. 'We filter, we block, we counter, but it's impossible to stop everything.'

'Can we do more?'

'We're always open to ideas,' said Jennifer cautiously.

'A media business in St Petersburg is behind a lot of this, right?'

'There are multiple actors involved,' Jennifer replied. 'Some state, some private.'

Topps looked down at his notes. 'But the TruNews agency is the most brazen. Its TV and radio channels and troll farms.'

'It's certainly a major player.'

'How do we stop it?'

Jennifer tilted her head at a slight angle, as she did when defensive. 'We closed the American TV channel of TruNews after the invasion of Crimea.'

'How do we stop it transmitting in Russia?' asked Topps. 'Because the garbage still gets out to the Russian population and from there it leaks out to the west.'

'I'm not sure there is any way to stop a Russian TV station,

Mister President.'

'Come on!' said Topps. 'We took on the entire Chinese cyber army and won.' He turned to look at Declan. 'You can take out a TV station can't you, Declan?'

Declan hesitated. The protocol did not grant a voice to advisers. They were lucky to get a sandwich and he hadn't even managed that. He was supposed to speak through Jennifer.

She gave him the nod.

'Defensively we are upping our game against Russian propaganda all the time. We do a great deal to counter the social media stories that do, as you say, leak out of Russia. We screen hundreds of thousands of news articles every hour. We're monitoring a hundred Kremlin orientated Twitter accounts. If we don't like the post, we stop it coming into the country.'

'So how come twenty percent of Americans believe the CIA assassinated Kristensen?' asked Topps. 'That's what I read in my daily briefing.'

'A lot of people are pre-disposed to believe in conspiracy theories,' said Declan. Out of the corner of his eye he saw Stotton smirk. 'We call them the Counterfactual Community.'

'We're getting a little off track here,' said Topps. 'I want to know whether we can hit TruNews offensively and stop its propaganda.'

'There have been several successful hacks into TruNews by independent news outlets,' explained Declan. 'They've briefly managed to show the real situation in Ukraine. But if you don't want to believe it then it's easy to dismiss these hacks as lies.'

'I'm not talking about hacking it,' said Topps. He turned to General Horn. 'Can we bomb it?'

The Chairman of the Joint Chiefs of Staff cleared his throat and rubbed his tight beard. 'Technically, yes. We could hit it with a missile.'

'We can't bomb a civilian target,' said Bex. 'It's totally out of the question. We must accept that we can't convince everyone all the time. Russian propaganda will be accepted by those who want to accept it. Including those in our country. It is what it is.'

Topps sought views elsewhere in the room. Eventually, he

sighed and nodded to show acceptance. 'Let's talk about objects we might be able to bomb. Over to you General Horn. What's the latest in Europe?'

'It's a continuation of the situation last time we met,' said Horn as his assistant put a map of the Baltics on the screen. 'It's not an escalation but it's provocation at the same high level of intensity.'

A photograph of a plane appeared on the map.

'Specifically,' continued Horn. 'Yesterday at zero nine hundred eastern standard time, a flotilla led by the Russian aircraft carrier Admiral Kuznetsov approached the Swedish island of Gotland. The Swedes scrambled everything they had and re-enforced the island, but it turned out to be another exercise and it ended with a mock marine landing back in Kaliningrad. However, they have positioned the fleet off the Lithuanian port of Klaipeda. Effectively blockading it.'

'But your assessment is that this is not an escalation?'

'Correct.'

'Not a prelude to invasion?'

'We can't rule that out,' said Horn quickly. 'Our assessment is just as it was last time we met. Pintov has enough on his plate with Ukraine. We think this is sabre rattling.'

'That's an awful big sabre and a lot of rattling,' said Topps. He turned to Jennifer. 'What's the intelligence assessment?'

'Everything we've talked about recently, including the propaganda, is part of the Gerasimov Doctrine. The murder of an anti-Russian politician, crashing a foreign bank, turning off the lights, troll farms, military sabre rattling. All are designed to exploit social divisions, sow chaos, and manipulate public opinion. Easier and just as effective as war. Sometimes more so.'

'We're back where we started,' said Topps. 'The propaganda, the other elements of hybrid war. The Russians seem to be winning that battle.'

'They've been at it longer than us,' said Declan. This was his bailiwick after all. 'Influencing elections, Brexit, the Catalan separatist movement, the French yellow vests. Russian cyber armies and bots pump out hundreds of fake articles targeting the young in Finland, Latvia and Estonia who speak Russian and have Russian heritage. They are too young to remember the bad Soviet Russia. They believe that Germany runs Europe now, and they should follow Britain and reject Germany's European Union. Russian's Eurasian Union looks more attractive. Certain ex-eastern European countries have good reason to prefer an eastern outlook. For example, the Czech Republic, Slovakia, Hungary, Romania, Bulgaria.'

'Thanks Declan. Any other views on this?'

Bex took up the running. 'NATO was set up to defend Western Europe from communism. That's long gone. Do we really care if Russia wants to redefine its borders at the margins in Finland and Ukraine and the Baltics?'

'But where would they stop?' asked the President.

'All Russia wants is a Eurasian Union centred on popular nationalism,' said Bex. 'Could be a useful counterweight to the European Union based on overly liberal socialism. It's not so clear to me that it is in the interests of the United States to defend and prop up a European Union that expanded too far.'

'So where do we draw our red line?' asked the President. 'Too late for Ukraine. Now you seem to be suggesting maybe not Finland. Not the Baltic states.'

'The red line is the former Soviet bloc. That's where we go all out to defend. Up until that red line we only assist, as we are doing in Ukraine.'

'Even NATO countries?'

'Correct.'

The President turned to Director Stotton. 'How do you see this in Langley?'

Declan cupped a hand behind his ear to catch Stotton's softly spoken voice. 'Europe grew strong with peace that Russia and the United States bought for them. Apart from Britain and France, the rest of Europe spent next to nothing on the military for decades. Russia fought an expensive cold war and various regional wars around the world, including against Islamic Fundamentalists, while the Europeans got fat and rich. The Russians are as angry about that as we are.'

'I don't see what Russia gains,' said the President. 'These

actions won't endear the Europeans to Russia? Germany is not going to jump into Russian arms.'

'They don't want Germany. They want the periphery. The core Europeans will stay the same. But the Russians guess that we won't help when they target its peripheral countries. Just like we didn't help Crimea or Eastern Ukraine until they overstepped the mark. If you are one of those peripheral countries you have a choice of being a peripheral member of a dysfunctional, less influential European Union, with Russia harassing you constantly, or joining the Eurasian Union with Russia as its head but on your side. This is the question facing Norway, Finland, Lithuania, Estonia, Latvia. Eastern Ukraine and Serbia have already slipped east. Bosnia is almost there.'

'All right,' the President interrupted. 'This is my point. Pintov is winning the ideological war. I regret not taking him out on that speedboat when we had the chance.'

'We made the right decision not to assassinate,' said Bex.

'So how do we get rid of Pintov?' asked Topps.

Heads turned to look for a volunteer.

Jennifer stepped up to the plate. 'We don't do regime change. We wait for him to die. Or for the Russians to push him out.'

'Let's help them,' said the President. 'Like we did in China. Turn the state propaganda machine in on itself. Turn the Russians against Pintov.'

'Let's not forget about the nuclear threat,' said Jennifer. 'We're at DEFCON level 2. We need to tread carefully with Pintov.'

The President wafted a hand dismissively. 'Pintov's dangerous. But he's not suicidal. I don't buy this nuclear threat.'

'It's real,' interjected General Horn. 'The Russians have repeatedly drilled the use of battlefield nuclear weapons. RAF sentinel have reported nuclear-capable Iskander-M missiles being deployed to Chernyakhovsk base in Kaliningrad.'

'Nuclear capable,' said the President.

'And just last week a Kalibr missile was fired from a submarine in the Barents Sea hitting a target five thousand kilometres away in Kamchatka.'

'Nuclear capable,' the President repeated. 'My understanding is that we would see any moves to ready and deploy battlefield nuclear warheads in advance. Have we seen that?'

'Not yet. But the risk is very real, Mister President.'

'Remind everyone of our response if he does.'

General Horn looked ready for the question. 'We have told Pintov that we would escalate exponentially in Ukraine, with the supply of an iron dome for defence, more F-16s and cruise missiles for offence. With that Ukraine would be able to take back Crimea and destroy the Black Sea fleet. The war is going badly enough already for him. But it would get a whole lot worse.'

'But we wouldn't respond in kind?'

'That wouldn't be our recommendation, Mister President. Better to use the first use of a nuclear weapon in eighty years to get China and India onboard with blacklisting Russia.'

'I accept that militarily we are squared up to Russia correctly for now.' He pursed his lips and drew a large question mark on his note pad. 'But I'd like ideas on how we win the ideological war. How do we turn the screw on Pintov?'

38

Mickey took a seat on a stool across the table from Olga. 'Hello again,' he said. 'Is this just a coincidence?'

'I came to see you. I want to ask why you are in Russia.'

'I'm running a Russian investment fund,' explained Mickey.

'That's what you are doing in Russia. But it doesn't explain why you are here.'

'I'm meeting management to discuss the businesses and review the strategy. That way I know which stocks to buy and which to avoid. Kazbegi Holdings is one I am looking at, which is why I wanted to look at TruNews.'

'I ran a security check on you before allowing you in to meet Bogdan and you don't have any background in Russian markets or businesses. You left the City more than a year ago. A fortnight ago you were selling vegetables in the market. Now suddenly you are interested in Russia. You've been sent by the British Police.'

'I haven't.'

'By Frank Brighouse of MI5.'

She had done her homework. Mickey decided it was safer to tell the truth. 'The reason I am in Russia is because I lost two million pounds when RSB bank collapsed. Money I was going to use to buy a house for my wife who is expecting our first child. So, I came up with a plan to make the money back. From the performance of the fund and consulting fees from Ivan Kazbegi for reviewing his businesses and advising him what to sell.'

She sat upright and her eyes widened. That magic Kazbegi wand trick had worked again. 'You're working for Kazbegi?'

'I've met him. I offered to look at Kazbegi Holdings and tell him which businesses to sell. Any that have illegal activities. His stake in TruNews for example. I recommended he sell that.'

'What did he say?'

'He doesn't want to sell right now.'

'Maybe instead of selling the investment Kazbegi could persuade Bogdan to clean up.' She straightened a crease in her suit. 'You see, I agree with your advice to Bogdan. There is no need for him to be involved in criminal activities anymore. He should concentrate on TruNews. I've been saying this for years. Maybe Kazbegi will put pressure on him if you show him evidence of the illegal activities. They used to be close.'

'But I haven't got any evidence,' said Mickey. In truth the only evidence of illegal activities he had was circumstantial evidence that the Baltika bank hacking had been done by someone in Olga's cyber division. And she'd made it clear she didn't see that as a crime.

'If I showed you the illegal activities, what would you do with the information?'

Mickey took a moment to think it through. 'I'd show Kazbegi and tell him he must either persuade Bogdan to stop or he has to sell his stake in TruNews.'

'Very well.' Olga got to her feet. 'Let's go for a tour.'

Angelina phoned Leonid and told him to bring the car out front. They stopped near the offices of TruNews and Olga disappeared into the building. She returned a few minutes later with a briefcase and no explanation of what was inside.

She gave instructions to Leonid and soon they were passing huge oblong warehouses and circular storage tanks on the way to the port. There, giant white cruise ships disgorged passengers at the end of their day trip.

'Before sanctions, nearly a million tourists a year arrived by boat,' explained Olga. 'The westerners no longer come but we still have the Asians. The ship pays a docking fee. Half goes to the state of St Petersburg. Bogdan, or one of the other gangs, takes the other half.'

The smell of rotting fish grew stronger as they drove on to the commercial port, where towering yellow gantry cranes stacked coloured boxes onto container ships as if painting by numbers.

'Some of those containers will be carrying people,' explained Olga.

'Cheap seats,' said Mickey. 'But no access to the bar so not for me.'

'It's no joke and it's not cheap. Migrants pay ten to twenty thousand euros to get to Europe. Some don't make it. Trafficking is just one of the criminal businesses down here. Two thousand people work in the docks. As well as mooring and stowing cargo there are hundreds of less obvious jobs. Inspecting, weighing, repackaging, supplying special straps, cleaning. Everyone gets paid but they also pay out protection money.

'The docks are carved up into mafia fiefdoms built up historically, randomly. If you want to work anywhere in the docks, you must pay protection money to someone.'

'Some countries you'd pay tax,' said Mickey, filming on his phone. 'Taxes fund roads and schools. Protection money just makes criminals rich.'

They drove on to a small island littered with scrap metal and timber. Like a fairground candy grabber, a crane dipped its claw into a stack of stripped logs, scooped up the pile and carried it to a metal basket on the dockside.

'Timber is ideal for smuggling,' explained Olga. 'They hollow out the wood and stuff it with drugs, cigarettes, and other things. The sniffer dogs can't smell them. Another one of Bogdan's businesses.'

They exited the docks and Olga gave fresh directions to Leonid. They were soon back on the tourist trail, passing the summer garden and coasting down the fashionable Vladimirsky Prospekt. Leonid pulled up at a five-storey building.

'What's next?'

'You'll see.'

They sat in the car for ten minutes until a man approached the building and paused at the entrance. He took out his phone, dialled, spoke, then went inside.

'About one hundred men go through that door every day.'

'I guess they're not visiting their mothers,' said Mickey. 'Is it a brothel?'

'It's called a salon for intimate services. But yes.'

'Does Bogdan own it?'

'Nobody owns it. It's like a worker's co-operative. But most of the girls have been trafficked here by Bogdan's men. They come from poor parts of Russia with the promise of a high life in St Petersburg. They owe money for the trafficking services. They end up working here to pay off the debt. Most never do. And Bogdan's men protect the brothel and of course make good use of the service as well.'

Mickey nodded but said nothing.

'You should go in.'

'Thanks, but no thanks.'

'Go to film and gather evidence.'

'They're not going to be happy with me filming.'

'I have some special glasses you can use,' said Olga. She opened the briefcase and handed them over. 'The lenses are neutral. The rim has a camera.'

A small camera lens was visible in the top right corner. He put them on as Olga produced a laptop from the briefcase and opened it. It took a minute to warm up and then as Mickey looked around the car the picture came up on her screen.

'Say something. Anything.'

'Something anything.'

Olga adjusted the settings. 'All set. Go in. Film a little. Then change your mind.'

'Are you coming with me?' he asked Angelina.

'Of course not,' she replied. She opened the glove compartment and fished out a face mask and a yellow beanie. 'Put these on.'

'I ain't wearing that hat. I'll look like a right plonker.'

'That's the idea. Nobody will look at your face. They'll all be laughing at your hat.'

He pulled it over his ears.

'And tell them Bogdan sent you,' said Olga. 'And he said you could have a free.' She scribbled some sentences in Russian and the English translation. 'Remember to only speak in Russian.'

'I'm not going to fool anyone,' said Mickey.

'Of course no one will think you *are* Russian. But it will be much more difficult to trace your voice.'

Olga opened Mickey's door. He still wasn't sure he wanted to do this.

'Don't be shy,' she said, pushing him out of the car.

A quick check for traffic then across the street. He caught the apartment block door just as it was closing, went through and waited in the stairwell for the tapping of footsteps to disappear upstairs. Then he followed on up. He stopped outside the flat. There was no name or number or bell. Just a doormat and a camera over a steel door. He hesitated. Angelina should be with him. There would surely be some big heavies on the other side.

He drew a deep breath and rang the bell.

An old woman with high cheek bones exaggerated by blusher opened the door. She waited for him to speak.

'Can I come in?' he asked in Russian, reading from his script.

'You don't have an appointment,' she said in English with an unexpected American accent.

'Bogdan sent me.'

She waved him in. 'You don't need to speak in Russian. We all speak English.'

He persisted, reading from the script. 'Bogdan said I could have it for free.'

She frowned. 'I don't care what Bogdan says, you will still have to pay.'

Mickey didn't have any Russian words to reply so he nodded.

'There's no need to wear a face mask.'

Mickey coughed and she took a step back. Then she shrugged and opened the door to a waft of apple blossoms. A security guard patted him down then went back to his phone. Brightly illuminated around the walls of the room were women of all ages in varied stages of undress.

'Which girl do you like?'

Mickey looked around the room. Some were only children staring back with empty eyes. Others were older with an air of sophistication but still empty eyes.

Enough already. He turned around and hurried back out the door and down the stairs, half expecting to hear the footsteps of some heavy behind him. But nobody followed.

'That was awkward,' said Mickey, climbing back into the car.

'It was worth it,' said Olga, turning the laptop to face him. 'Watch.'

She played back the recording.

'That's pretty good,' said Mickey.

'We'll get some more,' said Olga. She gave new directions to Leonid.

Twenty minutes later he pulled up at the kerb.

'Look,' said Olga.

'What is it?' asked Mickey.

'Watch.'

A black Mercedes parked up outside a café, engine running. A man came out the side entrance, walked over and threw a packet through the car window.

'Protection money,' explained Olga.

The car rolled about ten metres up the road and stopped outside an all-night convenience store.

'Put on the spectacles again.'

Mickey did as he was told, then Olga pushed him out of the car. 'Come on.'

She hooked her arm in his and snuggled into his head as they walked along the pavement.

'Keep looking at the car,' she whispered as they drew near.

The rear passenger window was down a couple of inches.

A girl walked petulantly out of the front of the store and pushed a brown envelope through the gap.

'Now look at the number plate,' Olga whispered in Mickey's ear.

The engine picked up a notch and the car rolled away. Olga turned Mickey round and they walked casually back to the car.

There Olga checked the video on her laptop. She made a note of the car registration then typed it into some search engine. 'The car has been leased from Nafkematze Automative. That's a subsidiary of Kazbegi Holdings.'

'Interesting,' said Mickey. 'That's another business Kazbegi needs to clean up.'

Mickey had seen a lot in the previous hour. All very useful.

They drove back to the hotel. Mickey offered to buy Olga a drink, but she wanted to get home. Did she have someone waiting at home for her? A partner? A child? She knew all about Mickey's private and professional life. He knew almost nothing about her.

'Well thanks for the tour of St Petersburg. I really appreciate it.'

She nodded. 'Make good use of the information. Get Kazbegi to persuade Bogdan to clean up.'

39

The TruNews reporter stood in front of a depressing block of Soviet-era red and blue concrete buildings. In the background were older, wooden structures whose paint had been blasted by arctic winds to hints of their original pastel. Beyond rose forbidding, barbed mountains.

She took a deep breath of ice-cold air and addressed the camera.

'For almost a century Russians have been living and working here in the mining town of Barentsburg. They have enjoyed good relations with their Norwegian neighbours in the main town of Longyearbyen some fifty kilometres along the coast. This harmonious relationship is a result of Svalbard being governed by an international treaty. Many Norwegians remember Russia as their liberator from the Germans in World War Two and the relationship between the two countries remains strong. However, NATO's increasingly hostile attitude towards Russia has changed this. NATO has stationed troops in Longyearbyen in contravention of the Treaty which states that the island must be demilitarised. And so Kazbegi Holdings has taken the precaution of bringing security personnel from its security subsidiary the Borodin Group to defend workers threatened by these NATO hostilities.'

* * *

'What do you make of it?' Declan asked.

'It's classic Russian disinformation,' said the monitoring agent. 'The Svalbard Treaty clearly established full Norwegian sovereignty over the archipelago. The international aspect relates solely to commercial activities. As for NATO stationing troops. Norway invited a handful of NATO observers to monitor a winter exercise.'

'They're using the same playbook as Crimea and the Donbas,' said Declan. 'Employing a sophisticated deception and disinformation campaign to hide Russian intentions as well as the timing and scale of operations. They keep any hostile intentions in Svalbard vague and activities below the threshold of NATO's collective defence guarantee. They can deny any military interventions because the Borodin group are private military contractors. And they are there simply to protect Russian citizens. Next thing we know there will be the arrival of supply ships with large civilian containers. But they'll be holding military equipment, including missiles. They can then jam electronic communications while they seize the airport and occupy Norwegian government buildings.'

'I think you're getting ahead of yourself, Declan.'

'Am I? Once they get away with the first move, they just keep pushing further.'

The agent shook her head. 'How on earth could they justify that?'

'The TruNews reporter just told us. They're claiming that Norway has breached the Svalbard Treaty by allowing NATO troops to be stationed there. So, they'll claim that they are taking over the island to prevent any escalation by NATO. And they'll demand NATO troops leave. Just like Ukraine. It's all our fault.'

'Who's going to buy that?'

'India, China, the southern hemisphere. Russia will already be on a diplomatic and informational offensive to justify its actions. They'll be telling everyone of the limited nature of their objectives. Purely to discourage NATO intervention, they'll say.'

'They can say what they like, but Svalbard is sovereign territory of a NATO country. Any hostile Russian action will trigger Article 5 and a response from NATO.'

'I'm not so sure,' said Declan. 'The Alliance does not regard the Arctic as a high priority. As for Svalbard, it's geographically isolated and barely populated. Its legal status is ambiguous and might provide politically expedient justifications for the allies to spurn Article 5.'

'So, the Russians are likely to get away with this, just as they did in Crimea?'

Declan shook his head. 'They may have come in under the Pentagon radar. But they've not come in under ours. That's the flaw in the Gerasimov Doctrine. It gives advance warning of the real intent.'

40

Pawel had arranged to meet Mickey in an Irish bar replete with barrels, brass taps, wooden tables, and loudspeakers playing something that must have been the missing link between music and noise. Mickey asked the bar girl to turn it down then surveyed the choice of a dozen draught beers. He plumped for a Blarney Stone. Angelina had never heard the Blarney legend, so Mickey explained that kissing the stone endows the kisser with the gift of the gab.

'Have you kissed it?' she asked.

'I'd be too frightened of what might happen.'

The beer was warm and looked as if it had been flushed out of a radiator. But it tasted fine.

'*Boodym zdarovy!*' said Mickey, raising his pint.

Angelina chinked it with her bottle of water. 'Your Russian is coming along.'

'I'm getting the important words sorted.'

She smiled. He realised that she didn't do that a lot but when she did, she really was very attractive.

'What made you become a bodyguard?' he asked. 'It's a dangerous way to make a living.'

'Life is so very fragile anyway,' she replied. 'For me it isn't much more dangerous than ordinary life. It's like being a racing car driver. If you know what you are doing, it isn't as dangerous as it looks.

Pawel appeared at the top of the cellar steps. He came down them one at a time, throwing his gammy leg first.

'What are you drinking?' asked Mickey, shaking his hand. 'I'm guessing vodka.'

'Once upon a time I would,' said Pawel. 'This used to be an old Soviet drinking den. It would have been vodka shots for all the comrades back then.' He pointed to Mickey's dark malt. 'Is that Guinness?'

'Blarney Stone. Same difference. Give it a go.'

As the barman poured Pawel looked up at the football on a large screen hanging incongruously from the wooden rafters. 'Russian rubbish. That's the worst thing about sanctions. We don't get the English premiership or La Liga. We can only get football from Russia, Serbia, Turkey.'

'And people say sanctions aren't working.' Mickey gave Angelina a wink.

Pawel took his pint, sank a good third and wiped the froth off his lip with the back of his hand.

They moved to the library snug room where the books and leather softened the noise from the main bar. Pawel continued his moan about the football on offer and then, as if he'd suddenly remembered why he'd come, his face turned serious. 'How did you get on with Bogdan?'

'Interesting,' said Mickey. He decided not to tell Pawel about Olga. She hadn't specifically said to keep her name out of it, but it seemed safest. 'He's clearly involved in mafia activities such as prostitution, extortion, smuggling. I don't know how much TruNews has to do with it but there is bound to be overlap. And in any case the cyber division in TruNews has some dodgy activities. I am very clear Kazbegi needs to sell his stake.'

Pawel nodded. 'You are right. That's one of the reasons I wouldn't recommend buying Kazbegi Holdings.'

'What if he sold the stake in TruNews?'

'He won't. But, even if he did, I still wouldn't buy.'

'Why not?'

'Did you bring the book?' asked Pawel.

Mickey took a hardback business book out of his briefcase. The middle pages were cut out and filled with five thousand dollars. He slid it across the table and Pawel slipped the book into his briefcase.

'Everyone in Russia already owns Kazbegi Holdings. Everyone loves it. It's overbought. Where are the new buyers going to come from?'

'If sanctions are removed.'

'But Kazbegi Holdings isn't under sanctions. Foreign investors can own the shares. If sanctions are lifted, then the whole Russian market will rise but Kazbegi will lag. That wouldn't be my pick.'

Even if Pawel did have a lazy side, he offered more than most analysts. They could all crunch numbers and understand businesses, but most were clueless on share price movements. Pawel was a good analyst who also thought like a trader.

'Then there is the risk from Kazbegi's closeness to Pintov.'

'Which he denies,' said Mickey.

Pawel shrugged and then continued. 'If those in power get rid of Pintov, then Kazbegi loses his protection.'

'Who is in power then if it's not Pintov?'

'The siloviki.' Pawel lowered his voice. 'Generals, senior FSB, the family. They are the board. Pintov is just the chief executive.'

'Which family?'

'It's a term left over from when Yeltsin's family, his daughter especially, ran the country. Now the family means a few oligarchs. If this board concludes Pintov needs to go, he goes.'

There was a lot of sense in that. 'But if the board put in place a new president who stops the war, sanctions will be lifted. Happy days.'

'If,' said Pawel. 'The oligarchs want to stop the war to stop sanctions. The FSB and some generals want to escalate the war and restore Russian pride. They agree with Pintov's aims but they think he's messed up the approach. It depends which side wins the power struggle.'

'But going back to what you said about Kazbegi being close to Pintov. The British and Americans seem to agree he's not close, because otherwise he'd be under sanctions.'

Pawel smiled. 'I don't know why he escapes sanctions, but he is close to Pintov. He was one of those who interviewed Pintov for his first position as prime minister, back in the Yeltsin era. He gave him the job.'

'Is Kazbegi on this so-called board?'

'He was on the old board, in the days of Yeltsin. It's a new board now. There's a lot of resentment of Kazbegi. A new government might seize assets. As happened before. They would for sure make Kazbegi Holdings pay tax.'

'It pays tax now,' Mickey pointed out.

'Practically nothing for a company so large. And where does all the cash go? Kazbegi Holdings generates billions and pays only a small dividend but doesn't build any cash in the balance sheet.'

'So where does it go?' asked Mickey.

'Extraordinary payments. Every year. Which, by definition, means they shouldn't be extraordinary. But there they are. All below the line so nobody takes much notice.'

'Except you. What examples?'

'Five hundred billion rubles this year for earthquake damage. That's seven billion dollars.'

'But you don't believe it?'

Pawel shrugged. 'There was an earthquake in March in Kamchatka, and they have operations there. There probably was some damage.'

'But not seven billion dollars' worth,' suggested Mickey.

'No. Last year four hundred billion in payments for hurricane damage. Other years losses for early debt repayment, litigation, restructuring charges. You get the picture.'

Mickey knew the answer, but he asked anyway. 'Where do the payments really go?'

'To Kazbegi's various offshore bank accounts and to those belonging to his mates. Pintov being one for sure.' Pawel laughed. 'It's ironic. Kazbegi is supposed to be fighting against corruption. But he's the worst.'

'Back in your offices you told me it was a red chip.'

'That was my colleague,' said Pawel. 'You never asked me what I thought.'

'So basically, Kazbegi is a crook.'

'We use the term avtoritet. The simple translation is authority. Some of these avtoritet are gangster businessmen. They have business portfolios stretching from the legitimate to the criminal. They dress well, have no tattoos, and mix with high society. But they are basically mafia.'

'Tell me about the criminal activities.'

'It's what you've seen with Bogdan. Kazbegi Holdings is also involved. Some of his joint ventures are with Bogdan. There are hundreds of companies in Kazbegi Holdings. Some are legitimate of course, the mining operations and the Borodin security group, though that's also something I don't understand how he gets away with. But some of the companies we just don't know what they do. Could be drug smuggling. People trafficking. Arms manufacturing.'

'Can you prove any of this?'

'I wouldn't dare. I wouldn't normally talk about it to an investor. But you're different.'

Mickey sipped his drink. The ball of thread was unravelling fast. The next question was what to do about it. He was rapidly going off the idea of investing in Kazbegi Holdings. A better plan of action was beginning to take shape.

41

Baked all afternoon by an unopposed sun, *The Cossack* at last gained relief from the seaward wall of Sochi harbour, which cast a shadow almost as far as the fading Olympic rings on the eastern wall. The Master dropped the anchor on the ninety-metre yacht laden with passengers decked out in new leather, fine garments, Rolex, and gold.

The vessel drifted until secure. The birthday party began within minutes. Kazbegi was pleased to see that his guests had taken enthusiastically to the Romanov theme. The Serbian Prime Minister flattered himself as Rasputin. The Czech opposition leader dressed as a Tsarina. The French National Rally leader surprised by attending as a modest vassal while the Polish opposition leader risked ex-communication from the Catholic church in the white robes of an Orthodox bishop. Others wore aristocratic vestments of uncertain origin.

Kazbegi himself would have dressed as Emperor Nicholas. But he had reserved that role for his illustrious guest, though given everything that was happening in the real world it was far from certain whether he would show.

White-liveried waiters carefully choreographed their movements around the deck, topping up champagne flutes and offering multi-tiered silver platters of scallops, anchovies, and langoustines.

As dusk fell the ship's fire-officer, against his better judgement, lit period candelabras. Tchaikovsky, Stravinsky, and other Russian greats drifted over the conversations.

The special guest had still not arrived when the chef announced that he could hold off dinner no longer, and so the banquet captain called guests to their allotted seats.

The chair on Kazbegi's right remained empty.

To his left sat the Hungarian Prime Minister, who asked mischievously. 'Would our special guest by any chance be Russian?'

'That is presumptuous,' replied Kazbegi, as he spooned the lemon croutons in his crab bisque. 'But tell me, how concerned should I be about these student protests in Budapest? You don't seem able to stop them.'

'I am not trying to stop them,' replied the Prime Minister. 'I want them to let off steam.' He then expounded on his view that allowing some protest was in fact essential in running an autocracy.

The butter-seared lobster tails had been dispatched with still no sign of the guest. When the chocolate mousse was served, Kazbegi reasoned that his special guest was not coming and beckoned the Czech first minister to fill the empty chair. Kazbegi's Hammers had beaten the first minister's favourite team of Chelsea, and he wanted to gloat.

The waiters were serving coffee and cocktails when, finally, a gathering drone rose over Prokofiev. On the helideck the Landing Officer signalled the bridge. Behind him a flight deck crew member held two luminescent sticks aloft. The rescue boat dropped into the water. Flashing red and continuous white lights approached from above. Tiaras and toupees were held tight as the helicopter hovered a full minute before lowering to the deck.

A posse of bodyguards emerged first and then President Pintov. He was not in fancy dress, but Kazbegi was simply delighted he had arrived. He was the first to greet him, with a polite bow, knowing the President disliked handshakes.

Robust applause accompanied the walk back to the tables. The President sat on the seat vacated by the Czech first minister. He took a black coffee and engaged in polite small talk with those fortunate enough to be in hearing range.

'Would you like to address the guests?' asked Kazbegi when he sensed the gathering was growing agitated for just that.

The President rose. The music cut. Tables fell silent.

'Thank you, Ivan. And happy birthday. I am sorry I have arrived late and that I will have to leave early. I am particularly sorry that I missed the magnificent dinner, but my duties are great in these times of relentless western aggression.

'I have come to extend the hand of friendship from Russia to the Visegrád Group. For we share a common cultural and political philosophy. We believe in sovereignty, independence, freedom, homeland, family, work, honour and, most important of all, we believe in God.

'The European Union stands for the opposite of all of these. Sovereignty, homeland, and independence are being overwhelmed by Federalism. Many of you are criticised and penalised for your proud nationalism and refusal to have your Christian countries flooded by Muslim refugees.

'The British saw these problems. They left. And they are now in a much stronger position. You are being told to stay in a position of weakness. France and Germany want a two-tier Europe. You will all be stuck on the bottom tier.'

The President spoke at length. Eyes began to flicker. A head dropped and then jumped back up. Whether the President knew or was coming to a natural end wasn't clear.

'I urge you to campaign for your countries to break away and join the Eurasian Union where you will be full members with Russia on an equal footing. This is my simple message for you tonight. Please enjoy the rest of your evening.'

42

Mickey edited the video clips and cut them into one reel. He added descriptive text then showed it to Angelina.

'Pretty good, don't you think?'

'We have …'

'A saying in Russia,' Mickey interrupted. 'Tell me.'

'Every sandpiper praises his own swamp,' she replied.

'I'll take that as a yes.'

He sent it to Uli, registered the blue tick, then gave him a few minutes to watch it. Meantime he paced the hotel room wondering about Ivan Kazbegi. Everyone he met in St Petersburg knew he was a wrong un. It was obvious really, because he'd have had to sell a lot of second-hand cars to have got so rich otherwise. But why wasn't he under sanctions?

The trill of his phone jump-started him back into the present. It was Uli.

'What do you reckon?' asked Mickey.

'I don't really understand,' replied Uli. 'I presume these are pictures of Bogdan's criminal activities.'

'You've got it.'

'Why would I be interested in this?'

'Because Ivan Kazbegi is in business with Bogdan.'

'He has a small stake in TruNews.'

'It's much more than that.'

'Are you sure?' said Uli, with slow deliberation.

'I'm as sure as you can be about anything out here.'

Uli paused. It was just possible to make out the tug on a pipe then the puff as he exhaled. 'So, I guess we're not going to be putting Kazbegi Holdings in the recovery fund.'

'There isn't going to be a recovery fund. I've got a better plan. We're going to go short. Sell shares in Kazbegi Holdings now at this high price. Crash the share price and buy them back at rock bottom.'

'How will you crash the share price?'

'We submit the video to the Foreign and Commonwealth Office as evidence that Kazbegi should be placed under sanctions. We also circulate the film on social media just to make sure.'

'Possibly,' said Uli cautiously. 'But I'm not sure your film is really proof that Kazbegi is involved in criminal activities.'

'They acknowledge Bogdan's name at the brothel.'

'Kazbegi isn't Bogdan.'

'How about all the film at the docks?'

'Very scenic.'

'The timber is used for smuggling goods. The containers people.'

'Who says?'

'Ok, I agree that's supposition. But the protection racket is clear. The car picking up the payments is leased by a subsidiary of Kazbegi Holdings.'

'So are hundreds of cars I expect.'

'TruNews also has a cyber division that is cover for a troll farm and the hackers that crashed RSB.'

'Have you got evidence?'

'I've got the name of the hacker who is already under sanctions and pictures of him celebrating with an FSB officer, who is friends with Bogdan, on the night RSB collapsed.'

'Interesting.'

'There was also all the financial chicanery in the accounts. Unconsolidated holding companies, extraordinary items, and the disappearing cash. I've also heard that Kazbegi is close to Pintov. He interviewed him for the job back in the day.'

'*Was* close.'

'Still is, apparently.'

'If he was close to Pintov, the UK government would know and he'd already be on the sanctions list. Or do you think you've spotted something that they have missed?'

'I don't know why he's not on the sanctions list. But all I'm saying is the market thinks Kazbegi is a saint and Kazbegi Holdings is a blue-chip investment. I don't think either is true. And I think we can sling enough mud to make some stick.'

'I'm warming to the idea,' Uli said eventually.

Beautiful. 'Before we do anything though, I must show this to the Old Bill.'

'Why?'

'They might not want us to make it public. They might want to use it as evidence for a criminal prosecution.'

'We can still short the shares though. If Kazbegi gets arrested the shares will collapse.'

'Sure,' said Mickey. 'But let's hold fire for now. Don't want to get on the wrong side of the law. And I don't want to do anything that might draw attention to me while I'm still in Russia. See you tomorrow.'

He finished the call and sent the video to Frank with some explanatory text. Finally, the fog was lifting, and he had a plan that should work. It *had* to work. He checked his phone for messages from Helen.

'I'm fine. Hope you are too. Stay safe. Xx.'

Brilliant. Kisses as well.

He texted a reply: *'All's well here, too. Been a useful trip. Coming home in the morning. Love Mickey. Xx.'*

He was glad to be going home. Russia really was the wild east.

It was some comfort to know that Angelina and Leonid were still sleeping in adjoining rooms. But also worrying that he needed bodyguards in the first place. He'd feel safer having one of them in the room with him. And Leonid wouldn't be the first choice.

He took off his trousers and tie and got into bed. He turned to his side to go to sleep when a new message pinged in. Helen?

It wasn't from Helen but from Olga.

'I must be in Moscow tomorrow so I can give you a quick tour of our marvellous capital before you fly out. Meet you outside St Basil's cathedral at 11am.'

Strange. He hadn't arranged to meet her. He'd got everything he wanted from the tour she'd given him of St Petersburg. And for that he was immensely grateful, even though he did feel guilty that the agenda had moved on from what they'd agreed. He was no longer going to use the film to persuade Kazbegi to clean up TruNews as agreed with Olga. Still, it might still have the desired effect if Bogdan was forced by the police or public opinion to clean up his act.

Perhaps Olga was going to show him that Bogdan's criminal tentacles reached Moscow. That might be useful to give extra footage for the video.

Why not go? He had Leonid and Angelina to look after him. One more outing before jumping on a plane home.

43

With nine flaming domes rising unexpectedly to the sky, St Basil's cathedral looked like it had been copy-pasted into Red Square from another world. It was nevertheless impressive.

Angelina was restless again. 'We're a perfect target for a sniper.'

'Relax,' said Mickey. 'If Bogdan wanted to kill me, he would have done it in St Petersburg.'

'Not necessarily. And he's not the only one who might want to kill you.'

That was increasingly true. 'Here she comes.'

Olga, reassuringly alone, walked up the hill to meet them. She offered a hand to shake. 'Good to see you again.'

'Likewise,' said Mickey.

'Are you ready for a tour?'

'Sure. I don't remember arranging one though. Did I?'

'I thought we should start at the best,' said Olga, ignoring his query. 'Come, we will walk out into the square so that you can appreciate the cathedral in perspective.'

Olga explained the history from the original church built by Ivan the Terrible through Soviet times, when it somehow escaped destruction, to its present status as a tourist museum.

After St Basil's, she walked them to the car. She gave a running commentary as Leonid drove them round the capital.

At the Cathedral of Christ the Saviour they got out to approach on foot. 'This is a perfect symbol of Russian history,' said Olga.

It wasn't as colourful as the others. Mostly white stone and marble. 'This is a replica of what was a new Cathedral in its day,' explained Olga. 'When built in the 19th Century it was the largest in the Russian empire. The golden domes used the latest technology of electroplating. It was built to celebrate the fusion between the church and the state.'

'What happened to the original?' asked Mickey.

'You've heard of Marx's famous expression: religion is the opium of the masses. Well Stalin agreed and he knocked it down. During the Soviet era, this area became a swimming pool.'

'Why did they rebuild it?'

'Yeltsin did. To demonstrate that the Soviet era was over. You see the contradictions. One government builds it, another destroys it, another one builds it up again. This could only happen in Russia.'

They returned to the car and a brief time later they came to a huge Orthodox cathedral with blue domes and gold plaits. More cupulas. If only he had the patent.

'This is The Holy Trinity,' Olga declared. 'The larger church is for God the Father. The middle one for the Son and the small one for the Holy Spirit.'

'Are you religious?' asked Mickey, realising that the tour had been dominated by cathedrals.

'My mother was Orthodox Christian,' she replied without answering the question. 'You?'

'Still trying to figure it out,' replied Mickey. 'Though I have heard that there are no atheists on a crashing plane.'

They did not get out at The Holy Trinity but continued driving, travelling past buildings already seen. Olga's commentary grew less enthusiastic. In a long tunnel she took out a piece of paper and wrote: 'Turn off your phones.'

Olga turned off her own while Mickey and Angelina did the same. She placed them all in a metal box.

'Now I will show you something more relevant to present times,' she said.

'What's that?' asked Mickey.

But she did not answer. Instead, she gave new directions to Leonid.

They headed south on a highway filled mostly with SUV's and BMWs. It morphed from six to ten lanes at will and was littered on either side with the typical paraphernalia of a large city. Cheap hotels, petrol stations, medical centres, banks, shops, restaurants, apartment blocks, a car store, a park, light industrial plants, a recycling centre.

After a time, Leonid turned off the highway and pulled up at a small park.

'I used to live here,' said Olga, pointing out the window.

'In a park?'

'Come,' she said without explanation.

They exited the car and Olga retrieved a shopping bag from the boot.

Mickey and Angelina fell in line behind as she negotiated her way through a grid of well-tended flower beds to a stone monument topped with a cross.

From her bag Olga produced a photograph of a young woman and lay it on the pavement. She took out a glass jar, placed a candle inside and lit it. Then she laid red carnations on the photo. She lowered her head and closed her eyes. Lips moved as she prayed in silence.

Finally, Olga pulled herself upright and wiped away a tear.

'I'm sorry for your loss,' said Mickey. 'Someone close?'

'My mother.'

'Oh. I am really very sorry.'

'Don't worry,' said Olga. 'She died when I was just a little girl.'

A list of names had been engraved on the monument. Maybe a hundred. Olga must have understood what he was thinking.

'One hundred and twenty-one.'

She said no more until they were back in the car. 'Nineteen ninety-nine. This is the site of the bomb on September 13th.'

'One of the Russian apartment bombings,' Mickey guessed.

'At five o'clock in the morning the third bomb blew up here,' she said. 'It was 6/3 Kashirskoye. That is the name of the highway. It was a nine-story building. A Khrushchevki, the nickname for that type of accommodation, after the Soviet leader Khrushchev. They were drab and cheap. But it was home.'

'You survived,' said Mickey, before adding, 'obviously.'

'I was staying with my father. My parents had split up. Papa got a phone call from my aunt. I could see on his face it was something terrible. He did not want to take me with him, but I insisted. When we got here there was this empty space in the middle of the building. Just air filled with smoke and rain. Firefighters crawled like orange ants over the rubble, looking for survivors. Big diggers pulled at metal and stone. We stood watching all day. I really thought she would be all right. Every time they took away a body, I still thought my mother would be fine. She was so strong. She was invulnerable.' She paused. 'We found out later that hers had been one of the first bodies recovered.'

Mickey remembered the loss of his father when he was a child. 'That must have been very hard, growing up without her.'

'The hardest part is not knowing the truth.'

'The truth?'

'I grew up a patriot, and an admirer of Pintov. I heard the rumours that he and the FSB were behind the bombings, but I dismissed them. I was sure that Pintov would never have had such cynical disregard for life that he would kill innocents for his own political ends. But I am no longer so sure.'

'What's changed your mind?' asked Mickey.

'The thousands of young soldiers being killed. Plus, my father, who worked for the FSB, has always believed that Pintov knew.'

'What do other Russians think?'

'Nobody dares to think,' said Olga. 'Anyone who links the bombings with Pintov doesn't survive very long. For the first few years on the anniversary there were protests here because many people did believe he planned it. I just thought they were upset and wanting someone to blame. But the protests don't happen anymore. People are too scared.'

'Is this what you wanted to show me?' asked Mickey. 'Not the churches. This bomb site.'

'Yes.'

He checked the time on the dashboard clock. 'I've got to catch my plane.'

He tapped Leonid on the shoulder, and they moved off. Olga seemed to be working through sad memories, so Mickey left her to it and watched Moscow pass by out the window. He was pleased to be going home. He knew there would be a better side of Russia that he hadn't seen, but what he had seen was disturbing.

As they approached the airport a plane coming into land roared over the car and disturbed Olga from her reverie. 'I showed you the apartment bomb site because I want to know whether British intelligence believes that Pintov and the FSB were involved in the bombings.'

'How will you find that out?'

'I'd like you to find out for me.'

'I don't work for British intelligence,' said Mickey. 'Genuinely. I am just a finance man.'

'I know who you are, Mickey Summer. Remember I did a security background check on you. You know Frank Brighouse.'

'Not well enough to ask a favour like that,' said Mickey.

'It's not a favour. I have information I could trade.'

'Isn't it best if you contact them yourself?'

'There is a CIA station in St Petersburg, but I don't trust it,' said Olga. 'Then there are routes I could take on the web using TOR and remote servers. But I'd prefer a human that I can trust.'

'What makes you think you can trust me?'

'Instinct. Find out what you can. If there is nothing, you tell me and we let it go. If you find there is evidence, we can discuss how to trade information.'

'I'm not sure I want to get involved.'

'Did you like the tour of Bogdan's criminal businesses?' Olga asked.

Where had that come from? 'I told you, I really appreciated it.'

'Then you owe me a favour, don't you think?'

So that was why she had taken him on the tour of St Petersburg. Or at least part of the reason. Now he didn't feel so guilty using what he'd filmed to crash Kazbegi Holdings. He could trade the information on Bogdan's mafia activities for information on the apartment bombings. That would be a fair swap.

'I'll ask the question,' he said eventually. 'And let you know what they say.'

44

On Declan's previous visit to the Washington Golf and Country club the mercury had been pushing a hundred. Now hoar frost covered the trees on either side of the heavily gritted driveway. He parked up and checked in at reception, where he was surprised to be directed to the men's locker room. There he surrendered his gun to the senator's protection team.

'You can change in here,' said a guard, handing Declan a pair of shorts.

'Change for what?' asked Declan.

'You're taking a sauna,' the bodyguard explained.

Declan smiled. Good counter-surveillance. Naked he couldn't film or record.

According to the sand timer, Senator Martin had been waiting five minutes. He sat on the top level. Declan didn't care for that much heat and took a low seat as far from the heater as possible.

'Thanks for coming, Declan.'

'Thanks for inviting me.'

'I'm sorry to meet like this. Once this enquiry is over, I'll invite you to lunch. Right now, we are not really supposed to meet at all. As you know.'

Declan nodded. 'Appreciate that.'

Senator Martin smoothed out a non-existent crease in his towel. 'I'll come straight to the point. I understand you've been pressurising Spitz to expand his prosecution further than Ladyman.'

'You shouldn't be talking to Spitz.'

'Neither should you. Do you really think you're better placed than Spitz to determine the terms of reference of the enquiry? He has thirty years of experience as a Special Prosecutor.'

'I think he should cast the net wider. Just as I did last time I was in this building.'

'Thing is Declan, this enquiry is disruptive. Which would be fine if it had a purpose. But it's not going to find anything. Because there is no Black Chamber.'

'You would say that.'

'I would. But you can understand how difficult it is to work with an enquiry overhanging. Not just for me but for all the others you accused.'

'I guess.'

'Imagine if there was an enquiry into your development of the GameOverRed malware that led to the collapse of Royal Shire Bank, and near collapse of State Financial. You'd find that quite disruptive, I'm sure.'

'I did nothing wrong.'

'You would say that.'

So that was the deal. Back off. Leave Spitz alone. Or they'll come after him.

'I think you understand where I am coming from,' said the Senator. 'That's all I have to say.'

Declan said nothing. He stood up and let himself out into the relief of a cool room. He dressed quickly and left the club faster. As he drove back down North Glebe Road, Senator Martin's warning turned over in his mind, like a hawk over roadkill. But Declan wasn't a quitter. If anything, it had simply renewed his faith that there was a Black Chamber. And he'd got its members running scared.

45

It was good to be back in England. Even better to find Helen well and relaxed. He told her about his plan to make good money from shorting Kazbegi Holdings, and even though she didn't fully understand the mechanics of the trade she could see that Mickey was cautiously optimistic, and that had pleased her. And he *was* optimistic. It should work. But he first needed to run a couple of things by Mishkin.

He didn't want to be seen going to Mishkin's castle, so he arranged to meet up in one of his old stomping grounds. Epping Forest had shed its leaves and visibility was good. He picked up his binoculars. Mishkin and a guard were negotiating the path he had directed them to take. Satisfied they had not been followed, he drifted deeper into the forest to the rendezvous; an old iron-age camp that he used to run around in as a child.

He waited for them to catch up, then stepped out from behind a holly tree. 'Wotcha.'

'Are you alone?' asked Mishkin, looking nervous outside his fortress.

'Just me,' replied Mickey.

'So, did you have a fruitful visit?'

'St Petersburg is a beautiful city,' said Mickey. 'Moscow too.'

'And the leads I gave you were helpful? Dina for example?'

'Dina approached me, remember.'

'But I called her to suggest she meet you. Never mind. It's not important. What did you learn?'

'You're right about Kazbegi,' said Mickey. 'He does have links to the St Petersburg mafia.'

Mickey walked Mishkin through the evidence he'd uncovered. He didn't mention the video because he hadn't yet decided whether to use it.

'Are you going to take this evidence to the police?' asked Mishkin.

'I'm seeing them this afternoon.'

'Let's see what happens, but I suspect they won't be interested. They don't want sanctions on Kazbegi.'

'That's really what I wanted to see you about. Why do you think he's not under sanctions?' Mickey asked, knowing his shorting plan would only work if he was.

Mishkin shrugged. 'I assume he is paying someone a lot of money to keep his name off the list. But if you publicise what you have found, especially his links to TruNews and its role in collapsing RSB, then the demands for him to be sanctioned will be impossible to ignore.'

'I'm thinking about it,' said Mickey. 'I'd rather go through official channels.'

Mishkin fell silent while he looked around the forest. 'What is the mood regarding Pintov in Russia?'

'The people I spoke to were tired of the war. Though mostly they were still supportive of Pintov.'

'I don't understand this,' said Mishkin. 'He is a monster.'

That nicely teed up the question he really wanted answering. 'What is your view on the Russian apartment bombings?'

'Why do you ask?'

'Someone mentioned it.'

'The official view is that Chechen terrorists killed hundreds of Russian civilians in a series of bombings. A terrible atrocity that required Pintov to call a state of emergency, abandon elections and start a second Chechen war that cemented his popularity.'

'But what's your view?'

Mishkin shook his head. 'It wasn't terrorists who organised the bombings. It was Pintov and the family, using the FSB.'

Mickey decided to play dumb. 'You think Pintov and the Russian security services killed their own people to start a war? The very people they are sworn to protect?'

'Correct.'

'That is as bonkers as the crazies who say the CIA were behind 9/11.'

Mishkin shrugged. 'Why not investigate? You can find the evidence.'

'Where?'

'British and American intelligence. I think they know the truth.'

'If they do then surely they'd make it public to destabilise

Pintov. Would have done so years ago.'

'Surely,' Mishkin repeated. 'And surely Kazbegi should be under sanctions. And surely all those murders I told you about would have been investigated.'

'Why would the CIA protect Pintov?'

'Why indeed? Ask your friend Declan. See if he can find out.'

'If the CIA don't want to publicise evidence of Pintov's involvement, then they won't tell Declan.'

'Ask,' said Mishkin.. 'I'd like to know. You'd like to know. And clearly the someone who mentioned it to you would like to know. Who was that?'

'I can't tell you.'

'I understand. But see what you can find about Pintov and the bombings. Let me know what you discover. I'm very interested.'

46

The meeting room at Vauxhall Cross was far more welcoming than the windowless underground box in which Mickey had last met Peter Jones. On a table in the corner sat flasks of coffee, tea, and milk beside a plate of plain biscuits.

He wandered to the window. Trains shunted in and out of Vauxhall station. A few hundred metres down Harleyford Road floodlights rose over the Oval. The rest of the view was typical of London south of the river: gardens, gasworks, red brick tenements, church spires sprawled haphazardly, all connected by badly surfaced roads.

The door opened. Peter Jones entered the room replete with trademark dandruff and nicotine-stained fingers and hair. Beside him, Frank walked somewhat sheepishly.

'Enjoying the view?' asked Jones.

'Very pleasant,' said Mickey. 'I'll have to knock ten percent off the asking price for backing onto a train line though.'

'We never hear them actually,' said Jones, shaking hands. 'Triple-layered armoured glass. Tea or coffee?'

'Coffee, please. Armoured glass to stop snipers, I guess.'

'Not just bullets. The windows are bombproof as well.' Jones carried a tray with the drinks over to a soft seating area and placed it on a low table. 'The room next door was once hit by an anti-tank rocket. It only caused superficial damage. It failed to penetrate the inner cladding. Reassuring, don't you think?'

Mickey remembered the story but not the detail. 'Someone fired an anti-tank rocket in London? So close to Westminster.'

'The Real IRA. It was an RPG-22, Russian made, as it so happens.'

Jones rambled on a bit more about the IRA and Mickey wondered if he was ever going to get to the point of the meeting. He decided to help him out. 'What do you think of the video?'

'The video,' Jones repeated. 'That is what we wanted to talk to you about.'

Talk to him rather than with him. There was a definite tone of disapproval.

'Sterling investigative work, I have to say. Getting under the skin of the St Petersburg mafia like you did. Very enterprising. And this hacker you uncovered. Dmitri. We've passed that on to GCHQ. I understand that they were already aware of him, but you've added to the mosaic. So, thanks for that.'

There was a 'but' coming.

'But it's the material on Kazbegi Holdings,' said Frank, who'd never been one to skirt around a subject. 'That's the problem.'

'Problem for who?' asked Mickey.

'It might be a problem for us,' said Jones, glancing at Frank as if to suggest he was back in the lead.

'In what way?'

'That rather depends upon what you plan to do with it.'

'I was planning to send it to the Foreign Office.'

'We'd rather you didn't.' Jones tried to smile but it came across more like a snarl. 'We'd prefer it if you kept it under wraps. At least for the time being.'

'But there should be enough on this for them to impose sanctions.'

'I don't think there is,' said Jones. 'A lot of it is circumstantial.'

'Shouldn't I let them decide?'

'We'd rather you didn't,' said Jones. 'There are complications and sensitivities you see.'

Mickey turned to Frank. 'What is he on about, Frank? In plain English.'

'The government don't want to place sanctions on Kazbegi,' said Frank, looking at Jones as if to say: see, that wasn't so difficult.

'Why not?'

'We really can't tell you that,' said Jones, before Frank could open his mouth. 'Let's just say it is a matter of national security.'

'National security,' repeated Mickey.

Jones nodded. 'Therefore, it would be very much appreciated if you could keep the video private. At least for now.'

'For how long?'

'Difficult to put a timeframe on this.'

'Are we talking about weeks or months?' asked Mickey. He didn't want to have to wait too long and miss the chance of trading Kazbegi Holding shares.

Jones furrowed his brow as if calculating something. 'Difficult to say.'

'Probably years,' said Frank.

Mickey nodded his appreciation of Frank's honesty. There was clearly not going to be an investigation into the bank collapse. Without the video he had nothing on Kazbegi. He might have to go back to the original plan and build a recovery fund. But that would take so much longer and contained much more risk. He suddenly remembered Olga.

'There's something else that came up during my trip. It's not in the video.'

'Really?' asked Jones, who looked delighted to change the subject.

'There's a woman who works at TruNews. Runs the cyber division. The troll farms, the hacking, ransomware …'

'Olga Federova,' said Jones.

'You know her?' asked Mickey.

'The name has come up,' he said vaguely.

'She lost her mother in the Russian apartment bombings. Some people think Pintov and the FSB had a role in the bombings.'

Jones' eyes displayed nothing.

'She'd like to know what information British intelligence has about it.'

'I'm sure she would,' said Jones.

'Can you give her that?'

Jones shook his head. 'Olga Federova is deep into the Russian intelligence apparatus. It is most probable that she is asking on behalf of Pintov. He'll want to know because he'll be worried about what might come out in the Russian public domain, once he's no longer in charge.'

'So, he was involved.'

'I've no idea,' Jones replied quickly. 'The point is that Olga can't be trusted. We certainly can't tell her what we know.'

She seemed trustworthy to Mickey, but he wasn't going to get in an argument over it. He'd agreed to ask the question. He'd done that. 'I'll let her know.'

There seemed no point in continuing the meeting. He stood up and Frank and Jones followed suit.

'I'm sorry we couldn't make more use of your investigation,' said Jones, as they walked out of the meeting room and into the corridor. 'And on behalf of his majesty's government I'd like to express our gratitude for your cooperation in keeping your findings under wraps.'

Mickey didn't answer. He hadn't agreed to be silent. He'd been thinking about doing so as a favour to Frank, who was a mate. As for Jones, he'd never really liked him, and he certainly wasn't doing anything for the King. Jones had chosen the wrong button to press there.

47

Kazbegi made the call from his 'black hole'. Built by former US National Intelligence staffers, its communications and telephones conformed to the highest TEMPEST specifications. Nothing on the electromagnetic spectrum emanated from that room.

Kazbegi had installed a similar set-up in St Petersburg for

communications with Bogdan, though he was less certain of the security at that end. He wouldn't put it past Bogdan to leave the door open. The old Vor was increasingly unreliable. This slip with Mickey Summer being just the latest example.

Kazbegi asked for an update on business in general and then turned to the real purpose of his call. 'Why did you talk to Mickey Summer?'

There was a moment of silence before Bogdan replied. 'He had a business proposal.'

'I told you not to talk to him. Do you remember that?'

There followed a longer silence.

'Is there a problem?'

Kazbegi ignored the question. 'I told you to frighten him out of Russia. Do you remember that?'

'Of course I remember. Beratov tried, but Summer didn't leave.'

'So, if I wanted to frighten Mickey Summer away because I didn't want him looking into our activities, why did you then meet him?'

Again silence. 'I was curious to hear his business proposal.'

'And why did you give him a guided tour of our activities?'

'I had lunch with him. That is all.'

'I assume you were drunk at this lunch.'

'I told him nothing.'

'He knows about the protection racket, the comfort house, the smuggling. He knows about the cyber team at TruNews and the hacking of Baltika.'

'How do you know that he knows this?'

'He's talked to Mishkin. And Mishkin is now making mischief with it.'

'We should have killed Mishkin years ago.'

'On that we can both agree. It must be done.'

'I'll tell Beratov.'

'Tell him to be prepared to make it two.'

'Who is the second?'

'Mickey Summer, if he doesn't go away.'

'I'll tell him. Now to more important matters. I am being baptised on Sunday.'

Kazbegi stymied a laugh. 'Why?'

'I am at the time of my life when I want to make peace with the world. I would like you to be there at the ceremony. We'll have a celebration after.'

'I cannot travel to Russia right now. But I will be there in spirit.'

48

The Yak-130 glided over a blue-green Volga and kissed the reconstructed runway at Saratov South Airbase. It taxied to the terminal, where the ground crew wheeled up a flight of steps. Beratov disembarked and walked slowly to a white Lada Granta driven by a plain-clothed GRU officer.

In silence they drove along the Syzran highway, passing through fine agricultural landscape for almost two hours before turning abruptly right at a signpost for Shikhany 4. Minutes later they passed through the ageing town with its run-down supermarkets and cosmetics stores, and then on to a welcome sign outside Shikhany 2: 'The town of chemists.' A flash of the driver's ID got him through the police checkpoint.

This smaller town was in better health. Carefully manicured flower beds lined the roadside, well-dressed patrons chatted in a newly opened cafe, the shops were full of modern goods and there was a military hospital and a school. A statue of Lenin had survived the purges and surveyed the surrounding streets named after war heroes.

They drove on past the deserted red-brick buildings where the first chemicals were developed in the seventies. At the new communications centre, the labs, pipes, and tanks were all hidden from view. The only hint of any unusual activity were the hazmat suits hanging in a cupboard behind the reception desk.

There a guard checked Beratov's paperwork then showed him to a windowless waiting room. After a time, a hook-nosed man with a postman's busy gait arrived carrying two bright-orange, hard-plastic briefcases.

He saluted. 'Colonel Dvinsky.'

'Lieutenant Colonel Beratov.'

'I understand you graduated in chemistry.'

Beratov nodded. 'From St Petersburg.'

'Excellent. You will be able to understand the briefing.' Dvinsky approached the table and set down the briefcases side by side. 'As you know. Novichok is a binary chemical weapon. We have two precursors. Each on its own is relatively non-hazardous. It is only when they are reacted together that we get the nerve agent.'

Dvinsky opened the first case to reveal a syringe holding a colourless liquid. 'Acetonitrile. A common solvent found in every chemical laboratory.'

Inside the second case another syringe held a yellow suspension.

'This is an organic phosphate such as is commonly used as a pesticide precursor. Both are designed to be undetectable for any standard chemical security testing. When combined they form agent A-245.'

'And how does A-245 affect the target?' asked Beratov, curious to know how Mishkin would die.

'Like the other agents, it inhibits the enzyme acetylcholinesterase, preventing the normal breakdown of the neurotransmitter acetylcholine. Acetylcholine concentrations then increase at neuromuscular junctions to cause cholinergic crisis …'

'More simply,' interrupted Beratov. It had been a long time since his last chemistry class.

'Cholinergic crisis is an involuntary contraction of the muscles. This is what gives the patient the appearance of a zombie. But what kills them is that it leads to respiratory and cardiac arrest, as the heart and diaphragm muscles no longer function normally.'

'Perfect. How long do the chemicals last?'

'Forever if kept apart. Even after reacting the agent will last for many years as it has a very low evaporation rate.' He passed over two bags, a sheet of thin black material and a ball of thread.

'What's this?'

'Impermeable material and thread. You should use this to line the gloves that you will wear. The bags are to dispose of the syringes and unused Novichok. You must dispose of them separately.

Flush the liquids down different toilets in different locations. The syringes go in the bags and into landfill. Not a public waste bin, like those idiots in Salisbury.'

49

Mickey phoned Declan's secretary and explained who he was and what he wanted. She rang back ten minutes later and put Declan on the line.

'Hi Mickey. How are you?'

'I'm good mate. How about you? Have you made it to President yet? We like our colonies run properly you see, and your last few leaders haven't been all that great. We reckon you're the man for the job.'

'I'll let President Topps know,' said Declan.

They played catch up on family and friends. Mickey was reluctant to say that Helen was pregnant. It was still early days. But he wanted Declan to understand why he was so desperate to get his money back. He left it with the simpler explanation that they needed a house because they planned to start a family. They then talked about work. Turned out Declan was now running a task force looking into Russian hybrid warfare. He knew all about Bogdan's troll farm, the cyber theft from RSB and other illegal activities, plus Ivan Kazbegi's links to TruNews. Nothing in the video that Mickey had sent had come as a surprise.

'You're probably understating the case,' said Declan. 'I think Kazbegi holdings is very much tied into Pintov and the system.'

'So why don't you go after him?'

'The collapse of RSB is viewed as a British problem, and realistically we can't prosecute anyone even if we did go after them. As for Kazbegi, he's very careful to never quite overstep the mark. We've got no clear evidence he's close to Pintov or Bogdan.'

'Is someone being paid off by Kazbegi?' asked Mickey. 'Cards on the table.'

After a suspiciously long pause Declan said, 'I don't think so.'

'So why is he not under sanctions?'

'Because he's denounced the war, he gives to charity and he's an anti-corruption champion.'

'That's the official line,' said Mickey. 'But it doesn't wash. What's the real reason?'

Another long pause. This time long enough to make coal. 'You didn't hear this from me.'

'Go on.'

'Net zero,' replied Declan.

'Net zero,' repeated Mickey. 'What has that got to do with it?'

'The west can't get there without the rare earth metals produced by Kazbegi Holdings. Plus, even at this early stage of the green reset the economy is very vulnerable to a supply shock. America can cope with higher oil prices. But not without lithium for phones and laptops, silicon for chips, cobalt for rechargeable batteries. So, we're turning a blind eye to his Russian connections.'

Finally, an explanation. Not a satisfactory one but at least there was some sort of logic to it. 'How do you feel about that?'

'Personally, I don't like it,' Declan admitted. 'He should be under sanctions, and we'll deal with the shortage of batteries and chips like we dealt with the shortage of oil and gas. But I don't set policy.'

'So, who is pushing this?' asked Mickey.

'It comes from POTUS. And those who advise him.'

Some might call it Realpolitik but, whichever way it was looked at, a criminal was being allowed to enjoy his ill-gotten wealth because some people at the top of the decision tree thought the economy trumped morality. 'Have you heard of the Russian apartment bombings?'

'I must have missed that. Which apartments?'

'This was way back,' said Mickey. 'Nineteen ninety-nine. A series of bombings of Russian apartment blocks that killed hundreds of civilians. Apparently done by Chechen terrorists. Russia went to war to avenge the deaths.'

'I was still at school. Why is it relevant?'

'Some think the bombings were the work of Pintov and his cronies so that they could cancel elections they were about to lose and whip up nationalist fervour. I've been told that Ivan Kazbegi supported the plan.'

'That's a hell of an accusation. Do you have any evidence?'

'I don't,' said Mickey. 'The bigger question is whether you do.'

'I just told you, I don't know anything about it.'

'Not you personally. American intelligence. I tried British Intelligence, but they won't tell me anything.'

'Why not?'

'They don't trust the Russian who's asking.'

'They know him?'

'Her,' Mickey corrected. 'She's plugged into Russian intelligence. I'm just the messenger. Her name is Olga Federova. She works for Bogdan, but I think she's a good sort. She wants him to quit his illegal activities. She helped me make the video. Check her out. If you're interested, and you find out you do have evidence of Pintov's involvement, she'd be prepared to trade information.'

'How do I know that name?' asked Declan.

'She runs the underground cyber businesses of TruNews.'

'I know her now. That is very interesting. The President has asked us to target TruNews.'

Mickey filled in more background, including that Olga's mother had died in one of the bombings and that her father was involved in the plot when he worked in the FSB.

'Well, I am interested in what she can tell us about TruNews. That's for sure. Whether I've got anything to trade I don't know.'

'Could you look into it?'

'You bet I will. Look, I must go now. But I'll get back …'

'Before you go,' interrupted Mickey. 'Do you have a problem if I make public what I know about Kazbegi? Because I'm confident it will crash the Kazbegi Holding share price and I can then get back the money that was stolen from me and buy a house for Helen.'

Silence. Mickey wondered if the line had been cut. Then finally Declan replied, 'You're a British citizen. I have no jurisdiction over you.'

'But I don't want to get you in trouble.'

'Don't mention my name.'

* * *

Mickey checked the video one last time to strengthen his resolve. It was convincing. Kazbegi would have to face sanctions. He called Uli.

'I've been expecting you,' said Uli. 'Have you made a decision?'

'Let's do it,' said Mickey. 'Release the video.'

'Exciting.'

'First, we put on the trade and prime the market to expect news on Kazbegi Holdings. Then we release the clip later today.'

'And the police are happy with this?' asked Uli. 'You were concerned they might want to keep it as evidence for the prosecution.'

'There isn't going to be any prosecution.'

'Sanctions then.'

'There won't be any sanctions either. Kazbegi is being protected from sanctions because Kazbegi Holdings is critical in the supply of rare earth metals for the green industry. The US government doesn't want that disrupted. So, he avoids sanctions.'

'In that case this isn't going to work,' said Uli. 'If there are no sanctions the shares won't fall.'

'I think when this video gets circulated the pressure to put him under sanctions will escalate. So just the threat of it will make the shares drop.'

Uli was silent except for the sound of him puffing on his vape. 'Are we going to get in trouble for doing this? With the police or Ivan Kazbegi?'

'We'll do it all anonymously. Kazbegi won't know.'

'But the police will know it was you because you showed them the video.'

'It's not illegal to report on illegal activity. We've nothing to worry about.'

They formulated a plan to short Kazbegi Holdings and hedge it with a long position against the MOEX index. From a stock lender they borrowed two hundred thousand ADR shares and then sold them immediately on the market at an average price of one hundred and forty-nine dollars. Mickey did some quick mental arithmetic. When the trade settled, they would have around thirty million dollars in cash. They would still owe the stock lender two hundred thousand shares. But if the share fell, say to one hundred dollars, they would be able to use the cash to buy shares in the market at the new lower price. It would now only cost twenty million dollars to buy two hundred thousand shares. Crosshair investments would make a cool profit of ten million dollars. Two of those would be for Mickey. And Helen and the baby of course.

Easy winnings.

The trick now was to make sure the share price fell.

* * *

Mickey scrolled down the list of contacts on his phone, writing down the name and number of anyone he thought might own shares in Kazbegi Holdings. Top of the list was a Russian he used to manage on the trading desk at Royal Shire Bank. LinkedIn showed he was now at a Russian trading house.

'Yuri. How's it going?'

'Who is this?'

'And you said you'd never forget me.'

'Mickey Summer? Long time.'

After a brief catch up Mickey segued to the purpose of his call. 'I'm thinking of buying some Russian equities ahead of sanctions being lifted.'

'There is no sign of that happening.'

'Pintov might go,' said Mickey.

'No sign of that either. And even if he does go that doesn't mean sanctions will be eased. It depends on who replaces him.'

'I want to have exposure to Russia, just in case,' explained Mickey. 'I'm looking for one safe Russian stock to put in my portfolio and …'

'There are no safe Russian stocks,' interrupted Yuri.

Yuri always saw the negative side of things. Particularly his bonus payments, no matter how large they were. 'You're probably right. But the safest Russian stock I can think of is Kazbegi Holdings.'

'Safe as you can get in Russia,' agreed Yuri.

'That's what I thought. But when I checked it out with Alexi Stepanchikov … you remember him?'

After a moment, Yuri admitted that he didn't recollect the name. Which had a lot to do with the fact Mickey had made it up.

'He reckons Kazbegi has some dodgy mafia connections.'

'Every Russian company has some dodgy mafia connections.'

'That's as may be. But apparently an investigative journalist is going to put something out on YouTube. Should I worry? Or is it just muck that won't stick?'

'Who did you say told you this?'

'It's just a market rumour.'

No trader could admit he hadn't heard a market rumour and eventually Yuri said, 'I heard it already, but I don't believe it.'

'They'll never be able to prove anything anyway, right?'

'Right.'

'I should go ahead and buy Kazbegi Holdings?'

'Maybe buy on weakness,' said Yuri. 'In case this rumour does pull the shares back a bit.'

'Good call, mate. Thanks for your help. Keep in touch with yourself.'

Mickey couldn't suppress a smile. Next, he tracked down an old colleague who ran a family office for a Russian Oligarch. Again, they played catch up for a couple of minutes and then Mickey asked him if he'd heard the rumour that there was a YouTube hatchet job coming up on Kazbegi Holdings.

'Where did you hear that?'

'Yuri Belovski,' said Mickey. 'Remember him?'

'Of course.'

'But I still reckon Kazbegi Holdings is a solid red chip, and any mud that gets thrown at it won't stick.'

'I agree,' came the unconvincing reply. 'Nothing to worry about.'

'How is the family in any case?'

'Fine. Look, Mickey. I've got to take another call.'

The line went dead. Mickey smiled again.

And so on, ringing around the market until the tables had fully turned. Now when he asked people what they thought about buying Kazbegi Holdings they told him to hold off: there was bad news in the pipeline. The share price was already falling.

Late in the afternoon he posted the video online. He didn't need to tell anyone. They would all have primed their alerts to look for any news on Kazbegi Holdings. It had started well. But they needed the share price to stay down for at least a few more days so they could close out the position. Fingers and legs crossed in the meantime.

50

Kazbegi first watched the video from a Russian perspective and satisfied himself that the average citizen would view it as western propaganda trying to undermine one of the country's leading industrialists. Moscow prosecutors would see the slim evidence of criminality as circumstantial and not worthy of investigation, though a pre-emptive raise in goodwill payments would be judicious. The liberal opposition would cheer, but the video contained nothing they did not suspect already, especially concerning his relationships with Bogdan and Pintov.

Then he watched the video again from a western perspective. This was more worrying. The suggestion that TruNews was involved in the collapse of RSB could not be ignored and would lead to fresh calls for him to sell West Ham, and for the government to impose sanctions.

'What was Bogdan doing!' He slapped both hands on his desk and stood up, turning to his lawyer: 'I told him to frighten Mickey Summer away but instead he shows him around TruNews and takes him out for lunch.'

'You think the video was made by Mickey Summer?'

'Who else?'

The lawyer shrugged. 'There are plenty of people who want to bring you down.'

'I need to do something about Bogdan. This is not his first mistake. And he has also allowed TruNews to be critical of the President. I can't protect him forever.' Kazbegi walked over to the window and looked out on Fleet Street, the birthplace of journalism. The window also afforded a view of the ecclesiastical façade of the Royal Courts of justice and a glimpse of the magnificent dome of St Paul's. He told colleagues that in these surroundings he felt he had the press, the courts and God on his side. He was going to need them now.

He turned back to the lawyer. 'How bad could this get?'

'Worst case you are designated under the Magnitsky Act and have sanctions imposed.'

Kazbegi nodded. 'How do we mitigate?'

'Move the company headquarters to a Special Administrative Region in Kaliningrad. It would still be an internationally registered company and retain tax breaks but will be out of reach of the UK government. So, they wouldn't be able to suspend your shares and freeze your assets.'

'I don't want to retreat from the UK. There must be other ways.'

'I can't think of any.'

'I'll call in a favour from our friendly Lord.'

'You're going to pray?'

'I'm talking about Lord Griffin.'

The lawyer nodded. 'What do we do about Bogdan?'

'I am afraid that it is time for him to meet with the real Lord.'

51

Olga smiled encouragingly at Bogdan, who wore a ceremonial white robe and heavy gold crucifix for his baptism. She was pleased for him. He had always had a strong spiritual streak and though he had undoubtedly sinned, who was she to judge? He was no less deserving of this rite than the other more conventional candidates. His desire for absolution was genuine. As for the final destiny of his soul, that would be for God to decide.

Bogdan stopped by the edge of the river and dropped his robe. His seventy-year-old body was now naked except for a white loin cloth. He flinched as the icy water rose over knees tattooed with stars. He had once explained that these symbolised his refusal to kneel before authority. On the still strong arms two knives wrapped in chains told of two violent attacks behind bars. The bulls on the shoulders symbolised Bogdan's intent to challenge, successfully for gang leadership. He stepped out further, gritting his teeth as the water rose to his waist.

Bogdan stood before the priest and closed his eyes. The lids were tattooed with the words 'Don't wake'. This had been not only a message to other Gulag prisoners to not disturb his sleep, but also a demonstration of his ability to endure the pain of such a marking.

The priest placed his hand on Bogdan's head, plunged it under and made the sign of the cross. Bogdan came back up gasping and smiling. Whether his sins had been absolved or not, he seemed to believe they had. And perhaps that was all that mattered.

The silence was shattered by two cracks and Bogdan's forehead burst open.

The crowd screamed. Some ducked. Some ran.

The priest prayed.

Still wearing his beatific smile, Bogdan fell back into the water. His feet bobbed to the surface as his body drifted downstream. Bodyguards jumped in and wrestled him back to shore.

Olga darted forward. She was afraid of more shooting, but she had to help if she could. She walked through the bubble of bodies. Someone had put Bogdan in the recovery position. But she could see that was futile. Half his head was missing.

She turned away and retched. And again. She wiped her mouth and shook her head clear.

May God rest his soul.

52

'We have a problem,' Mickey told Uli on the intercom.

'I know. The share price has moved back up to one hundred and fifty dollars.'

'I think I know why. Can you come round?'

It took Uli a minute to make his way to Mickey's office. He did a double take when he saw the man standing in torn jeans and a hoody.

'This is Paul Myers of Myers Detective agency,' explained Mickey. 'The private detective I hired to follow Kazbegi.'

Uli and Paul shook hands.

'Show Uli what you showed me,' said Mickey.

Myers readied the mouse on his laptop. 'Kazbegi had lunch today at Claridge's with Lord Griffin.'

He clicked through photographs showing Kazbegi getting out of his limousine below flags fluttering over the Roman façade of Claridge's. Then through the window photos of him meeting another man already seated at a table.

They greeted each other and exchanged pleasantries.

'How did you manage to record the conversation?' asked Mickey.

Paul hit pause. 'A directional microphone through the window.' He hit play and the two men ordered drinks and talked cricket and rugby for a time.

'It starts slow,' said Paul apologetically.

Uli glanced at the time on the wall clock.

'It's worth it,' said Mickey.

The conversation drifted towards politics and Russia. Finally, the mood changed. Kazbegi lowered his voice and Paul turned up the volume.

'I'm going to need help from your contacts in Washington.'

Griffin's reply was inaudible.

'I need you to broker a deal,' continued Kazbegi. 'London and Washington can impose Magnitsky sanctions on me personally and I will cooperate. I'll sell the football club if I must. You can freeze my London property. So long as there are no sanctions on Kazbegi Holdings.'

'I think they might buy that,' said Griffin.

'It's in nobody's interest to sanction the company,' said Kazbegi. 'The world economy needs my metals. And if the company collapses thousands of jobs will be lost, including many in America and Britain. You'll find sympathetic ears if you talk in the right corridors in Washington.'

'I suspect this will take a lot more than sympathy.'

‘I also understand that your house in Appleby needs restoration,’ said Kazbegi. ‘My building arm is ready to do that. As part of our outreach to preserve English Heritage.’

‘I’m afraid this will cost more than repairing a duck moat,’ said Griffin.

‘Whatever it takes.’

The conversation then drifted away.

‘That’s all that is relevant,’ said Paul. ‘But the full recording is on this.’

He handed Mickey a memory stick.

‘Good work. Keep following him.’

Paul packed up his laptop and left the room.

Mickey turned to Uli. ‘My guess is that is why the share price has rallied. Kazbegi has been able to convince the market that even if he personally faces sanctions the company won’t. That he has it all under control.’

‘It’s difficult to know what to do,’ said Uli. ‘We could release this video. That’s incriminating.’

‘I’m not so sure,’ said Mickey. ‘All he’s doing is asking a favour and offering one in return.’

‘Should we close the short position?’ asked Uli.

Mickey looked up the share price. One hundred and fifty-one dollars. If they bought shares to give back to the stock lender at this price it would cost slightly more than the thirty million dollars they’d got in cash from selling them. They’d lose money. ‘Let’s keep it on for now. Let’s get legal advice on whether this idea of only sanctioning Kazbegi personally will fly.’

* * *

No gown and wig for Veronica this time. Just a suit and a warm smile. ‘How was your trip to Russia?’ she asked.

‘Very useful,’ replied Mickey. ‘Beautiful city, St Petersburg. You ever been?’

‘I’m afraid not.’ She glanced at her watch.

‘I’ll get straight to the point,’ said Mickey. ‘You probably know that the government are considering placing Ivan Kazbegi on the sanctions list.’

'Only what I've heard on the news.'

'Right. Thing is I've heard Kazbegi is trying to do a deal where the sanctions are placed just on him personally, but they don't apply to Kazbegi Holdings. Could that work?'

Veronica's eyebrows narrowed and she pursed her lips. 'It's not my area. But I imagine that in practice, sanctions on the man, or the company would amount to the same thing.'

'Why do you say that?' asked Mickey.

'Because most banks and corporations would still avoid any financial interaction with Kazbegi Holdings.'

'Why would they?' asked Mickey. 'It would still be legal to deal with the company.'

'You can't separate Kazbegi the man from Kazbegi Holdings the company. The Head of legal at the corporate would make a risk-based assessment and order them to stop any dealings with Kazbegi Holdings. Maybe not all. You'd still get some corporates prepared to deal with the company. But I'd be amazed if any financial institutions would take the risk.'

'Love it.' Mickey rubbed his hands.

'I take it your enthusiasm comes from humanitarian sympathy for the Ukrainians.'

It took a second to realise she was being sarcastic. 'I've finally figured Kazbegi out to be a wrong-un. And I want him to get what he deserves and not wriggle out of it.'

'That's all?'

He shrugged. 'I'm also trying to get back the money that was stolen from me. The police aren't going to help me, so I'm doing it my way.'

53

Bogdan's death had raised many questions to which Olga had no answers. She thought of putting a sign up on the door: I do not know why Bogdan was shot. I do not know who shot him. I do not know who is now in charge of the business.

Although on this last point she did at least have an idea.

Bogdan's silent partner. Presumably he, and of course it was he, was now calling the shots.

Another matter troubling her was that her friend and TruNews anchor Ekaterina Albats had not been seen for days. She was said to be on holiday. But she wasn't returning messages. She had become more outspoken against Pintov. Bogdan had allowed that and had probably been protecting her. The partner must be more behind Pintov, and that was another cause for concern.

Dragan had been behaving oddly too. He'd hardly been at work and when he was in the office, he mostly walked around the floor talking to people. She finally discovered the reason when he called her into his office one morning.

He sat leaning back in his chair with his feet on the desk.

'I am your new boss,' he announced. 'I have taken over management of TruNews.'

Olga took a moment to process this declaration. 'Who says?'

'The person who makes these decisions. Bogdan's partner.' Dragan pushed his chin out. 'Your job doesn't change. You are still in charge of this floor. Instead of Bogdan as your boss you now have me.'

Olga wasn't sure if she could work for Dragan, but for now she'd have to go along with it. 'Who killed Bogdan?'

'I don't know,' said Dragan, without any great conviction. 'Bogdan had a lot of enemies.'

'Where is Ekaterina?'

'She's on holiday,' Dragan said with a mischievous smile.

'Don't harm her.'

'I have no influence over that. What I do have influence over is the new reporting style. We all need to make sure we follow the rules more closely in future. Including your staff. We are all under suspicion.'

'Suspicion of what?'

'Disloyalty to Pintov.'

'Who is Bogdan's partner?'

'You're coming with me to meet him at a strelka.'

'I never have anything to do with that side of the business. I only ever work on cyber.'

'The boss demands your presence,' said Dragan.

'Why does he want me involved?'

'I don't know. But you should be honoured.'

Dragan took his feet off the table and stood up. 'Come.'

Reluctantly Olga followed him out to the car park where Bogdan's driver was waiting.

On the drive to the meeting Olga tried in vain to think of a reason to be excused. Not only were the people she was going to meet deeply unpleasant, it was also dangerous. She was scared. Her mouth was so dry. They drove in silence out of St Petersburg and into the countryside. After a time, they turned through an arched gateway at the entrance to an estate. Along the causeway they passed kennels and stables, a lake, and a Japanese pagoda.

They drove past the heavily fortified and moated estate house to a log cabin in the middle of a field. It was surrounded by the cars of earlier arrivals, parked facing outward in the event the meeting turned acrimonious, and people needed to make a fast exit.

At a security desk they were asked to show ID, but worryingly for Olga nobody was relieved of weapons. In the simply furnished meeting room a dozen large, suited men sat around a long table. Bodyguards stood behind.

At the head of the table sat Ivan Kazbegi.

* * *

Kazbegi called the meeting to order with a minute's silence for Bogdan. This was respectfully observed by all except the dogs barking in the kennels.

'We live in hard times,' Kazbegi said. 'The war, the unrest, the sanctions. These things are making business difficult for us all.'

Around the room shrugs and nodding heads suggested general agreement with the sentiment.

'If we fight each other,' continued Kazbegi, 'our problems will be even greater. Outsiders will come in and we will all lose out. I understand some things must change after Bogdan's death. They are already changing. But it is best if we do this by negotiation. Do you agree?'

All stared impassively. No one spoke.

'Of course, you agree,' continued Kazbegi. 'So let us make a start. Dragan, tell us your situation.'

Dragan sat up in his chair. He was half the age and girth of the others in the room. 'Already we have problems in our supply chains. The Chechens transporting our heroin along the Baikal-Amur railway have switched to supplying the Tambov.'

'They approached us,' shrugged a man with a shaven head crossed with scars.

'But now we can't supply our clients,' complained Dragan.

'We will supply them.'

'Our dealers need business,' said Dragan. 'They will fight to win it back.'

Scar-head shrugged.

'There is no need for this fighting,' said Kazbegi. 'Dragan, you should talk to the Chechens. Tell them your people are still in business. Tell them the Tambov are also now in this business. They can supply us both. There is room for us both.'

Dragan nodded.

Scar-head said nothing.

'What else?' Kazbegi asked Dragan.

'The Papov gang are pushing in on our fishing fleet,' he said, looking at a man with a blue nose and thin lips. Dragan turned back to face Kazbegi. 'Remember Kovalev, the sea captain with the glass eye?'

Kazbegi nodded.

'They tortured him.' Dragan turned back to the Papov man. 'Then they buried him alive.'

A hush settled round the room, though Olga also noticed a few smiles.

'Why torture him?' asked Kazbegi calmly. 'What did he know? He was just a fisherman.'

'To send a message,' said the Papov man.

'There is no need for this,' said Kazbegi. 'Talk to each other. Split the fleet. Let everyone know that it is settled. If not, the Brotherhood will join in.'

Papov man said nothing.

'What next, Dragan?'

'The Brotherhood are already a problem. They have taken over some of our trans-Siberian haulage. That has caused us problems in Vladivostok.'

'You see,' Kazbegi opened his hands. 'This is how we all lose out. But this is not a matter for this strelka. I will deal with the Brotherhood. I might let them have the haulage so long as they stay away from the fishing. That would be good for the Papovs as well. Do you agree?'

Finally, Papov man nodded.

'What next?'

'The Bridge gang killed two of our men and captured a timber truck.'

'Two men for a truck of timber?' said Kazbegi, looking sideways at a man with leathered skin on his face and hands suggesting many years in the sun. Olga suspected it resulted from hard labour rather than lounging by the sea.

'It's not the value. It's to send a message.'

'You are also sending messages,' said Kazbegi. 'What are these messages everyone is sending?'

The Bridge gang leader said nothing.

Kazbegi answered his own question. 'You think that without Bogdan I have no control in St Petersburg. You think I have gone soft living in London.'

'It's not about you going soft,' said Scar-head. 'It's the video and the threat of sanctions. You are under attack. You have your global businesses to be concerned about. Maybe this is a good time to take a little of your local activities.'

'These local businesses are my life blood,' said Kazbegi, his voice rising. 'They are what I grew up with. I will not let them go.' He drum-rolled his fingers on the table. 'As for the video and the legal threats. That is all being taken care of.'

The meeting continued along the same vein, with Dragan raising problems and Kazbegi suggesting solutions. Other gangs also took the opportunity to air grievances. Nobody signed any contracts. Agreements were ironed out verbally. And it was clear that in this company Kazbegi was the first among equals.

When the meeting ended the participants departed in silence.

Kazbegi signalled for his own people to stay seated. Olga had made no contribution and still had no idea why Kazbegi had insisted upon her attendance.

Kazbegi ordered champagne, insisting everyone took a glass.

When they were all filled, he raised his own towards Dragan. 'The king is dead. Long live the king.'

The comment was meant to suggest Dragan was the new king. Nobody looked convinced. Least of all Dragan. Kazbegi was the power on the throne. And Olga had become an unwilling courtier.

54

From the cathedral's double-tiered towers the bells tolled uninterrupted as Semyon Bogdan made his final journey. His hearse rolled slowly forward, leaving tread-lines in the fresh snow. Black limousines followed and behind them on foot, dozens of men carrying wreaths with inscriptions honouring Bogdan:

Forgive us, we could not protect you.

The greatest Vor.

Grandpa Bogdan.

'All these mafiosi gathered in one place,' said Papa. 'One small bomb could solve a lot of problems. Not just in St Petersburg. There are mobsters from Moscow and across Russia.'

'Hush, Papa.' Olga was still not sure she'd done the right thing in acceding to his wish to attend the funeral. He'd not been passed fit to fly and so they'd had to drive from Moscow. Seven hours plus stops for the nurse to administer drugs and fluids.

'Bogdan was different from these others,' he continued.

'Speak quietly, Papa.'

'He was a good man,' he said, barely lowering his voice. 'True to his word. He treated his wife well. And his mistresses.'

Olga didn't point out the contradiction. She pushed his wheelchair through the gates of the Nikolskoe cemetery and followed the crowd to a white mausoleum, where two columns stood either side of a bas relief doorway displaying a topless, tattooed Bogdan in front of three cupolas.

Crows clattered in the silver birch trees as the priest began the ceremony. Only the immediate family listened fully. Olga studied the assembly. Many of the gangs she had seen at the strelka were present, uniformly dressed in black and dark sunglasses.

A few metres to her side stood Kazbegi. She'd been instructed to keep her distance in public, though when she caught his gaze, he nodded slightly. He didn't appear unduly troubled by the death of his old friend. But in his line of work, he had probably become inured to death.

From a silver aspergillum the priest sprayed holy water among the crowd. Bogdan's eldest son gave a short eulogy then the pallbearers carried the coffin through the doorway and laid it to rest. They re-emerged and walked back towards the hearse. The gathering fell in step behind.

Olga's departure overlapped with that of Kazbegi. He paused to let her push through with the wheelchair.

Kazbegi leant down to acknowledge Papa. 'Your father, I presume.'

'He has come from hospital in Moscow to pay his respects.'

'That is very good of you.'

'Who murdered Bogdan?' Papa asked Kazbegi, in as loud a voice as his Parkinson's allowed.

'I don't know.' Kazbegi turned back to Papa. 'He had a lot of friends. But he also had enemies.'

'Was it you? Or Pintov?'

Kazbegi turned away as his goons moved between him and Papa.

'We're going.' Olga raised her hands then wheeled Papa away. 'Why did you do that?'

'He killed Bogdan. Or he allowed Pintov to kill him. It comes to the same thing.'

She stopped walking and looked at him quizzically. 'Do you realise that Kazbegi is a very dangerous man?'

'He is evil. You will read about him in my letter.' He handed over a supermarket carrier bag.

'What is it about?'

'You will see.'

They walked on in silence. Arriving at the car Olga helped the nurse get Papa into the front passenger seat.

'I'll come visit very soon,' she said, before kissing his forehead and shutting the door.

The car pulled away and she walked in the same direction. In her peripheral vision she became aware of eyes following her. She turned to see Beratov staring expressionless.

55

Olga was pleased to return to the warmth of her flat. She made a hot drink and retrieved Papa's letter from her bag. She kicked off her shoes and sat on the bed. With a mixture of curiosity and trepidation she turned to the first page.

My dearest Olga. My most fervent wish is that you will forgive me for the part I played in the story I am about to tell.

To fully understand why these events unfolded, you would need to have followed Russia from the birth of the Rus state, through the Mongol invasions, the empires of the Tsars, the revolution, the rise and fall of the Soviet Union. But it is not so important to understand why these things happened. It is enough to know that they did.

I start in early 1999. You will remember the poor life we lived at that time. I felt guilty at not being able to look after my darling daughter properly. I could not afford meat or to buy you new clothes for your birthday. But we were not the only people suffering. The market reforms introduced by the siloviki and the stupid alcoholic Yeltsin were reckless. They only brought poverty to ordinary Russians while a handful of oligarchs stole billions and grew obscenely rich. There was great disillusion with the President, made worse when the police investigated him for embezzlement. His popularity was rock bottom. Revolution was in the air. The regions were growing increasingly independent. There was a danger that the communists, who had already failed in one attempted coup, would regain control of the country. The communists would have reversed the process of capitalism in Russia. So, the Oligarchs and siloviki installed one of their own as Prime Minister. They chose Pintov. But Pintov was a grey and obscure bureaucrat who had no chance of beating Primakov and Luzhkov in the upcoming elections. They were desperate. Desperate times call for desperate measures. They devised a plan named 'Storm in Moscow'. I quote from the memorandum dated 29th June 1999. (A copy of the original is in the folder along with the other documentary evidence for what unfolds).

"The Administration of the President has drafted a broad plan for discrediting Mayor Luzhkov with the aid of provocations intended to destabilise the socio-psychological situation in Moscow. The conducting of loud terrorist acts is being planned in relation to government establishments: the buildings of the FSB, MVD, Council of Federation, Moscow City Court, Moscow Arbitration Court. Also foreseen is the kidnapping of several well-known people and ordinary citizens by Chechen rebels. A separate program will set organized crime groups in Moscow against one another. All of these measures, taken together, will implant in Muscovites a conviction that Luzhkov has lost control of the situation in the city. This will then allow the introduction of emergency rule and cancellation of elections."

I do not know who precisely devised the 'Storm in Moscow' plan. But the family clearly must have known the outline if not the details. By family I mean President Yeltsin, his daughter Tatyana Dyachenko, who was effectively running the country at the time, and her associates: Boris Berezovsky, Ivan Kazbegi, Valentin Yumashev, Aleksandr Voloshin. Others who must have known include Prime Minister Pintov, Chief of Presidential Administration Aleksandr Voloshin, General Aleksander Korzhakov. Whether Deputy head of the Russian Presidential Administration Segei Zverez was supposed to know about the plan or happened across it by chance is unclear. But he did show the plan to journalist Aleksandr Zhilin. Zhilin wrote about it on 22 July 1999 in Moskovskaya Pravda, but he was largely ignored by readers and colleagues because his claims were unthinkable. He showed the plan to Sergei Yastrzhembskii, the deputy premier of Moscow. He also did not believe it and the police and other authorities took no action.

A gust of wind crashed the window shut and broke Olga's concentration. She realised how tiring the day had been. She set the manuscript aside. It looked to be an account of the apartment bombings. She was shocked to learn that Papa had some involvement though it was no great surprise that Ivan Kazbegi was involved. He had been very close to Pintov back then. And she'd come to realise that he probably still was.

She suddenly remembered that Beratov had seen Papa hand over the carrier bag at the funeral. He'd looked suspicious. Yet why shouldn't she take something from her father? What business was it of Beratov's? But if the letter was all about Pintov and the apartment bombings it would not be good to be caught reading it. It needed to be put in the safe.

Not the dummy safe built into the wall containing rubles and cheap jewellery to fool burglars, but the real safe space she had created outside in the stairwell. She slid off the bed, picked up a knife and walked out into the corridor. She stood still for a while to make sure nobody was listening then removed the loose brick. The carrier bag fitted neatly into the cavity behind.

56

Declan turned off the unusually quiet George Washington Memorial Highway and passed through the main entrance security before continuing down the road to CIA headquarters. In the parking lot were top-of-the-range Teslas, a Lincoln Navigator, and a Cadillac Escalade. All a notch up on his old Chevy and the typical selection at the Hoover building. The stereotype of CIA agents being Ivy league wine-drinkers while G-men drank beer could benefit from an automobile addendum.

As he was seeing the Deputy Director of CIA Analysis, there were extra security checks, so by the time Declan arrived at Stotton's office he was uncharacteristically late. Stotton waved Declan in and motioned for him to take a seat while he pretended to finish off some paperwork. Playing power games.

Eventually he set down his pen and looked up. 'You wanted to see me?'

'Are you familiar with Olga Federova?' asked Declan.

'Never met her personally but I'm aware of who she is. Why are you interested in her?'

'She runs the cyber division at TruNews. There's a possibility she's losing faith with Pintov and might be willing to trade information that could be very helpful to us. You'll remember POTUS asking us to see if we could attack TruNews somehow. This could be the somehow.'

'How do you know this?' asked Stotton.

'She contacted Mickey Summer. You remember …'

'I know who Mickey Summer is. Have you seen the video he made about Ivan Kazbegi?'

'I've seen the video. It wasn't clear who made it.'

'Did you put him up to that?' asked Stotton. 'Because that's causing a lot of trouble up on the Hill.'

'I've got nothing to do with it.' Not strictly true but true enough to sound convincing.

Stotton folded his fingertips under his chin and pursed his lips. 'I am going to ask you straight, Declan. Is Mickey Summer working for you?'

'Absolutely not. Mickey contacted me because Olga Federova wants to trade information with American intelligence. I'm here to see if you're interested.'

'Why was Mickey Summer in Russia?'

'I do know that. He has been working for Crosshairs Investments in London. Running a Russian equity fund.'

'Olga Federova knows ways to contact us. Why has she asked Mickey Summer?'

Declan shrugged. 'I guess she trusts him.'

Stotton sniffed and tipped his head sideways. 'What does Mickey Summer hope to gain with this video?'

'If it was Mickey Summer who released it then I assume

Crosshairs Investments has found a trade that makes them money. Crosshairs lost a lot of money in the collapse of RSB. Or it could be they just want to see justice done.'

'Justice!' Stotton laughed. 'Some things are more important than justice.'

'Is that why none of us are looking into the collapse of RSB?' asked Declan. 'All following the same orders from people above playing realpolitik.'

'I don't know about people above. I'm following orders from POTUS.'

'But who is he taking advice from?'

'Don't start on that again.' Stotton stood up and turned to the window. He looked out over the car park. 'You really think a conspiracy like your Black Chamber theory could be kept hidden from all the thousands who work in Langley and at the Cube.'

'And the Pentagon,' added Declan. 'It's possible.'

'And even Spitz's enquiry hasn't convinced you otherwise.'

'He hasn't dug deep enough.'

Stotton shook his head, came back from the window, and sat back down. 'Back to Olga. What does she want?'

'She wants to know what information we have on the Russian apartment bombings. She believes there may have been collusion with the FSB.'

'That's entirely possible.'

'And Pintov knew about it.'

'Also possible. Why is she interested?'

'Her mother was killed in one of the bombs,' explained Declan. 'Olga could give us some valuable insights into TruNews and even the Kremlin.'

'I can imagine, but the files are category-one classified. So, we won't be sending her those anytime soon.'

'It might be enough for me to read them and just tell her what's in them. If we've got nothing to trade, we'll say so and maybe offer something else.'

'Such as?'

'Money? Exfil.'

'That's a better proposition,' said Stotton. 'Though I'd want to tread very carefully with Federova. She's unreliable.'

'First I need to read the files.'

'Azimov says nobody can read them right now.'

'Why not?'

'Doesn't want anyone touching the subject. Worried about what Pintov might do if it came up again. He's unstable. He might fire a nuke. Or worse.'

'If it's all smoke and no fire then what's the problem? If there's something more substantial, you can decide whether you want to trade with Olga for information she has.'

'As I said, that's not my call.'

'How about Director Charles? Technically he doesn't report to Azimov. It is his decision.'

'Azimov has seniority over Charles, even though there's no reporting line. You know that. Charles could go against that if he really had to. But he is in no mood to do you any favours.'

'I think we're missing a big opportunity here.'

'Perhaps. But there's nothing we can do.'

57

On the flight to Moscow Olga was idly checking emails when she found one that she could scarcely believe. A notification that her father had been discharged from the European Medical Centre and transferred to the Serbsky. There was no explanation. She hadn't been consulted. An administrator simply notified her after the fact. She shivered at the thought of her father incarcerated in the notorious Soviet-era psychiatric hospital.

She made sure she was the first to exit the plane and ran through the airport to the taxi rank.

'The Serbsky Centre,' she directed the driver. And then, just in case there had been some mistake, she rang the European Medical Centre to check.

She got through to the ward sister and asked, 'Is my father, Papov Federova, still in your care?'

'Your father was discharged yesterday,' she replied. 'He was transferred to the Serbsky.'

'Why? And why wasn't I consulted?'

'The move was made because the party paying for your father's treatment is no longer in a position to pay for it.'

'I know,' said Olga trying to keep the image of Bogdan's bloodied head out of her mind.

'Someone who worked for Semyon Bogdan came to move him. All the paperwork was in order.'

'Can you tell me the name of this employee?'

There was a short silence broken by displaced voices from others on the ward.

'Lieutenant Colonel Beratov,' the sister said finally. 'As I say, everything was in order. And I know the Serbsky has a bad name from Soviet days, but it's really a very fine hospital now. I'm sure your father will be in good hands.'

* * *

The Serbsky had been the KGB's residence of choice for dissidents. There they were drugged, tortured, and re-educated back to correct thinking. In modern times it was a psychiatric hospital but the fact that a dementia patient like her father could be sent there was evidence that it was still a tool of the state.

'I want to see Papov Federova,' Olga heard her own voice faltering. 'He is my father.'

The receptionist tapped on her keyboard. 'This will be possible. You have been given permission.'

'Who has given permission?' she asked, even though she knew the answer.

The receptionist looked at a screen. 'Lieutenant Colonel Beratov.'

Olga was instructed to wait on a plastic chair. After a time, a tall, heavy-set male nurse arrived and asked her to go with him. There was no attempt at conversation from either party as they made their way along windowless corridors.

They arrived at a heavy metal door. Olga peered through the glass slit. The room housed five metal beds with thin mattresses. Two occupants lay reading books, another sat on the bed looking out of the small, barred window. A fourth stood staring at the wall. On the bed in the far corner her father lay on his back with his hands over his face.

'I want to talk to him.'

'That won't be possible just now.'

She knew better than to argue.

'When?'

'When Lieutenant Colonel Beratov gives permission.'

'I want to speak to Beratov.'

'Good,' said a voice behind. She turned to see Beratov smirking. 'That is the idea.'

* * *

The nurse marched Olga into a sparsely furnished room with white walls and bright lights on the ceiling. A plastic jug of water and three glasses were laid out on a trolley in one corner. Once the door was shut the room became eerily silent. She suspected it was soundproof.

Beratov held out a hand. 'Your bag please.'

There was no point in refusing. She handed it over.

Beratov unzipped it and turned the contents on the floor. Cell phone, wipes, pen, notepad, lip balm, nail file, powder, wallet, and car keys. Beratov picked up the phone.

'Password,' he demanded.

She told him. It was pointless to resist. He flicked through the list of phone calls and messages but was evidently disappointed not to find whatever he was looking for.

'How long have you known Mickey Summer?' he asked.

'I met him for the first-time last week.'

'But you looked into his background before that.'

'As a security check, yes.'

'Summer was sent to Russia by Nikolai Mishkin. To cause trouble for Ivan Kazbegi. And you helped him.'

'I know nothing about that. He had lunch with Bogdan. I went along as an interpreter.'

'Afterward you had communication on social media, and you took him on a tour of Bogdan's illegal activities in St Petersburg.'

'I just showed him the sites. He had a plan to clean up TruNews. Stop the illegal activities. He wanted to show the video to Kazbegi and get him to persuade Bogdan.'

'Well instead he posted the video online.' Beratov shook his head. 'You helped him make a video that is proving to be very troublesome for Mister Kazbegi.'

Beratov produced a folder from an attaché case. From there he withdrew some photos. Pictures of Olga at the Strelka. He showed her them one at a time.

'Associating with criminals is an offence,' he said. 'If you don't co-operate with us, I will show these to the police.'

She said nothing. Now at least she knew why Kazbegi wanted her to attend the strelka.

'If you co-operate, I will also allow the doctors here to resume proton therapy treatment on your father.'

Olga hit replay. 'You stopped his treatment?'

'It is expensive. Bogdan was very generous. Kazbegi is less so.'

'Leave my father alone,' she shouted.

'Co-operate and everything will be fine.'

'I will co-operate. I have done nothing wrong.'

He showed her another photo. Her sitting in the car with Mickey Summer. 'This was taken in Moscow. Why did you take Mickey Summer to see the site of the Chechen apartment bombings?'

'He wanted to see where I grew up.' She knew it was pathetic.

'Is he planning on making a video about the apartment bombings?'

'I have no idea.' This she could say with conviction. 'Why would he?'

Beratov ignored the question. 'Your father attended revolutionary demonstrations before he became ill.'

Olga shrugged. 'He campaigned for opposition political parties if that is what you mean.'

'It is a crime to support banned anti-Russia activists. Your father should have been locked up in Serbsky a long time ago. He only escaped because Bogdan protected him.'

'This is a psychiatric hospital,' said Olga. 'My father has cancer and Parkinson's.'

'You share his anti-Russian feelings, don't you?'

'I am a patriot.'

'You are against the war in Ukraine.'

'I don't like to see young men die.'

'You are against the state and Pintov.'

She knew better than to admit that. 'I work for the state and Pintov.'

'Young people like you don't understand,' Beratov shouted, thrusting his head forward. 'In Soviet times the KGB ran the country and the economy. We could see that communism wasn't working. We were happy for it to come to an end. We wanted to move to a market economy. But Yeltsin, that useless, drunken, mid-ranking party official somehow got into power.' He started walking around the room, waving his arms as he spoke. 'Yeltsin started giving away businesses to his friends. People who'd done nothing to help their mother country before. Siloviki like Pintov had given their lives for Russia. They had served honestly and put their own lives at risk. They were getting nothing in return.'

'But they do now.'

Beratov walked back and stood close again. 'It's taken time. But now they have a fair reward for their hard work.'

'My father worked for the KGB, but he didn't become a siloviki criminal.'

'Your father lost his way.'

'After all he did for the state, he should be allowed to have his final years in peace.'

'We can both agree on that,' said Beratov. 'And it is in your power to make this happen. What did he give you at the funeral?'

'Nothing,' she answered weakly.

'I saw him hand you a carrier bag.'

'Just papers. Rubbish.'

'Well, we will find out.'

'You are boring me as usual, Beratov. Stop talking and do whatever it is you have planned.'

'Very well.' Beratov nodded to the guard.

He opened the door. In walked a woman dressed in white. She

pushed a trolley loaded with saw, scalpel, pliers, handcuffs, tape, and black cotton sacks.

Olga tried but failed to make eye contact.

Who was this woman? What was she going to do?

A man dragged a dental chair with straps for arms and legs.

He grabbed one of Olga's arms, and the male nurse gripped the other. They pushed Olga down into the chair.

'No!' she screamed.

But they over-powered her and strapped her arms. She kicked out as they grabbed her legs, but they too were restrained.

The woman filled a syringe with clear liquid.

'Don't do this,' Olga pleaded. 'We are sisters.'

The woman turned slowly. Still avoiding eye contact, she approached the chair. She found a vein in Olga's upturned arm and inserted the needle …

58

Various dignitaries and officials slipped in and out of the Oval Office as Declan sat outside, hoping for a no-show or for a shortened visit that would allow the Chief of Staff to grant him entry. His stomach was complaining about the lack of breakfast or lunch when a red-faced senator left early.

The Chief of Staff checked his watch. 'Two minutes, Declan. And they've already started.'

The President smiled as Declan entered the room. 'Take a seat.'

'I would but I've only been given two minutes.'

'Ignore him.' The President waved a hand dismissively. 'He got out of bed the wrong side. What do you want to see me about?'

'I'd like your approval to access files at Langley relating to the Russian apartment bombings.'

'That's a new one on me,' said the President. 'I haven't heard of any bombs on the Russian mainland. Drones yes. But not bombs.'

'It was way back.' Declan gave a potted history. He was near the end when the door opened.

'Time up, Declan. Your next appointment is waiting, Mr President.'

'Who is it?'

'Senator Martin.'

The President raised his eyes to the ceiling. 'Tell him five minutes.'

'Thank you,' said Declan trying not to smile at Senator Martin having to wait for him. One small victory.

'Why are you interested in this?' asked the President. 'Ancient history, surely?'

'It's resurfaced in the Hybrid Threat Group,' said Declan. 'I'm looking at a potentially very high value asset in Russia. One who might give us insight into TruNews, which I know is something you wanted action on.'

'I do.'

'But I need to verify their motivation. It's mixed up with the apartment bombings. They lost a relative and they have always wondered whether Pintov was to blame. Because this individual runs the underground activities of TruNews she is plugged into the Russian security apparatus. If I can establish it's true, we might be able to trade valuable info, including things that might let us hit back at TruNews.'

The President sat back in his chair and cradled his hands behind his head. 'What does Langley think?'

'Stotton says Asimov has locked the files away.'

'Why?'

'Apparently, it's too sensitive,' said Declan. 'If we bring it up it might add fuel to the fire in Russia.'

The President shrugged. 'Why would we care about adding fuel to the fire?'

'Asimov thinks it would look like we're pursuing regime change and it might get Pintov so mad he'd do something crazy.'

The President nodded. 'No harm in you looking though, surely. Have you asked Asimov for the files?'

'Have I asked Asimov if I can look into a conspiracy theory about the deep state in Russia?'

The President frowned then chuckled. 'Like your Black Chamber theory here, right?'

'Precisely.'

'Azimov thinks you are a conspiracy theory nut, doesn't he?'

'Correct.'

'Are you?' asked the President.

'I don't believe I am.'

The President rocked onto the back legs of his chair. 'Where are we on this Black Chamber?'

'Special Prosecutor Spitz is ready to press charges, I believe.'

'I haven't been given a heads up.'

'You don't need one,' explained Declan. 'He'll probably only indict one person for misleading intelligence. He didn't find evidence of any Black Chamber group.'

'You sound disappointed.' The President's eyebrows rose. 'That should be good news. Am I right?'

'If there is no Black Chamber, then yes that's good news,' said Declan evasively.

The President nodded and rocked his chair forward so all four legs were once again firmly planted. 'If I say yes to your request and you read the documents and you conclude that Pintov was involved, then what collateral damage might I expect?'

Declan had to think about it. 'I really can't say until I've seen it. But apparently the evidence is ambiguous. Nothing proven. I'm not sure anyone other than this asset really cares any longer. I don't understand what the sensitivity is.'

'Neither do I. You have my authorisation.'

59

The peace in Regent's Park was disturbed only by rhythmic raking from a solitary gardener, the foraging of a bird, and Beratov's own breathing. He reflected on the pleasant stage he had chosen for Mishkin's final act. In the distance the low winter sunlight reflected momentarily off some glassy surface. Possibly one of Mishkin's minders checking through binoculars.

The watchers must have satisfied themselves that Beratov had come alone, for a man now approached from the north entrance heading directly for him. As he drew near, Beratov recognised Mishkin's chief of security. He motioned for Beratov to stand, then frisked him thoroughly. Collars, coat lining, shoes included.

Satisfied, he spoke softly into a lapel microphone, 'Clear.'

Beratov sat back down. The chief stood over him.

In his peripheral vision Beratov saw Mishkin approach, flanked by two more guards. One took up a position on Beratov's right. The other sat on his left. Mishkin sat far left.

'Still social distancing, Nikolai?' asked Beratov.

'In present company, yes.'

'It is understandable,' replied Beratov. 'Given the history. But times have changed. That is what I have come to tell you.'

'Pintov has given me a pardon,' Mishkin said sarcastically.

'Not that. Never. But he is concerned for your wellbeing.'

Now Mishkin laughed, so hard it turned into a cough. When he'd regained control he asked, 'Why is that?'

'He does not want you to be assassinated,' said Beratov.

'For once we share the same sentiment. But why is he suddenly concerned for my wellbeing?'

'The British would assume the order came from him and he does not want to alienate the support he has in this country.'

'Support?'

'In some quarters,' Beratov qualified. 'You know that. Public opinion is growing tired of the war in Ukraine, and many want a peace settlement. So, as I say, your assassination would reflect poorly on him at a sensitive time.'

Mishkin fell silent and studied Beratov for a while.

'I still don't understand why you are telling me this?'

'There are rogue factions trying to kill you.'

'Rogue?'

'Beyond the control of Mr Pintov. He does not want them to succeed.'

'Tell Mr Pintov that I appreciate his concern, and I will continue to take great care.'

'You need to change your security staff. One of them is

against you.'

Mishkin exchanged glances with his security chief then turned back to Beratov. 'Who?'

Beratov smiled and pointed to the guards. 'It could be one of them.'

'Never,' said Mishkin. But his eyes betrayed his uncertainty and the guards shuffled nervously.

'We intercepted a phone call between this person and Kazbegi's people.'

Mishkin stroked his chin. 'What did they talk about?'

'Your security arrangements and your diary.'

'Do you have a name?'

Again, Beratov glanced at the guards. 'I can give you the phone number used. You can then investigate further.'

Mishkin nodded consent.

Wearing gloves lined with the impermeable membrane, Beratov reached into the jacket pocket for the paper that had been laced with Novichok. Hiding his writing under one hand he wrote down a number, folded the paper tightly so the number could not be seen and handed it over. Mishkin hesitated. Then curiosity got the better of him and he removed his thick gloves, unfolded the paper, glanced at the number, showed it to his security chief then placed the paper in his pocket.

Beratov, got to his feet.

A guard pushed him firmly back onto the bench. 'Stay seated until we tell you.'

'Of course,' replied Beratov, crossing his legs nonchalantly.

Mishkin grimaced in pain as he stood slowly, then limped away. Soon he would no longer be troubled by arthritis.

60

The needle was six inches long. The white witch was laughing as Olga strained at the straps. The injection flooded her body with heat. Suddenly the wall was crawling with thousands of insects. They jumped onto Olga, smothering her so that it became impossible to breathe …

She woke up and opened her eyes. Where was she? At home. It had been another nightmare. A flashback. Her heart pounded. She reached for the glass of water beside the bed and drained it. Some noise from the window caused her to jump in bed. It was just the shutter rattling in the wind.

She felt so angry. But at the same time helpless and lethargic. What had they done to her? What had she said? Olga was sure she had held on to three important truths. The first that she had not known that Mickey Summer would post his video online. The second, that the package her father had given her contained a letter asking her to forgive his time as an FSB agent. She strongly suspected it said more but fortunately that was as far as she had read so far, and she had been able to say it with conviction. Finally, that she had not been party to any anti-Pintov activity. Yet. Though recent events were causing a rethink on that front.

In any event she must have satisfied Beratov because he had eventually let her go, issuing an apology of sorts and signing her into a private room in a hospital while she recovered. He seemed to think everything would return to normal. She knew it would not.

Now, safely returned to her flat in St Petersburg, she discovered, to no great surprise that it had been searched. Not ransacked. But it was clear that every drawer and cupboard had been rifled through and the bed stripped. She was satisfied that they would have found nothing incriminating because what they had been searching for was not in the room. She retrieved it from behind the brick in the stairwell.

On the presumption Beratov had now installed cameras in her flat she took the manuscript out to the park. She walked around for a full hour before she was confident nobody had followed her. Then she bought a small bottle of vodka and found an empty bench on which to sit and read.

When the Russian people suffered the apartment bombings the resulting horror and fear galvanised us into a desire for revenge. Pintov rose to lead us in a just and glorious war against the Chechen perpetrators. Our patriotism for the mother country was

renewed. Internal political and economic strife were conveniently forgotten. Most importantly, the elections were cancelled.
Some thought it all too convenient. They questioned the official version of events. These people often met an untimely end.
Most ordinary Russians, including you my dearest, dismissed these conspiracy theories because our country was reborn with a strong leader who was tackling corruption among the oligarchs and was admired on the world stage. We wanted to look forward. Only now, as I approach the end of my days, am I ready to look back and tell you what I know. And what I did. And ask for your forgiveness.
The first bomb ripped through an apartment in Buynask, Dagestan on September 4th 1999. It was my fiftieth birthday. I had a beer with colleagues after work then hurried to pick you up from school. I had just set a cake on the table when the news broke on the television. I turned up the volume. Dozens, mostly family members of Russian servicemen, had been killed by a car bomb. Grainy black and white photographs conveyed the horror. I remember the children's toys in the mud. It reminded me of you, and I turned the television off. I did not want you exposed to this senseless inhumanity and, if truth be told, Dagestan is two thousand kilometres from Moscow. This appeared to be another tragedy in the years of war against the Chechen rebels.
Of events in Buyansk I have no insight. Perhaps that really was the work of Chechen terrorists. It is in Moscow where I know for certain that things were not as they seemed. I know because I was involved.
I was the FSB banker for the operation 'Storm in Moscow'. Remember I wrote above that this was the plan to discredit Mayor Luzhkov with bombings and other provocations intended to show he had lost control of Moscow. My first role in April and May 1999 was to transfer money to the Nevynnomyssk Chemical Combine to purchase six tons of 'material'. This was hexane. Four payments of different amounts so as not to attract attention. I was also told to transfer one million rubles into a private account belonging to the deputy regimental commander because his authorisation was needed for any purchases of hexane. I also

transferred six hundred thousand rubles to the personal account of Vladimir Romanovich, who had been recruited to run the operation in Moscow and St Petersburg. I had known Romanovich for many years. He was a criminal who had helped the Chechens rent premises in Moscow for money laundering, extortion, and other activities. I have copies of all these financial transactions as well as the home addresses of the Chechen field commanders with whom Romanovich had contact and their addresses in Moscow and Moscow Oblast. These and other documents are in the folder. The evidence. The facts. But let me continue with the story.

Olga set down the notes. She had known that Papa worked for the FSB, but he had always said it was in some administrative role. Financing Chechen terrorists was administrative. But that wasn't the sort she had in mind. As for this 'Storm in Moscow' plan, she had never heard of it before. It was unbelievable, but at the same time, why would he make this up? Why would he lie to Olga about events surrounding Mama's death?

She read on.

On the night of September 8th, I was working late in the ministry. Shortly after midnight, I heard sirens. I turned on my radio and listened to control call in a major incident in Guryanova Street. I immediately wondered whether this was the first of the incidents that had been planned. But they were not to involve citizens.

The plan had been to bomb buildings belonging to the military, FSB, MVD, Federation Council, City Court, war memorials. Something that real Chechen terrorists would do. But this was in a residential suburb southeast of Moscow and I couldn't recall any military or government targets in that area. As I drove home it became clear that an apartment building had blown up. When the first investigators declared it to be a gas explosion, I was relieved. A tragic accident. But nothing to do with our 'Storm in Moscow' operation.

But the next day, as the hours passed and pictures emerged of bodies in smoking rubble, investigators declared that this was also the work of Chechens. Not in some mountainous Caucus outpost, but in Moscow. Not servicemen but ordinary people; women and children among them. I did not know what to believe. I could only think of two possibilities. That it had been an accidental gas explosion which we were opportunistically pretending to be a Chechen bomb to suit the narrative. Or it had been an accidental explosion of Romanovich's bombs that he had been storing in the apartment for later use on legitimate targets.

I thought about calling Romanovich to ask him directly. He was an early adopter of Moscow's infant mobile phone network, believing that Lebyanka could not listen to calls on this new technology. But he was wrong, and I knew for sure that his phone was monitored continuously. I would land in trouble for breaching security if I called him. So, I did not.

This was a terrible mistake on my part. Because I might have been able to stop the greatest tragedy of your life.

Olga stopped reading. It was true then. She set aside the manuscript. But why was Papa telling her of his involvement? Did he not realise he was opening wounds worse than those she had just received in torture. Was he trying to absolve himself of responsibility by claiming that the storm in Moscow plan was supposed to only bomb military targets and not civilians? But was that any better? Pintov and the FSB targeting their own brave soldiers.

She wanted to read on. She must. It needed to be done. But it would be like opening a coffin to identify a corpse. She just didn't have the strength for that right now.

61

Mishkin wretched again but only air escaped. His stomach had been emptied already. He sat on the floor, back against the iron bath, foam seeping from his mouth, yellow eyes rolled up to the ceiling.

'Where is the ambulance?' Julia screamed down the phone, a moment before the doppler of a siren came through the open window.

'Nikolai!'

'The boat is too full!' Mishkin screamed.

'Nikolai, there is no boat. You are hallucinating.'

'Get off the boat!' screamed Mishkin, wide-eyed momentarily before collapsing again.

The siren stopped. Footsteps drummed along the pavement and then across the parquet hallway. A paramedic appeared at the door and walked over calmly.

He knelt in front of Mishkin. 'My name is Dan.'

Mishkin said nothing. His eyes remained closed.

'I'm here to help you,' continued Dan. He took his bag off his shoulders, set it open on the floor and pulled on surgical gloves. 'Are you in pain?'

Mishkin nodded.

'Where does it hurt?'

He opened his mouth to speak but said nothing.

'He said it hurt inside all over,' Julia offered.

'Has he been ill like this before?'

'No.'

'How long has he been like this?'

'He started feeling ill on Monday, but it's been getting worse every day.'

'I see,' said Dan, slipping a pulse oximeter over Mishkin's finger. 'Did he eat or drink anything unusual on Monday?'

'Not that I know.'

'Has he changed any medication or dosages?'

'No,' replied Julia. She produced a cardboard box containing his medications.

Dan glanced over the contents then turned back to Mishkin. 'What's your name, friend?'

'Nikolai,' answered Julia.

'Nikolai. Do you know what year it is?'

Mishkin nodded but said nothing.

'What is your date of birth?'

Mishkin didn't answer. Dan looked at the reading on the device and then went back to Julia.

'How long has he been taking Baclofen?'

'Since we moved to London. Ten years ago.'

'And you are sure he has not increased his dosage?'

'Yes, I'm sure. I give him the medication. I'm a qualified nurse.'

Dan set a stethoscope round his neck and placed a cuff on his arm to measure his blood pressure.

'What's wrong with him?' asked Julia.

'It could be a reaction to medication.' Dan turned his head to read the display and then read the oximeter again. 'Where did you move to London from?'

'Moscow.'

Dan's calm veneer vanished. He read the displays again and then moved back and got to his feet. 'Is your husband involved in Russian politics?'

'He campaigns for democracy and human rights.' Her mouth dropped. 'You think he has been poisoned?'

Mishkin grunted and nodded his head.

'Can I have a word in the next room?' asked Dan.

'I can't leave my husband.'

'Just for a moment.' Dan led Julia by the arm into the corridor. 'I'm going to call for some specialist equipment.'

'I understand.'

He pulled his lapel mic up to his mouth. 'Command. I have a suspected nerve agent attack. I need a hazmat response.'

'He's going to live, isn't he?' asked Julia.

Dan didn't answer.

62

Ambitious people get promoted upwards until they reach a height where the lack of oxygen starts to tell. They just about cope but everyone knows they are struggling. That was the point at which CIA Director John Charles had arrived, and he had visibly aged since he'd taken over as head of the agency.

He set aside some paperwork on his desk and looked up to face Declan. 'You want to see me about the Hybrid Threat Group?'

'Indirectly.'

Charles sighed. 'This isn't about Stotton again, is it?'

'We're good,' Declan replied. Good enough anyway.

'Glad to hear it. So how can I help?'

'I'd like access to the library files on the Russian apartment bombings.'

'They are classified Top Secret and Asimov ordered them locked up out of sight.'

'I thought you ran the agency,' said Declan mischievously.

'Asimov is Director of National Intelligence,' Charles said pointedly. 'Why do you want to read them?'

'I want to see if the KGB and Pintov had any involvement.'

'The evidence is circumstantial,' said Charles.

'You've looked at them?'

'I was Director of Analysis when Senator McCain brought it up. I had to look at it.'

'And what was your opinion?'

Charles shrugged. 'You read it one way and Pintov's people turned a blind eye to a Chechen bombing campaign because it fit the narrative. You read it another and of course they didn't. It's preposterous.'

'It's twenty-five years old,' said Declan. 'It would be declassified by now if there was nothing in it. There must be a reason it is Top Secret.'

'The test for assigning material a Top-Secret classification is whether its unauthorized disclosure could reasonably be expected to cause exceptionally grave damage to the national security. One example of exceptionally grave damage is armed hostilities against the United States or our allies. If we release something that speculates Pintov was behind the Russian apartment bombings, he is likely to go off the deep end. And that is just one of the sensitivities.'

'What are the others?' asked Declan.

'Chechen separatists might gain fresh traction with a claim that the war was started by a false flag operation.'

'Is that such a bad thing?'

'I use the term separatists generously,' said Charles. 'They don't just want independence from Russia. These are Islamic fundamentalists. And the entire Caucus region is a tinderbox. Light up the Chechens and it spreads to Dagestan, Ingushetia, Azerbaijan. In fact, why stop there? We could have an Islamic state across the whole of central Asia. To give some credit to Pintov, if it hadn't been for him that's probably what we would have already.'

'I understand, but I still want to take a look and form my own opinion.'

Charles shook his head. 'I can't overrule Azimov on this.'

'But the President can.' Declan set a letter down on the table as if laying an ace. He suppressed a smile. 'This letter grants me unrestricted access to all information concerning the Russian apartment bombings.'

Charles studied the signature before handing it back to Declan. 'You can see the files. But you're wasting your time on another conspiracy theory.'

* * *

A librarian sporting an Einstein hairdo appeared to be as excited by Declan's presence in the library as he would be discovering special relativity. 'When I started working here these rooms were full of people. You had to book a slot.'

He chuckled at the thought and led Declan through the empty room to a white monitor in the corner. 'Everything from the nineties has been copied to film.'

'I'd prefer to see the originals,' said Declan.

'Microfiche is best. The originals have faded over time.'

'It's just an old habit from my background as an investigator,' explained Declan. 'I like to see original evidence.'

He wasn't just going to be looking at the Russian apartment bombings. Down in the basement nobody would be looking over his shoulder.

'As you like.'

The librarian led him across the floor and down two flights of stairs to a room lit by luminescent strips. The lighting slowly improved as they walked along metal racks stuffed full of cardboard folders.

'The archives are sorted by year and then subject.'

'Can you get me files on the Russian apartment bombings, nineteen ninety-nine.'

Carefully, as if sifting through ancient parchments, he worked his way along a row and extracted a large cardboard folder and handed it to Declan. He pointed to the corner of the room. 'Table and chair over there.'

Declan carried the file over and set it down. 'Top Secret–Limited Official Use.' He turned to the Executive Summary.

In September 1999 a series of explosions in apartment blocks in Buinaksk, Moscow and Volgodonsk killed hundreds of civilians. The prevailing view holds that the bombings were perpetrated by separatists from the Caucasus as acts of retribution for Moscow's military campaign in the republics of Dagestan and Chechnya. Another view holds that the Russian Federal Security service was behind the bombings, or at least complicit, with the objective being to make Russians rally around the flag and boost the popularity of Pintov, the new prime minister.

He then zipped through countless Department of Defence briefings and intelligence reports on the situation in Chechnya prior to Pintov coming to power. These included a number from Russian intelligence itself. The Russian authorities blamed the apartment bombings on Chechen rebels and thereby galvanized popular support for a new war in Chechnya. Pintov, the former head of the FSB, had just been named prime minister and achieved overnight popularity by vowing revenge against those who had murdered innocent civilians. He assumed control of the war and, on the strength of initial successes, was elected president.

But there were also reports and articles claiming FSB complicity. The evidence was mostly circumstantial except for two bizarre incidents that were difficult to explain any other way.

The first occurred in the town of Ryazan on September 24, 1999. Local police caught two FSB agents planting bombs in the basement of an apartment block. The then head of the FSB, Nikolai Patrushev, claimed that it was an exercise to test the readiness of the local police to prevent a real terrorist incident.

The second was an announcement by Gennady Seleznev, the speaker of the Duma and a close associate of Pintov. On September 13 on the floor of the Duma he announced the bombing in Volgodonsk. But this was three days before it happened on September 16.

On September 17 Vladimir Zhirinovsky, the Leader of the Liberal Democratic party, demanded an explanation of how Seleznev had known about the bombing in advance. But Seleznev avoided responding and Zhirinovsky had his microphone turned off when he persisted in demanding an explanation.

Declan read a transcript, obtained by CIA Moscow station, of precisely what Seleznev had said on September 13. "Here is a communication which they transmit. According to a report from Rostov-on-Don today, this past night, an apartment house was blown up in the city of Volgodonsk."

Declan read further and discovered that Russian human-rights defenders Sergei Yushenkov, Yuri Shchekochikhin, Anna Politkovskaya, and Alexander Litvinenko had all campaigned to shed light on the apartment bombings. But all of them were murdered. Two motions in the Duma to investigate the Ryazan incident failed in the face of opposition from the pro-Pintov Unity party.

It was fascinating. If true it was a cynically cruel early version of the Gerasimov Doctrine, before the general had coined the term. A false flag operation involving the murder of hundreds of Russian civilians coupled with manipulation of the domestic information space and assassination of political opponents who called out the crime for what it was. However, it was all pretty much as Director Charles had said. Smoke but no fire. The dim yellow light was worsening Declan's headache. He needed a change of scene. A change of conspiracy.

He returned to the filing racks and found the files on the Black Chamber that he had read during his last visit. He flicked through the first folder containing Defence Department briefings on the situation in Iraq before the invasion. Then those briefings suggesting Saddam Hussein possessed WMD. The claims from the defector Harith about mobile weapons labs. The engineer al-Haderia who said he'd been working on nuclear weapon storage. But the lie that was most interesting and the one he planned on slapping right down in front of Spitz was the claim from Biggerstaff that he'd seen a memorandum of understanding between the governments of Niger and Iraq over the supply of uranium. No such memorandum was ever uncovered. No evidence surfaced that uranium had ever been shipped. Declan knew it was fabricated.

But he couldn't find Biggerstaff's memo. He licked his fingers and carefully separated each piece of paper in the folder, laying them down in a paper mosaic on the carpet. If the librarian came now, it would be difficult to explain what he was doing.

He flicked through the rest of the files. Biggerstaff's memo was nowhere to be found. Something else was also missing. Asimov's presentation on P20G. This was the group set up by Donald Rumsfeld in the 1990s to bring together CIA and military covert action. There had not been any explanation why this document had been included in the Black Chamber file. But it seemed obvious that whoever had collated the files on the Black Chamber suspected it was related to P20G. And by extension to Azimov. That presentation was the smoking gun.

Someone had removed both Biggerstaff's memo and Azimov's presentation. It could only have been a member of the Black Chamber sanitising the files before Spitz got to examine them.

Declan put the files back in order and returned the crate to the shelf. He walked through the basement and up the stairs into the reference section. He wanted to scratch an itch about Pintov.

He sat down at the microfiche desk. He scrolled through a sea of slides, reading any articles he could find about Pintov's KGB career. He had been an atypical recruit. One of the so-called 'cohort of outsiders' that Yuri Andropov had recruited to bring fresh blood and critical thinking into the KGB. Pintov claimed that the new intake like him were able to question the direction of the USSR and see the incurable illness that eventually killed it. They permitted themselves to think differently.

Declan wanted to understand what Pintov had done in the KGB. In 1985 he was posted to Dresden in East Germany, seemingly an intelligence backwater, where he did unglamorous administrative spy-craft. He found copies of the West German authorities' analysis that the East German Stasi had funded and trained the far-left Red Army Faction as well as other terrorist organisations. All this happened when Pintov was stationed in Dresden, and analysis at the time, by the CIA station in Berlin, said the gang regularly met the KGB in Dresden. Pintov's name was not mentioned because he was an unknown then. But it seemed highly likely to Declan that Pintov was running this operation. If true, he had form in bombing innocent civilians in the pursuit of political ambition, and this was yet another example of the Gerasimov Doctrine.

Then it hit Declan. It was Pintov who ran KGB activities in Dresden. Pintov who recruited Gerasimov and moulded his thinking. The Gerasimov Doctrine was really the Pintov Doctrine. And if it were true that Pintov masterminded the Russian apartment bombings it was the evilest example of his doctrine.

He walked back out to reception. The librarian was still there. 'Found what you were looking for?'

'I didn't,' said Declan, knowing that would be reported back to someone. 'Just wasted five hours on a wild-goose chase.'

The librarian smiled. 'You have a good evening now.'

Back in the car Declan composed a message for Mickey to send to Olga.

I have read through the files on the Russian apartment bombings. The evidence that Pintov and the FSB were complicit is only circumstantial. I have no information to trade. But I would still like to talk to your friend about her workplace and we may be able to offer a reward of some sort for information on that. As for the bombings though there is no interest here in pursuing that story any further.

He then checked his messages and emails. One stood out. He'd been called for a vetting meeting. Routine. Just the usual biennial check to see if an agent remained fit for service. Except he'd had one only eighteen months previously. It wasn't routine.

63

'*... no interest here in pursuing that story any further.*' Olga couldn't believe the message from Mickey Summer. She stood up from her desk and shouted, 'Why not?'

She ran to the door then realised she couldn't go out on the floor feeling so desperate. She walked back and slumped down at her desk. Why are the Americans not interested? Was it because, like Papa, they knew the truth long ago.

Dmitri knocked on the door and opened a small gap. 'Are you okay?'

'Yes, of course.'

'I heard you shouting.'

'It was nothing.'

He took a step inside the office and closed the door behind him. 'You've seemed very agitated the last couple of days. Is it because of Bogdan's death?'

I've been tortured. You'd be a little out of sorts if you had been tortured. 'Yes. I've not been sleeping. I'm going to take the rest of the day off.'

'Good idea.'

She could sense all eyes looking at her as she hurried across the floor. Even on the underground it seemed that people were staring at her. She was relieved to arrive home. There she took the papers from the safe in the wall and walked to the park. This time she did counter surveillance for only thirty minutes before she sat on a bench. She braced then took the plunge.

When I woke on the morning of September 13th the news on the radio was of the third bomb. I heard it was a building on Kashirskoye Highway and feared the worst. I rang Mama and there was no answer. When I put down the phone it rang immediately, and I thought she had rung back. But it was Aunt Mila. She screamed that it was our building that had been blown up and she had not been able to reach Mama. She was hysterical. For some reason you woke up early and seemed to understand what had happened. I didn't want you to come but you insisted, and I was frightened to leave you alone. When we arrived at the apartment block and saw the smoke-filled hole in the middle where our flat had been I immediately feared Mama was dead. I wanted to join the firemen looking for survivors in the rubble, but they would not let me. So, we stood watching all day. Checking the faces of the injured. Praying that she was not one of the dead in the zipped bags. We didn't know that her body had been one of the first to be carried away.

Olga's eyes were too full to be able to read further. She folded the manuscript, stuffed it back in its envelope and walked around the park, trying to take comfort from watching other people, the birds, dogs, flowers, trees, anything living. Eventually, she had calmed down enough to return to the bench, and Papa's story.

After the bomb in Kashirskoye, Moscow was in a state of total panic. Residents searched storerooms for bombs. Some fled the city. But the next bomb did not come in Moscow. It was in Volgodonsk on September 16th. Whoever planted this, and it was not my man Romanovich, had used so much hexogen that it blew a crater fifteen metres in diameter. It was a miracle that only nineteen people died. Again, of course, it was blamed on the Chechans. But not everybody was convinced.

Newspapers speculated about FSB involvement. They now knew about 'Storm in Moscow', the plan to create conditions to avoid elections. Also, there was suspicion over why these bombings were happening undetected. Obshchaya Gazeta reported that Duma deputy Konstantin Borovoi had been tipped off by a GRU officer on the morning of the Guryanov street bombing and he had passed this on to the authorities. But those authorities dismissed it as rumour. People were asking why they had not evacuated the street instead?

But the most incriminating evidence that we, the FSB, knew that a bombing campaign was underway came three days before that bomb in Vologodonsk when the fool Seleznev spoke about it in the Duma. Three days before it blew! On the 17th at a plenary session of the Duma, Vladimir Zhirinovski, leader of the Liberal Democratic Party, challenged Seleznev to explain how he knew about the bomb three days before it occurred. Journalists were also asking the same question. Seleznev did not offer any explanation. Only silence.

About this time, I heard that some of the family, particularly Yeltsin's daughter Tatyana, had got cold feet with the high number of fatalities. As I said, the original plan had been to blow up military and civic buildings. But somehow, we had been tricked. I expected an order to instruct Romanovich to abort the remainder of his mission. But no order came. I knew that his next bomb was planned for the night of Friday 17th to September 18th somewhere in the Northern Administrative district of Moscow. I passed this information anonymously to the newspaper Moskovskii Komsomolets. They informed law-enforcement, and the municipal authorities undertook an immediate search of basements and attics in the area. On Friday at 1pm sacks containing hexogen were discovered at Butyrskii Val only hours before they were set to detonate. I don't know how many lives I saved by doing this, but the apartment contained nearly one thousand people. If only I had been able to stop the bomb in Kashirskoye and save Mama.

Papa was trying to portray himself as some sort of hero. That was not right. And it was making her angry. He had financed the bomb that killed Mama. Romanovich murdered her. But Papa was complicit.

Romanovich remained at large and undiscovered, but then Moscow police interviewed the businessman who rented out the Guryanov apartment to Romanovich. From him they compiled a composite photo, and it was clearly Romanovich. I have a copy of the original photo and you can see the high-forehead, sharp nose and piercing intellectual eyes. But we were able to convince the police that the photo was of a man named Mukhid Laipanov from Karachaevo-Cherkesiya. They hunted for him instead. It seemed that, despite all the mistakes and leaks, we had successfully covered our tracks. But then the Ryazan incident occurred.

Shortly after 9 pm on September 22nd, two residents of an apartment on Novoselov Street in the city of Ryazan suspected three individuals leaving the basement of the building. Two young men and a woman driving a white Zhiguli. Police arrived and discovered three sacks and an electro-detonator consisting of batteries, electric watches, and a twelve-calibre shotgun shell. The building was evacuated, and residents of neighbouring buildings fled their homes. Thirty thousand people spent the night on the street. Bomb squad officer Yuri Tkachenko disarmed the detonator which had been timed to go off at 5.30 am. His portable gas analyser got a positive reading for hexogen. Local FSB officers took the sacks away and the best possible outcome looked to have been achieved. The terror level had been raised, allowing Pintov to impose emergency law and cancel elections, yet this time nobody had died. But things began to unravel very quickly.

Composite photos issued by the local police clearly showed the three suspects were not Chechens but Russian. The white car was found abandoned. A short time later a call to Moscow was made from a telephone bureau for intercity calls, and the operator who connected the calls stayed on the line long enough to catch some of the conversation. 'There is no way to get out of the town undetected.' 'Split up and each of you make your own way out.' The operator reported the call to the police who traced the number and discovered it was to an FSB number in Moscow. Then two of the suspects were caught and identified as FSB agents.

And so, a most elaborate story was devised. That the FSB had been testing the readiness of the police and locals in Ryazan with a training exercise. Rice had been in the sacks not hexogen. The detonators were not real. The sapper who defused the bomb had been confused. (In the folder is a copy of the original police report stating the contents were hexogen mixed with TNT, and flammables including potassium nitrate, sulphur, and sugar).

It was a fairytale that few believed. But the idea that elements in the FSB had been prepared to blow up ordinary citizens was even more unbelievable. But it really should not be so hard to imagine these events taking place. During the Cold War the KGB regularly used terrorism in its fight against America. We stoked anti-Israeli and anti-American sentiment in the Arab world. We got our Stasi friends to open terrorist training camps in East Germany and across the Middle East.

We clapped when a bomb went off in La Belle discotheque in West Berlin and when the Red Army faction bombed and kidnapped and assassinated. And who was the KGB man in Dresden in those times?

None other than Pintov.

That was the environment he was working in. So, I say again, it should not surprise anyone that he would use the same tactics in Russia when his new citadel of power was under threat.

It worked. The elections were cancelled because the country was once again at war in Chechnya. Pintov grew in popularity. Few cared about the truth. Many, not just in Russia, had reason to keep it secret. It's time the truth was known. At least by you. I am sorry it has taken me so long. Please forgive me.

I love you with all my heart,

Papa.

Olga walked back, still processing what she'd discovered. The apartment bombings had been staged by Pintov and the FSB. She was now sure of that. But her own father had played a part in the murder. Had he really known nothing about the bomb in Kashirskoye that killed Mama? Was it just good fortune that he'd taken her to stay with him that night and so she had survived while Mama had died? Too many questions.

Once home she placed the manuscript in the brickwork under the stairs. She wasn't sure what to do with it. Mickey Summer had made it clear that American and British intelligence were not interested. She wanted to publish it, but she would meet the same fate as the others unless she left the country. Yet that would be difficult without a passport. She needed help. One candidate sprung to mind. And he owed her a huge debt.

64

Helen had gone to bed early so Mickey sipped a beer as he looked at the scan on his phone. It wasn't much to look at. More of a blob than a baby. But it was apparently implanted well and had a cardiac pulse. Not a fully formed heart yet, they'd said, but a pulse. And Helen's blood pressure was under control.

The only problem was that they still didn't have the money to buy the Marshall's house. The Kazbegi Holdings share price refused to fall. They could cut their losses and turn back to the recovery fund idea. But after what he'd learnt in Russia, he was no longer sure there would be any recovery.

There was only one other way he could think of to make a fast fortune. He scrolled through some racing odds. Desert Storm was eleven to two in the race at Haydock. But once bitten twice shy. He turned to the football. The Hammers were odds on to go down. But it was hopeless. He was never going to win big enough to buy a house. He needed the Kazbegi Holdings trade to come good. He needed him to face sanctions.

He checked his messages. There were a number about the Hammer's odds that he chose to ignore. There were also birthday wishes on Helen's family group chat for her aunt. He posted a picture of a birthday cake. It was the best he could do.

Then a message came in from Olga. Probably still annoyed that he'd not been able to give her anything on the apartment bombings. But no. This was something else.

Remember the tour of St Petersburg I gave you? You never told me you were going to post the video on the internet. I got into a lot of trouble helping you with that. But I have more content for you if you want it. Better material. More damaging for the subject. But for several reasons, I need to urgently leave the country. But I have no passport. I need help from your friends. Also, do you remember that rumour I asked you to investigate? And you said there was no interest in pursuing the story further. Well, now I have very good information to show that it is true. I will bring that with me. Maybe your friends will want that. Either way you owe me. Get me out. Please hurry. My life is in danger.

65

Mickey was thinking of getting another half when Frank finally appeared in the light of the doorway, peered into the gloom, and gave him a thumbs-up. He stepped lightly across the wooden floor and hung his raincoat on the back of the chair.

'How are you?'

'Mixed,' replied Mickey. 'Helen's expecting. Though I'm not

supposed to tell anyone. So that's the good news. The bad news is the video on Kazbegi Holdings isn't bringing down the share price. The market still doesn't expect sanctions.'

'Is that what you wanted to see me about?'

'No.' Mickey couldn't put his finger on why, but Frank looked different. Then it clicked. 'You've dyed your Barnet!'

'The missus instructions,' explained Frank, flushing slightly. 'She thinks it will help with promotion prospects. Looking younger.'

'Do you want promotion?'

'Not really,' Frank replied, with a shrug of the shoulders. 'So, what is it that's so urgent I had to skip my training run?'

'Olga Federova. She wants to defect. Her life is in danger and it's urgent.'

'She told you this?' asked Frank.

He showed Frank Olga's message. 'Because of her work she doesn't have a passport. She'll need to cross illegally. She needs help from you boys at MI6.'

'SIS,' Frank corrected. 'I can pass that information on to Jones. Not sure if anything will happen. He didn't seem interested in her before.'

'Can't you go through someone else?'

'It would come to his attention whoever I went through. But these things take time to put in place. If it really is urgent, she might be better off trying her luck at crossing without a passport.'

'Come on, Frank. You can do better than that.'

'I work for domestic intelligence. I've got as much idea of what to do as you do.'

'I can do foreign exchange,' said Mickey. 'But not exchange of foreigners.'

Mickey set his glass down. He studied Frank for a moment. 'Maybe I will do it myself. Seem to have to do everything that way.'

'Why are you even considering this, Mickey?'

'First, she says she's got more dirt on Kazbegi. If she has that will strengthen the case for him to face sanctions. Second, I owe her. She helped me make the video. She didn't know I was going to go public with it. I didn't know myself at the time. And it's the video that has got her into trouble.'

Frank said nothing. A silence settled. It seemed to spread through the whole bar.

'So that's why I have to go,' he said eventually, now resolved to do it.

'How?' asked Frank. 'I doubt the Russians will let you back into the country after the video.'

'Haven't thought it through yet.' Mickey leant back in his chair. 'Smuggle myself in somehow and smuggle her out in the boot of a car?'

'You can't be serious, Mickey. It's way too risky. And while we're talking of risks, there is something you should know. It's Nikolai Mishkin.'

'What about him?'

'He's dead. Poisoned. Novichok probably. We're trying to keep it out of the press, but we can't do that for much longer. Semyon Bogdan was also killed.'

'Bogdan? That might explain why Olga needs to get out of the country. I think we must help.'

'I'll mention it to Jones, but don't hold your breath.' Frank checked his watch. 'I need to get going. I've got a call at six.'

'Wait. If I do go – and I'm not saying I will, but if I do – can you give me some help? Unofficially. As a mate. Not as someone from MI5. Some people to get in touch with.'

'I should be able to do that for you.'

'Thanks.' Mickey took a deep breath. He could feel himself getting dragged into this madcap idea against his better judgement. But he did owe her, and she had the information he needed to smash the Kazbegi Holdings share price.

66

The biennial vetting review meetings were sold as friendly fireside chats for the employee's wellbeing. But Declan knew otherwise. They were designed to send a percentage of the workforce home. To demonstrate that processes were in place to weed out crackpots and crackheads. It was for the benefit of the establishment, not the employees.

He braced before the door. Whoever was behind it would have a truckload of intelligence on him. His phone calls, emails, medical and financial records, social media exchanges, internet searches. The whole package. Probably knew more about Declan than he did himself. But he wasn't going to be caught out. He was going to play the smart game. No smiles. Short answers. Give nothing. Leave no openings. Like the professional cons he used to interview.

Deep breath. He knocked.

'Come in!'

It was a woman. That was good and bad. Good because he was much less likely to get annoyed by over-intrusive questions. Bad, because they were generally better at this game than men.

'Hi, Declan, please take a seat. My name is Jacinda.'

First names. Cosy. Surnames would have been a red flag.

'Thanks.' He relaxed into a non-confrontational position.

'So, Declan. This is just a standard vetting review so nothing to worry about …'

'It's five months early,' Declan interrupted, and immediately regretted it.

'That's right. A couple of things have been highlighted so we want to make sure you're OK.'

'No problem,' he said as convincingly as possible.

'Declan, I know you're struggling financially. We can do a lot to help employees on that front. So, let's go through things.'

Declan looked away. He'd not been expecting this.

'Declan?' She waited for him to regain eye contact. 'I'm here to help. So, on your credit card we can see that your repayments are greater than your income and the debt is rising. We can pay off this debt and you pay it back at no interest through your wages over time. Would that be of interest to you?'

Was this a trick to tie him down? Make him more obedient. 'Could be.'

'Good. I'll arrange for you to see someone in Finance.'

She made a note on a pad. 'You see, we've made progress already.'

'What other things have been highlighted?' asked Declan.

'The Black Chamber.' She raised her eyebrows as if she expected some response.

'What about it?'

She looked down at her notes. 'You seem to be very personally invested in the enquiry.'

'I uncovered the Black Chamber. It was my investigation.'

'Tell me about it.'

No way. Might as well go and hang himself as start talking about something she presumably had been briefed was a conspiracy theory. 'Special Prosecutor Spitz has taken over the investigation. I'm no longer in the loop.'

'What is the Black Chamber?' she pressed.

Careful. 'We won't know until Spitz concludes his enquiry.'

'Can you tell me what you think it is?'

She wasn't going to let it go. 'It's possible that there is a deep state group of people in the CIA, the Pentagon and the Capitol that have a more right-wing view of the world than the typically elected President.'

'Is that a problem?' she asked. 'There are views held left and right of POTUS. That's what happens in a democracy.'

'The problem is only if this group manipulate and fabricate to influence the President's decision-making towards their world view.'

'Such as?'

He knew he was slipping down the slope, but he suddenly didn't care. 'Such as fabricating evidence that Saddam Hussein had weapons of mass destruction, and so influencing President Bush to go to war.'

'A war in which your brother died?'

She'd done her homework. But it felt intrusive. His brother had come home in a coffin. Never shot baskets with him again. Never drove him to the lake to skim stones again. Josh was none of her business. But he couldn't say that. 'Correct.'

'So, you are personally invested. As I suggested.'

Declan didn't answer.

She sat back in her chair. 'I guess your brother's death was difficult for you.'

Bat back. 'We were close.'

'Do you want to talk about it?'

Duck. 'I'm good, thanks.'

She smiled and withdrew her incisors. 'I see you have a prescription for Ambien. Are you having trouble sleeping?'

Why else would I be taking sleeping pills? 'That's right.'

'Why do you think you're having trouble?'

'Stress I guess.'

'What's bringing about the stress?'

'The money situation you mentioned. So, your plan should fix that. Thanks.'

'Is work also causing you stress?'

'I enjoy my work,' said Declan with some conviction.

'Even so, it can be hard to switch off. What do you do in your downtime?'

Declan thought through the last few weeks but couldn't remember anything. It had been work and sleep, or try to sleep. Repeat. He used to run. Used to watch football and baseball games. Go out for the occasional beer and shoot pool. He hadn't done any of that in months.

'What do you do in your downtime?' Jacinda repeated.

'I play a lot of sport.' Instinctively he pulled in his paunch.

She'd noticed but didn't comment. 'You do a very demanding job, Declan. Unless you have a way to switch off your brain becomes tired. Stressed.'

'I guess.'

'Can you remember any traumatic events you might have had?'

'Like when?'

Jacinda shrugged gently. 'Ever.'

'My brother's death was the most traumatic event.' And the injustice of losing him still burnt. And that's why he'd joined the Bureau. To fight for justice. 'He was my best friend as well as my brother.'

'That must have been very hard. Did you talk about it to anyone?'

Such as? Dad was AWOL. Mom couldn't talk about Josh. He

wasn't sure he wanted to talk about it to anyone even if there had been someone prepared to listen. What was there to say? 'Not really.'

'You know, people deal with traumatic experiences in different ways. Some scream and shout. Some cry. But eventually most people need to talk about it. That way the brain can process it all. People who are not able to do that will lock it away. It doesn't heal. It can develop into stress disorder.'

'Are you suggesting I have PTSD?' Declan bit his lip. Why had he offered that up? Tossed it up for her to smash out for a home run.

'It's a possibility. A psychiatrist would have to diagnose it after an in-depth assessment of your mental health. I think we should arrange an appointment. Do you agree?'

As if he had any choice. 'Might help.'

She jotted down another note in her pad, then turned the pages in his file and stopped at a sheet that she examined briefly. 'You haven't taken a holiday in a while.'

'I plan to,' he lied. 'Soon as I tidy up a few things.'

'Is the Black Chamber one of those things you want to get tidied up?'

'Like I said, that's all Spitz now.'

Jacinda let the silence hang. Just stared at him. Reading his mind. 'You need to let it go, Declan.'

'I have.'

'You need to take a holiday.'

'I will.'

'I'll need to see that booked into the diary before I pass you fit for work.'

67

Here he was again, doing things his way because the authorities were too wrapped up in bureaucracy and internal debate to do what was so clearly right. Having said that, Frank had managed to get the contact details of some Estonian smugglers. Mickey had to pay them ten thousand dollars upfront. Obviously, he'd had to tell

Helen that he was going back to Russia to tie up some loose ends. He didn't tell her he was smuggling into the country.

He did not fly direct to Estonia. After years of Soviet occupation, and more recently the invasion of Ukraine, most Estonians were wise to the reality that their easterly neighbour was not a friend. But with a quarter of the population native Russians, a good number of Russophiles remained to keep an eye out for suspicious arrivals in the country. Which is why Frank had suggested Mickey fly into Helsinki.

At the airport he hired an SUV and drove down to the harbour. At a canopy kiosk he got a coffee and a traditional multi-grain porridge. It was out of season but nevertheless the shoreline seemed strangely silent. Even the birds appeared to be holding their breath in expectation.

Along with hundreds of day trippers and tourists he boarded a ferry to Tallinn. He found a tourist guide for the Estonian capital abandoned at the bar. He took it to a comfy chair and flicked through the pictures. But he found himself drifting off, so set a thirty-minute alarm and had a snooze.

When he woke the room was shaking violently. The engines were in reverse, dragging the boat to the dockside. He returned to his car and entered Permisküla Puhkeküla into the sat nav.

As he drove through the capital the traffic seemed to make way for him. The highway southeast was empty and similarly wanted to hurry him along into the sparsely populated border region where the road became bound by trees, with no turn-offs to the side and home again. He was being drawn relentlessly forward.

After four uncertain hours he pulled into a holiday park with assorted wooden bivouac constructions. He was the only guest. The resort manager checked him into his room then left for home.

Mickey turned the heating up, lay on the bed, and waited.

Dusk fell. Birds crooned.

Finally, an engine approached. Heavy wheels crunched on gravel. A knock on his door.

Mickey opened it slowly.

A heavily bearded man stood in a baggy jumper and loose

jeans. He smelt of dog.

'Your passport,' he snarled.

Mickey wouldn't ordinarily give this man a virus, but he had to trust him. He handed it over and Beardie flicked a torch between it and Mickey. Satisfied, he handed it back and led Mickey to the lorry. He helped him up into the cabin where a large dog snarled and bared its teeth. He was on a short chain but not short enough for Mickey's liking. He settled down in the leather seats as far from the dog as possible.

Beardie pressed a catch, and an overhead locker sprang open. Mickey looked up quizzically.

'You go in there,' said Beardie, cupping his hands to give Mickey a leg up.

Reluctantly Mickey pulled himself up into the locker, then used his elbows to shuffle further inside. He pulled his knees up to fit his feet in, and then the door closed on total darkness. Mickey grimaced. Vertigo and claustrophobia in one neat package.

The truck pulled away and each bump in the road knocked his head against the roof. Every time the truck stopped, he prayed the locker would be opened. Every time it moved off again, he braced once more.

Finally, after a particularly long and hopeful rest, the locker opened. Hands tugged his ankles. His legs slid out and arms wrapped around his thighs to support his weight. He lowered his body back into the cabin.

'Where are we?' he asked, rubbing his limbs to get the blood circulating.

'You are in Russia,' said Beardie, passing him a phone. 'This has a number already entered. Call it if you have not been contacted in one hour.'

He opened the passenger door.

'I just wait here?' asked Mickey, climbing down.

'They should not be long. Walk around to keep warm.'

The truck pulled out into the empty road and the lights disappeared round a bend. He was in a lay-by, empty except for one truck with lights and engine off and presumably the driver fast asleep.

After a shivering thirty minutes a car approached. A door opened. The driver got out, walked up quickly, and demanded to see his passport.

'Everything OK?' he asked.

'I think so,' said Mickey. 'I'm safely over the border.'

'Yes, the safe part is done. Now is the danger.'

68

Declan pulled up across the road from his mother's dirty-white townhouse. Josh's rusting basketball hoop hung over the door. He'd loved shooting hoops. Preferred doing it on his own but would always let his useless kid brother play whenever Declan asked. Especially on birthdays and Christmas. Declan got to play with Josh for hours then.

He rang the doorbell. Mom's home help answered. 'Hey, Declan!'

'Daniella. How are you?'

'I'm still here, thank the Lord.'

In the hallway Mom stood with open arms, red lipstick, and eyeliner. 'My little boy.'

'I'm six two.'

'Give me a kiss,' she demanded, raising her puckered lips.

He cupped her small head in one hand and kissed her forehead.

'I'll make your favourite dinner,' she said, ushering him in.

Daniella raised her eyebrows. 'I've got dinner covered.'

Mom hadn't cooked a meal for over a year. One more sign of her deteriorating health. She was only sixty-three but acted twenty years older. The doctors said it was dementia and old age. But it was her heart. Broken when her oldest boy never came home from a war that should never have been fought.

'You'll go pay your respects to you brother.' It was said in a questioning tone, but it was a clear instruction.

'Of course.'

Declan went upstairs and into Josh's bedroom. Took a deep breath and turned on the light. It was the same as it had been for over twenty years. Stuck in a time warp. The college stickers and pennants on the ceiling. The high school diploma and school year photographs on the walls. On the shelf sat football helmets, stone souvenirs, toy racing cars and other assorted knickknacks. An American flag lay over the bed. His mother had not moved a thing since the day Josh had left for Iraq.

It was a war memorial. But like withered flowers on the roadside, it had gone on too long. When Spitz concluded his enquiry, properly, Declan would try and push Mom into closure.

He went back downstairs and found her in the living room. In the corner a couple of cardboard boxes were half-full of crockery that had been wrapped in newspaper. She'd made a start on packing for the move to Laurel, to be nearer Aunt Ellen.

'I've arranged for a removal company to take everything, Mom. You don't need to pack a thing. It will all just appear in the new house in Laurel.'

'I don't trust them with my best china,' she explained. 'And remember you said you'd pack up Josh's things.'

He wasn't looking forward to that. He'd rather leave it to the removal guys. But she insisted it was personal and that Declan needed to take care of it. 'I will.'

'Are they still treating you well at the Federal Bureau of Investigation?' She liked to use the full title, and Declan didn't have the heart to tell her he was now seconded to NSA.

'They're insisting I take my annual leave. Which is a sign of a good employer.' Or someone wanting him out of the way.

'That is good,' she agreed before segueing into the question he knew would come eventually, 'You got yourself a girlfriend yet?'

'Nope.'

'Why not?'

'Too busy to meet anyone.'

'I liked Mary, she was a kind girl.'

'I liked her too.' Thanks for bringing her up.

Mom then wandered down memory lane. It was mercifully curtailed by dinner. Daniella had made the meal stretch and Declan could have eaten all three portions. He made most of the running in the conversation through dinner. Then they sat back in the living room for rosemary tea.

They retraced a lot of the ground they'd covered over dinner. Eventually she hit the topic Declan had been dreading.

'You put away those men who sent Josh to war?'

'Still working on it.'

She sat up suddenly, more alert than she had been all evening. 'You arrested them all the summer before last.'

'It's a slow process.'

She clasped his arm, surprisingly tight. 'I need justice for Josh before I leave this house.'

'I'm trying.'

'You always said trying is what you do in kindergarten.'

He sighed. 'These people have the best defence lawyers that money can buy. They've thrown up a big smoke screen. It's difficult to see the way forward.'

'Where there's smoke there's fire.'

He laughed. Hadn't he been saying the same thing?

'Now it's time for bed.' She looked at the open door and called out, 'Daniella!'

'She left already.'

'That's right. My little Declan is looking after me tonight.' She grabbed her walking stick and put it in front of her. Got to her feet on the second attempt. She didn't need it, but she made Declan take her arm and help her upstairs and into the bathroom.

'I'll take it from here,' she said with a smile.

Declan stood on the landing and checked his messages to the accompaniment of gargling and the buzz of an electric toothbrush.

When Mom emerged from the bathroom she said, 'You'll pay your respects.'

'I already did, Mom.'

'Of course. You love your brother.'

She retreated into her bedroom, leaving the bedside lamp on and the door slightly ajar.

As Declan passed Josh's room he stopped. 'Love you Josh.'

69

Dawn broke in streaky pink over the forests and marshes of Leningrad Oblast. As the morning sun drifted higher, the wetlands surrendered to market gardens, pigs, cattle, and finally the morning rush hour on the outskirts of St Petersburg. Turning off the highway, the driver meandered through back streets, his eyes flicking from windscreen to mirrors as he checked for a tail.

He pulled up outside a flower shop. 'Buy flowers. When you come out of the shop walk around the corner and get into another black pickup. When you are ready, send a message on the phone. We'll take you both back across the border.'

'In the truck?' asked Mickey, not relishing the thought of the top locker route again.

'That won't work. The Russians use X-rays to scan vehicles leaving Russia. But don't worry. We have other ways.'

'What ways?'

'You don't need to know yet.'

That was true. Best to concentrate on the job in hand. He stepped out onto the pavement and the car pulled away. He entered the shop. A lady with blue glasses smiled.

He smiled back and looked around the flowers on offer. Red and yellow tulips. A purple iris. He normally kept it simple with Helen and bought roses.

'Do you have roses?'

'Sanctions,' she replied, then frowned and wagged a finger. 'You.'

He grabbed the nearest bunch of tulips, paid for them with cash and hurried out of the shop. Having been blamed for Russian sanctions he suddenly felt very exposed. He walked quickly up the street and around the corner. A black pickup stood with its engine idling. As he drew near, the door opened.

Angelina at the wheel.

He climbed into the passenger seat and handed her flowers.

'I know you wanted to keep the relationship strictly professional, but I couldn't help myself.'

She smiled and set them on the seat. 'Can you ride a bicycle?'

No-one had ever said that before when he'd given them flowers. 'Why?'

'Olga has arranged to meet you on a bike in some woods,' she explained.

They returned to the highway and took the ring road anti-clockwise around St Petersburg. After a few miles, they turned onto a smaller road passing through the north-eastern suburbs where factories, shops and petrol stations eventually gave way to forest. They pulled into a lay-by and Angelina took two mountain bikes out of the back of the pickup.

She threw a leg over her saddle with surprising grace. Mickey gingerly mounted his bike and followed her down a narrow trail through a gravel pit. She was pulling away and Mickey realised he was in too low a gear. He changed up and caught Angelina, though the effort left him out of breath. He was relieved when they came to a clearing where Olga was standing by her bike, looking around her nervously. Where had the confident and relaxed Olga gone?

Mickey was shocked to see the change in her, especially after such a short time. He started to dismount but got back in the saddle when Olga jumped onto her bike.

'Keep cycling.'

Olga raced off and Mickey struggled to keep up, but after about half a mile she slowed, and he was able to hang on her back wheel. Finally, she pulled up and dismounted.

She had bruising on her face.

'What happened to you?'

'I fell off my bike,' she said with tears welling up in her eyes. 'Now tell me. What is your plan for me?'

'I was helped into the country through Estonia. The same people will take us both out. They wouldn't tell me any details. I just have a phone number to ring when we're ready to go. Shall I ring them now?'

'Not yet. First tell me why British intelligence are not interested in the apartment bombings.'

'I don't know.' He reached down and picked up his water bottle. He was desperately thirsty. He sipped through the black plastic nipple then gave up, unscrewed the lid, and gulped down half the bottle before putting it back in its rack. 'But once you get to England you will be able to ask them yourself.'

Olga looked away. She looked unsure of her next move.

'I have the proof about Pintov's dirty secret. It sounds to me that the British and Americans don't want to hear it. So, there is not much point in me handing over my proof to them. I will have to find another way.'

Mickey nodded to the bruises on her face. 'You didn't really fall off your bike.'

'I was interrogated.'

'Why?'

'Beratov knew that I showed you around St Petersburg. I thought you were going to show your video to Ivan Kazbegi, not publish it on the internet.'

'I'm sorry. Once I realised Kazbegi was clearly mixed up with mafia I thought there was no point in showing him. We came up with a different plan.'

'You got me into a lot of trouble.'

'I'm sorry.' Again. 'I owe you. That's why I've come to get you out.'

'Beratov also saw my father hand me a package at Bogdan's funeral. He wanted to know what it was. He suspected it was anti-Russian in some way because of Papa's behaviour in recent times. In fact, it was evidence of Pintov's involvement in the bombings.'

'Did you tell Beratov?'

She rolled up her sleeves. 'The bruises are from the chair straps. But physical punishment is only the least of it. You are not allowed out of the cell. Not even to go to the toilet. The cell becomes disgusting. You are given no water. You beg for it. You are humiliated. But I told them nothing.' She spat on the ground. 'When they arrested me, I hadn't read my father's papers. I had nothing to tell them.'

'That was lucky.'

She nodded then looked away. 'I always was a loyal Russian citizen. I love my country. Look at my work. And now the right thing is for Pintov to go. When I show the people how he knew about the apartment bombings that will be the final moment for him.'

'Is your evidence convincing?'

'My father has written a confession. He was in the FSB and was involved in the plot. He kept quiet for all these years because he would be killed and maybe me too. But now he is near the end of his life he wants to speak out. For other reasons too he wanted me to know.'

'A confession might not convince people,' said Mickey. 'He could be making it up.'

'He also has documents. A copy of a secret order issued by Boris Yeltsin to initiate the Second Chechen War. A room leased in the Kashirskoye block using FSB money.' Olga looked away. 'Other documents as well.'

Suddenly she looked back. From down the trail came the sound of snapping branches.

'Come,' she said, jumping on her bike.

She raced off along the path again. Mickey and Angelina followed as fast as they could. Mickey's quads were soon burning, and his mouth was dry again. Olga turned down a side trail and kept up the pace even though it twisted and turned over rutted ground. Mickey nearly came off on a bend.

Finally, she stopped and held her finger to her lips. From the main path came the sound of tyres on gravel. The pace never slowed, and the cyclist soon disappeared into the soft emptiness of the forest.

'I also have full financial disclosure on Pintov,' she said as if there had been no break in the conversation. 'He has a five percent stake in Gazprom, thirty percent of Surgutneftegas and a majority stake in the oil-trader Gunvor, with the beneficial owner hidden behind a trail of successive ownership of offshore companies and funds, with the ultimate beneficiary being accounts owned by Pintov in Lichtenstein and Zurich. Everyone will see he is the richest oligarch of them all.'

'Will anyone be surprised at that?' asked Mickey.

'Some will. Some won't. Do you know who killed Semyon Bogdan?'

How had they moved on to that. 'Pintov?'

'Kazbegi.'

'Why?'

'Bogdan had turned against Pintov. I also have more information that proves Kazbegi is the main man in the St Petersburg mafia. He was also involved in the Storm in Moscow plot. With this information we can destroy him.'

'The west doesn't want to sanction Kazbegi,' said Mickey. 'Even after my video it's not clear anything is going to happen.'

'Do you know why?'

'It's because of his precious metals. Western economies can't transition to net zero without the metals. They can cope without gas. But they can't do without lithium, nickel and cobalt. That's why they pretend Kazbegi is a good guy.'

'Well, he isn't,' said Olga. 'Let's see what they think after they have seen this material.'

She unzipped the pocket on the back of her red waterproof jacket and pulled out a memory stick. 'Password is two thirty Chepstow.'

Mickey did a double take.

'I've had to watch you closely before I could trust you,' she explained. 'The stick has everything about Pintov and the apartment bombings. Also, Kazbegi's mafia links. And something that the Americans will very much want to know about, a copy of a contract between Kazbegi Holdings and naval procurement. They are going to build a naval base in Svalbard.'

He had no idea where that was. 'Why are you giving the memory stick to me?'

'Take it to the British embassy in Moscow and make sure it gets safely to Frank and Declan.'

A trip to Moscow wasn't in the agreement. Not even in the small print. 'I'm just here to help you over the border. Why don't you give the stick to Frank and Declan once you've got to England?'

'Because after what I am going to do, I might not make it out.'

'What are you going to do?'

'Start a revolution.'

* * *

The attaché at the embassy seemed to be expecting Mickey. He certainly wasn't surprised to see him. After checking his passport, he took the package without question, and promised to transmit the files to Frank and Declan. He then wished him a safe onward journey. As if he knew he wouldn't be getting a conventional flight home.

Mickey returned to the embassy foyer, put on a hat and a face mask, and pulled up his collar before exiting. Angelina had explained that Russian cameras watched all coming and goings at the embassy. That's why she decided he would attract unwanted attention if she had accompanied him. But he felt exposed without her as he walked quickly along the embankment, the Volga flowing grey down below.

In Novy Arbat he executed basic counter-surveillance, meandering in and out of the boutiques and shopping malls for twenty minutes, wary of anyone plugged in and talking. Eventually, satisfied he was not being followed he returned to Angelina in the pick-up.

Now it was time to get out of the country.

70

Declan was one of the first to arrive at the White House situation room. He watched it fill with members of the cabinet and representatives from every entity in US military and intelligence.

There wasn't a smile among them. Russian aggression and Pintov's continued threats to use nuclear weapons had put the US military at DEFCON 2. Bombers were on continuous airborne alert, submarines readied, and troops poised for combat.

Once all had gathered and settled, the President summed up the situation. 'NATO is experiencing confrontation with Russia on multiple fronts, with the high possibility of invasion of multiple countries including the Baltic states, Scandinavia, and Poland.' The President looked around the room and then he continued. 'Let's have a summary of what everyone is seeing from their perspective. General Horn.'

The Chairman of the Joint Chiefs of Staff cleared his throat, edged his chair closer to the table and read from his briefing notes. 'The 11th Tank Regiment, which has been manoeuvring on the border with Finland, has been reinforced by the elite 4th Guards armoured division and by units of the 6th tank brigade. Both these units fought in Ukraine and have experience of semi-covert infiltration.'

He pulled a map of the Baltic states on the screen and with a light pen circled the tanks on the border with Finland. He then circled another tank on the border with Poland.

'Meanwhile a battalion from the Russian 1st Guards Tank Army, stationed west of Grodno, has been constantly rolling back and forth to the border with Poland. It has crossed the border on three occasions. The last time by several hundred metres. The airborne units from the 76th Air Assault Division at Chkalovsk air base in Kaliningrad are in a state of high readiness. Elsewhere in Kaliningrad we have seen a substantial military build-up. Tu-22 long-range bombers continue to fly sorties just inside Belarus's border with Poland. They have flown every day for the last six.'

He then circled a warship positioned south of Iceland.

'The Russians have also moved a fleet into the GIUK gap. They would be able to engage any seaborne NATO reinforcements that we try to send into the Baltics.' Horn set down his notes. 'As you can see, there's a lot going on.'

He hadn't mentioned Svalbard. Nobody had. Then again, nobody else knew what Declan did. He didn't want to bring up Olga's information yet, but he needed to steer the thinking in that direction. 'There's also the Russian incursion on Svalbard.'

The President at first scowled at the interruption and then relaxed when he realised it was Declan. He turned back to General Horn. 'Is Svalbard a part of this piece?'

'The Russians have dozens of military incursions around the world. I was trying to keep the focus on the European situation.'

'Svalbard is Norwegian,' said Declan.

Horn nodded to concede the point. He moved his light pen up to the top of the board. 'As Declan pointed out, there is an ongoing incident at the Russian mining town of Barentsburg on the Island of Svalbard. Kazbegi Holdings brought in military personnel to protect its commercial interests. They blame NATO deployment on the island even though it is sovereign Norwegian territory.'

'I didn't see that in my security briefing,' said the President.

'They are employees of the Borodin Group, which is owned by Kazbegi Holdings. They are Russian troops or former Russian troops armed with Russian equipment. But they aren't regular troops. That's one of the reasons I didn't mention them. I think it's a distraction.'

'What if everything else is the distraction,' said Declan. 'What if the Russian fleet is in the GIUK to prevent NATO reinforcing Svalbard.'

'We've received no intelligence that suggests that. Svalbard is a coal mining operation run by a private Russian company. I think, with respect Declan, you've lost the plot on this one.'

'It could be just as we saw in Crimea,' Declan persisted, avoiding eye contact with Horn because he knew he was getting his back up. 'Pintov can deny that he is sending in troops. He can say this is just a Russian mining company protecting its employees. But the Borodin Group is an extension of the Russian army. Almost interchangeable with the GRU. Which is just one of the reasons I've been pushing for sanctions against Ivan Kazbegi.'

Jennifer's eyes flashed a warning for him to back off.

He persisted. 'We've monitored mobile phones and fitness trackers and some of these men have recently been stationed in Russian army bases. Some have fought in Ukraine. I don't think they are stationed there for defence purposes. Remember the Norwegians unequivocally consider Svalbard as sovereign territory. And Russian troops have been allowed to get on the island unopposed, below the threshold that would invoke article five, because we've all been so busy elsewhere.'

'That's correct,' said Horn. 'We have been busy with half the Russian army engaging European borders and we've been giving it a lot more focus than Ivan Kazbegi's private army.'

General Horn returned to the tank battalions near the Polish and Finland borders, and Declan's mind drifted. He wondered who had promoted the policy of turning a blind eye to Ivan Kazbegi. Was this another example of the Black Chamber making up policy instead of the President?

The usual conventions of truth and integrity did not apply to the Black Chamber. They knew best. Horn, Asimov, Bex, Stotton and whoever else was in the group. They knew better than the President.

And now they thought they knew better than Declan. But they were wrong about that.

'With all due respect,' Declan interrupted. 'I still think we're looking at this the wrong way round.'

The room fell silent. Jennifer glared. Declan caught a few smirks in his peripheral.

'You're looking at this in the old context of East versus West. I think the axis is North versus South.'

He let the silence settle.

'General Horn, would you be kind enough to put your map back on the screen.'

Horn shrugged then did as requested.

Declan walked over and pointed to the laser pen. 'May I?'

'I'm surprised you're even asking for permission, Declan.'

This brought a few chuckles from around the room that helped diffuse the tension. He had essentially accused the entire United States military and intelligence community of not being up to the job.

'I'd like to take you back to Svalbard. We've been monitoring Russian propaganda concerning the islands. For over a year now, they have referred to Svalbard as an international island that is administered by Norway. This is a subtle but very important change in emphasis. Svalbard is in fact Norwegian sovereign territory to which the treaty allows other countries access rights to mine for minerals and to fish. It is not an international territory like, say, Antarctica. But that's the idea the Russians have been promoting to their own people and to Europeans.'

'Go on,' said the President.

'Under the treaty, any of the forty signatories could turn up and start mining in Svalbard,' explained Declan. 'Russia, through

Kazbegi Holdings, wants to make sure nobody else does.'

'They want more coal. You're saying that's what this is all about?'

That's precisely what this is not about. But he didn't want to put it so bluntly. 'Their coal mining operations are loss making. Coal is not the future. So, this isn't about more coal. Why then are they building a new deepwater harbour?'

'For a Russian naval base,' answered Admiral Dare.

'Correct,' said Declan. 'The arrival of the Borodin group is the advance party sent to protect that.'

'Where did you get that information?' asked Stotton.

'I have seen the contract drawn up between Russian naval procurement and Kazbegi Holdings,' said Declan, deliberately not answering the question.

'What's the source?' Stotton demanded.

He wasn't going to reveal Olga as the source until she was safely out of Russia. 'Highly credible.'

Stotton was about to come back for more when Declan was saved by an intervention from Bex.

'The limitations of the Spitsbergen treaty prohibit naval bases,' she said. 'The Russians can't get away with that.'

Was she for real? Had she not been following events. As if Pintov cared about limitations in old treaties. 'They are already breaking the treaty.'

'Do we care?' asked the President. 'I'm with General Horn. We've got tanks massed on European borders and a war in Ukraine. Do we care about Svalbard?'

Declan wondered whether to point out that the President was demonstrating exactly how well the diversionary tactic worked. While he hesitated, Admiral Dare jumped in.

'It would be the Russian equivalent of Pearl Harbour. It would give the Russians control over the arctic.'

'Russia wants to shift its centre of gravity north,' said Declan. 'We got used to looking at maps drawn west to east. That's what we think when Russia is apparently threatening the Baltic states. But look again.' Declan gave everyone time to reposition to face the screen. 'Yes, the Baltic and Scandinavian states are west of

Moscow but more importantly they are also north. Moscow needs to secure its defences against NATO ships attacking from the north. St Petersburg is the forward operating base. Everything we are seeing is consistent with securing this defensive position on their north-eastern flank. But the real jewel, what Russia really wants, is the northwest route into the Barents Sea which will soon be ice free all year round. From there they can control the Arctic Ocean. The Northern Fleet is based in Severomorsk. And it has free access to the Arctic. But if it also had a base in Barentsburg then, as Admiral Dare explained, it would be like Pearl Harbour is to us.'

Declan stood back against the wall. Jennifer gave him the eyes. He'd not had time to tell her about the contract and she hated to be blind-sided.

'Thank you, Declan,' said the President. 'Very interesting. Thoughts anyone?'

'We need to see this new intelligence on the Russian naval base,' said Stotton sternly. 'And I want to know where it came from.'

'Of course.' Declan nodded. He'd have to show Stotton eventually. But given that Olga didn't trust CIA St Petersburg station, he couldn't tell him anything until she was out of the country.

'I think Declan makes a good point,' said General Slatterly, head of Northern Command. 'I've warned for some time that the Arctic is now the front line in our defence against strikes on North America. Russia has deployed cruise missile systems in the Arctic that have significantly increased its ability to control a large stretch of the Northern Sea Route.'

'The Northern Sea Route is international water,' said Admiral Dare. 'Moscow has no more control over it than we do under the terms of UNCLOS.'

'Which the United States has not ratified,' General Slatterly pointed out. 'In any case the Russians already use their special rights to protect marine life under Article 234 as an excuse to deny freedom of navigation to foreign vessels.'

'We sailed a task force right through just this June,' said

Admiral Dare.

'You can get through with a task force,' interrupted Declan. 'But commercial ships must give Moscow forty-five days' notice before entering the Northern Sea Route, and they're required to have a Russian maritime pilot on board. We've been saying for some time that this is another example of Russian hybrid war. They have captured the Northern Sea Route without firing a shot.'

'That's illegal.'

'It doesn't matter,' said Declan. 'They make it clear that ships found in violation may be halted, detained, or in extreme circumstances …' he paused for attention, '… eliminated. Faced with that threat everyone is playing ball. The Russians already effectively control the polar silk road. With a naval base on Svalbard that control will be absolute.'

The discussion once again circled the room. The hawks like Admiral Dare wanted to take out the Borodin group, while others felt there was no justification for any military intervention.

'How difficult would it be to kick these guys out?' asked the President, looking at General Horn.

'We're fully committed elsewhere.'

'QED,' said Declan.

'But the Norwegians have a training exercise ongoing on Svalbard,' said Admiral Dare. 'They could turn that training exercise into reality.'

'Would the Norwegians want to do that?'

'I'm sure they would,' said Bex.

'Put together a proposal,' said the President. 'Meantime, let's everyone rethink a little on this North-South axis. And we need to see this contract, Declan.'

'Mister President.'

The President drew the meeting to a close and Declan followed the other participants out of the room, upstairs and along the corridors to the White House exit.

71

Jennifer was waiting for Declan, standing behind her desk, chin slightly forward, nostrils more visible than usual.

'What's this contract between Russian naval procurement and Kazbegi Holdings?' she asked. 'And where did you get it?'

'It came in minutes before the meeting,' Declan explained, handing her a copy. 'I didn't have time to inform you.'

She studied it for a few moments. 'Where did you get it?'

'Olga Federova, via Mickey Summer.'

'We agreed not to pursue that.'

'I'm not pursuing it. Mickey Summer is doing this off his own bat.'

'Bullshit, Declan.'

He raised his hands. 'Okay. He's had encouragement from the British but not from me.'

'So why did he send this to you?'

'He assumed I'd be interested. And I am.'

She sighed. 'Langley will go ape over this.'

'Why?'

'Because they gave a very clear no. They don't trust Federova.'

'Why not? I've only had time to skim what she's given us, but it looks like dynamite. All the dirt on Ivan Kazbegi's mafia activities plus evidence that Kazbegi and Pintov and the FSB were complicit in the Russian apartment bombings. Plus, this contract for a naval base in Svalbard.'

'Declan, this woman works for the Russian propaganda machine. She's using you. This contract,' she waved it in the air, 'is almost certainly a red herring. As is the apartment bomb conspiracy theory.'

'Mickey Summer believes her.'

Jennifer smiled and took a seat. 'Mickey Summer is a civilian. And a Brit. Olga Federova knows the CIA liaison officer in St Petersburg. It's very suspicious that she is not using him.'

'We can verify the information she's given us.'

'The details on the troll farms will be useful,' Jennifer conceded. 'POTUS did want us to attack TruNews and we can with this. But even if we could confirm the evidence that Pintov and the FSB were involved in the Russian apartment bombings, that is just too provocative when we are trying to de-escalate. Not to mention the serious risk of wider contamination in the Caucus region.'

'The truth hurts. Let the Russians and the Chechens hear it and decide for themselves whether they believe it or not.'

'We can't get involved in regime change in Russia.'

'Why not. What's wrong with that? We all want Pintov out.'

'Regime change is slowly happening. We don't want a revolutionary change. We don't want tanks firing into demonstrators. Civil war. Separatists exploiting the situation to break Russia up. Not just Chechnya. Across the underbelly of Russia.'

Declan shrugged. 'Let's break Russia up. Where's the harm?'

'Russia has an important place in the world order. Especially in the European balance of power. It's played a role many times over the centuries. For sure it overstepped the mark invading Ukraine. Everyone other than Pintov and a handful of his most nationalist supporters knows that. But once Pintov has gone, the hope is that Russia will come back into the fold.'

'It's a pariah state. We should never let it back in.'

'If we don't, it will become even more closely aligned with China. That's not in our interest.'

'I can't believe I'm hearing this.'

'I'm telling you as I see it,' said Jennifer.

'And you go along with this?'

'I came up through military ranks in cyber command, so I'm programmed to respect orders from superiors.'

'I came up through investigative ranks in the Bureau, so I'm programmed to question anything. Including you.'

'In what way are you questioning me?'

'Like I'm wondering whether you are also in the Black Chamber.'

Jennifer swept her hair off her forehead. 'There is no Black Chamber.'

'Well solve this riddle for me. I took another look at the Black Chamber files in Langley the other day. Two key items are missing.'

'Enlighten me,' she said, hands on hips.

'In the Iraq inquiry, Biggerstaff testified that he'd seen a memorandum of understanding between the governments of Niger and Iraq over the supply of uranium. That was key to Bush agreeing to go to war. No memorandum ever turned up of course, because Biggerstaff made up the claim. Now that testimony has gone missing from the files.'

'Are you sure it was there in the first place?'

No need to answer that question. 'Also now missing is a presentation Asimov gave on the P20G group set up by Donald Rumsfeld to bring together CIA and military covert action. That was included in the files as a hint that P2OG was a precursor to the Black Chamber.'

'You can't be sure about that.'

'I know the presentation was there and now it's missing. Why would someone remove it, if it wasn't to cover their tracks?'

Jennifer took a deep breath then bridged her fingertips under her chin. 'When did you last take a holiday, Declan?'

'I don't know.'

'I do.' She looked at a piece of paper. 'April last year.'

'I've been busy.'

'You were instructed to book a holiday at your last review meeting.'

'I will. But I've got a live operation in Russia. Even if it is unofficial.'

She nodded her head reluctantly. 'As soon as.'

72

The drive back to St Petersburg took eight hours. More than enough time for the attaché to encrypt and send the files securely to Frank and for him to pass on to Declan. But there had been no reply from either. Not even an acknowledgement that the files had been received.

He rang Frank on his secure line in Thames House but got no answer. Next, he tried Declan in Washington and was put on hold for five minutes before he came on the call.

At first Mickey played the innocent tourist describing every building he'd seen, boring any eavesdropper into submission.

'Have you seen the manuscript from our friend?' he asked eventually.

'It's fascinating,' said Declan. 'I love the chapters set in Svalbard and St Petersburg. But there's still no interest in-house in the Moscow chapters.'

'Why not?'

'The topic is too sensitive, and the author isn't credible.'

'Your in-house team don't want the target subject to get upset. Is that it?'

'Yes. I'd still like to meet your author. She is clearly an incredible talent.'

'I get the idea that she's going to go ahead and publish in Russia.'

Declan was silent for a long while and Mickey left him to it.

'I wouldn't recommend that, but it's her call,' Declan said eventually. 'I still think it's best if she comes over and we all sit down and discuss what material we can use.'

Perhaps Declan was right. He was on the inside and Mickey was very much on the outside of the intelligence world. This sort of realpolitik probably happened all the time. 'I'll put that to her. I'd better get going.'

He cut the call. Removed the SIM card and dropped it down a drain. Now it was time to go home. With or without Olga. She could have one last chance.

73

The stairwell stank of urine and was littered with rubbish and things best left undisturbed. There were four flights to negotiate before fresh air hit them as they walked along an outdoor corridor to a metal door. Angelina set down the bedside table she had been inexplicably carrying and tackled the locks. She pulled open the door and walked into a small, poorly decorated room over-filled with cheap furniture.

'It's not for us,' said Mickey, turning on his heels. 'We were hoping for a mature garden.'

'Still joking,' said Angelina. 'Do you realise how dangerous your situation is?'

'That's why I'm still joking. Keep my mind distracted.'

'Well, you should be safe in here,' she said. 'We use this safe house when we need to keep somebody hidden. Off the grid. The residents in this area don't talk to the police and they turn a blind eye to everything going on around them. But even if anyone does see people coming and going, they think the flat is used for furniture storage.'

Mickey pointed to the bedside table she'd brought with her. 'That's why you were carrying that.'

'Exactly.'

'Will Olga be safe coming here on her own?'

'I think she can look after herself.'

Mickey found a kettle, and a basket of samovar leaves. He made the tea and let it steep while he cleaned some cups and freed a table from a pile of furniture in the living room. As he set the cups down on it, a knock sounded at the door.

Leonid looked through the spyhole. 'It's Olga.'

'Good timing,' said Mickey.

'She will have been watching and waiting for us to go in first,' said Angelina.

Olga took a seat but passed on the tea. She wanted to get straight down to business. 'Did you pass on the files to British and American intelligence?'

'I did. And I checked they arrived safely. Now we just need to get you out of the country. Shall I tell the Estonians we're ready to go?'

'Not yet,' said Olga. 'What do they think about the files?'

'They want to talk to you about them when you're in London.'

Her eyes drilled into Mickey's. 'What do they think about the files?' she repeated.

She deserved the truth. The whole truth. 'I think the information about Kazbegi is being taken seriously but I don't think they are going to do anything with the material on Pintov and the Russian apartment bombings.'

'Thank you.' She rubbed her forehead while staring at the floor. 'That is what I suspected.'

'Shall I call the Estonians?'

'No. I need to publish the files myself first.'

'Declan has advised against doing that,' said Mickey. 'For your own safety.'

'I agree,' interjected Angelina. 'It seems to me that the best thing to do is get you both over the border as soon as possible. Once you are in London you can discuss with the intelligence services and decide what to release. But there's nothing more you can do in Russia.'

'I need to make a video while I am still in Russia,' said Olga. 'That way I can turn the state's propaganda machine on itself.'

That was a big claim. 'Can you do that?'

'If I can get help from someone the Russian people trust.'

'Is there someone?' In a country brought up on a diet heavy in propaganda, was there anyone the people believed?

'Ekaterina Albats. The face of TruNews.' Olga stood up and walked to the door. 'I'll be back soon.'

'I think we should stick together,' said Mickey. 'I need to understand what's going on in real time, in person. I can't just sit still and hope everything is going fine.'

'I agree,' said Angelina. 'I don't like this at all, but if Mickey goes then of course I must go. And if I go, I want Leonid as well.'

'Let's all go then.'

'You go to your car first,' said Angelina, handing her the bedside table. 'Put your furniture inside then walk to the green Lada Granta parked in front of St Basil's church.'

* * *

In a car that had been selected for low cost and low visibility rather than comfort, they drove twenty minutes to a parade of shops, where Leonid picked up a bunch of flowers and a new phone. Olga entered the number in her own phone and then they continued across St Petersburg.

Leonid eventually pulled up outside a school. They were still a hundred metres short of the sat-nav's destination, a drab apartment block. Outside it, a dirty white Hyundai was parked with a man asleep behind the wheel.

'Ekaterina's highly professional police guard,' said Olga drily.

'Then why doesn't she just walk out and meet you?' asked Mickey.

'She'll be tagged,' explained Angelina, before Olga could answer. 'It will trigger the alarm if she leaves the apartment. Let's stick with the original plan.'

Leonid picked up the flowers, got out of the car and walked quickly up the street. He disappeared into the block of flats while the others waited. The sky darkened and it began to rain. With the engine off, condensation formed on the windscreen. Mickey wiped it with his sleeve, but it was still difficult to see out. There was no sign of Leonid, and he couldn't tell if the police guard was still in his car.

Eventually Leonid appeared, without the flowers, and returned to the car. Olga sent a message to the phone she had placed in the flowers.

A few seconds later her phone pinged.

Olga read out aloud. 'She asks: Who is this?'

'My reply: Your friend from the Nashi.'

A pause then, 'She has replied: Semyon's girlfriend, with a question mark. '

That's an old joke between us,' explained Olga. She looked away, her eyes tearing up. 'But it's no longer funny.' She pulled herself together and looked back down to her phone. 'I'm replying: Correct. I need to talk with you.'

'I am tagged and bugged.'

'Are you allowed out of the house?'

'So long as I stay on the island.'

'Shall we meet in the metro museum?'

'Okay.'

Olga dropped her phone back in her pocket. They waited around five minutes and then a young woman came out in heels and black leather trousers and jacket.

'That's her.'

Ekaterina walked off down the road. Hyundai man had presumably been woken by the alarm and followed in the car. Leonid took another route to the museum and pulled into a parking bay. He stepped out and fed the meter. A short time later Ekaterina arrived and walked casually into the museum. Hyundai man followed her in but returned to his car a couple of minutes later.

'I'll go in now,' said Olga. 'For this it's best I go alone.'

'I agree,' said Angelina, looking sternly at Mickey.

After Olga had left the car, Mickey rubbed his hands together. Was it from excitement or anxiety? Probably both.

They waited in silence. The windows steamed up fully. Mickey took encouragement from the length of time the two were together. Finally, Ekaterina emerged. She glanced in the direction of their car without showing signs of acknowledgement then walked away. The Hyundai followed.

Just as the museum was closing Olga emerged with a party of school children. She climbed back into the car.

'What did she say?' Mickey asked.

'Maybe,' replied Olga.

'Why is she only maybe?'

'She's scared. She's a newsreader not a revolutionary. What happens to her if she makes this film? Other journalists who've spoken out against Pintov were killed.'

'She can go into hiding. Russia is a big country.'

'They'll find her. Her face is very well known. She has a better idea.'

Something about the way Olga was looking at Mickey suggested he wasn't going to like it. 'Go on.'

'She wants to come with you and me.'

Mickey shook his head. 'Sorry. No plus ones.'

'Why not?'

'Because I only arranged with the Estonians to take two of us across. And I'm already worried that the arrangement might break down once you release the video. I don't need extra complications.'

'Ekaterina is not a complication,' said Olga. 'She's the key ingredient for what I need. I've already given you everything you need on Kazbegi. You still owe me.'

She was right. But it wasn't so much the extra person that was worrying Mickey. It was the fact he'd heard nothing from the Estonians. Plus one, plus two, it didn't matter if there was no party.

'All right.'

'All right what?'

'All right I'll tell the Estonians they've got onc extra to get out.'

'What if they say no?'

I go out on my own. He couldn't do that. 'We go to plan B.'

'Do you have a plan B?' asked Olga.

'I'm working on it,' said Mickey, with as wide a smile as he could manage given the tension.

'Take us back to the safe house,' Olga instructed Leonid.

He drove off slowly.

Hopefully they didn't need a plan B. If the Estonians could get two people over the border, they could surely get three.

But there was one more potential spanner in the works. 'There is one thing we haven't considered. Your father. They'll kill him if you use his evidence.'

'He's dying anyway. And he wanted me to use this. He is prepared to be sacrificed.' She looked away and was silent for a time. Then she turned back to Mickey. 'Plus he was involved in the apartment bombings. He killed Mama. He's as guilty as Kazbegi or Pintov.'

* * *

Back in the safe house Angelina watched the road from the window. Olga was busy working through her files. Leonid, sullenly silent, scrolled his phone. Mickey found a nearly empty bottle of vodka. He offered it round and fortunately no-one else wanted any. He poured it into a cup and knocked it back. It helped.

Olga's phone pinged. She smiled and looked up. 'Ekaterina is on. She asks if she should cut off the ankle bracelet.'

'That depends on what type she's wearing,' said Angelina.

'Did you get a look?'

'Sorry, no.'

'My fault,' said Angelina. 'I should have thought ahead. If she cuts it off, it will trigger the alarm.'

'She could wrap it in tinfoil to stop transmission,' said Mickey. He remembered that's what mates who were banned from Upton Park for fighting had done to get into the ground past the detectors. 'Then slip out the fire exit.'

'But Hyundai will be alerted when transmission stops.'

'If he's awake. Even then he'll think it's a transmission error. He'll go check but he won't go storming in.'

'Then what?'

'She goes down into the metro. She can cut it off there and leave it on a tube. When it comes above ground, they'll pick up the signal and go looking in the wrong place. That gives her time to get to the safehouse.'

Olga started texting. 'I'll tell her.'

'Have you heard back from the Estonians?' asked Angelina.

Mickey checked his phone. 'Not yet. But a plus one shouldn't be a problem. They were sociable types.'

Angelina didn't smile. 'Try them again. You can't get out of the country without them. And now you have committed to take Ekaterina.'

Didn't he know it.

* * *

Within the hour Ekaterina arrived at the safe house, dressed for a polar expedition. She'd brought along a nervous cameraman who declined to give his name and studiously avoided eye contact as he set up bright lights and an empty desk against the bedroom wall.

Under the thick coat Ekaterina wore a red jacket, white blouse, and no jewellery. She applied heavy make-up for the lights. She had no autocue, so had to memorise her script and film in short sequences. Over a couple of hours Mickey watched the documentary take shape. She also made clips for social media. Everything was in Russian, but Mickey could tell from reactions in the room that the content was explosive.

An increasingly heated argument built. Leonid began pacing the room, muttering, and shaking his head. He barked something at Ekaterina. She ignored him, but the cameraman swore at Leonid. Angelina stepped in to calm them both down.

Suddenly Leonid marched to the door, opened it and stormed out of the flat.

Now the cameraman started arguing with Angelina.

'What's going on?' Mickey demanded.

'Leonid didn't want to be part of this,' explained Angelina. 'He said that he's a bodyguard not a traitor.'

'I'm not a traitor,' Ekaterina protested. 'I'm doing this for my country.'

'I understand,' said Angelina. 'I'm just explaining what Leonid said. Anyway, it doesn't matter now. He's gone.'

'Probably to the FSB,' said the cameraman.

'He won't do that,' said Angelina.

She didn't look convinced.

'No more edits,' said Ekaterina. 'Let's go with what we have.'

'I'm ready,' said Olga. 'The social media clips I can release at the press of a button. For the documentary I need to work my way through TruNews security. I think it's best to interrupt one of the headline news programmes.' She checked the time on her phone.

'Six o'clock,' suggested Ekaterina.

'That's fine,' replied Olga. She looked at Mickey. 'Does it give you enough time to organise our escape.'

Organise? He'd sent a message to the Estonians. That's all the organising he could do. He checked his phone. Still nothing back from them.

'Should be enough time,' he said, convincing nobody, least of all himself. 'I'm on the case.'

He dialled Frank on the line he'd told him to only use in an emergency. Well, this bloody well was an emergency. It went to the answerphone. Although Frank's line was secure, Mickey knew to speak in code just in case someone was listening.

'I'm on my way home darling. Bringing two guests now so it would be wonderful if you could give them a warm welcome.'

* * *

With Leonid gone someone needed to drive and Angelina thought it would attract less attention if it were Mickey. That way it looked like a Yandex taxi taking three ladies out for the evening. He drove through St Petersburg rush hour and parked a couple of blocks away from TruNews headquarters.

'Good luck,' said Mickey, as Olga opened her door.

While they waited Mickey left the engine running so that the windows didn't steam up. He checked his phone. Still no message from the Estonians or from Frank.

Olga reappeared thirty minutes later.

'All done,' she said as she climbed into the car.

'Great,' said Mickey pulling out into traffic.

'You're heading in the wrong direction,' said Ekaterina.

'I'm going back to the safehouse.'

'We need to head straight for the border.'

'I haven't heard from the Estonians yet,' explained Mickey.

'What?'

'I haven't heard ...'

'I need to get out of the country!' Ekaterina screamed. 'I have just broadcast for Pintov's head on a plate. They'll be looking for me.'

'I understand,' said Mickey. 'We all need to get out. But I haven't been given any instructions yet.'

'We'll be ok.' Olga put an arm around Ekaterina. 'What about your plan B, Mickey?'

'I'm working on it.'

74

A teenager dressed in a traditional black Sarafan dress climbed the platform and took the microphone. 'I am the future of this great country.'

Her declaration drew cheers from some in the crowd. Others remained silent, suspicious that she was a Pintov stooge who had infiltrated the demonstration.

'Pintov has no future in my country,' she continued. Now

everyone cheered and waved placards vigorously. 'He has killed Ukrainian citizens. Bombed them to death. For that he is a criminal. But now we know that he bombed his own citizens. For that he is a monster. Pintov must go.'

Speaker after speaker grew bolder with each denunciation. The crowd swelled. This was not like the usual anti-war protests with a few hundred students and liberals. The ranks were now strengthened by an angry proletariat that had lost sons and brothers in Pintov's war, and by traumatised soldiers, including pardoned convicts, some psychotic even before their time as cannon fodder. It was a volatile mix. They hurled bricks at an army recruitment office and a billboard of Pintov. They set alight car tyres. The air filled with acrid black smoke.

The police watched and filmed but kept their distance. Waiting. Eventually, inevitably, the OMON arrived. A line of grey vans drew up and spilled a cargo of black helmets. Whistled into formation by commanders they stood behind riot shields, impatient and menacing, batons hanging on hips.

An officer climbed onto the roof of a police car.

'We demand that you stop these illegal actions and disperse,' he said clearly and calmly. Almost friendly. 'If you continue these illegal actions, you will be held liable in accordance with the current legislation of the Russian Federation.'

This produced jeers, horns, and whistles from the protestors. As the water cannon rolled forward the volume rose, and placards waved more vigorously. Bricks flew and clattered off the shields. A gun cracked. An OMON fell and was spirited away by colleagues.

The cannon fired. A woman holding a Ukraine flag was the first to be blasted off her feet. Others followed like ducks hit by water pistols in the fairground. The OMON marched forward, swinging batons at limbs and heads.

* * *

'We should be out on the streets with them,' declared Ekaterina, looking up from her phone. 'We shouldn't be hiding here like this.'

'An hour ago, you were screaming to get out of the country,' said Olga.

'We all need to stay hidden,' said Angelina. She turned to Mickey. 'But we can't stay here forever. They will be hunting us down. Studying CCTV, talking to people. Eventually they will find us. What is the plan?'

'I'm still working on it,' said Mickey. She was right that they had to get out of the safe house. Too many people had seen them coming and going. Eventually the police would be informed of the suspicious activity in the furniture storage flat. He checked his messages. Still nothing from Frank or the Estonians.

It looked like he'd have to trust the one person who never let him down. While the others went back to watching social media, Mickey downloaded Google Earth and zoomed in on the Estonia-Russia border. The security fence on the Estonian side of the Narva River looked impassable. He scrolled south to Lake Peipus. The red border line ran through the middle. There was no fence though. They presumably couldn't build a fence on water. It would be like a sea border. Patrolled by boats. So was the English Channel and plenty got through that. But he didn't have a boat.

He pulled up an ordnance survey app which relied on simple geo location. It came up in Hertfordshire. The last time he'd used it was trying to find out where he was on his way to buying the farmhouse. If they had only moved house a day earlier, he would never have been caught up in this madness. He scrolled east to Lake Peipus and looked for fishing villages on the Russian side.

His phone pinged. Finally, a message from Frank. With bad news.

'Your travel agent has resigned. They don't work with celebrities.'

The Estonians had lost their bottle over Ekaterina.

'What's the new travel plan?' he messaged.

'Will need time to organise.'

'How long?'

'Difficult to say. Maybe a week.'

No way was he living in the flat for a week expecting the police to come bursting through the door at any moment. *'We need to move now. Will go by boat across Lake Peipus.'*

'Wait.'

Mickey waited a few minutes and then Frank came back again.

'Drive to Samolva. Then walk west. The lake is frozen. No boat needed. Send your location when you are near.'

'Time to go,' said Mickey. He walked into the bedroom and pulled the duvets and covers off the bed.

'The Estonians have contacted you?'

'The Estonians have got scared. British Intelligence will help us over the border, but we'll have to walk over lake Peipus.'

'Walk?' said Olga and Ekaterina together.

'Yes. So, let's wrap up warm.'

75

Only the duty watch team was in the situation room when Declan and Jennifer arrived. The tapping of their keyboards appeared to summon the remaining NSC staff, who filtered into the room over the next few minutes.

President Topps appeared on video from an undisclosed location and called the meeting to order. He asked Jennifer to sum up the situation.

'I'm going to assume everybody has seen Ekaterina Albat's news report. Ekaterina is a popular and highly regarded newsreader on Russian TruNews and had been fiercely loyal to Pintov until recent months, when her subtle disapproval led to her being taken off screens. The fact that she has turned so fully against Pintov in this report has shocked the Russian population. The video provides clear evidence of Pintov's vast wealth and criminal links. That probably doesn't greatly surprise people, but what has shocked is evidence that he and the FSB were complicit in the bombing of hundreds of Russian civilians at the start of his reign. Ekaterina provided witness statements and other documentary evidence that are impossible for Pintov apologists to dismiss. The video has gone viral despite state censorship, and it appears to be the catalyst for demonstrations and riots across Russia.'

She pulled up pictures of crowds on streets littered with bricks and overturned vehicles.

'The protests have spread outside Russia to Chechnya, Moldova, and Georgia. And we're going to feel the effects of this video closer to home. A secondary target of Ekaterina Albats is Ivan Kazbegi. It's very clear from the video that he was aware of the plan to bomb Russian apartments, that he remains extremely close to Pintov and that he has substantial links to the Russian mafia. It is now inevitable that he is placed under sanctions. Precious metal prices are rising sharply to reflect this.'

The President then asked the US Ambassador to give the latest from on the ground in Moscow. She came up on the screen. Beside her was the Deputy Chief of Mission.

'The situation is very fluid and volatile,' she said. 'Outside the Kremlin a crowd of many thousands has been engaged in continuous advance and retreat from riot police who've used water cannon and live ammunition. There are reports that some of the protestors are also armed and have fired at the police. We also have a large anti-American demonstration outside the embassy compound here in the Presnensky District, because Pintov claims the video is the work of American intelligence.

'I was summoned to the Russian Foreign Ministry this morning where it was demanded that we hand over Ekaterina Albats. I told them that she is acting independently of any American office, and we have no idea where she is. That we are not trying to drive any political dynamics inside Russia.'

'Thank you, Tracey,' said the President. 'Before we go any further can I just check with everyone on this call. Has anyone been in communication with Ekaterina Albats?'

'Indirectly,' said Jennifer, looking at Declan. 'Her friend Olga Federova, who also works for TruNews, approached us to say she had information on Kazbegi and Pintov and the Russian apartment bombings. We said we were not interested, precisely because we did not want to be associated with regime change.'

'So, are we in communication with Federova?' asked the

President.

'We aren't,' said Stotton. 'The British are closer to her on this. They're not in communication with either Federova or Albats but they do have an in with a person trying to help them out of the country.'

The President nodded. 'Let me ask a follow-up question. Does anyone think we should be trying to communicate with Albats or Federova? Should we try to help get them out of the country?'

'I don't think we should go anywhere near them until they've crossed the border,' answered Bex. 'If we get caught giving assistance it will completely undermine their story. Pintov will win back support and it could very well send him off the deep end.'

'If the British are caught helping it amounts to the same thing.'

'The operation to extract Albats and Federova is not run by British intelligence,' said Stotton. 'It's a private arrangement. Fully deniable.'

'Do nothing then,' said the President. He'd phrased it as an open invitation to contradict him. But nobody did. He returned to the ambassador. 'Any signs of movement against Pintov within the Kremlin?'

'His inner circle is vocal in support,' she said. 'Denouncing the video as western fake news and Ekaterina as a spy. Ivan Kazbegi has also been equally vocal. But elsewhere the silence is deafening. They're waiting.'

'For what?'

'I think for someone else to break cover first. Or for Pintov to make a false move and inflame the situation.'

'That's what's worrying me,' said the President. 'How close are we to a catastrophic situation? Nuclear escalation, either from Pintov getting mad or calculating he's got nothing to lose?'

'We're monitoring that,' said General Horn. 'We see no developments at present. And we are comfortable with our own nuclear deterrent posture as it sits right now.'

'Should I call Pintov?'

'I don't think that's a good idea right now,' said Asimov.

'I agree,' said Bex.

'Do nothing then,' he repeated.

'We've got plenty to be getting on with,' said Bex. 'We need to batten down the hatches and get ready for rare earth metal prices to go through the roof. We need to prepare our responses to Russian republics declaring independence. We should be ready for the Caucasus to go up in flames.'

'I agree, we need to be ready on all those fronts,' said the President.

'There is something else,' interjected Declan. He glanced at General Horn before continuing. 'This is a perfect time to remove Russian forces from Svalbard. Kazbegi is in hiding. Pintov is distracted.'

'These Russian forces are employees of the Borodin group protecting a mining operation,' corrected Stotton. 'We've got no intelligence to say that Russia plans a naval base there other than the naval procurement contract that Declan received but we're unable to validate.'

'Ekaterina Albats has just validated it for us,' said Declan. 'It's the same source. And her information looks good.'

'Any other views on this?' asked the President.

'There is no justification for the Borodin group to be there,' said Bex. 'Their presence is illegal. The Norwegians have every right to remove them.'

'How difficult would that be?' the President asked General Horn.

'We believe there are just one hundred Borodin group personnel in Barentsberg and that they are lightly armed. The Norwegians should be able to overcome them relatively easily. They are waiting for the green light.'

'What about casualties? I'm particularly concerned about civilians.'

'Impossible to predict,' said General Horn. 'Barentsberg has a civilian population of around five hundred people. It's got a school, a bar, and a hotel. There could be civilian casualties. But Declan does have a counter hybrid idea to minimise that threat. I'll let him tell you about that.'

Declan stepped a little closer into the room. 'We send Borodin group employees notification that their contract on Svalbard is terminated. They may believe it and offer no resistance. It should at least weaken their resolve.'

The President looked around the room inviting other speakers. None came forward.

'The Norwegians don't need a green light from us. It's their country. They should defend it.'

76

They walked out to the car in pairs. Again, Angelina suggested it looked better if Mickey drove.

'Destination?' she asked, her index finger hovering over the sat nav.

Mickey checked his message from Frank. 'Samolva'.

Angelina entered that. 'Journey time three hours.'

'What's the plan from Samolva?' asked Ekaterina as Mickey pulled out into the evening rush hour.

'We walk. The lake has no fence and is frozen. We can cross no problem.'

'What about border guards?'

'They're at the road crossings,' Mickey replied with as much conviction as he could muster. 'Probably watching the news.'

Fortunately, any further inquisition was stopped by Olga who shouted in Russian and turned up the radio.

'What's happening?' asked Mickey.

'Radio Moscow is talking about the video.'

'There's no going back now,' said Ekaterina, catching Mickey's eyes in the mirror.

They drove mostly in silence, broken intermittently by Olga and Ekaterina discussing pieces on social media. Angelina didn't speak. She rarely did. But she looked anxious. Mickey didn't think it was about crossing the border. She never seemed scared for herself. He suspected it was fear for what would happen to her country.

77

Ideally the SRS advance force would have had a month to properly prepare a picture of the theatre the strike force was moving into. But they'd only had seventy-eight hours surveillance of Barentsburg before orders had come from Oslo to go in and remove the Borodin group personnel from the small town.

Svalbard was well into its two months of permanent polar nights and from the high bluff Lieutenant Colonel Olsen surveyed the sleeping town through night-vision binoculars.

The old mine workings and abandoned houses giving off no heat were barely distinguishable. But the coal brought up from the warm underground irradiated silently on the conveyer belts that were shut down for the night. The newer apartment blocks, the hotel, restaurant, and brewery displayed the warmth they garnered from the power station near the oil terminal.

All was satisfactorily quiet, and he turned his attention to the special forces moving in on skis to secure the port and surround the newly built Borodin group barracks.

Olsen signalled his driver. The Lynx growled and belched diesel fumes as it set off down the snowy decline. Hägglunds transporters were now spilling infantry onto the streets to make sure residents, some already twitching behind curtains, stayed safely indoors.

The Lynx took up a position one hundred metres from the barracks and was joined by a K9 Thunder howitzer, aiming directly over the Borodin machine gun mounted on the roof.

'Flank,' Olsen instructed and marines on snowmobiles raced around the rear of the barracks.

He signalled the translator to talk over the loudspeaker. 'Borodin personnel. Your presence on Norwegian Sovereign territory is illegal. You are requested to leave immediately. You are surrounded by overwhelming forces of the Norwegian army. It will be impossible for you to succeed against them. Come out with your hands up.'

After a few moments of internal debate some insults were hurled out of the window.

'They are swearing at us,' explained the translator, unnecessarily.

Olsen signalled the howitzer. It barked, firing a single round over the barracks and into the hills behind, from where the echo returned seconds later. The howitzer lowered its aim directly at the Borodin machine gun position which returned the gesture, even though this was a futile threat against the K9's armoured steel.

The warning produced another round of internal shouting. Then the barracks door opened. A man appeared with his hands on his head. He walked down the steps. Others followed behind and the line of men snaked over the snow. They were directed to an all-terrain truck and as the first climbed aboard it looked as if sense was going to prevail.

But then a machine gun rattled. Two Borodin men fell. The others threw themselves to the ground or took cover under the truck.

'Hold your fire!' Olsen shouted. But the rate of fire was too slow for a Norwegian Minimi. It had come from the Borodin gun on the roof of the barracks. Shooting at their own men. Men who were now his prisoners that he had a duty to protect.

On a signal from Olsen the howitzer barked again. The machine gun post was swept off the roof.

'Move out! Covering fire!'

The forward teams advanced and fired teargas canisters through the windows. After a short time, the door burst open again and more Borodin personnel spilt out. But Olsen knew there would be others inside, masked and prepared to fight.

'Assault!'

The polar night erupted with the rattle of machine guns and cracking of grenades. A few chaotic minutes later the advanced command officer reported the barrack secure.

'Hold,' Olsen instructed. He climbed down from the Lynx and walked over the snow to a groaning bloody mess.

'Medic!' he called needlessly. The medic was already running.

'Secure the town. Set up checkpoints and clear out any remaining resistance.'

78

Two killed. One Norwegian and one American. Nine wounded. Declan couldn't get the figures out of his head. The assault had been his idea. He'd called it in. The only crumb of comfort was that many more would have been killed if they'd had to engage the Russian fleet once it had built a naval base. He still felt sick though. And again, he had hardly slept. He did need a holiday. But he had one more task to complete before he could do that.

He arrived at Spitz's office right on time. He knocked on the open door and walked in. Spitz showed him a seat on the other side of his spotless desk.

'Thanks for taking time to meet,' said Declan. 'I'm sure you're busy.'

'No problem,' replied Spitz. 'I'd have thought you'd be the one who was busy, with everything going on in Russia.'

'Things are moving really fast,' agreed Declan. 'But to tell you the truth I'm actually now on leave.'

'But you're still working. Or is this a social visit?'

Declan smiled. 'Just want to tie up a couple of loose ends before I go.'

'Let me take a wild guess. They're to do with the Black Chamber.'

'That's right,' replied Declan. 'I have some important new information.'

'My report has been submitted, Declan. You've run out of time.'

'Who cares about the report? Let's just do our jobs.'

'What is the new information?' Spitz asked unenthusiastically.

'I looked at the Black Chamber files in Langley the other day. Two documents have gone AWOL. Two key documents.'

'Enlighten me.'

'Biggerstaff claimed to have seen a memorandum of understanding between the governments of Niger and Iraq over the supply of uranium. That was key to Bush agreeing to go to war.'

'And now you say it's missing?'

Declan nodded. 'Also missing is a presentation Asimov gave on the P20G group set up to bring together CIA and military covert action. That was included in the files as a hint that P2OG is a precursor to the Black Chamber.'

'A hint?'

'I believe so.'

'Why would someone only hint? Why wouldn't there be an explanation?'

'I don't know. But I know the presentation was there and now it's missing. Why would someone remove it if it wasn't to cover their tracks?'

Spitz nodded silently and waited for more. 'Are these your only whisps of smoke?'

'Where there's smoke there's fire,' replied Declan. Mom was right about that.

'If I could explain their absences to you, would you be able to put this pursuit of the Black Chamber behind you? Let it drop?'

'Can you explain them?'

Spitz removed some keys from his drawer and walked over to a filing cabinet. He fished inside and pulled out a folder. 'This is my submission to the Attorney General.'

He opened it, licked a finger, and began leafing through the appendices. He stopped, turned the folder round, and showed a page to Declan. It contained the letter from Biggerstaff to President Bush. 'I included this as proof of Biggerstaff's previous deception. The original will be returned to the library when the Attorney General has finished.'

Declan realised his mouth was open. He closed it. Then asked, 'What about Azimov's presentation?'

'I saw that. I also wondered why it was included in the Black Chamber section with no explanation.'

Spitz stopped. The silence hung. Grew louder.

Eventually Declan was forced to ask, 'Why was it?'

'I asked the librarian if he knew,' Spitz continued. 'He realised he had misfiled it. It should have been in the Black Ops section. Not Black Chamber. That's where it is now filed.'

Declan replayed Spitz's words. Processed them. Repeated them. He could feel the blood rushing to his cheeks.

'You're supposed to be on holiday, Declan. Go hit the beach.'

79

Mile after mile the highway was lined by unbroken forest. Whenever a car came towards them Mickey felt like stopping and running into the trees to hide. They looked so suspicious. A full car driving towards the border when the country was holding its breath. Finally, they came to a right turn and a narrow road that was only partly cleared of snow.

'Do you have chains?' Ekaterina asked.

'Do we?' Mickey asked in turn.

'Of course,' replied Angelina. 'This is Russia.'

Mickey was relieved when Angelina got out to put them on. He didn't have a clue. He helped lay them out in front of the wheels. Then followed her instructions and drove the car forward onto the chains before getting out to help Angelina fit them.

They made much slower progress on this new road, which was barely passable in places. Again, they were surrounded by forest except for the occasional village with a few houses and sometimes a church. Boats started to appear in driveways and dry harbours, which suggested the lake was near.

Finally, they arrived at the small town of Samolva. They passed a fishing museum. If they got stopped by the police, they could pretend they came to visit. At night? Realistically, if they were stopped, in the company of Ekaterina, they were all going to be arrested. And that would be the best-case scenario.

They continued to the west of the town and Mickey pulled into a cleared lay-by from where he sent his location to Frank, turned off the engine and turned to Angelina. 'I guess this is where we say good-bye.'

'While you are in Russia you are still in my care,' she said.

'You just can't face losing me,' said Mickey. 'But seriously, thanks.'

He checked their position on the map app then got out of the car. He was hit by an avalanche of cold. He retrieved the duvets and bed covers from the boot and handed them out.

A three-quarter moon lit the path as they walked. After thirty minutes they came to a turning. It ran west towards the lake. They proceeded cautiously. A light came up ahead.

'What is that?' whispered Ekaterina.

Mickey checked the map. The road came to a dead end at a collection of buildings. Farmhouse? Fish factory? Army installation? 'Let's keep to the side.'

They walked on more slowly now in the deeper snow, eyes and ears straining to understand what lay ahead. Now several lights. An engine purring. A vehicle without headlights, almost on top of them.

'Into the woods,' Angelina whispered.

They pushed through knee-high snow. Crouched behind trees, they watched a car rattle by on snow chains. The driver and any occupants couldn't be seen. Hopefully it was just a farmer going out for the evening.

A grinding metal symphony started up. This time with a squeal of a thousand dead mice. They crouched down again. A tank snarled as it approached then roared by like a beast with bottomless lungs.

It was clear now that the area was militarised. How stupid had he been to think the border zone would not be? He was out of his depth. And scared.

'Does everyone still want to go on?' he whispered through dry lips.

'What else?'

'Maybe we should go back to the safe-house?'

Ekaterina and Olga looked at each other and back to Mickey.

'I need to get out of the country,' said Ekaterina. 'I want to go on.'

'Me too,' said Olga.

Angelina shrugged. 'I go where you go.'

'We need to keep off the road then.' Mickey checked the map, took a line due west to the lake, pulled up the compass on his phone and pressed on into the woods. As the moon and stars disappeared under the canopy the world turned greyscale. One hand carried the phone, the other he stuck out in front of his face to defend against offensive branches.

It was much harder work walking off road. Occasional drifts

were waist height. The silence was heavy and misleadingly peaceful. They came to a clearing of cut trees. Mickey identified a particularly tall tree to aim for on the other side and walked round hugging the treeline.

A flash of silver stopped him in his tracks. Wolves. A pack. Little and large. They glanced over expressionlessly as they slid silently across the snow.

'Don't worry,' said Angelina. 'They are more afraid of us than we are of them.'

'I don't know about that,' said Mickey. 'I'm pretty scared.'

As quickly as the wolves had appeared they were gone, fading into the woods, untroubled by the humans, like everything else in the forest. It didn't seem possible that they had just seen a tank or that people all around were ready to shoot to kill other humans. Madness.

They circled the clearing, pressed back into the forest, and returned to darkness.

The snow had worked its way through Mickey's gloves and into his feet and despite all the exertion he was getting very cold. They should have reached the lake by now. Had they drifted south? He checked the map app.

'Are we lost?' asked Ekaterina.

'We're fine.'

'Listen!'

Mickey turned. Angelina was facing back the way they'd come.

'Can you hear?'

Mickey cupped his ears. The crests and troughs of light engines played out, like an orchestra of hedge trimmers.

'Snowmobiles,' said Angelina. 'Following our tracks.'

Mickey turned round and pressed on with renewed purpose, though it was impossible to move any faster. Slowly the trees ahead thinned and suddenly the light from the moon and stars returned. They were at the forest edge. Ahead was a gap of around a kilometre of open snow and then a thick line of trees on the other side.

Estonia. Safety.

But the snowmobiles were closing in.

'You go on,' said Angelina, standing behind a tree with her gun readied. 'I'll hold them up.'

'You can't fight soldiers,' said Mickey. 'Come with us.'

'Go.'

Mickey hesitated. Angelina fired a shot. And another. The strimming stopped.

Shots rattled into the trees around.

'What are we going to do?' asked Ekaterina.

'Stay here and be shot,' said Mickey. 'Or run over the border.'

Angelina returned fire. Silence. Then more shooting made the decision for them. Ekaterina and Olga ran out into the open.

'Come with us,' Mickey pleaded with Angelina again.

'We have a saying. No point throwing punches after a fight.'

'Surrender then. Don't get shot.' Reluctantly, Mickey followed the others, zigzagging round the drifts of driven snow.

Halfway across, a new sound approached. Whooping, ominously, louder, then breaking into the sound of a thousand birds flapping overhead.

The downdraft from the helicopter pressed upon him as he braced for the inevitable shots from above. What were they waiting for? Just get it over with.

* * *

'Hands to flying stations,' came the call from the flight deck of HMS Elizabeth. 'Hands to flying stations.'

'Runway is clear. Permission to launch the jet.'

'Launch the jet, foreship.'

The pilot of the F-35 Lightning followed the marshaller's hand signals until the jet was in position. The green circle light overrode the red cross but still he waited for the marshaller to drop down and point an arm to signal 'go'.

He hit full power and the jet took off, pulling 5G as it banked, screaming over the protective escorts in Narva Bay, heading for Estonian airspace …

* * *

A crack of thunder. Mickey ducked and threw his hands over his head. Waiting for the impact from whatever they had fired at him.

But nothing came. He looked up. A jet broke the sound barrier overhead, visible only by its after-burn. Behind him the helicopter was on fire, spinning and dropping. It crashed into the lake, breaking through the ice, and another explosion threw him forward. He picked himself up and ran. His lungs and legs were soon burning. Now he heard barking. He looked back to see two dogs emerge from the woods on the Russian side. Their handlers let them go. He ran on again. A hundred metres to go. But the dogs were quicker. He could hear them behind. Almost smell them.

A crack. A whimper. Another crack. Another whimper.

Then silence. He ran on, into the welcome of outstretched branches.

He crouched against a tree trunk. Cold air relieved his lungs. His legs shook uncontrollably. Exhaustion, adrenalin, cold. Over the cracking and popping from the burning helicopter came shouts and strimming engines again. The snowmobile soldiers were going to help their comrades. Their headlights circled the downed helicopter.

Snapping and crunching approached from the forest behind. Unquestionably coming in his direction. A half dozen camouflaged soldiers emerged.

One of them pointed a flashlight in his face. 'Come with me.'

Sounded like an American accent, but he wasn't sure.

They walked a hundred metres to a clearing, where a jeep sat with its engine idling. A soldier jumped out and handed him a silver space blanket. He climbed into the back of the jeep, where Olga was already sitting.

'Are you okay?' he asked.

'Fine.'

'Where's Ekaterina?'

'I lost her. She ran a different way from me. I heard an explosion.'

'That was the helicopter crashing,' said Mickey. 'Ekaterina wasn't there then.'

'I just hope she's all right.'

The driver spun the jeep round and accelerated away.

Mickey called out to the soldier. 'There was another Russian woman with us.'

'Yes, we picked her up. And her friend.'

'There's only three of us,' said Mickey.

'Sir, I'm just telling you what I heard. We've picked up you two. Another patrol has picked up two other Russian women.'

'That must be Angelina.'

'Of course,' said Mickey. 'Told you I had everything under control.'

80

Declan knew the agency would have picked up on his flight to McGhee Tyson Airport and assumed he was taking the agreed leave, hiking in the Smokies. It was partly true. But before he switched off entirely, he had one more itch to scratch. He drove south for an hour to Happy Valley and then headed into Nantahala Forest.

After another hour, the sat nav took him onto a gravel logging road that was icy in patches. Calvara's recommendation to hire a four-by-four at the airport had been a good call. He'd always had good judgement. Which is precisely why Declan wanted to see him.

Declan was less sure why he was so apprehensive about meeting the former CIA Director. Was it because Calvara was his last hope? The only other person on the planet who believed in the Black Chamber. His anxiety eased as nature overwhelmed his senses. Miles of leaf and bark, a moose drinking from a pond. Not a human to be seen.

Finally, he arrived at a clearing with horses and stables. Nestled up into a small incline was an Ark house; angled glass facing south, solar panels, a water tank collecting rainwater from the roof. Would never have had Calvara down as a tree-hugger.

'It was my wife's idea to move,' Calvara explained as he showed Declan around. 'She always wanted to live off-grid.'

'How are you finding it?'

Calvara shrugged. 'I could do without the bugs, but it's agreeable enough. I like my birds and fishing. I can still watch sport. We haven't done the deep winter yet. That'll be the test.'

After the tour they sat on a glass-enclosed veranda and Declan filled Calvara in on comings and goings back at Langley. He seemed uninterested. His life had moved on.

'You said you wanted to clear up a couple of things,' said Calvara. 'I'm going to take a wild guess and suggest it's to do with the Black Chamber enquiry.'

'That's right.'

'Let it go, Declan. It's not doing you any good getting eaten up by this and it won't bring your brother back.'

'It wasn't only my brother who died in Iraq.'

Calvara raised a finger to his lip and then cupped his ear.

From the trees came a hard kip-kip call. He set his binoculars to his eyes and pointed them at the wall of spruce. 'A red crossbill.'

Calvara made a note in his pad then looked back at Declan. 'The problem with criticising the Iraq war is that we have no control test. We don't know what would have happened if we hadn't gone to war. Maybe on the long view it was the right thing to do.'

'That doesn't alter the fact that Biggerstaff manufactured the evidence for weapons of mass destruction. And he misled the President over the Chinese cyberattacks. And he wasn't alone.'

'Spitz has closed that. It was Ladyman and Biggerstaff. Two rotten apples. That's all.'

'Except there is one thing that happened that still doesn't make sense.'

'Shoot.'

'If it was only two rotten apples, why did you resign?'

'I didn't know how deep it ran at the time.'

'But you felt the poison ran deeper and wider, didn't you?'

Calvara crossed his legs and folded his arms. 'At the time

there were a lot of things that looked out of place.'

'Precisely. Too many to be coincidence.'

'That's how it looked. I was worried you were right. That there was some deep-state faction in the agency and the pentagon. I figured I had to stand aside.'

'Hand on heart. Do you believe there is no deep-state body at work, even if it's not called the Black Chamber?'

'There's a deep state working in Russia,' replied Calvara, ducking the question. 'The former KGB security men who run the economy and the political and legal system. But they're hiding in plain sight. It would be the same way here. We'd know about it.'

'Maybe it's more subtle in America,' said Declan. 'We only see whispers of smoke. But where there's smoke, there's fire. Don't you think?'

Calvara smiled and pointed towards the hills. 'Mount Guyot. The second highest of the Great Smokey Mountains. Can you see the smoke?'

Occasional wisps of cloud rose from the green upper slopes. 'I can see it.'

'It's a natural fog,' explained Calvara. 'The temperature and pressure are just right so the vegetation releases a mixture of organic chemicals. That's the smoke that gives the mountains their name.'

'I never knew that.'

'So, you see,' Calvara paused. 'Sometimes where there's smoke …'

Declan finished the sentence. 'There's simply smoke.'

81

Mickey went straight from the airport to see Helen. He hadn't told her he'd smuggled his way in and out of Russia. All she needed to know was that he was back safely, and it had been a hugely successful trip. She wanted to hear all about it, especially because the situation in Russia was all over the news. He promised to tell her over dinner, but first he needed to get into Crosshairs.

It was time to cash in their chips. He caught the tube into the Gherkin, watching the share price of Kazbegi Holdings crashing with every rattle on the tracks.

In the offices of Crosshair Investments Uli, Vlad and Carmella were all waiting for him.

'What price now?' he asked as he walked in.

'Twenty dollars.'

He'd done the calculation so many times he hardly needed to use his brain. They could now buy the two hundred thousand shares they owed for just four million dollars, leaving the fund with a profit of twenty-six million dollars.

'I think they could fall further,' said Vlad.

'Maybe,' said Mickey. 'But they can't fall below zero and we've made plenty already. I think we should close out.'

'It's your decision.'

He nodded. 'Close it out.'

Uli placed the order to buy. Because of its size it took an anxious twenty minutes before it was completed. Uli constantly tugging on his vape. Carmella and Vlad staring at the share price on the screen.

'Done,' said Uli.

Vlad and Carmella were still staring in disbelief.

'It's all over,' said Mickey. 'We've made twenty-six million dollars. Well done everyone.'

When he took his five million out of that pot, he'd have more than enough to buy the Marshall's house and the rest he'd invest in US treasuries. He wouldn't be leaving it in any bank.

Vlad produced a bottle of champagne, popped it, and poured out four glasses.

'Here's to making money the socially responsible way,' said Mickey. 'Exposing a mafia oligarch who thought he was untouchable!'

'And here's to you, Mickey. Thanks for the ride and I hope you and Helen enjoy the new home.'

Should he mention it? Was it bad luck? There's no point

having the biggest gob in the City if you can't use it. 'There might be three of us moving in,' he said with a wink.

'Brilliant,' said Carmella, giving him a hug.

Vlad shook his hand.

Uli slapped him on the back. 'Now that really is something to celebrate.'

82

From the walls and ceiling, Declan carefully peeled the stickers celebrating Josh's college and local sports teams and packed them away with the pennants, high school diploma and school year photographs. Into the boxes went Josh's football helmets, polished stone souvenirs, bubbleheads, toy racing cars and other assorted knickknacks. Then the American flag that had lain undisturbed over Josh's bed all these years. Finally, the stuffed tiger and kangaroo.

Was it right to pack Josh's life up like this? It felt like a betrayal. 'Sorry, Josh. But it's time for us all to move on.'

He sealed the boxes with tape and carried them downstairs and into the removal van.

When all was ready to go Mom walked round the house one last time, tears rolling. Declan put an arm round her shoulder and walked her out of the door. They turned in the driveway to look again. Josh's rusty baseball hoop was still hanging out in front.

'Do you want me to get that down?'

'Leave it for the children moving in,' she said, walking toward the van.

He helped her through the passenger door.

'Good memories,' she said, as he pulled out into the street. 'And sad ones too.'

'Let's keep hold of the good ones,' said Declan. 'It'll be great for you to be near Aunt Ellen and the twins.'

'It will. Declan, will you tell me something?'

'Of course,' he replied.

'If you don't believe in the Black Chamber anymore. Where does that leave us with Josh's death?'

'I don't understand,' said Declan playing for time.

'Who can we blame?'

Declan didn't answer. He was thinking about the marine that had died on Svalbard. Would his mom blame Declan? It was only when they'd left the city and were on the highway that he felt he had an answer.

'Do you remember what Josh told us in his final letter? He said, don't go beating up on the guys who sent us to war.'

'I read that every day.'

'Well, be proud of Josh for doing his duty. And all the other soldiers who do their duty. And let's just leave it there.'

83

Mickey had been unpacking boxes all morning. So much for keeping the Sabbath holy. He needed a break, so he made a cup of tea and joined Helen on the patio. She was looking through photo albums. Fat lot of use that was, but it was important she took it easy.

He sat on a bench the Marshalls had kindly left behind and looked out at the garden. A huge pine tree stood at the bottom. On either side of a neatly mown lawn were shrubs and bushes he didn't know the names for. There was no colour, but it was winter. Helen had said that it would look beautiful in the summer.

The Summer's garden in the summer. He liked the sound of that.

Suddenly a buzz jarred the silence. 'Are we expecting anyone?'

'I'm not. Could be a delivery.' Helen started to get up.

'I'll get it,' said Mickey.

But Helen's curiosity had got the better of her and she came with him. As they walked down the hallway the buzzer sounded again.

'We need to change that horrible buzzer,' said Helen. 'We

need a good old-fashioned bell.'

'Sure.' Add that to the lengthening to-do list.

He opened the door to find Frank standing on the shingle drive.

'It wasn't me and I've got a dozen witnesses to prove it.'

'Morning,' said Frank, ignoring the joke and looking over his shoulder at Helen. 'How are you, love?'

'I'm well thank-you. And you?'

'Champion.'

Helen pointed to the parcel he was holding in his hands. 'Are you doing deliveries?'

'House-warming present,' explained Frank, handing it to her.

'That's very kind. Come on in. Would you like a cup of tea?'

'Please. White. No sugar.'

Helen showed Frank around the house while Mickey made the tea. It was ready just as the tour finished and the three of them sat out on the patio.

'How are you settling in?' asked Frank.

'We love it, mate,' answered Mickey, as Helen was occupied with opening the present.

It was a strange mixture of a framed picture and some writing.

'It's a history and coat of arms for the Summers family,' explained Frank.

Looking more closely, it had green swirls around a knight's helmet. 'Is it real?'

'It's genuine all right. Summers is an old Anglo-Saxon name. You can read all about it in the history there.'

'Brilliant. Tell Charlie boy I no longer need the knighthood. I'm sorted.'

'You probably do deserve an honour for what you've done, but you understand that it can't be acknowledged.'

'Well, I'm very proud of what you did,' said Helen, putting a hand on his knee.

'Me too,' said Frank. 'Strictly off the record, I think you did a fantastic job and so do some others.'

'Not everyone then?'

Frank ran a finger round the rim of his cup while he considered his reply. 'Some think you risked starting World War Three by destabilising Pintov.'

'That weren't me, remember. That was Olga and Ekaterina. And they're Russian. It's their country. They're entitled to do whatever they want.'

'I understand. And it looks to be working out reasonably well, doesn't it? Angelina is desperate to go back home but we've advised her to wait until the situation is more stable.'

'Funny ain't it? The Russian people knew that Pintov killed German industrialists in his KGB days, assassinated journalists and opposition politicians, massacred Ukrainians. They forgave him. When they discover he blew up his own people they decide that's unacceptable.'

'It was indiscriminate,' said Frank.

'How are Ekaterina and Olga?' Mickey hadn't seen them since their arrival in the UK.

'Both well. Olga's providing us with some very useful information on Russian troll farms and hackers. We are most appreciative. But we're having to tread carefully. Not everything she's given is stacking up.'

'Such as?'

'The main problem is the procurement contract to build a Russian naval base in Svalbard. The Norwegians can't find any evidence of that on the ground. Nor can we or the Americans find anything else to corroborate that. It looks as if she made it up.'

'Why would she do that?'

'To make sure Kazbegi faced sanctions.' Frank shrugged. 'It did help tip the case over.'

'And Ekaterina?'

'She wants to go to America. She is of course a famous face, so she'll probably need a new identity. She's made a lot of enemies.'

'They're both heroes in my book.'

'And mine,' agreed Frank. 'But there'll always be some who see them as traitors.'

'I guess it all depends on who is writing the history book,' said Mickey.

He thought about Olga. He had trusted her despite not really knowing her. A sudden realisation hit him.

Frank seemed to know what he was thinking. 'Pintov's involvement in the Russian apartment bombings?'

'How do we know whether Olga has faked some of that?' asked Mickey. 'Or even all of it?'

'It's clear she believed it. She wouldn't have risked her life exposing it otherwise. But did she embellish her father's account? Did she fake a few documents to strengthen the case? She's won in the court of public opinion and maybe that's all that counts. But with my detective hat on, I'd say a good KC would get the case against Pintov dismissed.'

'I'II guess we'll never know,' said Mickey. 'Is there anything we ever know for sure?'

About the Author

Michael Crawshaw grew up in Leeds, Yorkshire, England. He studied Chemistry at Manchester University and passed up the opportunity of a life exploding chemicals in favour of joining the so-called Big Bang.

He worked for several of the world's leading investment banks and became an award-winning Head of Research. Supervising analysts covering a range of industries and countries he acquired expertise in global money flows, politics and business, and an ability to quickly understand new subjects. When he left finance, he found these skills ideally suited to writing fact-based fiction.

His first novel *To Make a Killing* was published in 2012 and his second, *Cyber Wars – The Black Chamber*, in 2019. Both feature the indomitable joker Mickey Summer whose big mouth means nothing he takes on is more than he can chew. Mickey returns in book three of the series, *The Gerasimov Doctrine*, published in 2023.

Acknowledgements

Many resources were used in background reading, but special mentions must go to Catherine Belton for taking on the oligarchs with *Putin's People* and John B Dunlop whose academic study *The Moscow Bombings of September 1999* convinced me that Putin's darkest secret was true. Thanks also to James Robinson for the cover artwork and to those who gave editorial input: Helen Judge, Michael Roscoe, Jill and Karl Hancock, and especially Veronica Di Grigoli. And finally, thanks for the love and support of Carolyn, Joe, Sam, Ben, Bella and Alice.

Praise for Michael Crawshaw

A winner takes all murder mystery –
Sian Griffiths, *The Sunday Times*

A pacy thriller – Hephzibah Anderson, *Bloomberg*

Pick up a copy – Gary Parkinson, *The Times*

I really loved narrating this book. Highly recommended –
RC Bray, *Grammy award-winning narrator.*

This action-packed thriller is too realistic for comfort –
Helen Black, *author and award-winning script writer.*